SLAPPED!

SLAPPED!

A Novel
Based On a True Story

PAUL SWENSON

AuthorHouse™ LLC
1663 Liberty Drive
Bloomington, IN 47403
www.authorhouse.com
Phone: 1-800-839-8640

© *2013 Paul Swenson. All rights reserved.*

No part of this book may be reproduced, stored in a retrieval system, or transmitted by any means without the written permission of the author.

Published by AuthorHouse   08/07/2013

ISBN: 978-1-4918-0176-5 (sc)
ISBN: 978-1-4918-0175-8 (hc)
ISBN: 978-1-4918-0174-1 (e)

Library of Congress Control Number: 2013913223

Any people depicted in stock imagery provided by iStockphoto *are models, and such images are being used for illustrative purposes only. Certain stock imagery* © iStockphoto

Front cover Photo © *Fred Hayes*
Back cover Photo © *Ray Wheeler*
Author Photo © *Paul Schoenfeld*
Dancer Photo © *Douglas W. Carter*

This book is printed on acid-free paper.

Because of the dynamic nature of the Internet, any web addresses or links contained in this book may have changed since publication and may no longer be valid. The views expressed in this work are solely those of the author and do not necessarily reflect the views of the publisher, and the publisher hereby disclaims any responsibility for them.

Dedicated to all those individuals
whose inner beliefs and values
cause them to go up against great odds
for a cause they believe is worth fighting for.

And to nature, the great healer.

In Memory of Paul Swenson

EARTH YOUR DANCING PLACE

Beneath heaven's vault
remember always walking
through halls of cloud
down aisles of sunlight
or through high hedges
of the green rain
walk in the world
highheeled with swirl of cape
hand at the swordhilt
of your pride
Keep a tall throat
Remain aghast at life

Enter each day
as upon a stage
lighted and waiting
for your step
Crave upward as flame
have keenness in the nostril
Give your eyes
to agony or rapture

Train your hands
as birds to be
brooding or nimble
Move your body
as the horses
sweeping on slender hooves
over crag and prairie
with fleeing manes
and aloofness of their limbs

Take earth for your own large room
and the floor of earth
carpeted with sunlight
and hung round with silver wind
for your dancing place

May Swenson
Copyright May Swenson. Used with permission
of the Literary Estate of May Swenson.
All rights reserved.

Illustration by Alex Nabaum

Table of Contents

Prologue xiii
Chapter 1   Wind from the River 1
Chapter 2   The Horse's Mouth 13
Chapter 3   Something Wild 23
Chapter 4   Wrench in the Works 39
Chapter 5   Monopoly 49
Chapter 6   Damage 57
Chapter 7   Dinner on the Dark Side 63
Chapter 8   Year of the Ox 71
Chapter 9   Ox in the Mire 83
Chapter 10   After the Fall 95
Chapter 11   Ides of March 105
Chapter 12   Squawks, Lies, and Audiotape 115
Chapter 13   The Big Chill 119
Chapter 14   Hog's Wallow 133

Chapter 15	Crazy Like a Fox	143
Chapter 16	Fright Night	151
Chapter 17	Father's Day Massacre	161
Chapter 18	SLAPPing Back	175
Chapter 19	Bizarre Bedfellows	185
Chapter 20	Down by the Riverside	195
Chapter 21	Strange Encounters	209
Chapter 22	Desperate Housewives	219
Chapter 23	Popcorn Popping	229
Chapter 24	Costume Party	245
Chapter 25	Battle Scars	257
Chapter 26	Sweating It	265
Chapter 27	Big	275
Chapter 28	Poseurs at the Deposition	283
Chapter 29	A Brilliant Madness	287
Chapter 30	What Would Jesus Do?	299
Chapter 31	Heels, Deals, and Repeals	309
Chapter 32	Hardball	319
Chapter 33	The High Court Hustle	331
Chapter 34	Pyrrhic Victory	339
Chapter 35	Behind the Green Door	351
Chapter 36	Settlement	359
Epilogue		371
Endorsements		385
About the Author		389

Prologue

Long before white settlers arrived in the Salt Lake Valley, giving thanks for the river they found flowing northward from Utah Lake (which they dubbed "the Western Jordan"), the forty-mile waterway was a magnet for breeding, wintering, and migrating birds.

Before the advent of the Whites, Native Americans frequently crossed the river and camped on its banks. Later, when Catholic fathers came to visit Indian tribes in the region, they were nurtured by the stream, as were traders, trappers, and explorers.

For a century or so after European footprints appeared on its banks, it would remain one of the richest riparian and avian resources in the West.

Like its namesake in Palestine, the Western Jordan flowed into a dead sea, but in its most swollen stages it often crested dangerously. Returning from California in 1827, Jedediah Smith forded the river during spring flooding and reported he was "very much strangled" by the effort.

Both Brigham Young and Heber C. Kimball—among the first company of Mormon pioneers who arrived in 1847—are variously credited with naming the river. (The "Western" was soon dropped from its title). They regarded it as an oasis and a refuge in the desert, a beneficent reminder of the river where the New Testament records John having baptized Jesus.

As with the biblical Jordan, Kimball observed, this river flowed from a fresh lake through fertile valleys, providing irrigation water for pioneers' crops, and eventually emptied into an inland sea—in this case, the Great Salt Lake.

The Jordan River in Salt Lake County, Utah
Photo c. Anne-Marie Bernshaw

Herds of deer fed near the stream, along with beavers, foxes, squirrels, and other small animals. In the twentieth century, a couple of herds of buffalo were introduced into the area west of the stream as a commercial venture.

Pioneer families who chose the most placid stretches of the Jordan to baptize their children did not witness the descent of a dove, as reported at Jesus's baptism, but instead observed an occasional great blue heron, snowy egret, or red-tailed hawk.

Great Blue Herons and Snowy Egrets, Jordan River, Salt Lake County, Utah
Photo c. Ray Wheeler

Among summer residents of the river were white-faced ibis, double-crested cormorants, black-crowned night herons, American white pelicans, peregrine falcons, and turkey vultures as well as numerous species of game birds.

Cormorant Rookery, Jordan River, Salt Lake County, Utah
Photo c. Ray Wheeler

Often seen during the winter months in flights above the waterway (before the species became threatened) was the bald eagle, an American icon. A single nesting pair of the rare birds showed themselves near the northern extremity of the Jordan as recently as 2003.

A number of bird species once common on the river became increasingly rare or absent with the escalating encroachment of human activities within the area's ecosystem.

During the forty-year construction of the Mormon Salt Lake Temple, granite blocks were floated down the river to the city. The Jordan was again used to transport construction materials in 1869, this time by floating logs and ties for completing the Central Utah Railroad.

As the territory of Deseret became the state of Utah and communities stretched along the river's banks through Utah and Salt Lake Counties, the burgeoning human population found less salutary uses for the Jordan that cheapened and polluted the stream's holy antecedents and despoiled the river's aesthetics and sanitation.

Waste and sewage were dumped into the river, an all-too-handy route for ultimate disposal in the Great Salt Lake. And as late as the 1970s, industrial refuse from area slaughterhouses, packing plants, mineral reduction mills, and laundries was still being deposited in the Jordan.

Jordan River activist explores trash island in Jordan River, Salt Lake City, near 100 South
Photo c. Amy O'Connor

Citizen clean-up efforts yield truck loads of garbage in a 2-mile stretch of the Jordan River, Salt Lake City. Volunteers have retrieved over 300 shopping carts from the Jordan River
Photo c. Ray Wheeler

Tree branch captures floating litter in Jordan River
Photo c. Ray Wheeler

Although the Utah legislature created the Jordan River Parkway Authority in 1973 to protect and enhance the natural quality of the river and to develop park and recreational facilities, water conservation projects, and flood control measures, its establishment could not slake the thirst of corporate interests who primarily saw the stream as an avenue for commerce.

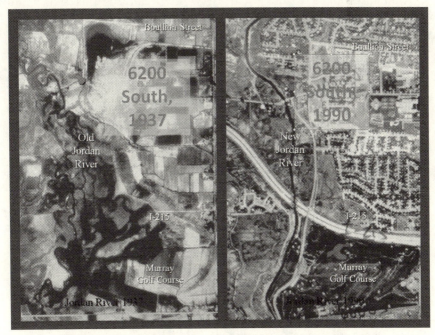

Photo c. Blueprint Jordan River report compiled by Envision Utah for Salt Lake County, page 7.

SOURCES The Jordan River Natural Areas Forum 2003 Strategic Plan.
The Jordan River Natural Conservation Corridor Report (2001)

In some ways, the story of the Jordan—its beauty and its exploitation—is the story of every major river in the United States. Fragile, life-giving, and once pristine waterways are threatened, fought over, and damaged by lack of foresight, all the while begging for attention and reclamation. The Utah river's name and spiritual provenance, however, would give the conflict surrounding its use a distinctive irony.

In the last decade of the twentieth century, verdant farmland on the Jordan's banks was eyed covetously by developers, who recognized its potential as lucrative commercial property. A critical step behind were conservationists and far-sighted citizens who sought the land's preservation as open space and wildlife habitat and opposed its exploitation.

The combatants were an odd lot led by two unlikely partnerships. One alliance linked a stocky man in Western clothing (black or white ten-gallon hat, pearl-button shirts, cowboy boots, and outsized brass belt buckle at his waist) with a silver-haired, dignified, and cloistered judge moonlighting as a real estate mogul. Under the jurist's black robes was a tailored business suit appropriate for government hearings away from the bench. Keeping largely out of the public eye, his quiet but intimidating presence, legal acumen, and low-key respectability could smooth the way for accomplishing one vision of the Jordan's future.

A rather different vision coalesced around two headstrong housewives. Crossing paths in a neighborhood near the river, they recognized in each other an appreciation for the natural world and a commitment to preserve a swath of it for coming generations, including their own children. Opposites in looks and temperament, their combined passion sparked a short-lived coalition of concerned citizens springing up like wild grasses at the water's edge.

The ensuing struggle and its aftermath would have far reaching consequences. Both for the abundant wildlife—multiple generations of which had made the river a home for centuries—and for the human populations near the Jordan's meandering corridor. A scuffle that started over land use and natural resources would spawn a roaring conflagration over citizen rights and free speech.

Once the battle lines were drawn, the chance for peaceful coexistence and a shared environment would give way to greed, selfishness, and a bulldozer mentality. Not consulted in the process, the nonhuman species would be given the hindmost consideration.

Chapter 1
Wind from the River

A bird's-eye view of South Jordan, Utah, in the summer of 1996 revealed a patchwork of old homes and new housing developments under a brilliant sun, interlaced with family farms, open fields, and tree-shadowed glades, all in the half embrace of the Wasatch Mountains.

A western gull from the nearby Great Salt Lake, swooping low over a suburban neighborhood, sensed breakfast, observing a feast laid out on picnic tables positioned in the middle of a curving, snaky street barricaded against automobile traffic.

Seated with her husband Ted and her children at one of the tables beneath the shade of a cottonwood tree, Julie Bell noticed the gull descend to peck away at a few crumbs that had dropped to the pavement from the plate of rolls she had baked for the picnic that morning. Then, bobbing its head, the bird lifted its orange beak and beady eyes to search for additional opportunities to forage.

What kind of people, Julie wondered, were her new neighbors. It was a welcoming sign that the Bells—just moved in—had been invited to this street party, but no one had yet made a fuss over their arrival. Later, it would seem fortuitous that Julie bumped into the blond woman at the salad table.

"Hi," the woman said. "I'm Jessica Ann Tobler." Then, poking her index finger between her lips, she appeared to be probing her teeth. Realizing the visual image, she withdrew the digit and clamped her mouth closed.

"I probably have some lettuce between my teeth," she said.

"Uh, no, not that I can tell," Julie said.

Then, attempting to cover the woman's embarrassment with a gesture of her own, she introduced herself. "I'm Julie Bell," she said, offering her hand.

Was it weird, or somehow oddly appealing, that a stranger had chosen to present herself by asking if she had food in her teeth? *Curious*, Julie thought. Was she insecure? Or was the woman's question a touching vulnerability, an anomaly in what seemed an otherwise jaunty, even flamboyant, personal style?

Julie was the stranger, after all. She had noticed the busty blond at an adjoining table, telling stories, laughing, and carrying on unselfconsciously. She had a pretty face, big sparkly hazel-green eyes, and shoulder-length hair.

A good-looking man sitting on the top step of the entry to a nearby house smiled indulgently at the conversation. Julie took him to be the woman's mate.

After a moment, the blond called the man over to introduce him. "My husband, Dave," she said, her fingers on his shoulder. Julie shook the hand he extended. "We live close by," Jessica said, "just around the corner and a couple of streets down—the house with the flagpole. Drop in when you get the urge."

It sounded like an open invitation, and while the woman's eagerness was a little overwhelming, Julie was grateful for the connection. She had a sparkle and a spontaneity that were hard not to like. *Friendly and talkative*, she thought. *My kind of person.*

"Oh, are these your kids?" Jessica asked as two of Julie's three children approached.

She introduced her daughters, Trish, five, and Cady, eleven. A few moments later, her son, Brandon, eight, also wandered over. Jessica reached into her pocket and gave each of them a piece of candy.

The street picnic had been a boon—a relaxing, no-pressure affair. Jessica Tobler's chattiness had buoyed Julie. Jessica was unlike anyone she had ever met, Julie decided with bemused fondness.

After the party, Julie and Ted helped clean and pack up the picnic tables and chairs. It was enough that Ted had shown up for the barbecue, although he hadn't gotten out of bed early enough to cook steaks and hamburgers on the grill with the other men. It had been after midnight when he arrived from Idaho, and he had slept in.

Ted's routine was to connect with his family on weekends after spending the week in Idaho, trying to make a go of the farm they owned, and then head north again on Monday morning. Why was it that Julie didn't mind going it alone on weekdays with the kids while catching the barest whiff of her husband on weekends?

Julie Acheson, now Julie Bell, had never needed to be taken care of. She had started earning her own money at age eight, babysitting at twenty-five cents an hour. Schlepping burgers and milkshakes on plastic trays fastened to her customers' car windows at a local drive-in had increased her pay to eighty-five cents an hour. Tips were rare, but she had put money away every week.

As a teenager—people said she was pretty—she had wanted contact lenses instead of glasses for her deep-blue eyes but knew her father couldn't afford them. That didn't stop Julie. She got a job to pay for them herself as a cashier at a mom-and-pop food store. The job might have gone to an older girl, but they had apparently liked her air of confidence.

Julie, third of four sisters and a younger brother, was the quietest of them all. Julie had developed her self-assurance despite her older sister's jibes. Her string of accomplishments at Jordan High School included first cheerleading for the Beetdiggers, a daunting task to create the clout to transform their infamous team name to something fearsome and respectable. She then went on to join the pep club, write for the school paper, and was elected president of her school's FHA (Future Homemakers of America). A pretty girl who could cook and run a house—it was the sort of reputation that appealed to boys whose expectations for domestic bliss had been shaped by a traditional upbringing.

She had a burning desire to graduate from college. She first attended classes at Snow College and continued on her undergraduate work at the University of Utah. She would not only do well, she would graduate (a first in her family) with honors. She continued on to earn a master's degree at the University of Utah—and had done it without student loans or parental financial support; although it meant managing a malt shop, cleaning college dorm floors, doing secretarial work on campus, and other jobs sometimes simultaneously.

Working hard had never bothered her. Independence and personal freedom came as naturally to her as her affinity for sunshine and mountain air.

Julie had married late—at thirty-two—not for lack of interest by the opposite sex. She had been determined not to end up in a smothering marriage of domestic dependence and emotional eclipse. It wasn't her idea of a fulfilling life.

When she had met Ted and began dating him, he didn't pressure her about defining the relationship or where it was heading. She had liked that. They were still seeing each other a year and a half later, and the destination of their developing bond remained unclear to her. She wasn't in any rush, she had decided. Matrimony was an option, not a priority.

Julie had a satisfying career teaching deaf children and had managed to build her own home, fighting through a whirlwind of obstacles. In sleepy, conservative Utah in the 1970s, where traditional gender roles were highly prized and deviations were suspect, young, unmarried women anticipated marriage as a way of obtaining a home of their own that their husbands would provide.

The idea that a single young woman might wish to reverse the process and buy a house well before she considered obtaining a marriage partner was virtually unheard of. Any notion that a woman would even dream of buying land and overseeing construction of her own home would be dismissed by skeptical authority figures. It had taken five years of enjoying her hard-won house and four of those years finding a comfort level with Ted before she was ready to take the plunge.

"You better realize," she had told him, "I'll never be the stereotypical farm wife—barefoot and pregnant. I won't be there just to make your dinner and rub your feet, if that's your dream marriage."

Now, the ironies of which parts of that promise had held true and which parts had been blurred to insensibility had come home to roost.

They still had the farm, but Julie wasn't cut out for the life; she wasn't *any* kind of farm wife. Which meant Ted was in Idaho with honest soil under his fingernails and she was in Utah with an unfinished house, fixing dinner, breakfast, and lunch for three kids.

The South Jordan neighborhood where they had just settled was quiet, cozy, and somewhat secluded—winding streets and little cul-de-sacs. While there were neat brick facades and well-groomed lawns typical of middle-class suburbia, domesticity was deceptive—an island in a wilder and more expansive landscape.

Nibbling at the extravagantly lush rectangles of Kentucky bluegrass on the Salt Lake Valley's desert floor were untrammeled fields of sweet flag, creeping bent grass, weeping love grass, and river oats. The wind carried the mixed aromas of the nearby Jordan River and wild growing things, including the sensual scent of sage. For those who cared to observe, there was a clear view of the mountains.

A semirural suburb southwest of Salt Lake City, South Jordan was a step up for Julie and Ted from their Taylorsville starter home, which Julie had struggled to build on her teacher's salary before they met and married. The battle to build this new house hadn't involved a court fight or devious contractors, as with her first home, but Julie was still grappling with most everything by herself.

Funny. She laughed. *Isn't that just how I seem to like it?*

Julie had made pilgrimages to the construction site every day during the summer of 1996, keeping a close eye on potential screwups until the house was finished. There were still empty lots in the neighborhood, and the new home had a semiprivate feel.

While it was being built, a few neighbors from down the street had stopped by to confess they were happy that civilization and green lawns would soon rescue the plot of land from what they perceived as only a looming weed-infested wilderness.

Some South Jordan residents seemed attracted to the area because it appeared to be on the verge of a growth spurt; it would be exciting to get in on the ground floor of development and progress. Wasn't it their destiny to see new restaurants, shops, boutiques, and office towers rise, finally putting them on the map? Otherwise, wouldn't they remain faceless residents of a generic bedroom community?

A survey had indicated, however, that most were pleased the town had retained its largely rural identity. For them, it was a good thing the community had thus far managed to resist power brokers who wished to exploit open land as merchandise—to buy, sell, or develop it for personal fortune. The landscape was still relatively pristine and a little wild—a place where their children could run free. They loved the view of the mountains, a sight they wouldn't fully appreciate until construction cranes thronged the skyline.

Julie felt the same.

She was willing to take her time getting close to anyone in the neighborhood. Trish, her youngest, was special needs and required a lot of attention and affection. The fact that she couldn't talk (and might never learn to speak) was difficult to explain to strangers who didn't understand.

The kids were used to their father's absences and their mother's self-sufficiency. Unless someone raised an eyebrow about the arrangement, it wouldn't occur to Julie that she was either too complacent about her long-distance marriage or didn't miss having a live-in husband as much as she should. While she was glad to see Ted when he showed up late on Fridays, it wasn't as if she pined for him all week after he said good-bye early on Monday mornings.

The change of scenery—figuratively and literally—was beginning to clear Julie's head and her vision. She was healthy and energetic and functioned nicely on four or five hours sleep. Now that they were getting adjusted to a new place, what would be her next challenge?

The location had its compensations. Their lot was perched on a hill that descended steeply from their backyard into a picturesque gully. And just a quarter-mile farther below were the Jordan River bottoms, teeming with wildlife. Often visible through a pair of binoculars were white-faced ibis, migrating osprey, foxes, and graceful deer and their fawns. For a fortunate, careful observer, an occasional eagle could be seen high up, surveying the scene. Think of it—the possibility of a fragile sense of peace and nature in what otherwise was suburbia. Maybe it wasn't a pipe dream.

The Jordan River Bottoms near Julie Bell's house
Photo c. Anne-Marie Bernshaw

The comforting feeling would help while they were settling in. Connecting with neighbors and new acquaintances could come soon enough; enjoying the natural world and her children seemed a sensible priority right now. And for Julie, the wonders of the environment had always been an extension of her spiritual life.

Unpacking boxes and getting furniture moved from storage after the sale of the Taylorsville house gobbled two weekends before Julie got the family to church. Any illusions of a period of privacy and anonymity vanished on that first church Sunday.

Being a Mormon and showing up in church made you part of a community, whether you were ready for social obligations or not. Welcomed warmly by members of her neighborhood ward (the congregational unit of The Church of Jesus Christ of Latter-day Saints—frequently referred to as "Mormon" or "LDS"), Julie realized she was ready.

If I'm anything, I'm a people person, she thought. Isolation had been part of the problem while feeling stuck on the farm.

The ward bishop quickly made it clear he believed in pushing new members to get their feet wet in church service. Normally when a new family moved into a ward, both parents were asked to speak from the pulpit in sacrament meeting, the weekly Mormon worship service. But when the Bells were approached on their second Sunday to accept a speaking assignment, Ted begged off, ostensibly because he couldn't always predict which weekends he could make it home from Idaho.

Julie knew it was more than that. Ted had made it clear that there were a few aspects of the Mormon religion he wouldn't participate in. He drew the line well short of standing behind a pulpit, except perhaps to say an occasional opening or closing prayer if called upon. As Ted offered his regrets to the bishop, Julie played along with a neutral facial expression.

"Yes," she said when the bishop turned to her; she'd be willing to accept the assignment.

Sacrament meeting—so called because its central ritual was the passing of bread and water as emblems of Christ's atoning sacrifice—was given over to sermons during its last hour. These were expected to be authoritative statements of doctrine, usually delivered by members of the all-male lay priesthood, who cited scripture and quoted the faith's general authorities. Their wives' talks, often less formal and more personal, had come to be dismissed by some as mere appetizers for the meat-and-potato sermons of their men.

None of this would have influenced Julie Bell in deciding how to shape her remarks. She drew on her personal spiritual outlook as the substance of her church life and made little distinction between personal, spiritual, and public experience.

As she stood at the pulpit on the following Sunday, more than one member of the congregation noticed she didn't defer to the priesthood or to custom by merely "bearing her testimony" or filling her allotted time with the story of her family's genealogy. Behind the microphone for less than fifteen minutes, she made clear, concise points about a hard-earned commitment to Jesus's instructions in the Sermon on the Mount.

Afterward, several people spoke to her warmly and thanked her for her remarks. Ted, who had happily turned up for his wife's talk and was elsewhere in the foyer, seemed also to be fielding friendly comments from ward members.

The following week brought visits from the ward's home teachers and sisters from the Relief Society, separate Mormon programs that brought male and female church representatives for monthly home visits to offer a spiritual thought or needed assistance. They made hesitant inquiries about Ted's work status and his absence. Julie and the children dealt with it straightforwardly.

"Daddy's a farmer, he won't always be in church since he can't make it down from the farm every weekend," eleven-year-old Cady explained.

Summer was sliding into fall, and Julie hadn't accomplished half the things on her list in finishing and furnishing the new house. The kids' need to spend time with their father eclipsed joint projects planned for the weekends with Ted. Private time with Ted came too far down on the list to get much attention. If they were to live under the same roof again, how would things change, and how much would it take getting used to? They couldn't stay apart indefinitely.

In mid-October, an official-looking letter showed up in the Bells' mailbox from South Jordan City. A new development was planned, and their property was within three hundred feet of the location for its launch. The heads-up was specific about the project's apparent inevitability but skimped on details. Would it ruin the ecosystem and impinge on the river corridor?

Julie called two or three neighbors and found none who had received a similar letter.

The sketchily described development didn't seem to meet requirements of the South Jordan master plan Julie had checked out before they bought the property. What was going on?

Always thorough about these things, Julie's inspection of the master plan at the South Jordan City Hall had yielded what she had regarded as reassuring news. It specified preservation requirements for the river bottoms and plans for a twenty-five-acre park on a piece of land donated to the city by the state of Utah, located directly behind the property they soon bought.

In the cul-de-sac adjoining the Bells' backyard, an opening had been left in the fence. After moving in, Julie and the kids had accepted it as an invitation to explore the countryside.

They followed a small dirt road that led down to a gate, obviously installed to block public access. But sometimes the gate was left open, and the Bells believed there was no harm in investigating the parkland as long as they caused no damage and left no litter. They were already imagining how the park would look once it was completed. Between fifty and seventy-five trees had been planted on the property by an ambitious Boy Scout troop. A disturbing sign, however—without maintenance and a water source, most of them had died.

Two or three nights after the letter from the city arrived, Julie had a strange dream. She found herself following a curving, dry riverbed. Her bare feet—hot and cracked—scuffed along in the thick dust. She wore nothing but her nightgown. Corpses of small animals littered the bleached-out riverbank. Around a sharp bend, she came upon a huge cottonwood tree that had fallen across the gorge and blocked her passage. She tried to climb over it, but her feet became entangled in its withered roots. In her dream, tears of grief and frustration filled her eyes and cascaded down her face. Looking down, she noticed her tears left droplets of water in the streambed, trickling among the deadened tree branches.

She awoke then and lay with her eyes wide open, blinking back the dream's vivid images and unresolved emotion. Shifting in bed, she turned to watch Ted stir and burrow deeper into his pillow. Careful not to disturb the mattress surface, she sat up cautiously and eased her feet into a pair of bedside slippers. Her eyes remained wet. Outside the bedroom window, the vegetation smelled good—fresh. After walking to the curtain, she drew it back and inched the window up another notch.

The sky was roiling with dark clouds moving from west to east toward the mountains. There was rain in the air, and she thought she could also smell the river. This wasn't going to be just a shower; an ominous storm was brewing. It had been a dry summer. They could use the moisture. This change in the weather felt almost personal.

Let it come, Julie prayed.

She returned to bed, shedding her slippers. Ted had turned to face her, but his eyes remained closed. On impulse, she stretched out to press her body against his sleeping form and put her arms around his neck. When his eyes flicked warily open, she saw a flash in the dark pupils. Lightning had struck somewhere close by. Seconds later, a peal of thunder followed. As his body responded to her touch, they could both hear the rush of the rain.

Chapter 2

The Horse's Mouth

The man who stood on Julie Bell's porch when she opened the door to his heavy, insistent knock was big shouldered, mustached, and wearing a huge black cowboy hat. "Hi, Julie," he said. He touched the brim of his Stetson but kept it clamped to his brow.

His head seemed lost in the oversized hat. A massive brass belt buckle gleamed at his waist. He looked as if he might have been a businessman, bulkily miscast in a "B" Western. But he was imposing, and he was confident.

What exactly have I gotten myself into? she wondered. *And why is he looking at me in that odd, familiar way?*

"You don't recognize me, do you?" he said.

Julie had half a houseful of people in her family room, and a stranger was at her door, asking her strange questions. *Oh,* she realized, *this must be the guest of honor.* But why should he expect her to know him by sight?

She motioned the man into her entryway and stepped back to allow him to squeeze through the door. It had been an eventful week, and she was already stressed before the main event she had planned could even get underway.

By mid-October, piles of autumn leaves still remained in colorful disarray in the Bells' front yard. Leaves hadn't been the only things stacking up in Julie's life, but unmet responsibilities at home were the last thing on her mind. If Ted couldn't find time on the weekend to rake leaves, oh well. She wasn't going to sweat the small stuff.

Her obligations to her guests had little to do with undone yard work and everything to do with how convincingly she would be able to follow through in helping to inform however many would show up in response to a flier she had sent to fifty households in surrounding neighborhoods.

An increasing anxiety over that letter from the city, with its unmistakable odor of double cross by city fathers, had eaten at her for days. Eventually she reminded herself of something she'd learned long ago: *if you don't know what's going on, don't wait for someone else to tell you.*

That aphorism had given her the courage to plunge ahead with the actions that had led to this moment.

Flier: Salt Lake County's Crown Jewel
Photo c. Dana Hagio

"The Crown Jewel of South Jordan"—that was the phrase Julie had used to designate the open space around the river. "A glass and concrete city is coming," she had warned in the flier. "Join us to learn about the proposed development, discuss our options, and take steps to guard our community's future."

What did she really know about the powerful forces pushing the development? If plans had been in the works for weeks or months, they had purposely been kept under wraps. Julie might as well have been fencing with shadows. That the master plan and the promised park were in danger obviously wasn't something the developers wanted known.

But who were the major players in city government, and who was pulling the strings?

Henderson Development Company was the firm the letter had identified as prime mover on the project. Poring through public records, Julie had learned that the firm's founder and CEO was a man named Geoffrey Henderson with an impressive résumé and "a proven track record of success," according to the company's literature. Did the name ring some distant bell?

The firm's "outside legal counsel" was listed as Marcus Hollings, a district court judge hired as a part-time consultant. According to company literature, he had once served as city attorney for West Valley City, Utah's second largest metropolis.

Julie mused that if one of a developer's goals was to wield clout in a small community with a craving for recognition, it might be advantageous to mention that it had a sitting judge on its team.

Up close, what might such a partnership look like? She couldn't quite bring the amorphous images into focus in her head, the dark shapes looming like funnel clouds in her consciousness. It felt as if she was dancing on the edge of a whirlwind that could suck her in and catch her up in it. *Okay*, she realized, *that was melodramatic. Maybe even paranoid.*

Start at the top. How else would she know who and what she was dealing with? Floating on a little surge of excitement once the flier had been distributed, she had placed a call to the office of the development firm's CEO.

It had taken some talking to get past Geoffrey Henderson's secretary. Eventually an impatient and distracted voice had come on the line and identified himself. *Keep the tone neutral but friendly*, she had told herself.

"Julie Bell here," she had said. "I received a letter from South Jordan City telling me about the development you have planned." In two or three brief sentences she had gone on to explain that she intended to host a gathering for interested neighbors regarding his project. Would he like to come and answer some questions?

"When would that be?" His husky voice had been annoyingly cozy, as if he knew something she didn't.

"October 15." There was a pause on the line. Was he checking his calendar?

When he cleared his throat and said he would be there, she had been a little surprised.

What kind of turnout would there be? Her fishing expedition had landed a big one; what if the gathering was a bust? Would only environmental kooks show up, believing they'd been recruited for radical activism? And would others decide to skip the invitation for the same reason?

By habit and tradition, Julie and all the Achesons in her birth family were moderately conservative Republicans. By definition, she reasoned, Republicans should be interested in conserving natural resources. How best could she approach her mostly conservative neighbors to solicit support?

Ted would be out of town, so it would be up to Julie to do it all—prepare an agenda, vacuum the carpet, bake the cookies, and eventually pour the punch and carry the conversational ball.

As the sunlight had faded, the doorbell had begun to ring. The first few people Julie had met at the door were unfamiliar—couples and singles. Friends and nearby neighbors had also shown up. There was going to be a good crowd.

Then came the knock of the man who had ignored the bell. In the entryway he stood staring at her with his dark brown eyes while she stole sidelong glances.

"You don't remember me, do you?" he asked.

SLAPPED! 17

"No, I don't. I'm sorry."

"Well, we went to school together. We were actually biology lab partners. I was in the eleventh grade; you were in the twelfth." He extended his hand. "I'm Geoffrey Henderson. Thanks for having me over."

Julie realized her face was reddening. Attempting to cover her embarrassment, she asked if she could take his hat.

"Uh, no, that won't be necessary," he said. "I like to keep it with me." Leading the way, she could feel his eyes on her as he followed her into the family room.

Approximately thirty people crowded the room, including State Representative Boyd Franklin, R-South Jordan. Some had come half an hour late, all too accustomed to operating on Mormon Standard Time. She used the delay to offer punch and cookies laid out on the coffee table. Making herself acquainted with people she didn't know, she was relieved to observe that many were chatting amiably with each other. No one seemed anxious about getting down to business.

Jessica Tobler had been one of the first to arrive, and she was brightening the room with her banter. Henderson seated himself between Jessica and another woman, who was attempting to talk around Henderson to Jessica. Julie noticed the woman was leaning a little unsteadily off her chair to avoid the visual obstruction of Henderson's hat.

For the very reason that everyone seemed engrossed in the conversation, Julie knew it was time to start.

Standing to face the group, she took a breath, smiled, and waited for the buzz to die. In welcoming her guests, she briefly read from the letter she had received and then turned to Geoffrey Henderson.

"We thought we should get the facts from the horse's mouth," she burbled, wondering immediately if the phrase would be regarded as playful or insulting but rushing on to avoid embarrassment. "Mr. Geoffrey Henderson of Henderson Development, would you mind telling us the details of your proposal?"

"Well," Henderson said, facing the room, touching his hat, and turning to prop an architect's drawing on a tripod, "it's more than just a proposal."

Compared to his audience of suburbanites, clad in chinos and pantsuits, his outfit and bearing made him a striking figure.

"We feel we have the city's backing and community support for the project," he said. "I'm happy to discuss our plans with you. I want you to feel comfortable about what this development will mean for your area."

The rough sketch was conspicuous by what it didn't show. It pictured trees and foliage on the riverbank and the entrance to what Henderson said would be the project area. The drawing was tinted green, implying a parklike environment. No buildings or parking lots for automobiles were visible. When questioned, Henderson painted a picture of a glass and concrete office complex—beautiful in its simplicity—studded with inviting restaurants and shops, interspersed with green space.

"You will see representations of the entire complex when the artist renderings are completed," he promised.

When asked to explain how the project would meet the requirements of the South Jordan master plan, Henderson parried a bit but eventually conceded there were differences.

"Plans are made to be evaluated and revisited or revised, even master plans," he said. "Citizens are free to alter them, if necessary, to accommodate new community needs and desires. This is how progress works in a democracy."

Some of the guests seemed mollified by Henderson's explanations. Others asked simple questions. Many remained quiet and unresponsive, although Julie believed she saw some skeptical looks. Julie hoped that someone besides herself would ask a probing question, and when Jessica Tobler raised her hand, the CEO seemed pleased that an attractive woman wanted to be recognized.

"I have kids who love the river bottoms, Mr. Henderson," she said. "We go there because there is space to run and enjoy the river. They also love the wildlife. So what do you say to a generation that loves that land precisely because it's still wild and pristine?"

Henderson looked a little miffed. He paused for a moment before he answered. "I wouldn't presume to tell children how to feel," he said. "I think thoughtful parents will know best how to deal with their questions," he added.

The Jordan River beneath the snow-capped Wasatch Mountains
Photo c. Dana Hagio

Jessica wasn't going to let him off the hook that easily. "Maybe I didn't make it entirely clear, Mr. Henderson," she continued. "The generation I'm talking about includes adults as well. I'm still a kid at heart, and I not only want open space for my children; I want it for me, my husband, my friends, and everybody."

Henderson's broad shoulders didn't sag. He stood tall and silent for a moment. "Ma'am," he began, "when you see our complete plans and the beautiful green space surrounding our plan, you'll want to bring your family and friends here more than ever."

Bent on summary, the developer rushed ahead to again pitch the advantages of the project. "What is good for the community and good for growth will be good for you," he said. It was boilerplate language drawn directly from Henderson Development literature, Julie and Jessica would later discover.

Sensing it did not have the full impact he had intended, he tried another tack. "There are some people who have the notion that a new development will spoil their view or alter their way of life. To some degree, that is inevitable. Have you considered that when you move in, you partially disrupt someone else's view? It's been true since the beginning of civilization."

The remark appeared to have drawn a blank.

Searching for a more positive note to conclude on, Henderson reached into his briefcase and extracted a framed photograph. Replacing the architect's drawing, he carefully propped it on the tripod. The image was of a ruddy-cheeked smiling septuagenarian with large ears who to another audience might have been reminiscent of Yoda in the *Star Wars* films. For most people in this crowd, however, the face had an instant familiarity and greater impact.

The late Spencer W. Kimball was the eleventh president and prophet of The Church of Jesus Christ of Latter-day Saints.

Henderson, however, had mined his writings for something else—a pertinent reference that could be used to imply that land development in the Salt Lake Valley was a sacred trust and calling.

"I want to make you aware," he said, "that President Kimball prophesied during his lifetime that the vast acreage of farmland and empty space in this valley would eventually be filled from rim to rim with homes and businesses. That prophecy is now being fulfilled."

As his audience sat in contemplation, Julie glanced at Jessica, who seemed to be reaching for some recollection. She was tentatively and then more boldly raising her hand.

Henderson took a moment to notice and recognize her. "Yes, ma'am," he said patiently, "did you have another question?"

"I'm just remembering something," Jessica said. "We also honor Brigham Young as a prophet, almost as a modern Moses. When he came to this valley, I believe he clearly stated that Temple Square would be the center of a vast network of homes, farms, fields, streams, and mountain havens that would be protected for the use of his saints and all of God's creatures. Shouldn't we be familiar with that saying as well?"

Henderson said he wasn't sure he had heard of such a pronouncement but smiled noncommittally. Oh well. Julie could tell from Jessica's expression that she suspected he had spun Spencer Kimball's words to suit his purposes, but neither she nor Henderson had been able to produce actual quotations. Sort of a case of dueling prophecies (or rather paraphrases thereof). At least she'd challenged his end-game strategy.

Thanking his audience, Henderson gathered his materials and sat down.

Julie made some concluding remarks, promising she would pass on continuing news and further developments. After a sign-up sheet on a clipboard was passed around, people drifted toward the door. Several thanked Julie as they left, including Jessica, who promised she would call.

Finally, Julie found herself alone with Geoffrey Henderson in the entryway. Although she was feeling anything but conciliatory, she apologized for not immediately remembering him. Henderson didn't seem overeager to leave. He launched into a long monologue, during which Julie realized, to her continuing chagrin, that she had other personal and awkward connections to the man.

It turned out that friends of the Achesons, who founded Draper Bank and Trust, had a son who was previously married to Henderson's current wife, Lila. How freaky was that? As Henderson spoke of other friends and acquaintances he had accompanied on hunting trips, some of the names were familiar, probably because Julie's brothers and sisters were active in a larger hunting community whose members hunted to procure meat for their families.

If you were Mormon and grew up in Utah, these often-invisible ties that bound you would eventually surface, sometimes in the least comfortable circumstances.

Having re-established connections with a pretty woman who had been his high school biology lab partner decades earlier, Henderson rambled on with ill-concealed buoyancy. Convinced he had made an impression by his willing participation in a neighborhood meeting, he saw their discussion of hunting and fishing expeditions as a natural segue to a more heroic adventure.

"Are you acquainted with Dick Munson?" he asked. Julie said she didn't think so.

"Well, he's the city administrator of South Jordan," Henderson said. "Very nice, very important guy. You should get to know him. We've been spending time together while putting together this development deal. I recently took him to Africa with me on a wild game safari. Thought he should get to see what real hunting is like." He chuckled.

Henderson was looking at Julie expectantly, as if his story should hold a special delight. While she had participated in hunting trips with her siblings, killing animals wasn't exactly what the outdoors signified for her. Not only that, she realized, but she had no clue what a city administrator exactly was and realized her facial expression didn't reflect proper excitement.

"That must have been something," Julie said vaguely. "Well, thank you so much for coming. We'll probably speak again."

Before turning to the door, Henderson glanced at his reflection in the hall mirror and adjusted the brim of his hat. Offering his hand, he seemed to be searching her eyes for a clue to her impressions. She managed a polite smile but kept her demeanor low-key. If her enthusiasm was lacking, he didn't seem to notice. She watched as he bounded down the steps and into the dark, headed for a huge white four-door pickup truck parked at the curb.

Ten-gallon hats, African safaris, and cozy relationships with city fathers, Julie thought. *What is this whole thing about? Could I have been thinking of the wrong end of the horse when I introduced him to the crowd?*

The possibility that the name Dick Munson could come to mean something to Julie Bell down the road or that Munson would later lie to the press and the courts about having accompanied Henderson to Africa did not cross her mind. She had dishes to wash and kids to get to bed.

Chapter 3
Something Wild

Julie Bell's garden echoed the surrounding landscape—partly domesticated but a little wild. It was all she could do to keep up with the weeds. When Jessica Tobler stopped by three days after the gathering at Julie's house and the encounter with Geoffrey Henderson, she found Julie chopping away at the undergrowth that would have to be cleared before fall became winter.

Welcoming her neighbor, Julie suggested they go inside for a Diet Coke. "Thanks but no thanks," Jessica said. "I'd prefer to be outdoors if you don't mind." Before Julie could reply, she noticed Jessica had found an extra hoe and was pitching in.

Julie watched her out of the corner of her eye as she worked by her side. Jessica was pretty, yes, yet no one would mistake her for a prima donna. She had energy and gusto, and she smiled when she talked.

Where did that commitment come from? Julie had been told that Jessica was pushing a campaign to inform the school board of the need for school buses in the neighborhood. After moving to South Jordan, she had helped to establish a neighborhood watch program.

"So," Julie said, "I hear about your community activism. I admire that. But I doubt you'll get much of a thrill working in my garden."

"Hey"—Jessica grinned—"I don't get *enough* of this kind of activity. I could use a lot more of it. I spend too much of my life indoors trying to change the world." She laughed self-deprecatingly.

"I'm interested," Julie said as she slashed at a greenbrier. "Tell me about what you do."

Rather than directly answering Julie's request, Jessica found herself confessing that despite her commitment to community issues, she often felt insecure and even jealous of women with jobs outside the home.

"Sometimes I feel less valued and respected than working women because I gave up the chance for a career in business for marriage and children," she said. "I guess I've channeled my embarrassment and some of my public relations skills into activism to justify my existence."

Jessica said she had worked on tax limitation, arts in the schools, volunteering for the Salvation Army, and child safety issues and had been involved in several Republican political campaigns. For years, she had lobbied state legislators on behalf of Second Amendment rights, pressing for expanded access to concealed weapons permits.

Julie glanced at her quizzically, wiping away sweat and a strand of her hair that was tickling her nose.

"But my real passion is open space," Jessica explained. "I suppose it has something to do with the way I was raised. When I was little, I really didn't think about how lucky I was. You don't think much about space when you've got plenty of it, when it's all around you."

Kids who grew up in the West in the middle to last half of the twentieth century—in small towns or on family farms in Utah and Idaho—stretched their legs whenever they felt like it.

Most didn't quite know what they had, except for the few who had visited their state capitals on school trips or, more dramatically, attended a Future Farmers (or Homemakers) of America convention in a large city, say Denver or Chicago. There, briefly perhaps, they felt a curious crimp, an uncomfortable lack of breathing room in a closed environment.

Some Western kids who went away to college were glad to escape the physical harshness and social isolation of rural life. Many put down urban roots and never returned.

Others, however, were only too happy to get back as quickly (or as often) as possible to open country, where nature's immensity seemed generous and inexhaustible.

When Jessica Ann Jones married Dave Tobler, they had an understanding that although his work would keep him near Salt Lake City's urban hub, they would eventually live in the country, or at least an approximation of the countryside that a semirural Salt Lake County residence could offer. South Jordan turned out to fill the bill.

Open fields, small farms, vistas of the mountains, pets and wildlife, the nearby Jordan River, a starry sky at night that wasn't obliterated by city lights—all of these were important to her, Jessica informed Julie. She wanted her children to experience some of what she had been fortunate enough to have while growing up.

Farm near Jordan River in So. Jordan, UT, 1996

Both her parents had spent much of their childhoods in the wilds and had worked to instill a respect for that legacy in their offspring. Jessica's dad, a World War II veteran, had been born in 1920 in quirkily named Show Low, Arizona. Jessica's father's family had helped to settle many areas in Arizona; the family's genealogy traced their roots to Mormon church founder Joseph Smith. The Swing-Hi Ranch ("Swing Hi in Show Low") had been in his family for generations. Its surrounding serenity and beauty had remained virtually undisturbed for more than a century.

Still there—after all these years—was a family swing, draped by twenty-foot-long ropes from two huge Ponderosa pine trees, that Jessica and her siblings had used to launch themselves into the sky, high enough to view the countryside.

Only recently when Jessica, her siblings, and their families returned with her parents for nostalgic visits, had they observed the changes brought by growth, development, and a ravenous forest fire.

The experience of Jessica's mother, born in 1926 in obscure Archer in remote southeastern Idaho, had been similar.

"My Aunt Olivia," Jessica told Julie, "always said, 'I love living here. You can go outside and holler as loud as you want and nobody cares.'"

Although Jessica, the youngest child in a family of three sisters and three brothers, was born and raised in Shelley, Idaho (where her high school's athletic teams were called the Shelley "Russets" after the famous Idaho potato), Archer had been her second home. There, the family barn was recognized as a landmark. There she swung from a rope with her siblings and cousins. She sometimes fantasized a "roll in the hay," which she took to have something to do with "making out."

Her mother's family had once received the Idaho Centennial Farms Award from the governor of the state; at that time their land had been continuously farmed by the same family for more than one hundred years.

"My grandfather on my mother's side always said that when he died, heaven would be no surprise," Jessica told Julie. "'Look,' he said, 'I lived in Archer, Idaho. I've *already* been in heaven.'"

Julie laughed in appreciation. "Hold that thought, Jessica. I need a minute to check on Trish." Her special-needs daughter required constant care. Whatever Julie was involved in during the day, Trish's needs were never far from her attention.

When Julie returned, Trish was with her, a slight brunette with freckles and a book in hand. She sat on the patio, where she seemed content to leaf through the picture book and watch them work.

Jessica picked up her story on the small farm her parents had built in Shelley, where she had grown up. When Jessica wasn't practicing the piano and flute, attending rehearsals for music productions, or performing in choir and band concerts, she was riding her bicycle for hours on dirt roads, she said, seldom even meeting an oncoming car. There was unending space for riding horses.

Life was to be lived outdoors—in all seasons. She ran with her dogs and played baseball, tetherball, and hide-and-seek with other farm kids. They built caves in the sand and forts in the snow, leaped from haystacks, had water fights, and jumped with as many as ten other children on a trampoline—one of the few indulgences that cost their parents money.

Some of these activities would have tantalized sheltered city kids; others might have been shunned as perverse or dangerous by parents who wanted more restraint. "In those days"— Jessica laughed—"no one ever worried about being sued."

Jessica swam in the same canal where cows peed upstream and never gave it a second thought. She rode in the back of pickup trucks with her dog, staged cow pie fights with her friends, hooked sleds onto the back of automobiles in the winter, lit firecrackers in tin cans, and helped burn the weeds on the canal bank every spring. She also pitched in with her family to burn garbage in huge fifty-gallon metal drums.

While chores were chores, if they could be done outdoors they were fun. Even tasks that required real effort—weeding the large garden where Jessica's family grew its own produce or lugging irrigation pipe for farmers.

"After the work was done, we had plenty of rewards," she said. "We thought there was nothing better than hiking in one of the canyons or roasting wienies over an open fire."

Then there was the river—the mysterious Snake. The fertile farms of Shelley were built on its banks. They drank from it, as dozens of other communities did, upstream and down. The view was something Jessica drank in as well. It was splendorous, although she could see only a piece of the stream that wound for more than a thousand miles from Idaho to Wyoming.

The river's wildness was both intimidating and captivating.

"I learned to fear it and respect it," Jessica said. Also absorbing was the wildlife that grew, swam, flew, crawled, and wriggled along its banks. Loving her dogs and cats—which regularly produced new litters of puppies and kittens—was one thing, but wild animals held a special fascination.

Nature's influence in childhood had been as directly responsible for nurturing her as her own parents had, she realized.

It was as if she had been chosen and sensitized to the healing power of the natural world. Singled out, in a way, for whatever might be around the next bend. Transplanted from Idaho to Utah, to the banks of another spectacular river—the Jordan—she felt at home.

"I have to tell you, Julie, the other night when I saw the view of the river bottoms from your picture window, and then from your terrace, I was a little jealous. The wildlife and the birds—what I wouldn't give to look out on a vision like that every morning. So stunning."

The view of the Jordan River from Julie Bell's picture window, 1996

"Better stay that way," Julie said, "if I have anything to say about it. What good is a master plan if the city won't stick to it?" She paused to wipe the sweat from her forehead. "This is our heritage. No matter what Henderson seems to think, they can't change the plan without public hearings for comment or opposition."

But why would anyone want to change a plan that was only four years old since its adoption in 1992, made at the time after thorough public review?

"I like your attitude," Jessica said. "You give me hope. If they try to sneak a bad decision past the community, well—we're the ones to hold their feet to the fire."

Henderson had tried to convey the notion that his development was *fait accompli*. No question, Julie and Jessica agreed as they talked. This time he was whistling in the dark when he implied that grateful citizens should praise the god of economic growth and thank their lucky stars that far-sighted men of financial means were in charge.

An arrogant assumption—yet to be tested in the marketplace of public opinion.

"This is *not* a done deal," Jessica said. "And you know what? I'm the one to help you fight this thing. I know how to do this kind of stuff. We can fight this together."

Eventually deciding they'd had enough of the weeds, they went inside, where Jessica accepted a second offer of Diet Coke, and their digging turned to information on members of the South Jordan Planning and Zoning Commission and South Jordan City Council—names Julie had collected from the phone book and calls to "information."

By the time Jessica left to continue her walk, they had put together a flier for a second neighborhood meeting. Using their own money, they would Xerox it at the nearby copy shop, Not Just Copies, and then distribute it in person around the neighborhood, drawing on contact information gleaned from the sign-up sheet.

Later that week, Jessica bought a new cordless telephone and gifted it to Julie. "If you're going to be an activist, a cordless is essential, as well as call waiting and caller ID," she said. It was more than generous, Julie thought, but how could she turn down a gift from the woman who was becoming her friend and mentor?

The second gathering, again to be hosted by Julie, would attract many of the same people who had shown up initially. But there would be new faces as well and hopefully a much larger turnout.

Lacking a guest speaker, Julie's plan was to get the attendees down to business quickly. Upon surveying the activity in her packed family room, she was pleased to realize that was how it had worked out.

Brainstorming in small groups to choose a name for their grassroots group, they came up with several possibilities and then reassembled to make a final selection. "Save Our South Jordan River Valley" was an early favorite, as was "Save Open Space" (SOS). A vote finally settled on "Space Preserves a Clean Environment," which left the acronym as SPACE.

The prospective activists agreed they had a lot to learn before taking on Henderson Development. Grassroots solidarity and organization would be crucial. Research assignments and other tasks were allocated among volunteers.

The attendees again broke down into small groups, one to probe traffic repercussions from the development, another to brainstorm advantages of preserving open space and wildlife habitat, and a third to evaluate potential impact on emergency responses to potential natural disasters.

Jessica tutored her group on the habits and foibles of community leaders she was acquainted with, plus the most effective methods of applying constituent pressure.

Looking up from her own group on traffic, Julie observed with satisfaction that the room was abuzz.

At the close of the evening, a petition was drafted and signed, supporting preservation of the riverbank land as open space:

> *We, the residents of South Jordan, petition the South Jordan City Council and the South Jordan Planning and Zoning Commission to preserve and protect the Jordan River Parkway in South Jordan, which has been designated as open space, including a twenty-five-acre park. We demand that zoning adhere to the current South Jordan master plan.*

Julie would continue research on traffic, which they expected to be heavily impacted by development. While there were long-range plans to widen 10600 South from the little two-lane road that now served the area, the effects of a vehicle surge would clearly overwhelm it before it could be enlarged.

The developer had also floated a hazy suggestion that another highway might be built—a huge five-lane north–south artery—parallel to the river. What was that about?

Next was the monthly public hearing of the South Jordan Planning and Zoning Commission, scheduled for November 20. The river project was sure to come up. Volunteers would have to do their homework.

Some SPACE members were to investigate potential water and air pollution and the environmental impact on wildlife. Henderson's vague references to parking had raised suspicions about how many parking spaces were actually planned and how large an area a parking structure would occupy.

Lip service Henderson had paid to green space was also suspect; the phony green tint applied to the preliminary sketch could have been a bluff.

Should the planning and zoning commission inquire if SPACE had realistic alternatives to the disputed project, they would be prepared. One such possibility was a nature education center for children—a natural for one of the most verdant and picturesque settings in the West. Ogden City had constructed such a center, which according to all reports was a thriving public success.

Rather than rent a Disney video or trust their kids to a dry classroom lecture, wouldn't enlightened parents welcome a resource that used the surrounding hills and fields as a living laboratory of nature? As an educator, Julie saw the idea as a natural.

Working together into the night, Jessica and Julie kept themselves awake with Diet Coke and speculation on the depths of the avaricious ambitions of the developers they were taking on.

They were occasionally interrupted by questions from Jessica's inquisitive children, Sydney, five, and Lexi, eight. Julie placed several calls to her own kids, checking on homework assignments and Trish's well-being.

Geoffrey Henderson was a big talker, the women decided, but even though the company bore his name, he was a front man. He wasn't smart enough to have drafted the grand strategy for manipulating politicians and sweet-talking the public. Marcus Hollings must be the brains of the outfit, the man behind the curtain who pulled the strings while keeping out of the limelight. What the men seemed to share was a certain ruthlessness.

"They're bullies is what they are," Julie said.

"Bastards more like it," Jessica said. She blushed, and they both laughed.

What might others think of the words that came to the tongues of exhausted Mormon housewives?

"Look," Julie said, "if we keep this up and our kids catch on, they'll never listen to us again." Jessica suggested a "cuss jar," a bottle with a slot in the lid where every swear word they caught each other using would require a twenty-five-cent fine.

"Damn right." Julie laughed. "If we get mad enough, we'll have enough to open a bank account for SPACE."

Alliances can be strangely organic organisms. Jessica and Julie quickly fell into a pattern of nightly meetings. They were not only forging a friendship but also a partnership. Julie purchased a "cuss jar," and it seemed to give them permission to talk openly and frankly, bolstering their courage for what was to come. They had to be ready.

A single wrinkle of their preparations—an effort to locate home telephone numbers of members of the planning and zoning commission—had taken hours to track down and install in a file on Jessica's computer.

The finished list, passed on to their volunteers, had an immediate impact, some of it difficult to evaluate. Callers reported commissioners told them they had never been called at home before and some of them were mad about it. A few let it be known they weren't sure they wanted public input before they had made up their own minds.

Jessica, Julie, and their children, along with other allies, got together to distribute hundreds of fliers to homes in surrounding neighborhoods. They canvassed shopping centers, gaining permission to plaster car windshields with fliers. Some store managers even allowed them to place petitions inside their shops.

Local Businesses show support for SPACE petitions

When an early storm dumped snow on the valley, they bundled their kids in mittens and boots, donned their winter coats, and trudged to cover the areas they hadn't yet reached. Physical exertion got their hearts racing and their juices flowing.

Nearing the meeting date, just as momentum was building, Jessica and Julie had a tiff.

Should they publicize their plans by calling the media?

"We need all the help we can get to get the word out," Julie maintained.

"No," Jessica said. "Just ask me what happens when you get reporters questioning your life."

Julie looked at her inquiringly.

"In my experience, if you let them in, it's a double-edged sword. Our lives may never be our own again. Reporters insist on getting both sides of the story. If they dig dirt on Henderson Development, they'll be poking into our affairs too. I don't want the grief."

Julie thought that one over. "Well," she said, "even if that's true, it's a risk we have to take. They'll eventually get the story anyway. This way, we make the first move rather than reacting. We can at least have a little control if we make contacts with journalists—more than we would otherwise have."

Couldn't Henderson and the city blanket the media with press releases, spinning the story to their advantage?

No, Jessica said. At this point, the developers wanted to operate in relative secrecy, without public awareness. But if that were the case, it made sense for SPACE to launch a preemptive strike with the media. "I've talked myself into it," she replied. "I guess you're right."

Having lost the argument, Jessica accepted the job of media liaison. After all, she had the best contacts.

Neighbor kids show support for nature

November 20 was overcast and cold. Arriving at city hall before the 7:30 start time, Julie and Jessica were barely able to squeeze into the hearing room. Within minutes, a line of people including neighbor kids with signs extended into the hallway.

As Julie approached the commission chairman to examine the meeting agenda, she heard someone remark that it was the most people he'd ever seen show up for a public hearing. There must have been more than one hundred in the room.

Last on the agenda. Julie couldn't believe her eyes. The lineup on the clipboard was a joke. They had intentionally pushed them as far back as they could, hoping they'd all go home. Some people she knew had taken time off work to attend the hearing. Several frivolous or inconsequential matters were scheduled to precede them.

A Boy Scout troop that supported a public park had been able to secure seats on the front row. That seemed like a plus, but only momentarily; contrary to custom, the meeting chair ignored their presence.

At least one TV cameraman was in the room, and Jessica recognized a *Salt Lake Tribune* reporter.

While the commission was purportedly conducting serious business, they sat unselfconsciously munching on a series of taxpayer-provided snacks. The treats included soda pop, bottled water, and cellophane cups of cookies, pretzels, trail mix, and animal crackers fancied up with pink and white frosting.

"What is this, a tea party?" Julie whispered to Jessica. "We drool while they eat?"

"Nobody told them it's rude to eat in front of guests," Jessica said.

Nearing 10:00 p.m., the commission was still haggling over mundane business—unweeded yards and citations issued to residents who had failed to plant trees in the parking strips beyond their front sidewalks.

Deadlines for the next morning's *Tribune* had passed. Several people left in impatience or disgust. But a surprising number appeared willing to stick to the bitter end. If the commissioners planned to make excuses for the late hour before announcing a postponement of further proceedings, they were going to have a mob of angry constituents on their hands.

After a hushed conference with his colleagues, the commission chairman declared, "Public comment on development plans for the Jordan River bottoms will now be heard."

The semipacked hall appeared to rouse itself. Was it a rustle of anticipation or relief?

Invited to the podium, black-hatted Geoffrey Henderson was accompanied by two younger men in dark suits, who erected a number of exhibits on portable stands.

Having been exposed to his earlier pitch, the repeated spiel appeared anticlimactic to Julie. He had learned enough to show a little environmental sensitivity and to mention employment and economic growth, but that was about it.

Deferential commissioners pitched softball questions to Henderson, allowing him to reemphasize his previous points.

By the clock on the wall, Julie noticed, he droned on for almost ninety minutes. Then Marcus Hollings followed with a statement of his own, and Janie Kisselman, the city's long-range planner, got in her two cents' worth.

Nearing midnight, the chairman announced that individuals in the audience who wished to make public comments for the record would be limited to two minutes each. Planning and zoning? This was a rerun of the *Twilight Zone*. And it was clear who was being zoned out. Audible discontent rumbled through the audience.

Trooping to the microphone for their allotted stints, Julie, Jessica, and others were cautioned about the time limit and then often cut off while raising their most salient points. A pathetic spectacle.

The hearing was officially closed just before 1:00 a.m. Several more people had left the hall, including one of the five commissioners, whispering an apology to his colleagues. "Here it comes," whispered Jessica. It would make strategic sense for the chairman to cite the lateness of the hour and announce a "no decision."

Astonishingly, he called for a formal vote. Requesting votes to affirm the project, his face registered surprise; only two hands were raised. "And in the negative?" The two remaining hands went up.

"A tie vote in this body requires us to pass this matter on to the South Jordan City Council for determination," the chairman said. "And we're going to schedule another planning and zoning meeting next Tuesday to hear more of your comments." There was a collective sigh in the room— mixed surprise, relief, disappointment, and anger.

It had been a wild night. But strangely, there was more to come. Jessica and Julie later realized that everything of lasting importance seemed to occur after the meeting was over—a total switch of what Jessica's mother had always told her. "Don't expect anything good to happen if you stay out after midnight."

A thin, intense man in his forties wearing a dark blue backpack cornered Jessica and Julie in a corridor and introduced himself as Jack Fitch, saying he was excited to meet "the ringleaders" of what he referred to as "a grassroots revolt."

Fitch said he was the chairman of an organization called Friends of Cottonwood Creek and was committed to helping educate the public about endangered land and water resources. He offered information and contacts that would bolster their campaign. Specifically, Fitch suggested that an organization called Utah Open Space might be able to step up as a key player, possibly helping to purchase the river bottoms property and protect it in perpetuity.

"I've been trying to phone these guys, but they won't return my calls," Fitch said, displaying an open folder of names and numbers.

"Why don't you let us borrow the folder and I'll see what I can do?" Jessica said. He gratefully handed it over.

As the man melded with the crowd, Julie watched with a mixture of interest and curiosity. His looks were not striking, and his clothes were standard thrift shop, but he had energy and a straightforwardness that were appealing. When she later learned that Fitch was reputed to devote himself to various liberal causes, it would not have occurred to her that he would become a close ally or that the time would come when supporters would drop like flies and the loyalty of someone like Fitch might be greatly appreciated.

Next in line in the crowded hallway was one of Julie's neighbors, who produced an article he had clipped from *The Enterprise*, a weekly Salt

Lake business tabloid. The story reported that South Jordan City—as well as officials from Sandy, Riverton, and Draper—had been working with Henderson Development for more than a year.

Apparently, a series of meetings to which the public had not been invited had laid the groundwork for the project, sometimes hyperbolically referred to as the "other downtown." The article implied the deal was virtually signed, sealed, and delivered—not cheery news but, if credible, damning evidence of the city's preference for secret meetings and of its contempt for public input.

Another supporter, a man named Tim Patterson from Parkway Palisades, a neighboring subdivision where he owned his own business, said he had a little extra money and would pay to have bright fluorescent armbands of orange and green material made for volunteers to wear, imprinted with the SPACE logo. A step up from ludicrous little orange dots advocates for open space had been wearing on their foreheads to invite public inquiry and group solidarity.

And then (although neither were eager for a prolonged conversation) there was Julie Bell's introduction to Dick Munson in his official capacity as South Jordan city administrator. Someone had pointed him out to her during the hearing.

Bumping into the tall, dark man—well groomed down to his mustache—as they headed for the exit, Julie asked abruptly, "Are you Mr. Munson, the city administrator?"

"Why, yes," he said.

She found she couldn't keep herself from asking. "Dick," she began, assuming a chatty familiarity, "didn't you and Geoffrey Henderson—the developer—go on an African safari together?"

Blame it on the lateness of the hour, Munson's surprise at being confronted on the issue, or an irritable disposition, but his reply sounded edgy and defensive.

"Yeah," he said, pausing as if to wonder at her impertinence. "But I paid for it myself."

As he huffed toward the door, Julie asked herself a question. *What suddenly possessed me to drop the "Mr. Munson" and call this guy "Dick"? I don't even know the man. Nor do I think I want to.*

Chapter 4
Wrench in the Works

Henderson Development functioned like a giant earthmoving machine with well-oiled moving parts. Some of the parts were mechanical, some financial, some political, and some judicial. Others were geared to public relations and wheedling cooperation or influence from key individuals who might otherwise stand in the way.

Early on, the company had seemed to spin its wheels, landing some small projects and moving cautiously to increase its bottom line. But those days were over. Geoffrey Henderson hadn't allowed himself to fully connect the firm's success—it's surge in new business—with Marcus Hollings's arrival.

There was some prestige, of course, involved with having a district court judge on the payroll, although a lot of good that cachet did when Hollings insisted that no press release be issued and no fuss made.

"The media can be stuffy about these things," Hollings had said. "Some people think that because a judge wears a robe he shouldn't be involved in business or in making money."

But soon Hollings was suggesting expansive moves and a variety of public relations ploys aimed at making friends and acquiring helpful contacts in communities where projects were underway or about to be launched. Occasionally, Henderson wondered who was working for whom. But he didn't complain.

It was secretly thrilling to be shelling out big bucks for a sitting judge to help move heaven and earth, not to mention local politicians.

Mayors, city council members, and zoning commissioners were sometimes among the easiest to move. These were folks whose livelihoods depended on a growing tax base to finance their fiefdoms. Development was the lifeblood of a healthy tax base, and public officials often found it flattering that a successful firm went out of its way to woo them for a public-private partnership.

In bucolic South Jordan, before Henderson Development began lobbying the city's public officials for a huge river park office complex on the banks of the picturesque Jordan as a way of putting their community on the map, it hadn't hurt that (at Hollings's suggestion) Geoffrey Henderson had induced South Jordan City Administrator Dick Munson to accompany him on a fully funded safari to Africa.

Munson was a pliable guy, affable and well-liked by his constituents. His gratitude and friendship were an even more significant trophy than the wild boar's head they had brought back from Africa. While the biggest game would be bagging the project that would surely follow their return, no one could prove undue influence had been applied.

South Jordan was a small, trusting community. "Conflict of interest" was not a polite phrase to bandy about in relation to such respectable figures as Dick Munson or Marcus Hollings.

A smooth harmony among the moving parts of the Henderson machine allowed it to acquire huge swaths of property, quickly manage to get the land re-master-planned and rezoned according to its liking, and then launch development. Once work was underway or completed, the property and project could be sold at tens of millions of dollars before Henderson Development could move on to a new venture.

SPACE (Space Preserves a Clean Environment), a collection of housewives, amateur activists, environmentalists, and hangers-on, was more than an irritant. Be damned if they hadn't become a monkey wrench in the works. Jessica Tobler, Julie Bell, and Jack Fitch had inspired others

SLAPPED!   41

to delusions of grassroots grandeur. They would need to be exposed. If the group refused to take the hint—to back off—it would be crushed.

The mechanism the firm had perfected to deal with such contingencies was the threat—and if necessary, the actuality—of litigation. The tactic would eventually be employed in a variety of communities, including Bluffdale, Riverton, Park City, Fruit Heights, Provo, Orem, West Valley City, and Erda, where opponents of Henderson Development projects would fail to buckle to such warnings and would be sued.

Although he would remain largely behind the scenes as long as he was a judge, Marcus Hollings was confident his knowledge of the law gave him adequate legal clout; he wouldn't hesitate to wield it with impunity.

One of Hollings's young sons came home from a Hollywood movie (*Judge Dredd*), excited to recount the plot for his father. He had identified with the main character, played by Sylvester Stallone, whose unlimited authority allowed him to serve as judge, jury, and executioner in dealing with anyone who dared to wreak havoc in a futuristic lawless state. "He's the bomb, Dad," the boy said. "Is that something like what you do for a living?"

While Hollings had explained the American justice system to his family and what they could and couldn't do under its prohibitions, he smiled in secret satisfaction at his son's naive comparison of him to Sly Stallone. Yes, Hollings was powerful. But if anything, he was the blond blue-eyed antithesis of the Italian Stallion—Aryan, upright, moral, and dedicated to the public good. Stallone should be so lucky.

That didn't mean he wouldn't exert his resources and expertise to make opponents of the capitalist system uncomfortable about appearing in court. Should Bell, Tobler, and their camp followers continue to cause trouble, credible threats and/or legal papers would be at the ready.

Meanwhile, Henderson Development would proceed steadily and prudently, taking care of business, advancing on several fronts simultaneously.

A possible snafu that could impede progress had recently come to the firm's attention. The 110 acres on which the development would be built—at approximately 700 West, stretching from 10600 South to 11200

South in South Jordan—was still largely under private ownership. Some farmers were hesitating to sell a few of the smaller parcels.

Henderson Development had elicited a verbal agreement with Brad G. and Delores D. Wilkerson to obtain the "Wilkerson property," as it was known—by far the largest chunk of the area. But before the deal could be completed with the entity known as the "Wilkerson Trust," several steps would have to be taken.

Word had gotten back to the developers that Brad Wilkerson was blabbing to neighbors that he had backup offers (three of them) pending on his property should Henderson Development's offer fall through. The firm would have to move quickly to lock up the land.

With crucial negotiations hanging fire, Marcus Hollings had supervised the drafting of an application for master plan and zoning changes regarding the Wilkerson property, the southernmost piece of ground the company was after. On October 7, 1996, the firm submitted paperwork to the South Jordan City Council, anticipating the land would fall like a ripe peach into its hands, with the council gladly agreeing to rewrite the master plan and revamp zoning. After the initial October 15 SPACE meeting at Julie Bell's house, the pace quickened.

By October 28, the developers had taken the first step—entering into a real estate purchase contract with the Wilkersons (later to be known in court documents as the "First REPC"). While the landowners signed the contract as "individuals," signaling an intention to sell to the developers, nothing in the document ensured they were doing so as representatives of the Wilkerson Trust. Stipulations in the agreement made it clear the sale wasn't a slam dunk.

> *Seller agrees to assist Buyer in the application and necessary filings to obtain necessary zoning to accommodate among other uses, the construction of class A grade office buildings within the city of South Jordan … The sale can be canceled by the Buyer or the Seller if the city of South Jordan does not grant the necessary zoning and master plan changes by June 30, 1997. Zoning also needs to have specific approval of the Seller.*

The contract also stipulated that the sale couldn't proceed until Henderson Development obtained ownership or rights of purchase on neighboring lands to the north, intended by the master plan for a city park, held by the city of South Jordan. Here, Henderson Development wanted to trade this parcel for land encompassing the Jordan River Trail System. This, as SPACE pointed out, would be an "empty trade" since state law forbade development of the meander corridor.

As the development firm moved to tie up loose ends, its allies passed along news to Hollings and Henderson that the opposition was continuing to meddle in the public arena.

On November 19, Julie Bell had spoken with South Jordan City Councilman Robert Warren to discuss the potential traffic impact of the commercial development. She had reportedly passed along information from the Utah Department of Transportation (UDOT) and the Wasatch Front Regional Council that the proposed development would produce 23,000 additional vehicle trips a day. Warren had reciprocated with advice to contact various state and private agencies that might be interested in preserving the river bottoms.

Julie and Jessica had also reportedly contacted the office of Governor Mark Legler for support and intervention based on the campaign promises Legler had made that he would boldly operate as "Utah's Open Space Governor."

But in actual fact, since the governor loathed being caught between powerful developers and small-town interest groups, he had asked his deputy of intergovernmental relations to handle the issue.

When Jessica and Julie kept the pressure on, Legler passed them off to his state director of public recreation. As if he was offering a final favor, he suggested, "Work with your local mayor." (There wasn't much chance of that, since hearing-impaired South Jordan Mayor Thayne Hollings (no relation to Judge Hollings) was a figurehead who seldom took a stand on anything.)

Instead, Julie and Jessica had written a letter to South Jordan City Administrator Dick Munson requesting that the city grant the residents of South Jordan a three-month grace period to allow them to develop "a better plan for development of the Jordan River Parkway" and that citizens be allowed to present it to the South Jordan City Council in March 1997.

That letter—Geoffrey Henderson was aggravated to learn from Munson—also requested that Henderson Development be required to "gather information concerning traffic impact that its mammoth project would generate on 10600 South and the surrounding roads, including quiet residential streets located nearby."

After this report was relayed by Munson over the phone to Henderson, the developer thanked him and was ready to hang up when Munson stopped him. "There's more," he said, "actually a lot more." Getting madder by the moment, Henderson worked to keep his voice under control. "Fax me the whole damn thing," he said.

Scanning the text of the letter (dated November 26, 1996) a few minutes later, he discovered three additional bullet points:

- *We also ask that Mr. Henderson complete a comprehensive environmental impact study with particular interest paid to the viable ecosystem along the Jordan River Parkway.*

- *In order to make the landowners and residents confident in Mr. Henderson's ability to finance the project, we ask that he show proof of funding. Residents have a concern with all the problems associated with building on a flood plain. More importantly ... the Jordan River Parkway is located in a dangerous earthquake zone, where liquefaction is at its highest danger. Given these and other obstacles, Mr. Henderson may not be able to obtain financial backing and/or insurance.*

- *We also request Mr. Henderson hire an architect to do a rendering of his proposed project so that the city of South Jordan and its residents may more fully understand how fourteen office buildings and restaurants will affect the quality of life in South Jordan.*

As if Henderson hadn't already informed these women during the meeting at the Bell residence that a rendering was being done. He'd damn well produce it on the company's own timetable, not theirs. *Calm down*, he told himself. This was nothing to get excited about. Did they think Dick Munson was going to scurry to do their bidding? It didn't hurt to have loyal friends in city government.

As Henderson was photocopying the letter for Marc Hollings, he noticed two other mentions he had missed. The letter requested "no vote be taken" on changing the master plan until Henderson Development and the residents of South Jordan had "completed their homework." In addition, the letter to Munson referenced an enclosed copy of the original petition, signed by hundreds of South Jordan residents, to keep the land zoned as outlined in the master plan. A "cc" at the bottom indicated copies had been sent to South Jordan's mayor and members of the city council.

Just how much trouble could two supposedly stay-at-home Mormon housewives stir up?

Later that afternoon, when Marc Hollings showed up after a day in court and was ensconced in his development office, he stood reading the document Henderson had handed him. And then, scowling, he invited Henderson in for a sit-down.

"Can you imagine what the press is going to do with this when they get hold of it?" Hollings said. "We could be playing catch-up and doing damage control for a long time. These women are more trouble than they're worth. They're not going to stop on their own. We're going to have to stop them," he said, glancing sharply at his partner.

Henderson could almost guess what was coming next. Hollings had used the plural pronoun "we," but what it usually boiled down to was something less inclusive.

"Get the bare bones of a lawsuit ready," Hollings instructed. "You're going to need to do a ton of research to identify where they're most vulnerable. They think they've got this town by the tail, but they are sadly mistaken. As soon as a court case is mentioned, this town will *turn* tail. And eventually, so will they."

An expression of disgust on his face, Hollings started to stand to indicate the conversation was over, that he had other things to do. Henderson was relieved to realize he hadn't been caught rolling his eyes, but he was annoyed at his partner's tone. It was cavalier and disrespectful.

Barrel-chested and imposing—wearing his black hat—Henderson was pleased to observe as they both stood that he was both taller and wider than Hollings—*his* employee after all. But the well-dressed shorter man had the manner of a ranch boss telling one of his cowhands to clean out the stables. Judge or no judge, Henderson decided, he didn't like that.

Could Geoffrey Henderson have conceived of the shameless prank Jessica and Julie would spring sometime after he had arrived home from work, it could only have further inflicted hurt on the CEO's tender ego.

Wracked with exhaustion from too little sleep and nerves frayed from days of pressure, the women were looking for a break. Spur of the moment, they stopped with their kids at a 7-Eleven on Redwood Road for Slurpees. There, Jessica spotted a scruffy felt fox on a rack of kids' toys. She tugged at Julie's sleeve and pointed. Looking at each other, they laughed and had a similar thought: *why not?*

They purchased the fox and gave it temporary habitat in a shoebox, cutting a ragged asymmetrical hole in the box lid. Making up what they were doing as they went along and giggling at the emerging prank, they placed a little covering of black paper over the hole and peeled back one corner. Then Jessica scrawled a note and attached it to the box: *Please, Mr. Henderson, don't cover up my foxhole with blacktop.*

It took a while in Jessica's trusty 1989 Acura Integra, weaving the streets of a largely Mormon middle-class Sandy neighborhood, to find Geoffrey Henderson's home. If the brown house stood out from its neighbors in any way, it might have been the peeling paint and a few missing shingles—not exactly what they had expected.

The women got out of the car, glancing nervously over their shoulders to make sure the coast was clear. Jessica carried the fox box to the front step, where they intended to deposit it on the doorstep and beat a hasty retreat. But the long rectangular window running the length of the front door seemed to invite their attention, and both women found themselves shielding their eyes and peering inside.

Something was staring back!

It was a huge stuffed bear, seven feet tall or more, standing on its haunches, baring its teeth. Within a few feet were other stuffed animals—a bobcat poised to spring, a deer, and an antelope. Jessica and Julie would later disagree about the monster bear: was it a black bear or a grizzly?

They abandoned the fox in a box on the welcome mat, soon to fend for itself before the more menacing menagerie. Bouncing over speed bumps in the Acura as they exited the neighborhood, the women noticed that the Hendersons had acres of open space nearby to run their horses—the one animal species Geoffrey seemed to prefer alive rather than dead.

Photo c. iStockphoto PhilipCacka

Chapter 5
Monopoly

Ringleaders. Buzzing in Julie Bell's head, the word Jack Fitch had used to describe the South Jordan homemakers he had just met woke her in the bathtub one cold predawn November morning. She had gone there for warmth and comfort, drifting intermittently between wakefulness and sleep.

Julie Bell was in her forties. Somehow she still burned with idealism fed by her education and her instincts. How could she not try to protect the natural world that had been so good to her and her family?

She found herself laughing out loud at the insinuations of the word. *Ringleaders.* Maybe it was a straight-out compliment, since in the beginning she and Jessica had barely been a gang of two. Fitch's word implied the strength and solidarity of a more significant throng.

Blinking widely, the only ring she laid eyes on was the faint one encircling the tub, which made her laugh again. One more thing she didn't have time for around here.

Was Julie a rebel at heart, a rabble-rouser? Well, the growing band of people (about two hundred now) who had so far rallied to their cause was certainly not rabble. Not many of them belonged to an established power structure, but a few (like Jessica) were informed about open space as well as the laws and governmental bodies regulating land development and its preservation. Most were solid civic-minded individuals.

Members of SPACE weren't exactly a ring, but they were becoming a circle of friends. Friends of the earth perhaps, despite the rude response an agitated neighbor had uttered when Julie had tried to hand him a flier: "You're all a bunch of space cadets!"

If she and Jessica were to be dubbed "ringleaders," they would have to earn the title. Standing up to a huge development firm and an entrenched political establishment wasn't exactly ring-around-the-rosy. The odds were all stacked in favor of the people on the other side, who possessed almost everything that mattered: money, prestige, political power, and the arrogant will to grind their foes underfoot.

Well, a few things on Julie and Jessica's side mattered too, she realized. Big things. For one, it was the right thing to do. They were doing it not just for their kids but also for the bumper crop of other children Utah boomer families were raising. *And what would their own lives be like without open space?*

Once they had gotten their children to bed, often late when the kids resisted their 9:00 p.m. bedtime, it was becoming commonplace for Julie and Jessica to work as late as 1:00 or 2:00 a.m., making to-do lists of contacts and assignments, composing fliers, and planning strategy. A couple of times, their sessions had stretched to all-nighters—until 4:00 or 5:00 in the morning.

After Julie drained the tub, scrubbed it with cleanser, toweled dry, and slipped into a T-shirt and jeans, she stood in front of the mirror, brushing her hair. Dark, full, and flowing, it touched her shoulders. She had a pleasing oval face, although she noticed there were now creases below her eyes, obviously the result of too little sleep. Makeup could serve as short-term camouflage. As a mother of three, she had retained her figure.

She considered the contrasting double image she and Jessica presented as they made public appearances together: the sleek and flamboyant blond with a wide smile and mischievous eyes and the laid-back brunette whose calm articulateness could occasionally sneak up on male power brokers. Some of them seemed to habitually take her lightly as a seemingly detached stay-at-home mom. Not a bad thing, since it often worked to her advantage.

It was funny in a way, she thought. If only those deep-pocketed developers in their plush offices (as well as their collaborators—those small-town politicians at city hall busy feathering their own nests) could see what really went on behind the shutters of their chief antagonists' homes, they might laugh themselves sick.

She could safely bet her fake Gucci boots that those captains of industry—unrolling expensive blueprints on a long walnut conference table in preparation for ripping up the elegant contours of the Jordan River—weren't worrying about child care. That was what their *wives* were for. Business and family were separate realms—not meant to cross paths.

Can't be helped, Julie thought. Wasn't that the way of the world? *This* world, at least. Most women—certainly most Mormon women—did most domestic chores, cooked the meals, raised the kids, washed and ironed their husbands' clothes, not to mention took on the lion's share of church service. And then if they desired to poke their pretty noses into community life, they had to find a way to do it that didn't detract from their family image or clash too openly with traditional expectations.

It was fortunate that Julie's oldest daughter, Cady, was both willing and competent to care for younger children. Most evenings, she had become the de facto babysitter for both Julie's and Jessica's kids when the women got together. Jessica would drop her daughters off at Julie's house and pick up Julie for the short hop to Jessica's place. Then in the wee hours, she would drive her back and make the exchange.

With Ted in Idaho for most of the week, Julie had grown accustomed to functioning as a single mother. Potty-training her five-year-old special-needs daughter, Trish, would have been difficult enough without the added stress. Now it was just part of the mix. Huddled around the bulky computer at Jessica's place (among the few local households where the electronic age was beginning to dawn), Julie came to expect the almost inevitable phone call from one of her children around 10:00 or 11:00 p.m. asking, "When are you coming home, Mom? I can't go back to sleep."

If Trish had pulled her diaper off and managed to leave a deposit somewhere on the kitchen floor—or worse, on the family room carpet—the tenor of such a call was made to sound like an emergency. So Julie felt obliged to salve her conscience, making a guilt trip home to clean up the mess and make sure everything was okay.

For Julie, a nightly neighborhood road rally often followed a day of chauffeuring Cady and Brandon to karate, Brandon to baseball practice, and Trish to dance and physical therapy. It was a comparable story for Jessica, who planned around getting her kids to dance, piano, and music lessons.

But it wasn't all a downer. Julie got a curious transfusion of energy from watching her kids perform. She wasn't going to use exhaustion as an excuse to cave to business-suited bullies.

Jessica had been involved in this kind of runaround for years, and she was still very much alive—alive and kicking. Julie realized that for her new friend the proposition had always involved kicking some butt, a skill Julie found inspiring.

As a motivator and an organizer, Jessica knew how to absorb inspiration as well as dish it out. At one of the SPACE meetings at Julie's house, now regularly attracting between thirty and fifty interested people to brainstorm strategies, a fund-raising suggestion caught Jessica's attention.

"How many people are here in South Jordan?" a woman asked. "If there are twenty thousand people here who would be willing to chip in twenty dollars each, that would be four hundred thousand dollars. Why couldn't we buy the land ourselves?"

It was true that the development company hadn't yet acquired all the property it required. There were still some holdouts who weren't agreeable to a sellout. Maybe the property owners—mostly farmers who had struggled for years to make a living off their properties—were looking for a better return on their labor.

Julie had learned that, previous to the recent planning and zoning commission hearing, the Utah Conservation Council had taken soil samples on the land and found that it had an acidic base. With water purification and other reclamation work, the area could be returned to wetlands habitat and a refuge for migratory birds. The UCC had offered $25,000 an acre to several of the landowners.

Henderson Development, however, had gotten wind of the UCC's incursion and had stepped in to inform the farmers that they would be willing to up the ante by $10,000 per acre.

It was clear the developers wanted to leave the impression that they could throw around cash with abandon so as to intimidate anyone else eying the land. *Compared to our resources, you might as well be offering play money* was the implication.

If Monopoly was the game, more than one could play, however. Since Jessica often indulged in the board game with her kids, she sensed that bravado might be able to carry the day, even for those with the fewest resources.

Applying the scenario to real life, the owners of Park Place and Boardwalk were treating the little guys as if their property was the slums (e.g., Baltic Avenue) and therefore relegating it to a lowball bid. What they weren't telling them was that it would soon skyrocket in value.

The upcoming November 27 South Jordan Planning and Zoning Commission meeting would offer a venue to educate people on the value of preserving open space. But there was also an opportunity to have some fun, using theatrics to liven things up and grab public attention.

On meeting night, Jessica dropped some Monopoly pieces into her purse, along with a wad of fake one hundred dollar bills.

It appeared a majority of the large crowd that stuffed city hall was there to speak in favor of preservation and in opposition to a glass and concrete city on the banks of the Jordan. Jessica's and Julie's networking and leafleting seemed at least to be paying off in warm bodies.

When city business from the podium concluded and the meeting was opened to public comment, those addressing the question of development versus open space favored the latter over the former by something close to a four-to-one margin. A window of opportunity had opened in the room.

It was Jessica's cue. She had delayed her remarks for ultimate impact. Approaching Commission Chairman Bart Morley at the front of the room, she withdrew a Monopoly bill from her purse and raised it high above her head.

"The developers of this proposed project want to buy the Boardwalk property of this city for Baltic Avenue prices," she said, glancing at Morley. "We can have some say over that. I will put up the first one hundred dollars toward a fund to allow us all to retain a stake in our heritage. If enough of us contribute, Henderson Development won't be able to 'Monopolize' our community."

Jessica held up a map of the property, to which she had attached rectangular strips of tin foil. "Under Henderson Development's plans, the greenery that now lines the riverbanks will be replaced by something as ugly as this tin foil—parking lots," she said.

Placing the map on a table, she spilled a handful of little plastic houses and hotels from her purse onto the map and arranged them inside the foil strips.

"If you think we deserve better than a collection of tacky buildings on this precious land, now is the time to respond." Then she removed the fake one hundred dollar bill and replaced it with a real one, showing it—front and back—to the audience before depositing it in front of Morley.

Almost immediately, individual members of the audience began to come forward—some with cash, others with pens and checkbooks in hand.

Had this been an alter call or a "come to Jesus" rally in a born-again church, the masses thronging the center aisle would have thrilled the pastor.

As unofficial referee of this secular congregation, Morley himself was apparently getting the spirit. He couldn't seem to suppress a grin at what was happening.

Within minutes, a sloping stack of currency and checks was heaped in front of the council chairman. "Will you take a credit card?" one woman asked, drawing audience laughter. She plopped down a fifty dollar bill.

Morley took out his own wallet and added another one hundred dollar bill to the stash. He said a fund would have to be established in a bank account under the supervision of the South Jordan Parks and Recreation Department.

SLAPPED!   55

Was this all a little too rosy, Jessica wondered. Was there a fly in the ointment? Oh no, there she was—a dark woman in a pink suit, seated at a table behind the podium.

Introducing herself as Gladys Hastings, the ranking planning technician for the South Jordan Parks and Recreation Department, she interrupted Morley to dash cold water on the building enthusiasm.

"There's really no way," she said, stepping brusquely to the podium, "that we can issue receipts for these contributions tonight. You will need to retrieve your money. It may take some time to get authorization to set up a fund. After a few days, if you're still convinced you want to be involved, you can bring in your money to our department office, where we can properly receipt you. But for now ..." she trailed off, nodding toward the stack of currency and checks that appeared to wilt at her words.

The air had gone out of the room. Once seated again, Hastings looked irritated that people were staring at her. Eventually, a slow stream of abashed and disappointed individuals trickled up the aisle to collect what they had offered up.

During a break in the proceedings, just as the sudden reversal was settling in for Jessica and Julie, an affluent-looking man from Parkway Palisades approached them to report he was willing to donate as much as $10,000 once a fund was officially established. He said he was certain that tens of thousands of additional dollars could be raised from others he knew in his neighborhood.

After profusely thanking the stranger, Jessica whispered to Julie, "If we told people what happened here tonight, they would think we were making it up."

Maybe Monopoly was a game of both chance and revelation. Failure to land on and acquire properties in the most affluent neighborhoods didn't necessarily spell loss or dishonor. That obscure and often overlooked space on the board called "Community Chest" might be the answer. *Could a community of people of differing means but similar goals come together to save a perceived heritage?*

Chapter 6
Damage

A mistake (no question) to count chickens before they were hatched, or cash before you have a place to stash it. *Why were all the best clichés metaphors from farming life? And why did they all seem to apply? As exciting as the prospect was that money and hope were mounting, wouldn't it be foolish to put the prospective eggs in one basket?*

Jessica had been tracking several officials at Utah Open Space and had finally gotten a bite from a friendly board member in Park City named Mandy Fletcher. After Jessica detailed the opportunity for a wildlife preserve on the Jordan River, Fletcher had agreed she'd be willing to make a formal presentation to any landowners who were willing to gather.

It was premature, Jessica realized, to get too excited about the possibilities—putting the cart before the horse, so to speak. (*There was another one!*) But it was encouraging that a powerful environmental organization whose mission centered on preserving open space and that presumably had the funds to accomplish their goals was taking a look at the Jordan bottomlands.

But what would the landowners say? Several of them had shown up at public hearings and had let it be known that they favored the proposed development.

Was my Monopoly stunt just a cute gimmick that will end up cutting off our noses to spite our faces? Some of those people had to feel outnumbered and chagrined.

What was it her mother used to say? *When in doubt, let people know you care.*

Corny but true and no connection with farming as far as she could tell. The practical application of that maxim was an easy one, she realized. Jessica had used it on many occasions.

When the girls arrived home from school the day after planning and zoning, the aroma from the kitchen reached their nostrils as soon as they opened the door. Chocolate chip and oatmeal cookies warm from the oven. They mildly resented their mother rationing them only two cookies each before dinner but agreed to help wrap the rest. Because of her gluten allergy, Lexi would get the best of it, as usual. The separate batch of rice cookies Jessica had baked would be hers alone.

Julie had been gifted with cookies from Jessica's kitchen before and had never complained. Virtually no one in the neighborhood had missed out. Would Julie be willing to accompany Jessica on a "cookie run" to landowners they had met at public meetings? She could hardly refuse after accepting her own plate of goodies.

Fresh baked goods were nurturance to farm people. They could serve as an unspoken apology should anyone have felt ganged up on. It worked with urbanites too. Jessica recalled she had once taken cookies to some gangbangers at a run-down apartment complex who had befriended her during a gun rights march. With the gift, their tough exterior melted away.

"It's not as if we're opposing the landowners," Jessica told Julie as they headed out the door. "But what if they think we hate them? We care about their land, and we care about them as well. They need to know we respect them."

Nobody was home at the Brad and Delores Wilkerson residence. They placed the Saran-wrapped cookies on the doorstep with a note:

SLAPPED! 59

As your neighbors, we want to let you know we care about you. We'd like to help preserve your land while ensuring you're properly compensated.

Sincerely,
Jessica and Julie

A teenage son answered the door at the Glen Edwards residence. He eyed the cookies eagerly and said he would tell his mom and dad. The message the boy agreed to pass on to his parents was a variation on the contents of the note.

Glen Edwards's father, Ken, opened the door at the third house. A former mayor of South Jordan, he invited them in. His wife, Sarah, took the cookies and placed them on the coffee table in the living room, inviting her guests to sit. The conversation meandered over a number of topics and led to a virtual history of South Jordan, narrated by Ken. Then he brought them up to speed on current events, recounting the visit of the representatives of the Utah Conservation Council and their offer of $25,000 an acre for the land.

Edwards said they had seriously considered this bid but were then approached by Geoffrey Henderson, who pitched an additional $10,000 per acre. Presently, this was the offer they intended to pursue.

Jessica mentioned that she and Julie were hosting a meeting to present other options and that Mandy Fletcher of Utah Open Space had agreed to attend. She asked if Ken and Sarah would be interested in hearing what she had to say. They said they would consider it.

Sarah Edwards served Jessica's cookies on good china and with a pitcher of cold milk. While Jessica and Julie had already eaten, they could hardly say no.

The visit ended with mutual smacking of lips. Whether the cookie run had accomplished anything besides encouraging goodwill was hard to tell. But wasn't that what good public relations were about?

Theoretically, but maybe not. How were they to know the gesture would later be turned against them and used in court?

Christmas was coming. The way things were shaping up, there would be precious little time for celebration. The neighborly visits might be the closest thing to feeling the holiday spirit Julie and Jessica would have.

On December 5, the date for the evening meeting with the landowners, which Tim Patterson had offered to host at his home in Parkway, a heavy snowstorm blanketed the Salt Lake Valley and surrounding environs. While Julie was watching the progression of the storm and wondering how it would affect attendance, Mandy Fletcher of Utah Open Space called from Park City.

Parley's Canyon was an icy mess, she explained, saying she wasn't willing to risk driving down from Summit County. They'd have to make do without her.

It couldn't be helped, although Fletcher was supposed to be the featured speaker. The storm slacked off toward evening, and a reasonable number of landowners showed up at Patterson's place. Julie and Jessica made apologies for their absent guest. Fletcher had faxed information on conservation easements, which Jessica detailed to the group.

The purpose of the meeting, Julie assured the gathering, was to inform the landowners of possible alternatives if rezoning was not approved and all master plan provisions remained intact. All of the participants, including Brad and Delores Wilkerson, seemed interested in preserving open space. The meeting broke up early to afford time for nervous drivers to negotiate the tricky roads.

Two days later, at the Republican State Central Committee meeting at Sandy City Hall, Jessica connected with Utah Congressman Elect Farrell Brooks, with whom she had a long-standing political relationship. Over the years, she had worked with him on tax and term limitation initiatives and other GOP gambits. Brooks, the genial, anti-establishment, high-energy owner of an explosives company, had won elective office after a legendary string of campaigns.

"Is there a possibility you could find federal funds to help save the Jordan River bottoms?" Jessica asked in her direct mode, softened by feminine charm. Brooks looked at her and smiled. After a little wheedling, Brooks agreed to drive with her to take a look at the site. While strolling on the banks of the Jordan, Brooks and Jessica ran into Ken Edwards, one of the nearby property owners. The three of them talked, and Edwards seemed impressed with Jessica's explanation that the congressman was considering how federal funds might be used to preserve the land. Brooks didn't confirm her assessment, but he looked pleased by the combined attention of a pretty woman and a down-home constituent and former mayor. As they walked to their cars, Jessica pointed out a red-tailed hawk winging overhead.

The next couple of weeks offered a flurry of activities and events— some of which Julie and Jessica had set in motion—offering SPACE a window for public relations impact in the push before the holidays. SPACE members and other concerned citizens met at the South Jordan Middle School to hash over ramifications of the commercial development and prepared for a city council meeting a week later, scheduled at the middle school to accommodate an anticipated large crowd. The council would again take up development plans for public discussion.

Julie and Jessica had advertised the meetings by flier and had also written a letter to Dick Munson and the South Jordan City Council, asking for time on the agenda to address traffic and environmental concerns.

They had been taking care of business. Since Jessica and Julie felt run almost ragged from Christmas preparations for their families and by their obligations with SPACE, they weren't inclined to look over their shoulders at the prospect of more trouble.

On December 17, the morning of the scheduled city council meeting, they found early Christmas gifts in their mailboxes—identical letters bearing both their names, signed by Geoffrey Henderson. Dated Friday the thirteenth of December, the missives had obviously been mailed late to arrive at the least convenient moment. The letter, sloppily written and oddly rife with compositional errors (*didn't these people employ a literate secretary?*) amounted to a thinly veiled warning to back off.

> *I will review some of the activities that concern us ... asking*
> *South Jordan city officials to violate our due process right*
> *to decision on our application for master plan and zoning*

so... that options on properties would expire... and that you would have more time to raise money to attempt to purchase the land yourselves ...

Your ... effort to delay our due process at South Jordan City clearly extend beyond the limits of the law ... Any effort by you... or anyone else interfere with any our rights may subject each person involved... to the possibility of litigation and the payment of damages. Damages literally could be in the millions of dollars.

In other words, *if exercising your First Amendment rights by speaking out at city council is worth being sued, get ready to rumble.*

Interesting that the same big shots who had difficulty putting together a proper English sentence for an important business letter knew how to juxtapose a few well-chosen words so loaded with menace that it went straight to the gut. *Litigation, damages,* and *millions* did the trick.

While the early 1990s psychological film thriller *Damage,* starring Jeremy Irons, was centered on sex rather than greed, the mental abuse dished out to its female lead could have been a model for land barons taking pleasure in tightening the screws on hapless housewives.

This kind of damage would be inflicted on the mind, the gut, and the pocketbook. The financial resources of the public-spirited individuals involved were tenuous at best.

Real-life Monopoly—they were now in over their heads in the game with professionals who played for keeps. Jessica later told Julie that as she read the letter, a little shiver ran down her spine. People who had the money and the power intended to soon acquire all the property they needed. Jessica and Julie had landed on the square that read, "Do Not Pass Go. Do Not Collect $200."

Chapter 7
Dinner on the Dark Side

They had been ambushed—plain and simple. If you were an admirer of the dark arts of political gamesmanship, the timing was exquisite.

With its less-than-subtle scent of coming litigation, the letter's arrival on the morning of the city council meeting was a shot across the bow, just as they were ready to sail into the teeth of an important engagement.

Once Jessica and Julie talked, they realized the maneuver was meant to knock them off balance, scare the fight out of them. But now, as they picked themselves up off the deck, both were consoled by the fact that they weren't so much frightened as angry at being blindsided.

"How dare they threaten us!" Julie fumed.

"These guys are *assholes*," Jessica responded, forgetting to look abashed at what had just come out of her mouth. It was a word she had warned her children of appropriate punishment for should they ever use it or any of its common euphemisms.

"Here," Julie said, producing a fifty-cent piece from her handbag. "I'm paying for this one." She dropped the coin into the slot of the cuss jar on Jessica's breakfast bar. "You deserve a free one."

Once they had vented to each other, the two women considered their immediate options. Should they simply go about their business at the meeting, giving no indication anything had happened or that their composure had been rattled? Wouldn't that be the best way to handle it? Did they owe any immediate heads-up to SPACE supporters? Or should they consult with an attorney before figuring out what to do?

As it turned out, the illusion that they could keep the matter to themselves for any length of time quickly evaporated. In the late afternoon, while helping Lexi prepare for her Christmas piano recital, Jessica heard her daughter Sydney calling from the floor above. "Mom, some TV guy's on the phone for you."

She picked up without considering what such a call might mean and immediately recognized the voice of Kent Huffaker, a long-time reporter at KTVX, Channel 4, who skipped the pleasantries to ask, "Is it true Henderson Development has notified you that they're considering a lawsuit?"

Caught slightly off guard, Jessica spilled the beans. Well, she said, she and Julie were in receipt of a letter from Henderson Development but weren't ready to talk about it in any detail.

His voice empathetic and reassuring, Huffaker took the stance of a friendly advocate for the public's right to know. "If they ever tried to sue you for speaking out, the media would come down on them like a ton of bricks," he said. "It would be a bigger story than whirling disease at Governor Legler's family fisheries."

Jessica found the comparison amusing, but she recognized that his diplomacy was aimed at assuring her that SPACE had allies in the press so as to elicit any scrap of further information she might be willing to divulge. She thanked him for his interest but firmly restated her position that she wasn't able to discuss the letter's contents. Whatever Huffaker had gathered about the situation—lacking strong visuals and usable quotes—wouldn't make much of a TV story.

The afternoon disappeared on Jessica's computer as she sorted through remarks for her presentation at city council. Later, in rummaging through her closet to decide what to wear, she realized she would barely have time

SLAPPED!

to fix something for the kids to eat but no time to eat herself. Oh well. She had a nervous stomach anyway. Maybe she and Julie could grab something after the hearing.

That evening, on the way into South Jordan Middle School, Julie Bell rounded a corner into a crowded corridor. Even from the back, there was no mistaking the man a few feet down the hall. Boots, cowboy hat, wide shoulders—Geoffrey Henderson. His hat was *white* tonight rather than black, a subtle image change—perhaps for the benefit of expected press coverage?

He turned from the man he was chatting up just in time to meet Julie's eyes. "Hey, Geoffrey," she said on impulse as she passed. "Your letter showed up. What's the deal with this stuff about a lawsuit?" Henderson shrugged, looking a little undone by the breezy affront.

Inside the packed auditorium before proceedings began, Jessica and Julie circulated another sign-up sheet among interested citizens with the intention of acquiring new names and contact information.

For once, SPACE supporters were given adequate time to present pertinent information on the proposed development's potential impact on infrastructure, property values, tax base, city parks, buffer zones, wildlife, pedestrian access to parks, and options for locating such a development on an alternative site. The community members who spoke from the podium seemed a solid cross section of South Jordan citizens.

Julie's detailed analysis of traffic impact in the community, drawing on information she had procured from the Wasatch Front Regional Council and Utah Department of Transportation (UDOT), made clear that she had done her homework. As the clincher for her remarks, she reported that UDOT was officially recommending that a traffic impact study be conducted before any construction could commence.

Jessica presented a laundry list of concerns about the need for open space preservation and the loss to the community should the master plan's guarantee of park space be abandoned. She offered the possibility that federal funds might become available to support creation of a park. For these and other reasons, she said, the city should oppose zoning and master plan changes. Applause was generous in response.

Only a couple of individuals spoke in favor of Henderson Development's plan. Overwhelmingly, it appeared, the community had spoken—in solid opposition. How could the council ignore the odds?

After huddling privately for a few minutes, council members took the easy way out. They tabled Henderson Development's request to amend the master plan and zoning ordinances and referred the issues to a subcommittee "for review and recommendation."

After all, it was almost the holidays, and while their hopes that the advent of Christmas might discourage a large public turnout hadn't panned out, could anyone blame them for postponing difficult decisions for a more propitious time?

It wasn't a defeat, but for Jessica and Julie the result tasted flat and unsatisfying. It did manage to delay immediate action by the developers, which might give SPACE some time to maneuver. But what would happen once the word got around about the threatened legal action?

Shambling toward the exit of the middle school as Jessica confessed she was starving and suggested they stop someplace to eat, Julie felt a tap on her shoulder.

Breaking stride and turning to look, she faced the tight-lipped smile and impeccable grooming of Marcus Hollings. She was unnerved but hoped she didn't show it. Then she noticed Geoffrey Henderson a step behind, his hands on his hips. She called ahead to Jessica, who was almost to the door.

"Ladies," Hollings said as Jessica backtracked, "we thought it might be a good idea for us to have a little informal talk."

Sure, go ahead and have it, Julie thought sarcastically. *Don't mind us. No, he's inviting us to chat as if we were friends and as if a late-night tête-à-tête is the most natural thing in the world.* "What did you have in mind?" Julie asked, glancing at her watch. It was almost 11:30 p.m.

"Well, maybe over a cup of ..." Hollings paused. "...cocoa?" The two women looked at each other. "Our treat," Hollings clarified.

"If we go to a restaurant, I'm going to eat real food," Jessica said. Julie was tired but also curious. She liked Jessica's brash interpretation of their offer as an invitation to dinner, and if *she* was up for it, why not? It would be a bizarrely perfect ending to a perfectly bizarre day.

"Oh, by the way, Geoffrey," Jessica said, turning to Henderson. "I got your letter. What a piece of crap." Henderson pulled his hat farther down over his eyes and appeared to be biting his tongue as he strode toward the door.

Nearing midnight, restaurant choices in the south valley were limited; in fact, there may not have been more than *one*—a downscale Denny's on 10600 South. Weirdly, the trip was made by convoy—in four separate vehicles.

Julie and Jessica walked in together from the parking lot. Entering the restaurant, they noticed the men had staked out a corner booth covered by Denny's distinctive orange fake leatherette.

Geoffrey Henderson was just removing his black ankle-length trench coat to drape it over the back of the booth. Jessica had noticed it at the middle school. With the boots, oversized belt buckle, and ten-gallon hat, the retro duster made him look like a member of the James Gang or some other infamous outlaw from *Maverick* or maybe an episode of *Gunsmoke*. He hadn't removed the hat.

Julie observed both men's eyes on Jessica as she took off her wrap. She had chosen to wear a black fitted zipper-down sweater and a black skirt—it came to her mid-thighs—with black hose and high heels. Julie wore heels as well, but her smart fitted pantsuit didn't draw as much attention. Hollings's conservative dark business suit with a striped tie was his usual public garb. The late-night denizens of Denny's, always a curiously eclectic lot—truck drivers, construction workers, young couples, teenagers, a few drifters or homeless, plus wannabe Goths with multiple piercings—must have had a ball trying to figure the focus of this foursome.

The first few moments were the most awkward. To make room for the women, Henderson had slid into the center of the curved booth, uncomfortably close to Hollings, who didn't seem willing to move any closer to the outer edge. Jessica was next to Henderson, with Julie on the near side. They all busied themselves with examining menus even though Julie had already announced she was only having a Diet Coke.

68   *Paul Swenson*

When a waitress mercifully interrupted their forced chitchat, Hollings ordered a Malibu chicken sandwich and a cup of hot chocolate and Jessica a chef's salad and "Moons Over My Hammy," a ham and scrambled egg sandwich on sourdough. (In the wonderful world of Denny's, bad puns passed for creativity.) Henderson said he was fine with ice water.

Once the waitress left the table, Hollings turned to the women. "We wanted to have this talk to ask if there isn't a way we can all work together to solve this community issue to our mutual satisfaction."

"Well, Judge Hollings—" Julie said.

"No, please," Hollings interrupted. "Call me Marc."

"Well ..." She paused. " ... Marc, let's look at it this way: if the changes in the zoning and the master plan don't go through, then there might be something for us to talk about." Julie glanced at Jessica, who, after a moment's hesitation, nodded her assent.

"Oh, the amendment to the master plan *will* go through," Hollings deadpanned. Henderson seemed visibly irritated by the interjection but didn't contradict his partner's assertion.

There was a brief pause as this news was absorbed and processed.

"We have a different opinion about the likely outcome," Julie said. "But for argument's sake, say you turn out to be right about that. If the project is finally built on the riverbanks, wouldn't a different kind of architecture with native materials be more compatible with the surroundings? Not so much glass and concrete."

"Yea, how about something more like the San Antonio River Walk or The Hotel Hershey in Hershey, Pennsylvania?" Jessica suggested.

Both men looked dumbstruck. How could housewives, their expressions seemed to say, imply that they had the expertise to evaluate the aesthetic choices of professionals? "We already have a team in place to make those decisions," Hollings said.

"Judge Hollings ..." Jessica said. He raised his hand to protest her form of address, but she waved him off. "Judge, the smartest thing you could do if you're successful in pushing this project through is hiring us to work on a committee to help make the project something we can all be proud of. Think of what Deena Cassalino did when she got in trouble."

The controversial Salt Lake mayor had hired Rod Yarich to defend her, the very attorney she had been under attack from all along, Jessica pointed out. "It was a brilliant public relations move," she added.

At the mention of Democratic pillars from the decadent capital city, the development partners' moods appeared to darken.

"While we appreciate your interest, Mrs. Tobler—pardon, Jessica. May I call you that?" When she didn't answer, Hollings rushed on. "We have our own people who are eminently qualified," he said. "Where we could use your help is in convincing your neighbors that our plan is in their long-range interest and for the benefit of the community."

"In that case," Jessica replied, "we'll have to fight you every step of the way." She smiled as she said it, and for a moment the men appeared to wonder if she was going to add, "Just kidding."

When the waitress came with the food, Jessica was telling Julie about the time she had brought her family to Denny's and all the kids had attempted to order hot fudge sundaes. Hollings forced a smile, and Julie noticed Henderson was rolling his eyes.

Having completed their part of the transaction, the women relaxed, in contrast to their somewhat disgruntled dining companions. As Julie sipped her Diet Coke and Henderson nursed his ice water, Jessica kept glancing enviously at Hollings's plate, where the pile of French fries served with his sandwich hadn't been touched.

"Something of mine you want?" Hollings said, the faintest edge in his voice.

"Why thank you, Marc. You mind if I have a couple of your fries?"

"Help yourself," he said, slightly put off by her switch in form of address and unbelieving she would go beyond yanking his chain. No civilized person would take food from another person's plate.

"Excuse me, Geoffrey," she said, reaching across Henderson's barrel chest to pluck two fries from the stack Hollings had ignored. She noticed Henderson almost flinch when she accidentally touched his wrist.

As Jessica calmly consumed her purloined potatoes, Henderson removed his wallet and was extracting a credit card when he stopped to ask, "I don't suppose anyone would like some dessert?"

He looked annoyed when both women hesitated before answering. "No thank you," Julie said.

"Actually," Jessica spoke up, "I would." There was an audible sigh. It was hard to tell whether Hollings or Henderson had uttered it. Neither man seemed resigned to spending another half hour in the booth.

"Don't worry," Jessica said. "I'm getting a hot fudge sundae to go. I'll take it home to my kids."

Despite reprieve from extended incarceration at the table, there was some impatient shuffling of feet by the hosts at the cashier's station as they waited for the waitress to add the to-go order to the check and bring the Styrofoam carton of food. While Hollings was trying to make nice by shaking hands, something occurred to Henderson.

"I got your shabby little fox," he said in a half-hearted final flourish.

"Who? Us?" Jessica teased. "Would we do something like that?"

"It was *cute*," he said, stressing the word with an ironic tone. "And I saw you peeking in the window."

As lame as it may have been, it wasn't a bad exit line. It even stung a little, Jessica realized as she walked Julie to her car. They paused briefly to watch the men's expensive vehicles wheel out of the parking lot.

"Why don't you just get this whole thing over with and sleep with Geoffrey Henderson?" Jessica said sarcastically. As black humor, it was more acerbic than anything she had ever said to her friend, or anyone else for that matter. Knowing she was not the target, Julie laughed.

"Oh, I do have my standards," she said.

Chapter 8
Year of the Ox

Christmas was tough. The carols were beautiful, but the words rang false when the nights were ... what? Jangling or raucous rather than silent. And all was far from anything that could be called calm. Opening presents with her family, Julie Bell was struck by the fact that even her kids' excitement was getting on her nerves.

What in past celebrations had been welcome and rewarding now seemed like a diversion, or worse, a cruel hypocrisy. Although present physically, she realized the attempt to block out everything swirling in her head (even for a day, even on Christmas) resembled torture.

As thankful as she was for an excuse to ignore the telephone for a few hours, even that reprieve obviously wouldn't last. Dead ahead, there would almost certainly be another looming crisis. She and Jessica were involved in what felt like hand-to-hand combat with an occupying force—a force intent on taking over not only open land but also their lives as well.

How long can a war last? How much resilience will it take to see it through?

As the red ribbon slipped away from the green wrapping paper on the package Julie was opening, something loosened in her psyche. A brilliant image of the Great Salt Lake revealed itself—the cover of a nature calendar, a present from her son, Brandon. Flipping through the pages with their gorgeous color photos, she perceived that some of the reverence she had always felt for the natural world may have been passed on to (and appreciated by) her children. Now, that would be a gift.

What she failed to observe and would only notice late in the coming year was the calendar's designation of 1997 as "The Year of the Ox," borrowed from the Chinese calendar and zodiac.

For the time being, she would also remain unaware (fortunately perhaps) of what the year would bring—a series of seemingly repetitive events, many without satisfying resolution. In the week between Christmas and New Year's, she would dream, bizarrely, that she and Jessica were yoked together in a vast field, plowing the same patch of ground over and over again. When she woke, Julie would laugh at her instant interpretation, deciding the patience of an ox would be required for this fight, as well as a sense of humor at one's own expense.

The day after Christmas, grasping for straws, Jessica reached out to Governor Mark Legler by letter, appealing to his self-designated title of "Open Space Governor" and asking him to throw state support to preserving the South Jordan master plan from amendment or change. The letter was predictably destined for the round file.

Its footnote was a call from a flunky in Governor Legler's office who said the governor wanted her and Julie to know that "the governor feels your pain." But respectfully, he asked, "where can our children expect to build homes if all open land is declared off-limits?" Jessica found herself practically screaming into the phone, "This is a riparian river bottom, not an alfalfa field!"

Seven days into the New Year, as Jessica walked to the microphone of the weekly South Jordan City Council meeting, wearing a fashionable silk dress and heels, a strange apparatus dangling from her left hand by its canvas straps caught the eye of several people in the room. City Administrator Dick Munson eyed her warily. She took heart in the fact that the names of several SPACE members had appeared on the agenda.

Alicia Ross had preceded her, describing an ambitious plan for establishment of a Jordan River Parkway Ecology Center supported by private donations and grants. Such a nature center would preserve open space, reestablish a riparian ecosystem, and expand recreational and educational opportunities.

Although thorough and professional, Ross's presentation left the council members and the audience only politely engaged. Something was required to shake things up, and Jessica had anticipated the need.

Placing the mysterious equipment on the sloping podium, somewhat obscured from audience view, Jessica began, "One thing I love about South Jordan is that it is clean and peaceful. Fortunately, our community hasn't yet been swallowed up in clouds of industrial pollution and the overproduction of carbon dioxide produced by high volumes of automobile traffic. That could change, of course," she added. "A major by-product of a poorly situated development is increased carbon dioxide exposure for residents.

"What is it like in other areas of the valley?" she continued. "I recently found myself in downtown Salt Lake City."

With this, Jessica retrieved the apparatus from the podium and strapped it over her face. Recognizable as a gas mask, the device transformed her appearance frighteningly. Green and ghastly, the old-style military mask featured a protruding nose like an elephant trunk and bulging "fly" eyes. For aging members of the audience, the image might be eerily familiar from old newsreels on chemical spills; for others, it was a first. But the device looked grotesque on a nicely dressed woman.

A few nervous snickers rippled through the crowd. "I am driving south on I-15 from downtown Salt Lake," Jessica continued. Her muffled voice was oddly distorted by the gas mask. "There are trucks, cars, smog, and congestion around me. Through the haze, I glimpse ugly, poorly planned developments on both sides of the freeway. I'm feeling oppressed."

Something was going on in the audience that the speaker could not grasp. She was perplexed. People were stealing nervous glances at each other as if uncomfortable or embarrassed. Jessica plunged on.

"I feel like I cannot breathe, but I keep driving. I'm starting to choke. I'm going to suffocate if I can't get a breath of fresh air soon. When I think I'm going to die, I see the sign for the South Jordan 10600 South exit. I'm almost there. Maybe I can make it.

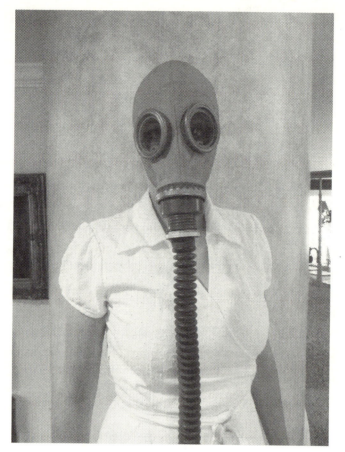

Jessica making presentation on pollution in a gas mask

"As I exit the freeway and start driving west on 10600 South, my head begins to clear." She unbuckled and removed the mask. Her voice assumed its normal timbre. "Oh, smell that country air! I can breathe." Here, Jessica took several greedy breaths, looking exultant and relieved.

It was a virtuoso performance, but the audience was strangely ambivalent. There was scattered applause, but several people laughed. Others were trying to contain their amusement, and a few more looked bewildered. When Jessica glanced at Julie Bell, hoping for a thumbs-up, she saw that her friend was covering her mouth with her hand, her eyes wide with … confusion? Shock? Mirth?

Worst of all, on the face of Dick Munson was an expression of … what, exactly? *Distress? Or is it actual concern?* "Are you all right, Mrs. Tobler?" he asked. *It bodes ill when someone who has made it clear he doesn't have your best interests at heart suddenly inquires about your emotional or physical health.*

Jessica hesitated, attempting to cover her uncertainty, and then spent a few moments citing statistical evidence from the Utah Board of Air Quality and the Utah Department of Transportation on traffic volume and air pollution. To a smattering of applause, she walked to her seat, the gas mask tucked protectively against her midsection.

It took a few moments after Jessica sat down and the next presenter began to speak for her to get her bearings. When she glanced at Julie, it was clear her friend was straining to control herself but could not contain her laughter. "What am I missing?" she asked, now a little peeved. "What is so funny?"

"It was hysterical. Every time you inhaled, the top of the gas mask sucked down like a bullfrog and then ballooned out when you exhaled," Julie whispered. "We couldn't tell if you were getting enough air. Not only that, but your voice sounded like Darth Vader."

As an attention-grabbing stunt, Jessica admitted to herself, it *was* successful—*too* successful. But an inadvertent comedy act (wildly entertaining as it may have been) might not have translated to a convincing demonstration of pollution dangers. No question, it had lacked the drama and impact of the Monopoly gambit.

"Oh my heck," Jessica said after the meeting. "I'm so embarrassed."

"Oh, that was great," Julie tried to reassure her, a grin still tugging at her lips. "You made your point."

At least it was something Jessica and Julie could laugh about. "As many times as I've been called an airhead, did I have to prove it in public?" Jessica asked.

"Apparently." Julie smirked.

Later, their amusement was tempered when Jessica and Julie learned that Geoffrey Henderson had written a January letter to Dick Munson (now obviously regarded by the developers as their "inside man" at city hall), demanding a "positive master plan vote" by the end of the month. Henderson's letter warned that "other developers," including single families, were attempting to make "backup offers" should the project fall apart by January 31.

Henderson admonished Munson to vigorously oppose the plans of "some vocal private citizens who desire to build a nature center," since that would mean the Wilkerson property would not be "re-master-planned."

A confidential phone call from Robert Warren to Jessica brought the news that the developers had threatened the city council with litigation should the members decide against rezoning the property.

Spurred to action, Munson submitted a recommendation to the South Jordan City Council on January 28 to amend the future land use plan map to designate an area for an office park project on property running south from 10600 South to the northern boundary of the South Jordan City Park.

Falling quickly in line, the city council unanimously passed the resolution, subject to certain conditions regarding zoning, Class A office space, office park design standards, building criteria, open space, streets and traffic, site plan, and public improvements. It included a "reverter" clause should those public improvements not be met within eight months.

Significantly, it excluded (for the time being) the Wilkerson property and the land for a city park they wanted to develop. Henderson Development still had an option to buy the park property and Wilkerson land but chose not to, preferring to wait for an expected city rezone.

Despite cozy relationships and easy wins at city hall, the absence of the Wilkerson parcel and the designated park land was a frustration for the developers and a win for SPACE. Missing puzzle pieces in the bigger picture, these land parcels would continue to elude them over time. And the longer they failed to nail them down, the more hope and maneuvering room the SPACE supporters could draw from the situation.

Unable to negotiate with the Wilkersons but probing every possibility, on February 21, SPACE forces managed to cement a get-together with the major players—Geoffrey Henderson and Marcus Hollings of Henderson Development and Dick Munson, Kenneth Manley, and Robert Warren of South Jordan City. Julie Bell, Jessica Tobler, Alicia Ross, and Tom Branson—a neighbor of Bell's—represented SPACE.

Having grown dubious about city fathers' commitment to providing accurate records of important meetings, Julie smuggled a tape recorder into the session, hidden in her purse.

On the ambitious agenda was discussion of a proposed bid by SPACE to purchase options on the Wilkerson property from Henderson Development for an eventual educational nature center. It was a long shot to at least be able to save a small plot of ground. In the long run, it could turn out to be the *only* shot. Should the developers ultimately get their way with their RiverFront project, half a loaf would be better than none.

At first, the cautious conversation seemed surprisingly congenial. When Alicia Ross told Henderson and Hollings that SPACE members had spoken with Mandy Fletcher of Utah Open Space and Janie Kisselman, economic development director for South Jordan City, regarding conservation easements, the developers appeared unruffled.

Assertively, Julie stepped in to suggest the developers allow Fletcher to talk directly to the Wilkersons, since Jessica and Julie had disavowed communication with them until the REPC expired on June 30, 1997.

"That would be appreciated," she said.

Henderson adopted an air of nonchalance. "As far as I'm concerned, you can talk to Wilkersons all you want," he said. His acquiescence seemed strangely out of character. Was he baiting a trap?

"You mean you're not going to sue us?" Ross asked. There was a moment of silence as the developers glanced at each other. *Was she trying to get under their skin? Or was her interjection naively innocent?*

Henderson held his tongue, not bothering to answer. He seemed to ignore the remark as frivolous.

The city fathers asked a few questions but were mostly mum, deferring to Henderson and Hollings. The exchanges went round and round without notable resolution. While the developers didn't dismiss out of hand the possibility of further negotiations, a comment by Henderson near the end of the session most likely spoke volumes.

Looking him in the eye, Jessica had said, "You know, Geoffrey, we've stayed away from working with Brad Wilkerson, and now we're trying to work directly with you. It would do wonders for your relationship with the community if you step to the plate as Mr. Nice Guy and sell us the Wilkerson property, if and when you acquire it. Or allow us to find a buyer for it. Supporting construction of a nature center on that land would demonstrate your respect for South Jordan."

"You know," he said, looking vexed, "we're not in this thing for charity. We're in it to make money." The blatant honesty of his confession was almost refreshing.

Jessica made one more pass. "Wouldn't you like to show your good faith by donating some land for open space development?"

"This is about profit," Henderson said. "You should know that, Mrs. Tobler. Your husband is a developer."

"And when I think he's wrong, I protest *his* developments too," she replied.

After a sudden burst of audience laughter, everything stopped dead for a moment. When Jessica broke the tension to pass the cookies she had baked and brought to the meeting as a peace offering, Henderson paused before reluctantly accepting one.

Then, mouth open, he hesitated again. Was he going to take a bite or not? "I promise," Jessica said, "I didn't lace them with ex-lax."

One morning in March, Jessica answered her doorbell to find the large frame of Jack Fitch shuffling his feet and hugging a doorpost. He wore an old dress shirt with long sleeves (partly rolled) and cotton trousers.

"Oh, excuse me, Mrs. Tobler," he began. "I was just driving through your neighborhood and decided to stop and say hello. I hope you don't mind." He held a book and some papers in his hands. "I have something for you," he added when he saw her gazing down.

"Jack, please call me Jessica," she said. "And of course, please come in."

Seated at the Tobler breakfast bar, Fitch explained that it was his habit to avail himself of public records to keep track of government actions that bore on conservation issues and other political matters.

"I've made copies for you of the minutes of the last several city council meetings," he said, handing over a sheaf of papers. "Three copies for you and three for Mrs. Bell. I thought they might be useful. They are public records, you know. I always make copies in triplicate for myself."

Pleased by his generosity, Jessica averred that such records would indeed be valuable and thanked him for his support. Shyly and tentatively, Fitch volunteered information about his community activism and his admiration for what Jessica and Julie were accomplishing.

"Anything I can do to contribute to the cause would be my privilege," he said.

"Thank you. Wait just a moment," she said, impulsively excusing herself to run to her office.

Returning to the kitchen with the Henderson "threat" letter in hand, she said, "I wanted you to see this." Fitch read it carefully, his brow darkening.

"Well," he said, "perhaps this explains why I brought you this." He placed a book on the breakfast bar. "It's something I thought you might want to read."

The hefty paperback was titled *SLAPPs: Getting Sued for Speaking Out* by George W. Pring and Penelope Canan. Jessica didn't want to appear ungrateful, although researching a text about lawsuits wasn't something she intended to squeeze onto her to-do list anytime soon. She thanked Fitch for the gift but apparently without proper enthusiasm.

"No, wait," he said as she started to turn away. "You're going to need this book if they actually sue you."

Jessica caught his serious gaze. Did he know something she and Julie were not aware of?

Reading her expression, Fitch said, "Look, I've dealt with people like this before. I have an idea of how they operate. I don't mean to be pushy, but I just think you ought to be prepared."

Making eye contact and thanking him again, Jessica added, "Please feel free to stop by again. Oh, wait," she said and returned from her freezer with her own gift, a loaf of Winder Dairy bread.

At the door, she watched him head for a rusty truck at the curb. Were neighbors watching the midmorning exit of an unfamiliar male from the Tobler household?

A little guiltily, she placed the book on the back of a bookshelf. This wasn't the time, she thought, to anticipate other another worrisome development down the road.

Only later would Jessica learn that the book's title referred to "strategic lawsuits against public participation." She hadn't a clue the volume would soon move to the front of her bookcase, usually reserved for scripture, and would eventually be consulted and applied as avidly as if it *were* holy writ.

In early April, SPACE was informed that Henderson Development's request for a zoning change on property north of the South Jordan City Park (not including the Wilkerson property) would be discussed at a meeting of the South Jordan Planning and Zoning Commission on April 24.

Julie and Jessica distributed a flier announcing a strategy session at Bell's home on April 23 and notifying concerned citizens of the public meeting.

SPACE leaders had strategically decided to cut off any and all contact with Brad and Delores Wilkerson. They would refuse to take Geoffrey Henderson's bait. It had become clear that the developers were itching for ammunition to prove SPACE was interfering with a legal contract. As long as the REPC was in effect, it would be best to regard the Wilkersons as *persona non grata*.

Explaining this and other battle plans to SPACE members at the strategy session at the Bell home heightened anticipation for the scheduled zoning hearing the next night. Hopefully, everyone would be loaded for bear.

A few minutes into the Thursday night hearing, Jessica sprang a surprise. She not only cited research supporting the importance of preserving wetlands and open space but also suggested it would make better sense for Henderson Development to move its proposed commercial development

SLAPPED! 81

to a location near the Bangerter Highway. She asked that the commission table the request for rezoning and give serious thought to alternatives.

Julie pointed out that although an initial request for a survey of citizen attitudes on the future of the river bottoms had been denied, the city was now conducting just such a survey. No decisions should be made before results of the survey were known, she said. A nature center, a planetarium, or a children's museum were possible options.

Julie said she had spoken with the director of the Salt Lake Children's Museum, who reported she was seeking a new location and thought fast-growing South Jordan was an excellent possibility with its large population of children.

It soon became evident, however, that despite the new information, nothing the SPACE representatives could have said would have made any difference. Call for public comment was only pro forma.

The commissioners had already made their decisions. They proceeded to vote unanimously, recommending the city council rezone the land to office/service and allow eight months for the developer to submit site plans and enter a development agreement with South Jordan City.

The next afternoon, a Friday, picking up some papers at city hall, Julie spotted a public notice on a bulletin board. "The South Jordan City Council will meet on Monday, April 28 in council chambers." After inquiring at the clerk's office, she was told the notice had been posted minutes earlier.

Public meetings on Monday nights had always been verboten in South Jordan and most Utah communities. Mondays were reserved on the calendars of the Mormon majority for "Family Home Evening," an LDS Church program that encouraged family gatherings in homes. Public officials unofficially deferred to their devout constituents.

A last-minute posting of a public meeting for a Monday night ensured that few citizens would learn of it and that even fewer would attend. Business could proceed without the inconvenience of a packed hall and voices raised in opposition to city council decisions on controversial issues.

Any assumption that because South Jordan was a small town, local politicians weren't as slick as their big-city cousins had to be questioned,

Julie mused ruefully. It was sheer luck she had seen the notice. What it meant was another postmidnight session with Jessica, cranking out fliers they would have to distribute on foot Saturday morning.

On Monday night, city council members looked baffled at the respectable turnout. They quickly got over it, however, and marched to the same tune and the same drummer as the zoning commissioners, rezoning the land to office/service. Careful to cover their own behinds, the council members certified in small print that if the owner or developer failed to comply with all provisions of the agreement within eight months, the zoning would revert to agricultural A-5.

It had proved a dispiriting spring for SPACE. While summer would bring brief surges in optimism, they would be inevitably followed by dashed hopes.

Totally on his own hook, Brad Wilkerson continued to play "footsie" with Utah Open Space, suggesting on one hand that if some issues could be resolved, a possible sale to a preservation organization wasn't out of the question and revealing on the other hand the existence of a standing offer for the land from a firm called McMillan Homes.

Which would it be—a gigantic development or maybe a collection of tacky little boxes? A Hobson's choice. Were the Wilkersons merely trying to jack up the ultimate purchase price? Whichever—they had obviously grown adept at playing all sides against the middle.

Chapter 9
Ox in the Mire

Jessica's Tobler's activist hot plate was always full, sometimes bubbling over with several projects at once. Long before she had ever heard of Henderson Development, there had scarcely been a time when she didn't have something cooking. In June, while the river bottoms fight continued to simmer, she briefly moved it to a back burner.

A rising star in gun rights controversies, she agreed to participate in a panel discussion at the Tower Theater in downtown Salt Lake City. It followed a screening of the hard-hitting documentary film *Waco: Rules of Engagement*, which chronicled the federal government's disastrous encounter with David Koresh and his fanatical followers at their Texas compound.

As a conscientious conservative, Jessica was amused to find herself yoked with two notorious liberals on the panel—Connie Gnavely of the Utah Chapter of the ACLU (American Civil Liberties Union) and Lowell "Lefty" Gunderson, a private attorney involved in civil rights cases and a former Democratic candidate for Congress. Ironically, Jessica had opposed Lefty, actively campaigning for his Republican opponent, Farrell Brooks, who had been elected in a bitterly contested race.

Surprise, surprise. Although the trio squabbled during the panel discussion over several firearms issues, all three expressed dissatisfaction with the feds' intervention at Waco.

Walking out of the theater, Gnavely—who had previously shared a microphone with Jessica during a couple of radio interviews—paused on the sidewalk at 9th and 9th to formally introduce her to Lefty.

"You would appreciate the work she's been doing on open space issues," Gnavely suggested to the handsome attorney. He looked Jessica over appraisingly as he shook her hand.

Two days later, long-time right-wing maverick Craig Peazy, who had been present for the panel discussion, called Jessica and suggested she use her newly acquired "in" with Lefty to explore forming a coalition of power players from the left and the right to accomplish a variety of local political goals that the conservative establishment hadn't had the guts to tackle.

It was such a crazy idea that it immediately appealed to her. Something about Lefty's passionate opposition to abuse of power had struck a chord with her. With characteristic impulsiveness, Jessica fast-talked her way through Lefty's secretary to reach him by telephone. Seemingly equally impetuous, he agreed to meet with her.

Her success in setting up a sit-down was followed by characteristic self-doubt. En route to the meeting, Jessica had butterflies. What of importance did she really have to say to an accomplished civil rights attorney?

In a boardroom at Lefty's law firm on West Broadway, as she waited for him to exit a meeting, it was a curious feeling, sitting quietly with Peazy, looking at the art on the walls. Peazy was not as impressed as she was with the subject of the paintings—portraits of prisoners in the state and federal systems who Lefty had gone to bat for in court to challenge correctional abuses.

It was an effort Jessica could appreciate. Her butterflies were abating. It occurred to her that she would have to set him straight about gun rights.

Once Lefty entered the room and they had pitched their idea, he didn't seem closed to the possibility that some kind of alliance on certain issues might be in his self-interest. Their conversation veered to a discussion of the open space controversy in South Jordan and then, eventually, to guns. Peazy looked bored and then peeved.

While averring to Jessica that the Second Amendment's guarantee of the right to bear arms applied more directly to a "well-regulated militia" than to individuals, Lefty suddenly remembered something and left the room to return with a copy of the December 1995 issue of *Playboy* magazine with Farrah Fawcett on the cover.

"I picked this up at a barbershop where I get my hair cut," he said. "It has an article in it about gun rights, with quotes from the Founding Fathers."

Knowing what she thought she did about *Playboy*, Jessica was surprised that anyone actually *read* articles in the magazine. Lefty was thrusting the publication at her and suggesting she bone up on the nation's framers' opinions on firearms. With cover art of the half-dressed actress Farrah Fawcett, the slick periodical seemed hot to the touch and almost slipped from her grasp.

"Uh, the Founding Fathers in *Playboy*?" she asked skeptically. "I'm not sure they'd want to be there."

The connection with Lefty had taken an odd turn—not what she had expected and certainly not what Peazy had intended. Had the lawyer merely been polite in appearing to be interested in an alliance with a couple of brash conservatives?

The next day, after her husband had left for work, Jessica retrieved the magazine she had hidden in a basket of laundry. She felt surreptitiously self-conscious to be handling it. Skimming past the glossy color photographs of a nude Fawcett, she found the firearms article and read it. Some of the quotes from the nation's founders the *Playboy* article had chosen to highlight she could interpret to support her view that the right to bear arms was sacrosanct and should be applied to individuals.

Buoyed by this happy thought, she found herself contemplating something trivial and outrageous, complete with absurd images. A ridiculous plan was forming, but did she have the nerve to pull it off?

In one of her daughters' bedrooms, Jessica located two long-since-discarded Barbie dolls at the bottom of a closet. After stripping them of their pretentious outfits, she superglued red high heels on their little feet.

Next, at her sewing machine, she constructed ingenious miniature ammo belts with tiny slots, in which she placed real .22 shells.

She placed one of the belts around the waist of one Barbie. She crisscrossed the other, a shoulder harness, over the second Barbie's pale nude chest. It took a trip to DI (Deseret Industries), the notorious Mormon thrift store, to find a toy machine gun and a neat little army Jeep. Seated in the Jeep, the machine gun resting between them, the Barbies looked— what? *Ready to rock 'n' roll.*

En route to Lefty's office, bearing a large and bulging brown paper sack, Jessica suffered another invasion of butterflies. What kind of a fool's errand was she pursuing? She pushed away the absurdity that she was somehow infatuated with the liberal attorney. It was her playful nature, she decided, to tease her political opposites about their misbegotten views.

At the law firm, Lefty's secretary regarded Jessica and her package skeptically but informed him of her arrival. The attorney invited her into his office, where she rolled the sack's vehicular contents out onto his desk. She had attached a little sign to the grill of the Jeep, which read, *Lefty's Version of a Well-Regulated Militia's Right to Bare Arms.*

Lefty meticulously examined the gift in minute detail—as if it were a legitimate piece of pop sculpture—and then began to laugh. First tentatively and then uproariously. He called several people on the intercom, including his secretary and law partners, insisting they come in and take a look. It took twenty minutes for everyone to troop through the office, laugh their lawyerly heads off, and be formally introduced to Jessica. In minutes, he had cleared an entire bookshelf and mounted the gift as an exhibit that would entertain countless future visitors.

When Jessica left the attorney's office, she knew she had made a friend. In a curious way, left and right had bonded—not by finding common political ground but through an appreciation for the scandalously absurd.

Although neither had a clue of their connected future, within months the liberal lawyer would offer leads to competent counsel and eventually volunteer *pro bono* legal assistance himself. For two embattled conservative

Mormon housewives, the lapsed Mormon lawyer's interest in their case would seem like manna from heaven.

The increasing rarity of a pristine natural paradise near an urban or suburban center had been a huge motivating factor for the South Jordan housewives in their crusade to save the bottomlands. With their kids adrift in summer vacation, Julie and Jessica decided to bring them along, mingling research with pleasure on a day trip to the Ogden Nature Center.

Forty-five minutes by car north of Salt Lake City, it was surprising to come upon a serene, 125-acre swath of wild country carved out of an otherwise urban area near downtown Ogden.

"See the building with a pitched roof and grass growing on top of it?" Julie told the carful. It seemed to blend seamlessly with the surrounding landscape. The kids were clamoring to exit the vehicle before it was parked.

While Jessica's daughters and Julie's son, Brandon, examined the displayed birdhouses and exhibits of birds, insects, butterflies, snakes, and a variety of flora and fauna inside the grass-topped building, Julie noticed her daughter Trish had discovered a back door, and she followed protectively.

As Trish turned the knob to step outside, she glanced back at her mother and beckoned. A boardwalk path led into nature, and Julie abruptly realized her daughter wasn't going to wait. She had taken off and was heading down the boardwalk.

Jessica joined Julie in the doorway.

"Look," Julie said, pointing.

Six-year-old Trish, often shy and reticent as a special-needs child, was running freely and with abandon, her arms raised exultantly to an overarching tunnel of trees.

Watching, her mother found herself overcome with sudden emotion. "I've never seen her run like that before," Julie said, tears falling. She turned to make eye contact with her friend. "What's gotten into her?"

Jessica didn't reply, but her own eyes were wet.

Whatever it was, Trish was happy and excited. She was running into the embrace of peace and safety.

Once the rest of the two families had caught up with Trish and joined the nature walk, they found almost too much to absorb in a single outing. Observing a variety of wildlife (ducks, great blue herons, white-faced ibis), it reminded them of home but with a pang of realization that such sights could soon not be as common on the Jordan.

Ogden Nature Center Tree Tunnel

The kids were fascinated by frogs, toads, bird eggs, and hives of bees and happy to discover a giant tree house and a rope swing over a pond.

SLAPPED! 89

After the children had all taken their turn on the rope, Julie successfully made her crossing. Jessica, wearing a dress, tucked it between her legs and grabbed the rope. Halfway across, she fell into the water.

With everyone convulsing with laughter, it took a few minutes before Julie helped her friend out of the pond. Jessica managed to laugh at herself as hard as anyone else had, and said she would allow the sun to dry her on the rest of the walk.

En route home in the car, Julie told Jessica she felt as if she had witnessed her daughter coming to life. "It's as if," she said, "Trish was saying, 'Here I am, God. I'm free.'"

What might it be like to transplant what they had seen to the Jordan? Julie was thinking. *Nature is powerful. Nature is a healer.*

The summer and fall slipped away for Jessica and Julie in a continuing series of repetitive encounters with SPACE supporters, city fathers, and other politicians, as well as with their adversaries at Henderson Development. Jack Fitch, the slim, intense director of Friends of Cottonwood Creek, had become a close and valued ally of the SPACE cause and was making frequent visits to a copy center to crank out fliers as well as duplicate government documents crucial to informing the public.

Fitch's wife, June, however, was not so enthused about her husband's activist activities.

"Please don't let Jack spend money," June had begged Julie Bell in a phone call out of the blue. "I don't know much about what he's doing with you ladies, but his family's needs come first." After that conversation, whenever Fitch offered to pay for supplies or extra copies of documents, Julie and Jessica tried to discourage it.

"You need to keep as much as you can for your household situation," Julie said. "You need to do what you need to do."

Although Julie Bell didn't learn of it until later, in the same week June Fitch had spoken to her about her husband's use of family money to fund a crusade for open space, she had also contacted Marcus Hollings. She complained to the judge about what she regarded as Jack's fruitless obsession with wetlands and small animals. It did not occur to her that she could be accused of playing both sides against the middle.

She was merely addressing the "powers that be"—people her husband was messing with—appealing to what she hoped were their better natures to protect family finances. June Fitch, after all, had an inoperable brain tumor. It wasn't necessarily fatal; in a way, it was worse than that. She had been told she was going to be around for a long time: would there be any money left to take care of her and her kids?

So when Julie Bell answered the phone in a pleasant but harried voice within weeks of Jack Fitch fully merging his efforts with those of SPACE, June Fitch asked her point-blank: "Do you know that my husband is mentally ill?"

Julie was caught off guard. "No," she said. "I don't really know him that well. He's come to a few of our meetings."

Would "Mrs. Bell" have time to listen to "a few facts"? June Fitch proceeded to report that while her husband was "in the service" after they were married, he had been diagnosed as having "a mental illness." Only later would doctors begin to call his particular ailment "bipolar disorder."

She said Jack had received a medical release from the service and hadn't been employed for years. She also alleged "some violent episodes in the family," declining to describe them specifically.

"He's really good at doing things, but he gets so far and then he quits," June said. "I just wanted you to know about his illness. You should be careful about believing anything he says. Would you please tell him not to spend money on making copies of documents as I know he has been doing for you?" She explained that her husband's expenditures put a strain on family funds.

Troubled, Julie listened but made no commitments.

How should the appeal June Fitch made be regarded? Jack Fitch had been a loyal, knowledgeable, and generous contributor to SPACE's efforts to resist the development of the river bottoms. He had shown up at one of the group's early meetings, described his own environmental organization (Friends of Cottonwood Creek), and offered to partner with SPACE in opposing Henderson Development.

While his efforts to inform Salt Lake County citizens of the issues might have been seen by some as obsessive (he made multiple copies of every relevant public document he could get his hands on, using them to update the press and petition public bodies), he had been a good friend and an invaluable resource.

Was it suspicious that Jack invariably wore secondhand clothing and drove a rattletrap 1969 truck that had survived far in excess of one hundred thousand miles? His habits (if one discounted his addiction to copy machines) seemed noble and remarkably frugal.

Jack's interactions with Julie and Jessica had been professional and gentlemanly, and what's more, his calmness and rationality belied the notion that he was mentally unstable. What was the significance of bipolar disorder? Weren't there thousands of people diagnosed with the ailment who—with medication—lived perfectly normal lives?

When Julie described her conversation with June Fitch, Jessica's response was typically Toblerian: "Well, let's do something to help the family." Direct action was Jessica Tobler's specialty.

The box of canned goods, frozen foods, and fresh vegetables and a wardrobe of adult and children's clothing that Julie Bell delivered to the Fitch household were accepted graciously by June Fitch. Julie had called ahead to say she was stopping by with some things.

The thin woman who met her at the door of the modest home had short brown hair and ruddy cheeks and wore a housedress and loafers. She invited Julie in and gave her a tour of the residence. Family photos were displayed on the mantle. The bedroom appeared to contain only feminine items. Without hesitation, June explained that Jack had chosen to move his effects to the basement (where he now slept) after a series of intense disagreements. She then claimed that the violence she had earlier referred to included a fight in which Jack had "thrown a chair" at her.

While this was distressing, the details remained cloudy enough that Julie refrained from making a definitive judgment. The visit did allow her to get a bit of a feeling for Jack's wife. She obviously loved her children and recounted personal details with enthusiasm. She was confused about her husband and didn't really understand why he was devoting his time to what seemed to his wife to be foolish and lost causes. And while June Fitch didn't say so directly, Julie picked up some resentment and hurt that her husband was choosing to spend many of his waking hours in the company of married females.

On another front, in July 1997, Jessica faxed Congressman Farrell Brooks a renewed appeal that he attempt to find federal funds to preserve the river bottoms. But Utah was far from Washington, and a freshman congressman could remain silent and oblivious amid more pressing concerns.

Ironically, although SPACE had purposely severed all contact with the Wilkersons, Delores Wilkerson—Brad's wife—asked to look at the video Jessica and Julie had made during their visit to the Ogden Nature Center. She showed up at Jessica's house one morning to borrow it, explaining that Jack Fitch had told her about its existence. Realizing this seemed to imply that the couple still retained a modicum of interest in considering potential buyers other than Henderson Development, Jessica handed it over willingly.

As autumn approached, Jessica and Julie met with Salt Lake County Commissioner Andy Nakamura, a maverick Democrat who always seemed to be juggling a number of pet projects. He seemed eager to assure them that he believed he could find county money to purchase the Wilkerson property. (Nakamura was reputed to talk a good game, but could he actually deliver?)

He said the county might come up with about $300,000, which would fall short of purchasing the ground surrounding the meander corridor. An October meeting to persuade Kent Overman, another county commissioner, to get on board for help confirmed Nakamura's intentions.

On a Saturday evening in late October, Julie and Jessica learned from a friend at city hall that Henderson Development had decided to train its opportunistic hooks on South Jordan City Park. Admiring the attractive property, the firm had surreptitiously offered a land trade with South Jordan City to enlarge its commercial development. SPACE was hoping to combine the Wilkerson property with the park to create a sixty-acre nature center.

Would city council schedule another quickie meeting to approve the trade? Julie and Jessica would have to devote most of Monday to

SLAPPED! 93

gathering intelligence on the possible sneak attack and getting it into citizens' hands.

That presented a dilemma: work all night Saturday in cranking out an emergency flier and show up for church in a semicomatose state or bend (if not break) the Sabbath to produce the flier after church Sunday afternoon and evening?

This seemed to be the sort of practical catch-22 that more and more overcommitted Mormons were dealing with weekly. And although it had been a century and a half since the pioneer era when Brigham Young had accepted the excuse for Sunday labor as the need to rescue an "ox in the mire," the phrase and the justification still had wide currency—especially in rural communities.

It appeared to Jessica and Julie that if there ever was a reason for getting down and dirty on a Sunday, this was it. Their ox might be over its head by Monday. The attractive flier was called "Save Our Park" and appealed to citizens to apply their influence to prevent another potential landgrab.

It took several hours of legwork on Monday to distribute copies in surrounding neighborhoods. The partners later learned that at least one copy had provoked interest at city hall. For whatever reason, any potential enthusiasm for a land swap failed to materialize, and no secret meetings were attempted. Jessica and Julie were convinced, however, that this didn't mean the "dirty tricks" squad at the South Jordan City Council had decided to disband.

At a mid-November meeting of the council, Mandy Fletcher of Utah Open Space had been slotted to speak about resolving a road issue that would free up a possible UOS buyout of the Wilkerson property. When Julie and Jessica arrived at the meeting, they were informed that Dick Munson had unceremoniously bumped Fletcher from the agenda for two priority guests (no surprise)—Geoffrey Henderson and Marcus Hollings.

Then, prior to the November 25 meeting of the council, Brad Wilkerson secretly signed a new real estate purchase contract (eventually to be known as the "Second REPC") with Henderson Development. Had Jessica and Julie known, the report would likely have sounded a death knell to hopes that the property might eventually pass to friendlier hands.

In December, although SPACE opposed it, the city council granted Henderson Development four additional months, until April 1998, to comply with the new zoning ordinance and avoid the land reverting to open space—the seeming *coup de grace* to a year of hard blows.

Was it good news or bad news that this fight was destined to stretch into an unforeseeable future? On the downside, maybe it gave the developers time to get all their ducks in a row—in order to pick them off one by one. However, time might instead allow the grassroots movement to gather momentum in educating the public about wiser uses for the river bottoms. SPACE wasn't about to sit back and wait for further development.

Geoffrey Henderson would have plenty to celebrate at his upcoming forty-seventh birthday party. Born in 1949—a previous Year of the Ox (designated every twelve years by the Chinese zodiac), his Oriental astrology chart described Ox people as "mentally and physically alert," patient, confidence inspiring, of few words yet eloquent once having opened their mouths. He tended to ignore the rest: "Ox people tend to be eccentric and bigoted. They have fierce tempers and can be remarkably stubborn. And they hate to fail or be opposed. They are most compatible with Snake, Rat, and Cock people."

When Julie ran onto her nature calendar's notation on The Year of the Ox and then researched the particulars of the Chinese zodiac, the sentence listing the characteristics of so-called Ox people seemed to jump off the page. With Geoffrey Henderson in mind, the nomenclature struck her as funny. She knew his age because she had gone to high school with him. *Compatible with Snake, Rat, and Cock people*, she mused. *That's Geoffrey all right.*

Now a brand new Year of the Ox was coming to a close, Julie realized. Wasn't it all too clear whose ox was being gored?

Chapter 10
After the Fall

To all visible appearances, Marcus S. Hollings led a charmed and highly respectable life. On his office wall above his neat and orderly desk was an elegant photograph of his handsome family in semiformal attire. He and his three sons wore dark suits, white shirts, and ties. His beautiful wife, Tamara—dark hair to her shoulders—and their three daughters were clad in long flowing white gowns.

His golden-blond hair, parted on the left, was now tinged with a distinguished silver-white. The patrician nose and classic profile gave him the air of an aristocrat or a judge, which he had in fact been for fifteen years. In the time he had been involved in real estate with Henderson Development while remaining on the district court bench, no one of importance had dared question the ethical balancing act he was performing.

The Mormon Historic Places Endowment, which listed him as a trustee, rather indelicately blurred the line between his two professions, noting on its literature that Hollings "practices law in the area of real estate development in Sandy, Utah." But no one seemed to care. Or maybe some people began to get a clue what that description may have meant when he started filing lawsuits for Henderson Development against various individuals and communities as a way of clearing opposition to the firm's sweeping advance.

Only a few close friends, including Elder L. Roland Blaylock of the Council of the Twelve of the LDS Church, had any intimate knowledge of the painful irritations that sporadically seemed to erupt under the unruffled surface of Hollings's life.

On a hike with Marcus and the children in a nearby Wasatch canyon, Tamara Hollings had been standing on a small outcropping of stone (her husband close behind her) when she fell. Since the kids were farther up the trail and not in the immediate area of their parents, they saw nothing. But they heard their mother cry out as her head struck a rock several feet below. It was a tragic mishap. She was hospitalized with a serious concussion, and at first there was concern for Tamara's life and then briefly for possible brain damage.

Marcus had come to the hospital, and as customary in the Mormon tradition, laid his hands on his wife's head, applying a drop of consecrated olive oil before offering a priesthood blessing—a prayer for her recovery. Several of their worried children hovered nearby, eyes welling with tears.

With heavy responsibilities crowding his double-booked calendar, it was several days before Hollings found time to check in at the hospital again, although he always made sure to call. Tamara's mother remained by her bedside, morning and night. Remarkably, Tamara began to show signs of steady improvement. As she sat up, sipped a cup of soup, and began to ask about what had happened and inquire about her children and her husband, the nurses noticed she was regaining color. But when her children were allowed to visit, they observed that something in her face had changed—something beyond bruises and a shaved head that revealed a scar from her brow to the back of her skull.

After Hollings's second visit to the hospital, he told Geoffrey Henderson and others that his priesthood blessing had healed Tamara. The word got around that there had been some sort of miracle. Marc Hollings (more and more he himself used the less formal name and invited others to adopt the shorter version) said nothing to challenge that impression.

Before her fall, Tamara had been doing some accounting at her husband's real estate office from time to time. She had found it dispiriting to always sit at home while her children were in school. Since Marcus was so busy, she saw him rarely and decided they were never going to have more than a few minutes a week together if she didn't create a presence at the office.

After her hospital stay, she stopped pressing to see her husband beyond his nightly appearances, usually just shortly before she dropped off to sleep. She couldn't quite remember the circumstances of her accident or what had preceded her plunge off the side of the mountain. But something had changed between her and Marcus. (She stubbornly resisted using the shorter version of his name). She resented his lack of attention to her while she had been hospitalized.

It was if she had suffered a loss of innocence. Tamara had always identified with the Mormon teaching that Eve had made the difficult but correct choice in eating the forbidden fruit from the tree of knowledge of good and evil. While the sudden comprehension of her husband's indifference left a bitter taste in Tamara's mouth, she preferred it to ignorance.

Isolated, lonely, and depressed, she had to find something to get out of bed for in the mornings. Since her college accounting degree was going to waste, why not put it to use?

Marcus seemed surprised when, without his secretary's approval or announcement, Tamara stuck her head in the door of his office one day just before noon.

She noticed he didn't seem particularly glad to see her. But on her request, he agreed to put her to work in an adjoining room. An accounting student in college, Tamara quickly began an inventory of a file Marcus had provided for her.

A few minutes later, she saw him leave with two other men, presumably for lunch. At about 2:15, he showed up just ahead of a tall, thin, plain woman with short dark hair, who his secretary ushered into his office. The door between the two offices was slightly ajar, and from what Tamara gathered from snatches of conversation, she was able to pick up that the woman's name was June Fitch. He was speaking to her in a tone of subtle persuasion; perhaps he intended it as personable and reassuring. From personal experience, however, Tamara had another sense.

The woman seemed emotional and confused, and when Tamara took a peek through the crack in the door (the woman was visible but not Marcus), her head was down and her gaze was on the floor.

Then Tamara Hollings noticed her husband's tone change, and what he said was so direct and confrontational, it shocked her.

"You need to divorce your husband," he announced. "He's a threat to your family."

Suddenly, Tamara Hollings didn't want to hear another word. She softly retracted the knob and eased the door closed. Had her husband—she wondered sarcastically—taken up marriage counseling in his spare time? She found herself unable to concentrate on the column of figures she had been perusing on a company data sheet.

When Marcus showed up at home that evening, Tamara was seated in the living room, reading, still clad in the neat blue pantsuit she had worn to his office. Her newly-grown hair was attractively groomed. She was relaxed and yet expectantly alert.

For a few minutes she heard the sound of utensils on china in the kitchen as her husband presumably picked at the meatloaf she had left waiting in the microwave. When he exited the kitchen, he passed the living room as if he were headed upstairs to bed.

"We need to talk," Tamara called after him. He turned and ambled (casually, she thought) back into the living room, his face a mask.

After she brought up the woman from the office (what was her name … Fitch?), something registered on his face. He was clearly getting the picture that she had overheard some of their conversation.

Sitting forward in his chair, Marcus Hollings smiled in a way that suggested either admiration or condescension; Tamara wasn't sure which. "Okay, Tam," he said, "You probably need to know what's been making me so crazy lately."

She remembered his periodic complaints about the environmental wackos in South Jordan who showed up at every city council meeting, every zoning hearing, every public opportunity to criticize and embarrass Henderson Development and its RiverFront project, didn't she? Two housewives and a crazy loner (maybe literally crazy) with a copy machine addiction—a guy named Jack Fitch, who cranked out enough paper to flood the offices of every elected official with fliers and petitions.

Tamara's husband explained that Fitch, Jessica Tobler, and Julie Bell wanted to create the impression they were the vanguard of a huge grassroots movement. *It was anyone's guess why they wanted to stop progress. Maybe to protect a few squirrels and other stray wildlife?*

They called their group SPACE (Space Preserves a Clean Environment), appealing to that aspect of Utahns' longtime cultural expectations of an abundance of open land in and around the state's communities for their children and grandchildren to enjoy.

It was a selfish and naïve assumption, Marcus had said on numerous occasions, a notion that didn't take into account the need for new jobs, an expanding tax base, and the opportunity for people to make a living.

"June Fitch is a troubled woman," Marcus said. "She came to me because she is concerned her husband is involved with these people in South Jordan who are fighting my project and because he is spending family money on a worthless cause. He has a mental illness that makes him irrational and impulsive. I'm trying to advise her."

Tamara Hollings stared at her husband. "Isn't this a situation for *them* to work out?" she asked. "What do you or your firm have to fear from a poor man with a mental handicap and a difficult marriage?"

"Oh, Tammy, you are so touchingly naïve," Marcus said. He paused to look at her with pity. "While it isn't a bad thing that you overheard some of what went on today, if you're going to spend time at the office, you need to prick up your powers of observation. If stupid people are allowed to muck around with public perceptions of our business plans, it could be very damaging. You've met Tobler and Bell. You know what they're like." He paused.

"Please realize, it's a godsend that since June Fitch is having trouble with her marriage, she has come to me for help. I can steer her in the right direction, and perhaps she'll keep us informed about her husband's activities to ensure he doesn't get into much deeper trouble."

Tamara Hollings had been mulling the irony: her husband was messing with someone else's marriage while virtually ignoring his own. It took a moment for her to get her head around what he was trying to say.

"What exactly do you mean?" she asked.

"I mean I'm tired of worrying about how to get these people—Jessica Tobler, Julie Bell, Jack Fitch, and all the rest—to shut up. They're stirring up all kinds of lies in the media. If I can't get them to shut up, I'll sue them. Simple as that. When people run up against the justice system, they tend to back off. They're not so eager to pursue their little causes anymore. I haven't spent my time on the bench without learning that simple lesson. The law has power."

Tamara Hollings considered. So with all the prestige, security, and financial independence that came with marriage to a man with a law degree and the privilege of wearing judicial robes, this was what it came down to. *This* was the payoff? This was the promise she and her children had invested their trust and family survival in? Maybe Marcus wasn't far from the truth after all: she *had* been a credulous fool.

Meanwhile, Jessica Tobler was recalling with nagging and guilty clarity how confidently she had connected her disdain for Hollings to the beautiful trophy wife he squired around to show off when they appeared at city council meetings.

Strange, she thought, how respectful and deferential almost everyone seemed to be to the handsome judge who was thought to care enough to grace community functions with his presence. (Jessica had found herself repelled by what others considered handsome in Hollings.) Once his plan of action became clear, was everybody afraid of him except for her and Julie?

Maybe we were stupid not to be intimidated.

She couldn't lose the flawless image of Tamara Hollings—long dark hair, perfect nails, slim, attractive body—but what was it in her eyes? Something hurt or vulnerable.

Having dinner with her family at Ruby Tuesday a few weeks earlier, she had caught sight of Tamara and Marcus Hollings in another dining room.

They hadn't seen her, but she had seen Tamara's face, and it haunted her.

Now she wondered, *Is Tamara really the "trophy wife"? Or is that simply my way of dismissing her because she is loyal to her husband?*

After a long-ago city council meeting, Jessica remembered, while she was headed for the drinking fountain, she had looked up to see Tamara Hollings blocking the way. "Why are you opposing my husband's project?" Tamara had asked, steadily meeting Jessica's gaze.

"I'm sorry," Jessica had replied. "Who are you? Do you live here?"

Why don't you go to the mall or something and spend time getting your hair done? Jessica hadn't said it but had bitten her tongue not to speak out loud. When she had called Julie the next morning to report what had gone on at the meeting, she had been almost screaming. "I can't stand Marcus Hollings's wife."

My gosh, she thought now in retrospect, *I hated her.*

Jessica Tobler's sister Cassandra, or "Cass" as Jessica often called her, was charmed by her proximity to prestigious and powerful people in her Mormon ward. She often had stories to tell her sister about her association with the righteous and the successful, often mistaking one for the other. One family particularly intrigued her—Griff and Ann Walters, an eminent attorney and his proud wife; they had four attractive children.

As the mother of five kids of her own, including a severely disabled daughter (she brought her to church weekly in a wheelchair), Cass was grateful for any attention the Walters couple paid to her or her daughter (or any member of the family). It made her feel that she and her family were noticed and valued by important people.

Several months ago, when Ann Walters had chatted amiably with her after Relief Society, Cassandra had suggested that Ann call Jessica about a project she was involved in because Jessica had public relations experience. On the phone with Jessica, Ann had radiated sweetness and light. In deference to her sister, Jessica had agreed to help her with a couple of press releases.

Cassandra now felt herself a designated confidant of the wealthy and well-known Mrs. Walters, who occasionally leaked tidbits of her personal and family life.

"Oh, my family is in such turmoil," the woman told Cassandra one Sunday. As she rushed on, Cass felt the muscles tightening in her face and something shifting in her gut. "My husband is a lawyer for a judge who works for a developer, and they are considering suing some people. These ladies are not very good Mormons; they're gaining so much media attention. And my husband has to handle it."

It couldn't be, Cass thought. But how could it *not* be? Adopting a tone of pretend empathy, she toughed out the rest of the conversation.

When Ann Walters next spoke to her at church, it was clear the woman had figured out who Cassandra's sister was and that she herself had been involved in some kind of personal dealings with her.

"You might pass on to your sister if she doesn't know," a noticeably cooler Ann Walters offered, "that Marcus Hollings's wife had a tragic accident. She's alive. But it's only because of the righteousness of her husband, who healed her with a priesthood blessing."

In their next encounter, Ann threw out an even sharper jab. "It might be a good thing if your sister Jessica showed up at homemaking meeting on Tuesday nights instead of getting herself in trouble at city council." Homemaking, an LDS Relief Society function, was held one Tuesday each month to assist women in developing domestic skills.

So much for a relationship with the ward's elite, Cassandra reflected. Was she being used as a conduit for condescension and veiled threats she was expected to channel to her sister?

One more encounter with Ann Walters was still to come—the strangest of all. As ward Relief Society president and Cassandra's "visiting teacher," she showed up on Cass's doorstep one afternoon for what she called her "last visit."

Asked by Cass what she meant, Mrs. Walters said, "Because blood is thicker than friendship, I can't assign myself to visit you anymore." She paused briefly and then added, "If your sister's actions are hurting my husband—and they are—I'm going to side with him."

Not the sort of visiting teacher's message Cassandra had come to expect.

And then, as if Cass hadn't gotten the message clearly, she would soon hear it more directly—from Griff Walters himself.

Taking a walk in her neighborhood one afternoon, she was surprised to observe a big luxury automobile slowing down as it rolled up alongside her in the street. She waited as the tinted driver's side window glided down.

"Hi, Cass," a squeaky voice said from behind the wheel with a tone of assumed familiarity. She recognized Griff Walters's intonation immediately. "Your little sister—why is it that she can't be quiet?"

Startled and perplexed, Cassandra stared at the partially obscured face behind the wheel.

"Perhaps you should pass this on to her: we're going to go after her husband."

Cassandra, whose friends had often marveled at her self-control in keeping her cool in tense situations, found herself enraged, yelling at the little man in the window. "Now look," she said. "You stay away from Dave Tobler. Dave is a good person. You stay away from him!"

She thought she saw a beet-red Griff blink in surprise. The window rolled closed, and the car lurched down the street.

It was not going to be pleasant disclosing this scene to her sister, as well as Cassandra's changed evaluation of the people she had once admired.

Suddenly—fighting hot tears—her community felt uncomfortably closed. Maybe it was like this for Mother Eve on introduction to "the lone and dreary world" after expulsion from the Garden. She had innocently stumbled on what was beginning to feel like the incestuous weirdness of a Mormon subculture. Could some of these relationships—convoluted and poisoned as they seemed to be—get any stranger?

Chapter 11
Ides of March

Who stabbed whom in the back? "Was it really Brutus who murdered Julius Caesar, or is that only in Shakespeare's play?" Cady Bell asked her mother while doing homework one snowy afternoon in January. "And even if he did kill him, wasn't Cassius ultimately responsible since he recruited Brutus to the murder plot?"

"Well, I believe the play is accurate about the essential facts," Julie said. "You should realize that Brutus was a sincere but naive man. He wanted to believe that those around him were essentially good and that their cause was just. He was of noble birth—meaning highborn—which assured him a powerful political position. In a conspiracy, it's hard to determine who bears the most responsibility and the most guilt."

Cady pondered. "What does Shakespeare mean when he says Brutus 'had rather be a villager than to repute himself a son of Rome'?"

"He believed that what he was about to do—kill Caesar—would signal his loyalty to his own community," Julie said

Cady read aloud from Act III, Scene I: "Only be patient till we have appeased the multitude, beside themselves with fear, and then we will deliver you the cause, why I, that did love Caesar when I struck him, have thus proceeded."

"Everyone," Julie told her daughter, "is capable of denial, even those of keen intelligence and high birth."

Julie, Jessica, and Jack Fitch—who had made himself an increasingly visible presence in the SPACE cause—had launched the 1998 New Year with a petition drive. Frustrated by the South Jordan City Council's obstructionist tactics and tired of always being told no by local politicians, they had opted for direct democracy as their best option.

"If those elected to represent you in government refuse to act in response to their constituents' wishes, what do you do?" Jessica asked rhetorically. "You go directly to the people."

Seeking to challenge the city council's decision to grant Henderson Development a four-month extension of contract proceedings (Ordinance 97-20) that avoided river bottomlands reverting to open space, the trio, with the help of two other residents, submitted an application to circulate a referendum petition repealing the extension.

At city hall, the action made a lot of people nervous. What would happen if such a referendum petition actually got on the ballot? So far, the city council majority, backed by the planning and zoning commission, had succeeded in inching the business park project toward approval and ultimate fruition despite the community brouhaha, while keeping a partial lid on negative publicity.

But now, nosy newspaper reporters and troublesome TV types looking for ratings were digging into the controversy. A two-page *Deseret News* article that appeared on the front page of the local section in December, titled "River-Bottoms Battlefield," stirred the pot. In the lead color photograph, Julie Bell and Jessica Tobler stood shoulder-to-shoulder on the snow-shrouded banks of the Jordan River in business suits, looking formidable and determined.

"We're not just a bunch of tree huggers out singing 'Kumbaya' along the river bottoms," Tobler was quoted as saying. "We like our open space, and we're willing to pay to preserve our quality of life."

Geoffrey Henderson was also pictured in a two-and-a-half column photo (this time wearing his white cowboy hat), marking up a map of the area. Quoted extensively in the piece, Henderson alternately sounded combative and defensive.

"The SPACE people have tried to generate as much clamor as possible, thinking that's the basis for the city making its decisions," he told the newspaper. But the project would move forward, he declared. "We have no other choice now, because we own the land. We're not philanthropists. We're not going to donate the ground for a park."

Deep in the entrails of the story (the fiftieth paragraph) was a mention of SPACE members' concern that Henderson's partner, Marcus Hollings, was a third district court judge and that that his long legal shadow may have reached into city council deliberations. Despite its innocuous placement in the article, the mention broke a media embargo on a little-reported fact of which thousands of *Deseret News* readers had been unaware.

A less extensive piece in the *Salt Lake Tribune* was accompanied by a four-column color shot of Tobler and Bell on the riverbanks—up close and personal as if they had commandeered not only the foreground of the photo but also the center stage of the controversy as well.

Meanwhile, Lowell "Lefty" Gunderson, the Salt Lake nonconformist lawyer, had actually lauded the city council for "genuinely listening" to the concerns of residents in his weekly column for *The Enterprise* business tabloid. Dealing with the council's decision to delay a vote on the request of Henderson Development to remove restrictions on the size of the fourteen-building complex previously approved, the piece became less complimentary to the council as it went on.

Lefty wondered if he would soon pick up a newspaper to learn that the council had found "the guts and integrity to stand up against the developers." Or would the headline read: "Business and Politics as Usual—Developers Win Over Public Interest Again"?

Naturally, considering this kind of scrutiny, the city council was becoming sensitive to potential criticism that it was stacking the deck against citizen opposition to the project. At a council meeting on January 26, 1998, it took steps to attempt to alter this perception, approving unanimously a proposal to form negotiation teams to settle land issues.

Newly elected Mayor Max McClellan and Councilman Robert Warren would steer a team that would deal with parks and open space. McClellan would also head a second group, along with Councilman Chase Champion, the city attorney (as needed), council staff, and representatives of "any community groups that might be appropriate." The move was meant to encourage an image of the council as both populist and cooperative.

In late January, on the wings of increased news coverage, Jessica and Julie recruited State Senator Deron Blevins, R-Riverton, to again attempt a preemptive strike at the governor's office. The governor agreed to meet with the three and several of their supporters, along with conservationists in his inner circle.

When Mark Legler assumed the governorship in 1992, fresh from a career as an insurance executive and son of a longtime folksy southern Utah legislator, his looks were so quintessentially rural Mormon that some of his constituents had pegged him as a poster boy for an entire way of life.

As he walked into the governor's boardroom on Capitol Hill, Jessica noticed how much Legler's face seemed to have changed. He was paler now, not the apple-cheeked, ruddy outdoorsman he had once appeared to be. In addition, he had a much more fashionable haircut and wore a pair of rimless designer eyeglasses. He had always been good at pressing the flesh, and his smile brought back some of his boyish charm. His eye contact—whether natural or practiced—was strong and his handshake firm as he made his way around the table.

After inviting Julie, Jessica, and Blevins (who were a little self-conscious in fluorescent orange SPACE armbands) to share their views, Legler listened attentively, interrupting only to ask an occasional question. About thirty minutes later, his chief of staff stuck his head through the doorway to remind the governor that he had another roomful of people down the hall, waiting to meet with him on another matter.

"I want to express my appreciation for your efforts to save open space," the governor said, standing to leave the room. Then, remembering something, he called his secretary on the intercom and asked her if so-and-so was available.

Was he passing them off to an aide for further discussion? The man who entered the room carried a camera, and the governor said, "We want you to have a photographic record of having met with us today. Thanks so much for coming. We'll consider what you had to say."

SLAPPED! 109

Obediently, the visitors lined up abreast for their photo op with the governor and smiled when they were asked.

It was Public Relations 101, and when Julie, Jessica, and Deron Blevins descended the swell of concrete steps in front of the capitol, all of them had the impression they had been let down gently, with nary a hope the governor cared to risk political capital on a prickly confrontation in an obscure briar patch in southwest Salt Lake County.

Dick Munson didn't have the governor's PR skills; he was, in fact, a bumptious public servant who managed to come off boorishly even in the most innocuous circumstances. But at least you knew where he was coming from. A Sunday school teacher and soccer coach in his off hours, his financial planning and public administration degrees from Brigham Young University gave him the overweening confidence that what was good for business was good for Munson and good for South Jordan.

As a devoted and willing conscript in a public-private cabal to push new development that would purportedly attract new jobs and tax money to the community, he was happy to accept the role of city council hatchet man.

He valued his close and cooperative relationship with the developers, who had put up millions to finance the project, and trusted their intentions for his city's improvement. Down the road, when those same developers would offer Munson a position as a consultant in their firm for considerably more money than he had made in local government, it would not occur to him as anything but a hard-earned opportunity that rewarded his diligence.

In mid-February, it was an abrupt and tersely worded letter from Munson—acting not only in his role as city administrator but also as acting South Jordan city recorder—that informed Jessica Tobler, Julie Bell, and Jack Fitch that the city council had formally rejected their application for a referendum. He wrote that he was refusing their status as referendum sponsors for the referendum petitions, citing the Utah Code and moving to thwart the entire process.

What now? Jessica Tobler drove to the state capitol one frosty morning, hoping to find something in the Utah Supreme Court Law Library that could serve to guide a layman's attempt to file a petition of extraordinary writ with the Utah Supreme Court since they couldn't afford an attorney in order to bypass South Jordan City's lockdown of the referendum process. Standing at a counter, poring over a dense passage of legalese in the Utah Code, her frustration boiled over in tears.

Oh my gosh. There's no way for a citizen to get justice. Unsuccessfully, she was trying to stifle a sob.

"Mrs. Tobler, what's wrong?" a male voice asked at her elbow.

State Senator Deron Blevins touched her arm. Dabbing at her eyes with a Kleenex, she vented her aggravation. Calmly, Blevins took a business card out of his suit pocket and wrote a name and a number on the other side. "An activist with Protect Our Canyons—she might be able to help," he said. "She's done some work on environmental issues."

The name was Alice O'Reilly. Later that day, after Jessica dialed the number, the voice on the other end turned out to be male rather than female. "I'm sorry she's not here right now," the man said when Jessica gave the name. "Can I help you?"

After identifying himself as Doyle O'Reilly, Alice's husband, he listened to what she had to say. He seemed interested and asked a question or two. "Well, I'm a criminal defense attorney," he said, "but I'll help you." Not only would he help, but he'd do it without pay, he said.

With O'Reilly's assistance, Tobler, Bell, and Fitch filed a petition for extraordinary writ with the Utah Supreme Court on February 19, seeking an order to require the South Jordan city recorder to accept their applications and furnish them five copies of the referendum petition and five signature sheets as required by Utah Code. The petition maintained that the Utah Code allowed referenda when rezoning can "drastically affect the character of a community."

On March 5, the SPACE leaders and several additional citizens pressed their case with South Jordan Mayor Max McClellan. They maintained the proposed five-lane highway to be built through Parkway Palisades and the construction of fourteen six-story buildings on the riverbanks would damage the environment and pollute the air and water. The vacillating McClellan listened but made no commitments.

As it turned out, Geoffrey Henderson and Marcus Hollings at Henderson Development had apparently had enough of the back-and-forth sparring. From their perspective, no amount of battlefield casualties and supposed discouragement had convinced the presumptuous housewives to back off from their losing campaign. It was time to haul out the heavy artillery.

On a Friday night (March 6), Jessica answered her doorbell to find a uniformed constable standing on her porch, holding an envelope. "Could I ask your name please, ma'am?" he said. When she responded, he handed her the envelope and then asked if she knew Julie Bell and could direct him to her address.

The envelope contained a summons. Dated March 5—the day of the citizens' meeting with Mayor McClellan—it was obviously more than a warning shot. Later to be referred to in court records as the "Original Complaint," it included a copy of a $1.7 million lawsuit Henderson Development intended to file within ten days. Tobler and Bell, along with twenty "Jane and John Doe" unnamed supporters of the women, were to be named as defendants.

The suit alleged that SPACE, among other things, illegally tried to induce landowners to breach earnest money contracts they held with Henderson on the 110-acre site.

"He (Geoffrey Henderson) wants to sue the neighbors, everybody connected with SPACE," Jessica Tobler was quoted in the *Salt Lake Tribune's* front-page story. "I'm sorry. The buck stops with me and Julie Bell. I'm not going to permit a developer to turn our neighbors against each other. I'm not turning in the names of the people who have been helping us."

The article reported Marcus Hollings had denied involvement in the lawsuit. "He's full of malarkey," Jessica told the *Tribune.*

"I'm appalled," Julie Bell told the press. "I feel I'm back in elementary school and a bully wants to force me to do his bidding. But we're not willing to sit down and shut up."

On March 12, Penelope Canan, coauthor of *SLAPPs: Getting Sued for Speaking Out*—the book that had gathered dust on Jessica Tobler's bookcase for a year—said in a front-page interview with the *Tribune* that the pending lawsuit was a classic example of a SLAPP. An associate professor of sociology at the University of Denver, Canan said strategic lawsuits against public participation are typically used by developers to chill public discussion and intimidate and silence their critics.

"We say our communities are only as good as we make them," Canan told the *Tribune*. "And here we have some people who want to keep opposing viewpoints away from the democratic debate."

Griff Walters, Henderson Development's attorney, was quoted in rebuttal: "I've never filed a SLAPP suit in my life," he said. Yet he acknowledged that the summons was indeed served to keep Henderson opponents from interfering with his client's business dealings.

In the days leading up to March 15, Henderson Development's deadline to file the lawsuit with the courts, March 11, turned out to be a double whammy for SPACE. Since the city had rejected SPACE's referendum petition, O'Reilly advised filing an initiative petition. This petition required a public vote on a proposed ordinance to restore the rezoned property back to agricultural use and forbid construction within the Jordan River's five-hundred-year flood plain. Not unexpectedly, the South Jordan City attorney's office again advised city officials that they were within their legal rights to reject the group's second application to circulate an initiative petition. SPACE's appeal to the Utah Supreme Court on the voter referendum question continued to hang fire.

March 11 was also the day the newspapers reported that all five South Jordan Planning and Zoning commissioners had voted to approve plans for the developers' commercial development, thus recommending the city council approve the conditional use permit and conceptual site plan for the project.

With the shadow of the suit hanging over Julie and Jessica, Doyle O'Reilly's proffered help was soon augmented by Salt Lake attorney Lowell "Lefty" Gunderson, who also agreed to represent them *pro bono*, an arrangement he embraced "because I am so outraged by this suit," he told the *Deseret News*.

"This is an abuse of the justice system and an effort to discourage citizens from community activism. It has a tremendous chilling effect … It's difficult enough to find people willing to take a stand on issues."

In a last-minute attempt at a truce, Lefty was to meet with Griff Walters and the principals from both sides on Saturday, March 14 with the aim of forging a settlement agreement and avoiding a lawsuit. Any settlement would have to preclude payment of any money or giving up any citizen rights, Lefty had informed Walters by letter. In addition, Julie and Jessica had asked that the developers commit to preserving at least a token amount of the river bottoms and work with SPACE to help save open space statewide.

Walters, meanwhile, wanted an apology from Tobler and Bell and a promise to forego public discussion of the project and any contact with landowners. Also he demanded attorney fees and a fine—all of which were instant deal breakers.

Nevertheless, Jessica and Julie showed up for the noon meeting at Lefty's law offices, Jessica clad in a blue-checkered silk business "skort," matching jacket, and high heels and Julie in a fashionable pantsuit and heels. All dressed up and no place to go for closure. Walters and Marcus Hollings were no-shows. Lefty, Doyle O'Reilly, Julie, and Jessica sat around the black marble conference table and waited. When it became obvious they were more than late, Lefty called Walters.

"We're not coming," Walters told him on the phone. "The deal breaker was your clients sending out petitions for people to sign to save the river bottoms. Brad and Delores Wilkerson got one in the mail this morning."

"We've been waiting here for an hour, and you haven't had the courtesy to call?" Lefty demanded. "You're an asshole."

Walters wheezed an offended gasp. "You just said a four-letter word."

"Seven letters, Griff," Lefty replied. "It's a *seven*-letter word."

It was a good thing they hadn't gotten too excited about the likelihood of a settlement. While hope for progress had supposedly been scuttled by the petition drive, if Henderson hadn't chosen *this* excuse, it would have been three others. Although Dick Munson had denied their right to petition, Doyle O'Reilly had advised them to proceed with the mail-in petitions and appeal (again) to the Utah Supreme Court if necessary.

It would be only a matter of days before Julie and Jessica would learn that despite the difficulty of reading and comprehending a six-page petition, signing it in the presence of a witness, and returning it by mail, hundreds of citizen responses had flowed in.

Litigation, however, would proceed. Beware the Ides of March. In South Jordan, they would come a day late, since March 15 had fallen on a Sunday. Filed in third district court, the lawsuit sought at least $200,000 in general damages from Jessica and Julie and more than $1.5 million in punitive damages.

Julie wondered what Cady's teacher would think if his student submitted an essay updating the Shakespearean tragedy for modern times with her hometown as the contemporary setting. Could her instructor blame her if she cast Dick Munson as Brutus, Geoffrey Henderson as Cassius, and her own mother as the victim of the backstabbing?

Chapter 12
Squawks, Lies, and Audiotape

The hot water from the showerhead felt good and comforting to Jessica on a windy March morning. But like almost everything pleasurable of late, she was interrupted before she could enjoy it for long. The ringtone of her cordless phone on the hamper just outside the shower insisted she shut off the water and draw back the shower curtain.

Recognizing Lefty Gunderson's cell phone number from her caller ID, she stood dripping wet, holding a towel in one hand and the receiver to her ear with the other.

"Jessica," Lefty said, "I'm calling from San Francisco. You're going to have to drop whatever you're doing right now and get down to RadioShack and buy a tape recorder—that is, if you don't already have one." He sounded unusually stern and serious, and Jessica couldn't resist trying to take the edge off.

"If you could see what I am doing," she smiled, vigorously toweling her face, hair, and torso, "you probably wouldn't want me to drop it. Or, I don't know—maybe you would," she added. He sputtered something profane. Thank goodness he didn't ask what she meant. Whatever had possessed her to say such a thing?

"A tape recorder?" she questioned.

115

"Look," he said, "this is important for the case—crucial enough for me to interrupt my business here to call you. After you've obtained the recorder, call Julie and have her come over to your house. The two of you need to call every landowner in the river bottoms. Once you've broken the ice with casual conversation, you need to ask if at any time you ever asked them to break their contract with Henderson Development. You need to record what each of them says."

Jessica had now fastened the towel around her body and felt a little less conspicuous.

"Yes, sir," she replied as if she was taking orders. "But may I ask why this is necessary?"

"Here's the situation. Fact is, none of the allegations they've made against you have merit, except potentially the claim that you persuaded their clients to breach their contracts with Henderson Development."

"But none of the landowners *did* break their contracts with Henderson," Jessica said.

"I know," Lefty answered. "But they will lie about this in court. Unless—unless you can produce tape-recorded evidence of their previous admission that you never asked them to breach."

"Do we have to do it today?" Jessica wheedled. "I've got a million things to do."

"Today, now—immediately. This is the most important thing you will do today," Lefty said. "People lie in court all the time. You've got to get to them before their attorneys do and start coaching them on what to say and how to form their arguments in court."

"Isn't tape-recording a phone conversation against the law?" Jessica objected.

"Not in Utah. The law says as long as one of the parties knows the conversation is being taped, it's legal. You must do it now. I'm taking depositions all day here and then going to dinner with a friend tonight before I take a late flight back. I'll call you in the morning to make sure you've done it. Are we clear?"

Around noon, at Jessica's kitchen table, tape recorder and telephone in hand, the two women argued amiably about who was the least competent in grasping how to operate electronic equipment.

SLAPPED!

"Here," Julie said. "I think I've finally figured it out. Call my house phone from this phone, and we'll see if the recorder picks up the message on my answering machine."

After the test, with Jessica on the kitchen phone and Julie installed in Jessica's office on an extension, the calls began.

"Mr. Schmidt?" Jessica began. "Good afternoon. This is Jessica Tobler and Julie Bell. Do you remember who we are? You may have heard the news that Henderson Development has launched a lawsuit against us. We wonder if you could answer one simple question?"

The man said no and that he was sure they had never requested that he break his contract with Henderson Development.

With an exception or two, the pattern was repeated, call after call. One man couldn't grasp the purpose of the inquiry. "Who are you, and what exactly are you doing?" he asked. But he did agree that they had never spoken to him before.

Many expressed their sympathy over the suit and their disgust at the maneuver. Julie and Jessica offered their thanks. One man said that while he'd never talked to either of them before, he had *heard* of them and knew their situation. Another advised that they should be very careful of Brad and Delores Wilkerson, since they had the reputation of "playing" the landowners against each other to get the best deal.

Most of the conversations were short and to the point. Surprisingly, the Wilkersons quickly agreed they had not been asked to break their contract and afterward chatted amiably for a few minutes.

After completing the list, Julie and Jessica glanced at each other in congratulation and relief. They had reached all the landowners. No one had balked or been unwilling to confirm that they had not been pressured to invalidate a contract.

"Lefty should be very proud of us," Jessica said.

"Let's listen to the tape," Julie enthused.

"Oh no! Lefty is going to kill us when he hears this," Julie exclaimed.

The responses of the landowners came through clearly. But what were those occasional strange noises?

"Oh, crap," Julie said. "It didn't work."

"Wait a minute," Jessica said. "That's Mr. Green and Mrs. White."

"*Squawk*," a familiar guttural voice intoned. "*Tweet, tweet, cheep*," a few seconds later. "*Squawk*" again. It sounded as if the landowners had been interviewed in a jungle. Moments later, came the *prrrrrthunk* of a nail gun plunging into Sheetrock.

"Oh my gosh," Jessica said. "How stupid of me. I didn't even think of the recorder picking up sounds in the house."

"This is supposed to be a public record. How can we explain that it includes your parrot, Mr. Green, and your cockatiel, Mrs. White, not to mention the contractor in the basement?" Julie asked.

It was as if the squawks and cheeps were the vocals of some exotic Latin American samba being played in the background with the repeating sounds of the nail gun as percussion.

As the tape continued, there was also laughter and idle chitchat by Jessica and Julie between calls and the clear sound of an interruption when two Mormon missionaries rang the doorbell. The recording would enter the annals of evidence as the epitome of amateur hour.

When both women had quit laughing at what they heard, they congratulated themselves.

"Look," Jessica offered. "If anyone tries to lie in court, we've got audio evidence to the contrary. And anyway, isn't it appropriate that our proof is accompanied by the sounds of nature?"

"Only you—or another blond—could look at it that way," Julie snickered.

Chapter 13
The Big Chill

"Kick ass and take names," Geoffrey Henderson had once told his twelve-year-old son, Douglas, when he asked his dad what to do about two brothers a grade behind him in school who were giving him trouble about a video game he had borrowed and lost. "If you can't scare them off by threatening to beat them up, report them to the school cop."

Henderson's wife, Lila, had protested that crude language was uncalled for from a man who replaced his pearl-button Western shirts on Sunday with starched white ones to meet with his fellow high priests. But her reprimand was merely obligatory; she wouldn't have gone so far as to question whether it was a good idea to groom his son as a vindictive informer.

Geoffrey, meanwhile, thought it good business practice to take notice of who was expressing public opposition to his firm's projects so he could do something about it. In advising an underling to follow through on such matters, he sometimes forgot to take precautions so as not to be overheard.

All of this would become publicly relevant on the same day Julie and Jessica conducted their telephone survey of neighboring landowners, played out for an observant audience a few hours later at a South Jordan Planning and Zoning Commission meeting.

When Lew Chambers appeared at the microphone during the public comment portion of the meeting, Julie and Jessica—seated near the front of the hall—noticed that Henderson seemed to shift in his seat on the row in front of them.

Might he be remembering that the guy was trouble? Although the witness's neighborhood did not directly abut the planned Jordan River development, his known reputation as a SPACE supporter might have been on Henderson's mind.

A lean, graying man with a strong presence, Chambers had actually been a rock in the shifting grassroots opposition, showing up at SPACE gatherings and public meetings to speak his piece. On this occasion, he not only made a forceful presentation on preserving a public park but also decried Henderson Development by name for choosing to sue environmental activists.

Chambers's remarks—which the planning and zoning commissioners had heard in one form or another before—might have been just another footnote in the public record were it not for what followed.

Loud enough for several people around him to clearly hear his words, Geoffrey Henderson turned to an associate to instruct, "Write his name down so we can add it to the lawsuit."

Jessica Tobler noticed that Chambers, among others, had obviously picked up on the aside. Several people turned in their seats to make certain who had spoken. Even commissioners who overheard the order looked chagrined. Henderson was staring straight ahead, Jessica noted, acting as if nothing unusual had happened, his smugness covering any embarrassment.

After the meeting, out in the hall, Julie and Jessica stood discussing the incident and what had followed. Brad Wilkerson's son-in-law had come to the microphone to invite the audience to join the lawsuit with the developers against Jessica and Julie. He had also managed to include a few well-placed insults aimed at the targets of the suit.

"Nice, eh?" Jessica said. "The planning and zoning commission sits by and allows us to be denigrated."

From somewhere behind them across the corridor, an angry woman's familiar voice carried the room and caused them both to turn.

"Why, Jessica," asked a beet-red Delores Wilkerson, "can't you and Julie just leave us alone?" Was she taking her cue and her tone from her son-in-law's comments?

"You're just selfish," she continued, speaking as she advanced. "What this is all about is 'Not in my backyard.' You guys keep harassing us and asking us to breach our contracts with Henderson Development."

So why the switch from this afternoon's telephone conversation? Several people in the hall were staring. Had Delores somehow just gotten the memo that what she and her husband had disclosed on the phone could damage their relationship with Henderson Development?

"What are you talking about, Delores?" Jessica said. "You just admitted to us we've never asked you to breach your contracts. And this isn't about my backyard. I have my own ducks and wildlife there. This is about preserving something beautiful for the community."

"Well," said Delores, glancing at her husband hovering close by, "we have plans for those wetlands!" Then, seeming to notice the exchange was drawing a crowd, she put her hand over her mouth and headed for the door. Brad Wilkerson was a few steps behind, hurrying to catch up.

The next day, on the heels of major stories about the lawsuit in both Salt Lake daily papers, Jessica's telephone started ringing. Even though she had been quoted in the *Salt Lake Tribune* as refusing to supply names of neighbors and other SPACE supporters, it was clear dozens of people who had aided the cause were not reassured.

"We can't get mixed up in any sort of litigation"—or words to that effect—was a repetitive mantra that Jessica and Julie Bell heard directly or by voice mail several times during the week.

When the "John and Jane Does" detailed in the SLAPP suit began to be identified—notified by letter and subpoenaed to appear in court—almost everyone who had attended a SPACE meeting or spoken up at city council and planning and zoning now confessed to looking over their shoulders. Alicia Ross, Brent Ray, Ross Davidson, and Rita Baylor, among other prominent citizens served with subpoenas, were suddenly conspicuous by their absence from public meetings. It became obvious that they were also making a point to avoid contact with their former allies in the cause.

Davidson had been a stalwart advocate for open space and, like a variety of others, had donated money on more than one occasion to keep SPACE afloat. Now, after being subpoenaed, he was among the no-shows. Ditto Baylor, who had only recently told the *Deseret News* that "The city council is trading the environment and the wildlife for a fast buck. I saw seven deer down there at the river bottoms just the other day."

Presumably, the deer would now have to fend for themselves. It was heartbreaking in a way. Selling out the environment worked like this: Big boys who made big bucks on previous deals acquired the land and then convinced city fathers that their own share of dollars would flow to public coffers once their projects were completed. And those who objected in public would be threatened with legal action suggesting they might have to shell out their own hard-earned bucks to defend themselves.

An extra wrinkle was maybe the toughest to take. How sad it was—understandable as it may have been—that public threats of financial damage could freeze the blood of decent people.

To top it all off, within a matter of days, an ugly spate of vandalism kicked in.

Jessica and Dave Tobler discovered someone had sabotaged their automatic sprinkling system by breaking off the heads and pouring sand into the pumping mechanism. In addition, their healthy lawn was suddenly covered with huge yellow blotches, perpetrated (the police said) by someone familiar with farming chemicals.

Jack Fitch discovered one morning that someone had shot out a window on his truck the night before.

This was only the prelude.

Some charming individual had thought to insert garbage into the Tobler mailbox, as well as distribute it on the fading front lawn. Dave's truck window was shot out; vehicles were egged and paintballed and auto tires flattened. House cats went missing, and those that returned had obviously been tortured. Then there were the anonymous telephoned death threats.

SLAPPED! 123

In addition, for the entire summer to come, phone service would mostly be out at the Tobler residence, and a repairman, called for the umpteenth time, would say, "I swear your phone is bugged."

In coming days, Julie and Ted Bell would be awakened one morning between 1:00 and 3:00 a.m. to the sound of breaking glass and discover upon searching the house a five-by-five-inch chunk of blacktop on the floor of their basement office. Drawing back the vertical blinds, Julie would find the gaping hole in the window and screen and glass on the floor.

Luckily, the missile had missed the computer. Another chunk of blacktop would leave a ding in the office door. The Bells' sprinkler system would also be hit by the vandals, copycatting the decapitation of sprinkler heads at the Toblers' place and the clogging of the pumping mechanism.

As the dark cloud of desertion by friends and destruction by antagonists spread, Julie and Jessica looked for a silver lining and found one in Lew Chambers. He refused to buckle or back down to mounting pressure.

"It will take more than a lawsuit to scare me off," he said. "I'm not doing this for my health but for the future of my kids."

The residual warmth of that loyalty kept the two women going once they noticed that many of their neighbors were also headed into hibernation. Not only weren't they showing up at SPACE gatherings, but they were managing to steer clear of personal communication on the street or even at the grocery store. Financial contributions to the cause from neighborhood sources—once generously given and gratefully accepted—were drying up.

The temperature at church had also cooled. When Julie called her ward Relief Society president one evening, she had barely identified herself when the woman said, "Sister Bell, I am so sorry to have to tell you this, but my husband and I have talked, and we must beg off supporting your open space group." There was an awkward pause on the line that Julie did not rush to fill. "We have five children to consider. With the lawsuit and all this threatened difficulty, we can't afford to be sued."

What could Julie say? *With everything unraveling, we need your help more than ever?* No, that wouldn't do. It had been comforting that neighbors and LDS ward members had rallied to the cause and was now all the more devastating that they had been intimidated into running for the tall grass.

What Lefty Gunderson had told the press about the chilling effect of an abusive lawsuit aimed at shutting people up now seemed almost prophetic. Henderson Development's game plan was working like a charm, at least on a community level. There was one glitch in the strategy, however—the stubborn refusal of the grassroots movement's leaders to admit defeat. It hadn't managed to back them off, even that a growing number of recruits among the battalions of their volunteer army were AWOL or waving white flags of surrender.

In fact, one afternoon when Jessica inadvertently encountered Geoffrey Henderson and Marcus Hollings in a parking lot while waiting to pick up her daughters from school, she was feeling just feisty enough to set up her adversaries as objects of ridicule.

Watching from her car as the two emerged from the mayor's business office, she called out the window, "My, my, imagine seeing you two this time of day. Shouldn't Judge Hollings be in court?"

Geoffrey Henderson glared in her direction, but Hollings, looking abashed, ducked into his car and drove away.

"Hey, Geoffrey," Jessica said, stepping out of her vehicle. "Did you notice the ribbon I'm wearing?" She pointed to her chest. It said, *Kiss Me. It's My Birthday!* Henderson continued to glare. "Well, aren't you going to?"

While the developer was opening his mouth to respond, Jessica's daughters and several classmates ran up to the car and hugged their chauffeur. "Hey, kids," Jessica introduced, "this is the man who is suing me."

"Really?" one of the kids said. Another put up his dukes as if he was ready to confront Henderson.

"See what you're up against, Geoffrey," Jessica said. "You've sued the Kool-Aid mom."

Henderson turned to find his car and then looked back. "When I'm through with you," he said, "you won't have any Kool-Aid left."

The encounter worked like a little pick-me-up. Jessica, Julie Bell, and the intransigent Jack Fitch all seemed more determined than ever to dig in their heels for the long haul. It was maybe a blessing that they didn't yet know how long that haul would be.

When Jessica decided to challenge a state representative in her district for his seat in the Utah legislature, she noticed the surprise among fellow Republicans. At the state GOP convention—stressing the importance of preserving open space as well as an urgent need to craft legislation to limit SLAPP suits against citizens engaged in the democratic process—she drummed up enough support to force Representative Boyd Franklin, a seventeen-year incumbent, into an unexpected primary fight.

The word got around quickly to Marcus Hollings and Geoffrey Henderson. Didn't the Tobler woman have enough to worry about as the target of a lawsuit without trying to stir up trouble in local politics? What if the unthinkable were to happen and she actually got elected? Wouldn't that give her a power base for more shenanigans?

Aware that the body of the antidevelopment movement might be losing energy while the brains of the outfit (Tobler and Bell) were still very active, city fathers and Henderson Development decided it was time to pull some political strings. Couldn't top GOP power brokers apply a little pressure from above?

One spring Saturday afternoon, Jessica opened her front door to find GOP Congressman Farrell Brooks on her porch, briefcase in hand. He was smiling a little too brightly to suggest a social visit.

Not that Brooks hadn't dropped in on her unannounced before. Once he had shown up near midnight, fresh off a plane from Washington, DC, seeking commiseration and a listening ear. Considered a maverick in his own party because of his support for term limits and other heresies, he complained to Jessica that he had been called to the office of the speaker of the house and "beaten up" for his independent ways. Jessica had listened and had somehow become Brooks's designated confidante.

But something about his less-than-relaxed manner this time around suggested to Jessica he was seeking something other than support or consolation. Invited in, he somewhat reluctantly accepted cookies and milk Jessica offered at her kitchen table. What had he come for? It wasn't evident, although he casually mentioned a conversation with Governor Legler and the first lady at the recent governor's ball.

"By the way, Jessica," Brooks said, wiping cookie crumbs from his lips with the back of his hand, ignoring the napkin at the side of his plate, "the governor asked me to pass along his greetings and a message to you. He said, well … he said if you were willing to back off the river bottoms emphasis of your open space convictions and compromise a little bit on your gun rights activism, he could promise his endorsement for your legislative bid."

Pausing to await a response from his hostess—who handed him his napkin—Brooks rushed on. "In addition, I recently had a conversation with your mayor, Max McClellan, and you know, I believe he would do the same."

Jessica sat for a minute without speaking, contemplating the curiosity of her friendship with the robust congressman. She had never considered Farrell Brooks pathetic, but he looked small and weak at the moment, his expression alternating between nervousness and hopefulness.

"Oh, one more thing," Brooks said. "The governor asked if you would reconsider using a Democrat as your attorney. Since the governor has staked out open space as one of *his* issues, he said it makes him look bad in particular and Republicans look bad in general that you're chumming up to Lefty Gunderson."

"Well," Jessica said, trying to control the anger in her voice, "I haven't noticed a single Republican attorney willing to step in to help us on a paying basis, let alone *pro bono*. And as far as the governor goes, I'm not the type of person who deserts my friends or a just cause I believe in so as to get elected. We're trying to protect something priceless, and we have a small window of time. I'm not going to stop trying to do that."

This time it was Brooks who remained silent.

"If the governor and the mayor want to meet with me personally to offer their endorsements, I might be willing to hear what they had to say," Jessica suggested. Brooks looked momentarily encouraged. "But my attorney would have to be present in those meetings."

SLAPPED! 127

"They'll never go for that," he blurted.

"Of all people, Farrell," Jessica said. "You're one who ought to know I don't compromise principles. Didn't you run against corruption in your campaign for Congress? I supported that pledge. Now you're telling me I need to sell my soul in order to get elected?"

Brooks looked down at his hands that were folded across his expensively suited belly. "You can't do any good until you *do* get elected," he said. "I ran for office many times until I learned you have to do what the big boys want. That's just the way it works. You should learn this lesson now: *play the game.*" When Jessica made eye contact but said nothing, Brooks broke her gaze and looked down.

Uncomfortable pause.

"Just tell them I said they can go to hell," the housewife suggested.

Moments later, as Brooks headed down the sidewalk to his new and stylish vehicle, Jessica had the feeling that a lull was coming in her dubious status as favored recipient of impromptu house calls. Strange, she thought, that an insecure congressman would willingly serve as errand boy for political cronies.

A week before the primary election in June, Mayor Max McClellan wrote to Republicans in the district, endorsing Boyd Franklin, Jessica's opponent. In addition, McClellan's plump nosey-parker wife, Rhonda, she of the Brillo Pad hairdo, entered the fray. The mayor's wife had often sat in the back of city council meetings, scowling during SPACE supporters' testimony, often following them into the corridors to ostentatiously listen in on their conversations.

Now, as her contribution to the political process, she campaigned to persuade friends to find and remove all lawn signs supporting Jessica Tobler's candidacy. Surprisingly, however, Farrell Brooks chose to challenge the establishment by mailing a batch of postcards supporting Jessica's run.

Next, Governor Legler took the highly unusual step of mounting a joint press conference with Representative Dale Jonas, the Democratic minority leader of the state house, to single out four legislative candidates to accuse of holding "extreme right-wing views" and to urge their defeat at the ballot box. Jessica's name led the list.

A few astute observers found it ironic that this alleged "right-winger" had mounted a tough environmental campaign to preserve open space—a cause attracting individuals from both sides of the political divide. There was the added irony that this was an issue the governor himself had embraced and then proceeded to turn his back on.

Days before the primary, the governor's campaign committee shelled out $16,000 for a vast telemarketing campaign blanketing Jessica's district with personal telephone calls endorsing her opponent, painting her as an "extremist," and advocating her defeat.

After listening to the voice message on her answering machine, Jessica pushed a button to save it for posterity (and the media). As a memento of a campaign that had obviously been sandbagged before primary voters ever would see her name on the ballot, the sound bite might mean something to her kids once they got interested in politics. She had, after all, managed to spook a vindictive governor into a preemptive strike, even though it would ensure the end of her short-lived quest for public office.

The papers, TV, and radio all picked up on the paradox, some stories brimming with amusement that the most powerful man in the state felt threatened by a stay-at-home mom who wouldn't shut up. In what she thought was an off-the-record chat with a *Salt Lake Tribune* reporter, Jessica blurted that she felt as if she had been stomped on by "a big fat elephant." When the quote (and a photo of Jessica) showed up on the front page of the paper the next morning, she realized she wouldn't be patching things up with the governor any time soon.

Results that trickled in for the noticeably leaner—but calculatedly meaner—SPACE forces through the spring and summer were no more encouraging at city hall and at court than they had been at the ballot box.

Not content to sit still for a SLAPP suit's painstaking progression through the justice system, Lefty Gunderson had filed a counter action on behalf of SPACE, charging that the rezoning ordinances, approved and then extended by the city council in April 1997, were illegal because the city had failed to post them in three public places as required by law.

SLAPPED! 129

However, on April 22, Third District Court Judge Horace Wilkins ruled that city officials had basically followed proper procedure, and dissolved a temporary restraining order he had issued a week earlier that had stymied council action on the RiverFront project.

On the same day, the city council voted four to zero to approve a conditional-use permit and general site plan for the project.

"It's not over yet," Jessica bravely told the *Deseret News*. "The city has ramrodded this project through, but we're going to continue to fight."

As if willing to take no chances that SPACE might rally a last-minute public protest that could persuade council members to reverse positions, city fathers pulled another agenda switch, hoping to do the public's business out of sight of the public. Late on Friday afternoon, April 24, notice was posted that the council would meet just before dinner hour the next day, at 5:00 p.m.

The strategy was foiled when both Salt Lake dailies caught wind of the move and published brief items in morning editions. However, the good-sized crowd who showed up with picket signs for the Saturday surprise had barely caught their breath before the council gave final approval of the eighty-six-acre business complex. Twenty minutes after gaveling the meeting to order, the council voted and left the room.

In a wistful mood that turned mischievous, Jessica and Julie left their seats in the hearing chamber and, as the crowd filtered out, made their way to the front of the room and installed themselves in chairs occupied a few minutes earlier by council members.

"It's our community, not yours," Jessica said as if she were speaking to the departed city officials.

On a whim, they deposited picket signs they had brought ("Save Our River Bottoms" and "Preserve the Jordan's Wildlife") on the vacant council chairs and decided to leave them.

"Look," said Julie, "they were so eager to do their business and get out of here that they didn't even eat their silly little treats." Dainty cups of pretzels and trail mix and bottles of Mt. Olympus Spring Water remained untouched. "We buy these refreshments for them," she pointed out. "We ought to have a taste."

"Not on your life," Jessica responded. "Mere mortals aren't allowed to touch food of the gods."

On May 5, the Utah Supreme Court ruled four to zero that SPACE had failed to present a completed referendum petition within the thirty-five-day time limit specified by state law. The court did not rule, however, on the Jordan City Council decision to deny the petition request on the argument that state law prohibits referenda on local zoning issues.

While concurring with the opinion, Justice Maurice Zundell criticized the decision of South Jordan City Administrator and Acting City Recorder Dick Munson to delay the request to prepare petitions while he awaited a legal ruling.

If cities started the referendum clock when an ordinance first passed, a "clever local government" could avoid referenda simply by enacting more statutes on top of the original, Zundell said. "We should not allow unauthorized delays by city administrators, those most likely to hope a referendum would fail, to make the process even more difficult."

Easy for a concurring justice to say now that he and his fellow justices had greatly increased the level of difficulty for out-gunned citizens seeking a direct voice in the democratic process.

"There's no hope," the usually ebullient Tobler told the press in a moment of despondency. "The supreme court has ruled against the citizens."

By late July, however, the *Deseret News* was asking its readers: "What are three things that never give up?" Its flippant answer was "Mosquitoes, junkyard dogs, and the group of South Jordan residents that goes by the acronym SPACE (Space Preserves a Clean Environment)."

The story reported that the ad hoc group had launched yet another initiative petition drive. The expanded initiative, if approved by voters, would compel the city council to return the twenty-five-and-a-half-acre Jordan River Park to state ownership and kill the RiverFront project. SPACE was already gathering signatures despite the fact that city officials had again denied an application, contending that state law denied permit initiatives on "individual zoning issues."

Once again, SPACE was prepared to carry the case to the Utah Supreme Court.

"We need 1,209 signatures to place the initiative on the ballot," Jack Fitch told the *News*. "We're about halfway there."

On another front, Lefty Gunderson had filed a motion with Third District Court Judge Theodore Haslam, seeking to dismiss Henderson Development's litigation against Jessica and Julie on the grounds that his clients had not in any way interfered with the firm's contracts with landowners—the very foundation of the lawsuit.

As Henderson Development attorney Griff Walters made an opening statement at the initial hearing, the judge—looking upset—suddenly halted proceedings. At the plaintiff's table, Geoffrey Henderson was absent. Sitting next to Walters and another attorney was Marcus Hollings, who was scratching his head.

Staring in the plaintiffs' direction, Haslam uttered a very injudicious oath. "Oh hell," the judge said in open court. "I can't hear this case."

As backbenchers gasped, *Salt Lake Tribune* reporter Joe Orr whispered to Jessica, "Oh goody! Judges never swear."

Haslam went on to confess a sudden realization. His third district court colleague Hollings was a minority shareholder in Henderson Development. "I can't wave a potential violation of the judicial canon of ethics," he said.

Walters explained that Hollings intended to resign from the bench later in the year. "Later in the year isn't now," Haslam said. The hearing was abruptly gaveled to a halt.

After the principals and spectators spilled out of the courtroom and into the corridor, Walters told Orr of the *Tribune* that while he was well aware of how large of a share Marcus Hollings held in Henderson Development, he wasn't about to divulge the information.

If Haslam had to bow out of the case because of his association with Hollings, wouldn't every other judge in the district be disqualified for the same reason, Jessica and Julie asked Lefty. True enough, he replied. If the case remained in limbo, it couldn't be prosecuted, but it also couldn't be dismissed. Whose interests did that serve?

Chapter 14
Hog's Wallow

It was just one letter to the editor in the *Tribune*. After all the acrimonious stuff Tobler and Bell had foisted on the press and hornswoggled the dailies and others into publishing while their cause was floundering, what harm could an outrageous rant by some stupid environmentalist sympathizer from Orem (of all places) do?

But the tone of the damn thing got under Geoffrey Henderson's skin. Was it possible there were smart-ass hippies in Utah County who had nothing better to do than sit around criticizing progress and disrespecting creation of wealth and the American Dream?

"Political Hog's Wallow" was the crude headline.

Henderson tugged at the sweatband of his black Stetson, pushing the brim back from his forehead. Damn, the thing itched even in the air-conditioned office. Reading with increasing irritation, he finally ripped the hat off his head in disgust and plunked it on the desk.

> *Call it the "oink" factor—or call it what you wish—but a couple of hefty developers are eating high off the hog along the Wasatch Front, and the rest of us piglets are left with the hind tit. What's going on here, guys? We all know that*

money talks. But in this case, it's screaming "Sou-weeee!" With buckets of influence money spilling over our officials' heads like so much swill, our political landscape looks more like a pigsty every day.

It really chaps my hide—and it ought to chap yours too— that heavy-duty developers are waving bucks under the snouts of former city administrators, city attorneys, city managers, economic development directors, county planners, top building officials, judges, and who knows who else and pushing through their big commercial and/or housing projects. Often contrary to the public's best interest or desire.

I say we butcher this hog and keep the bacon. I say we make it against the law for government personnel to dine on one side of the regulatory trough one day and gorge themselves from the opposite side the next. Our bureaucratic barnyard reeks of greed, and we need to hose off a few of our piggish municipal officials.

Make cronyism illegal. Chop it up. And maybe—just maybe—we can make this veritable sow's ear into a silk purse.

The letter was signed "Sam C. Hastings, Orem."

Henderson fleetingly wondered how South Jordan City Administrator Dick Munson would like being called a pig. He couldn't help smiling at the image of a deep flush darkening Munson's handsome face beneath his head of styled hair. But he quickly suppressed the emotion when it forcefully dawned that the underlying targets of this attack were Marc Hollings and himself. Despite the letter writer's reticence to name names, people would get the point: they were as much as being accused of bribery.

But how foolish to pay attention to a nobody. This guy had no standing in the community, probably some resentful outsider spreading his venom for the saints. Henderson Development was fast becoming the most respected and influential development firm in northern Utah, and Marcus Hollings and Geoffrey Henderson were not only successful business leaders but also priesthood leaders in the LDS Church as well. Who could stop them?

Before Geoffrey got into land development, he had run a boudoir photography business out of his home (Jessica's hairdresser had informed her of this salacious facet about Geoffrey's life) and sold fire extinguishers. While some salesmen went broke or made a shambles of their lives trying to grub out an existence, he had hustled his way to making money—an eventual tidy sum that allowed him to get into developing. Of course, he had to spend a lot of time on the road. The traveling played hob with both of his early marriages.

Elaine, his first wife, had never let him forget that he got her pregnant before their marriage. And when he had to spend time selling out of town, she implied he was ashamed of the kid he had conceived. That wasn't true, but he couldn't stand her nagging. Wasn't it primarily a woman's responsibility to raise the children? The two boys they had together should be grateful he kept as close to them as he was able, considering the demands on his time to provide a comfortable lifestyle.

His second marriage produced two more sons but also constant friction, and after his second divorce, he found Lila, a blond, uncomplicated woman who seemed to like the fact he wore Western snap-button shirts, shiny bronze belt buckles, and his signature hats. She even tried to match him in flash with tight little spandex outfits. Best of all, Lila usually managed to keep her fingers out of his affairs.

Once he had married Lila, he had been able to take some risks with his early development deals without telling her the details. She had been aware he was looking into buying some property with friends, but that was about all she had needed to know. It was, after all, *his* business, and she didn't ask a lot of unnecessary questions. She brought a twelve-year-old daughter from a previous union into the marriage.

The girl was as obedient as her mother and caused him no problems. The couple had been married in an LDS temple ceremony, bestowing an ultimate respectability on their merger. And to anyone who was critical of a third marriage, Geoffrey could point to the fact that since he had been given the church assignment of temple worker, he obviously had done nothing to upset church authorities.

Lila would soon have reason to be truly grateful and appreciative for all the hours he had invested to build wealth and security for her and their family, since they would leave the drabness of their Dimple Dell neighborhood for a new splendorous home farther up the hill. It had a backyard built for barbecues and a large deck where the family could watch fireworks in the summer and enjoy an expansive view of the Salt Lake Valley.

Geoffrey Henderson put the newspaper away, cleared his desk, and for a moment thought he felt a comforting glow of pride. But why, then, was there still a dull ache in his gut? What was stirring around down there beneath the stain this Utah County yokel had tried to impute to his reputation? Whose pretty face was he seeing in his memory from thirty years ago?

That brunette in his high school biology class—Julie Acheson was her name. She had briefly been his lab partner. Now she was Julie Bell. And at the meeting to explain the benefits of the Jordan River project to her neighbors, she hadn't even remembered their past association! Wasn't even charmed by his willingness to include her in his circle of acquaintances!

Now Henderson acknowledged his hurt—perhaps the reason why these South Jordan women could get to him the way they did. It wasn't just that they were meddlesome housewives messing with a business deal they didn't understand. They were supposed to be *his* kind of people— not as well off, of course, but ordinary Mormon girls from good homes, married with families, subject to authority. Instead they were flaunting their dissent, sticking out their tongues at priesthood authority. No wonder he felt betrayed!

Jessica Tobler was a blond cheerleader type who thought she could do cartwheels in public and get attention. But that serious, smart Bell, whose high school boyfriend had wrestled on the school team with Geoffrey's brother, Max—what the hell was she doing in his business life? Betrayal wasn't too strong a word.

This feeling, he realized, wasn't something he would ever share with anyone, least of all his mother, Gwendolyn, who had always made him feel strong and for whom he could do no wrong. Bell and Tobler weren't going to sap the confidence his mother had given him. His plans for progress would roll over them like the bulldozers poised to carve up the Jordan bottomlands. There, a shining new business park would rise on the river's banks as a monument to his vision.

Gwendolyn Henderson, although built like a pear, was a stately five foot nine. She had beautiful olive skin, meticulous nails, a broad nose, and short brown hair back-combed up in a fluffy feminine style. Gwendolyn worked payroll at the Granite School District and wore dark polyester pantsuits with short-sleeved buttoned-up cotton blouses. While her fashion statement could be described as "Molly Mormon," self-assurance and dignity transcended the look.

The fact that Gwendolyn was having her hair done at that very moment at a nearby salon wouldn't have concerned her high-powered, preoccupied son. Geoffrey was proud of his mother's well-preserved appearance. Never, however, would it have occurred to him to wonder how she maintained it.

Had he known whose nimble fingers were washing, snipping, and drying her coiffure as Gwendolyn and her stylist chatted, it would have been reason to recoil with a brand new spasm of perceived disloyalty.

Sammie Moench—formerly Sammie Acheson—had been Gwendolyn's hairdresser for more than twenty years. Their conversations were the stereotypical gossip/gab sessions that customers who didn't get enough attention at home often had with stylists who had become their confidantes. At almost every appointment, Gwendolyn persistently steered their chats around to the mounting accomplishments of her powerful son.

Sammie was politely attentive, but she had listened with only half a mind until lately, when she began noticing details of the real estate mogul's professional life that seemed familiar. She asked Gwendolyn what she felt were genuine and noninvasive questions about her son's development firm, but her client began pausing briefly before answering as if she sensed something underlying the queries besides a natural curiosity.

When Gwendolyn raised the subject of a lawsuit launched by Henderson Development against two South Jordan housewives, Sammie put down her scissors, swiveled her client's chair slightly, and met her eyes in the mirror.

"Gwen, I believe your son is suing my little sister."

There was an awkward silence as Gwendolyn broke eye contact and looked away.

"That's not possible," she said finally. "Those women he's fighting are troublemakers."

"Well," Sammie said, catching a grin on her own face in the mirror, "my sister Julie *is* sort of a troublemaker when she believes she's doing the right thing. She really cares about that land in the river bottoms and wants to save it."

"I can't believe your sister would do such a thing," Gwendolyn scoffed. "Geoffrey doesn't like it at all that they've come out against him in public." Her body was now stiff and resistant as she twisted away from Sammie's fingers in the chair.

"Look," Sammie said, trying to meet her eyes, "we've been friends forever. I don't really know enough about this thing to understand what is going on. But I'm not willing to lose a friend over this. Let's just not talk about it."

Gwendolyn was silent for a moment. Had her feelings been mollified? Then she bit her lip. "Just remember," she said, "Geoffrey takes everything as far as he can go. The fact that he's filed a lawsuit—he's the kind of person who will never quit." There was a hint of pride in her voice.

It was at that auspicious moment—as if irony were working overtime—that Sammie glanced up to see her mother opening the door of the salon, bursting with some kind of news.

Before Sammie could get a "shush" finger to her lips, her mother enthused, "I just got off the phone with Julie, and I've got to tell you what's going on."

"Mom," Sammie said, "I'd like to introduce you to Gwendolyn Henderson—Geoffrey's mom." And her mother said, "Oh, hi." Suddenly, the only sound in the salon was the drone of a hair dryer.

The latest word Julie Bell's mother was eager to spill likely wouldn't have meant all that much to Gwendolyn Henderson, who hadn't taken serious interest in the intricacies of local politics or their relationship to her son's business. But once her customer had left the salon, Sammie Moench was more than enticed by the news.

Julie had just learned—and passed on to her mother—the fact that Henderson Development had hired a new employee and that South Jordan City had lost a city administrator. Dick Munson had resigned in order to work for Henderson.

Earlier in the week, the *Deseret News* had reported that Munson was on the verge of leaving city government "to accept a private sector job." It took some reading between the lines and several phone calls to the few friendly sources Julie had developed in city government to learn the truth.

If birds of a feather flock together, could the same metaphor apply to barnyard animals? she wondered. This little piggy had gone to market, where the bucks were bigger than those available at the public trough, where Munson would not be subject to public dissatisfaction, and where his buddies were clearly wallowing in their success.

Interviewed for the *Deseret News* piece, and knowing he no longer had to hold his tongue, Munson had taken some inflammatory parting shots at citizens who had stood up to support SPACE and oppose riverbank development.

"This is a very militant citizens group that has done more to hurt the cause of open space preservation than to help it," Munson asserted. "They've personally lied to me and misrepresented the city's position on numerous occasions."

Munson hoped, he said, that citizens would study the issues and make their own decisions based on community needs, "not on one person's view outside a family room window."

It was clear to Julie that she was meant as the target of that last fragmentary quote, as if an entire citizen's movement could materialize out of her personal objections to the obliteration of a nature scene from her picture window.

Wouldn't most people be able to see through Munson's obvious personal stake in attacking conservationist forces? Having come out of the closet of public impartiality, he had put himself on record as a partisan of commercial interests that belied his previous guise as an unbiased public servant.

The fact that he was being welcomed aboard the Henderson bandwagon at this particular time must mean the developers believed the battle was won at city hall. Munson's usefulness as a friendly insider was no longer required.

In early August, another "inside man"—long able to fly under the faulty radar of an ethically lazy press and a complacent public while conducting a lucrative dual career as a powerful judge and stealth partner in a growing real estate empire—announced he was coming down for a soft landing.

Marcus Hollings was suddenly getting far too much negative press and public scrutiny for his own peace of mind. Before the year was out, he would resign from the bench to "pursue other interests." Those interests, of course, were full-time land development, where he could bring his legal mind and muscle to bear as an unencumbered operative for Geoffrey Henderson.

He was reported to have been particularly irate over complaints signed against him by Jessica Tobler and Julie Bell before the Utah Judicial Conduct Commission.

Having been "outed" by fellow Third District Judge Theodore Haslam in a particularly embarrassing way—as an obstacle to Haslam presiding over court proceedings in the suit Henderson Development had brought against Bell, Tobler, and an assortment of John and Jane Does—Hollings concluded he needed to quit the bench while his faultless reputation was still intact.

With legal assistance from Lefty Gunderson, Tobler and Bell's complaints with the JCC pointed out that Hollings had notarized his own signature on several real estate purchase contracts; had made appearances at city hall during court hours; and had sent letters to South Jordan City on third district court letterhead.

With one or two exceptions, including a Channel 4 report of Hollings adding seven days jail time to a misdemeanor sentence when a woman questioned his judgment in court, local media were still tiptoeing around the judge's conduct, characteristic of their longtime deference to the dignity of the judiciary.

Outside of the unfortunate "Hog's Wallow" letter in the *Tribune*, Hollings had heretofore escaped—as had Dick Munson—the ignominy of that rude phrase, "conflict of interest."

After the Utah Judicial Conduct Commission took a look at the complaints against Hollings and sent him a copy of the allegations, off-the-record conversations with members of the JCC indicated a full-scale investigation might be forthcoming. His eventual resignation from the bench stifled the inquiry.

Simultaneous with Hollings's low-key announcement of giving up his judgeship, Theodore Haslam had removed himself from handling Henderson Development's $1.7 million suit against Bell, Tobler, and assorted John and Jane Does. The third district jurist informed both parties to the lawsuit that they should request a new judge—either retired or from another district.

His reason? "I want to avoid even an appearance of potential conflict," he said.

"Judge Haslam increased my faith in the judicial system," Julie Bell told the press in response. She added that it increased her hope that other judges in the system were as ethically grounded.

What she left unsaid, however, was another thought. Too bad the now most prominent of his third district colleagues hadn't acquired the requisite scruples to separate commercial gain from the public interest.

Chapter 15

Crazy Like a Fox

"Crazy? Jessica is crazier than you are, Jack."

Doyle O'Reilly winked at Jessica Tobler as he said it and then transferred his gaze to Jack Fitch, who had noted that the five-letter word was the hammer in the rumors Marcus Hollings had been spreading about Jack's mental state.

Seated with Julie Bell around O'Reilly's desk, both Jessica and Jack knew the lawyer was teasing them, trying to lighten the mood. Black humor for sure, but in a jocular vein. Jack had already accepted the whimsical tag Jessica and Julie had applied to him: "Evil Genius." It spoofed their opponents as well, referencing Jack's knack for getting under their skin.

Jessica and Julie had quickly become comfortable with O'Reilly's sense of humor, and now Jack was also getting a dose. The attorney wasn't yet an "insider," but having waded into their case with enthusiasm, he had quickly won their trust.

Among the small coterie of legal counselors who had stepped up to offer free assistance to the open space warriors, O'Reilly had a more colorful reputation than even Lefty Gunderson. Tall, thin, and jovial, he often wore plaid shirts and cream-colored trousers. It had once fallen to him as a public defender to represent Ted Bundy, the notorious kidnapper and mass murderer of young pretty coeds. Salt Lake City had been one of Bundy's grisly stopovers on his cross-country killing spree.

Although Jack had managed a smile at O'Reilly's tease, the lawyer looked unsure about whether his breezy comment might have been taken the wrong way.

"Sorry," he said. "You know I despise the tactics of these bastards as much as you do, Jack."

"What they don't know," Jack Fitch replied dryly after a pause, "is I'm crazy all right—like a fox."

And then they all laughed.

Effects of Jack Fitch's bipolar disorder, previously referred to as manic depression, were evident only periodically to Jessica and Julie. There were times when he became moody or fidgety. And yes, he *was* obsessive about some things—his curious few prized possessions: a three-hole punch, a binding machine, and a stapler. But since he used these tools for his political activism—an "obsession" Jessica and Julie could also be accused of—they scoffed at the idea that this qualified him as a loony.

It was apparently inconceivable to Henderson Development that anyone who wasn't crazy would write Marcus Hollings a letter asking the firm to add his name as "John Doe No. 1" to the lawsuit Henderson Development had filed against Jessica and Julie, as Jack had. In effect, he was saying, "Sue me." It was his way of commenting on the cruel absurdity of the suit.

Then there were Jack's thrift store clothes and rusty old truck. But so what? If SPACE could be stereotyped as an unlikely and "ragtag" David in standing up to the financial and political Goliath of Henderson Development, Jack Fitch was the poster boy.

But wasn't it ironic that although Jack's shopping habits ran more to DI (Deseret Industries) than designer labels, his wife portrayed him as a wastrel?

Although Jessica and Julie showed up at city council meetings and other public events dressed nicely, their own vehicles were not new or shiny. So what exactly was the fuss? In Jack Fitch's case, it wasn't clothes (or a "nice ride" as the kids said) that made the man but commitment and unselfconscious decency.

*Jack Fitch's trusty rusty 1969 Ford F250 truck—
shoveling chicken manure for garden*

It wasn't a secret that Jack was having troubles at home and in an unguarded moment let it slip that among other things June was not happy with was his lack of skill in the bedroom. Hoping to help out, Jessica and Julie found themselves offering tips toward creating a more romantic atmosphere—some practical, others provocative.

In addition to traditional flowers for Valentine's Day, why not buy a bag of chocolate and cinnamon lips from a shop called The Chocolate Wagon, Jessica suggested.

"Oh, and here's an idea," she enthused. "Get the soundtrack from *Ten*—the Dudley Moore movie with Bo Derek. Remember that song, 'Bolero'? It's good to make love to."

Julie mentioned a Sears ad she had seen in the paper for boxer shorts embossed with red hot chili peppers.

Jack looked dubious but thanked them. He neglected to mention which (if any) recommendations he accommodated and which he discarded. But for a time after that he looked less distracted and left the impression that things were going better at home.

Maybe June Fitch was beginning to appreciate Jessica and Julie's intentions. She sent a note at Christmas thanking them for the clothing and food they had brought over. But when Jessica ran into her at the grocery store, there was a reserve in her manner as they briefly chatted.

As Jessica and Julie eventually learned, June felt a lingering jealousy over her husband's absence from family duties. These absences seemed to coincide with the hours he spent in the company of the South Jordan housewives. And contrary to June's liking, these women seemed far too preoccupied with extracurricular activities outside their homes.

At first she had chiefly mistrusted the brunette, with her long legs and her open-toed summer sandals with little clicky high heels. But then her suspicions shifted to the blond. Jessica's freewheeling, showy personality had grated on her. And wasn't it the blond's bold maneuvers in the public arena that her husband often admiringly commented on?

Earlier, Jack Fitch had informed Jessica of his intention to offer $50,000 of family money to Brad Wilkerson for his land. Concerned for his family's finances, Jessica decided she must warn Jane Fitch, who appeared to be grateful for the heads-up. Later, Jack did pursue the $50,000 offer to Wilkerson, who suggested the move was a breach by SPACE of the REPC contract. Jessica invited June to attend a SPACE meeting at Julie's home as their personal guest. If she got a sense of what went on, maybe she would feel like less an outsider and more a potential supporter.

Somewhat surprisingly, June accepted the invitation.

She seemed slightly ill at ease during the meeting but didn't look bored or eager to leave. She appeared to be waiting for something to happen that would connect the dots for her. Near the end, several people expressed their solidarity and support, indicating a willingness to continue to fight for the river bottoms. Curiously, the emotions in the room were familiar, Julie decided. They could have been mistaken for the bonded feelings of a Mormon testimony meeting.

Then something unusual happened. As the gathering was breaking up, Julie noticed June Fitch standing alone and motioned her to her side.

SLAPPED! 147

Jessica and Jack had joined Julie in a spontaneous group hug, and they invited June into the circle. She allowed herself to be included. It appeared as if nothing else needed to be said. When the Fitches left in apparent good spirits, a corner in their relationship seemed to have been turned.

Sadly, the momentary connection soon appeared to have been a passing fancy, or possibly wishful thinking.

Had Marcus Hollings knowingly set out to drive a wedge between the Fitches and use it to his advantage? Or had June made the contact to seek Hollings's help to lean on Jack to give up his activism while falling into the developer's web of insinuation about a relationship between Jack and Jessica?

In any case, as Hollings inserted himself more aggressively into the picture, June became a receptacle for all her old fears and jealousies, and Hollings was more than willing to feed the fire. It was easy to exploit June's conviction that her husband was mentally unstable. Why else, she had asked herself, would he drain money from their joint account to support a lost cause and pick a fight with a powerful and respected development firm? And it took only another small stretch of the imagination to suspect that he may have made a fool of himself over a mouthy, boisterous blond who didn't care who she hurt—personally or professionally.

The document that Mormons unofficially referred to as a "temple recommend" was more than a piece of paper one kept in one's pocketbook or purse. It was an official verification that one had been found worthy to participate in the most sacred ordinances and rituals of one's religion, available only within the walls of holy temples. It was a passport to participation in those rites, granted only after extensive interviews with ecclesiastical authorities.

So when Jessica and Julie learned that Jack's bishop had denied him a temple recommend—and refused to tell him on what grounds approval was withheld—they were shocked and mortified on his behalf. When Jack had the temerity to inquire about his status in the ward, his bishop had left the room without a word.

Gossip and rumors about Jack's mental health and close companionship with two married women from South Jordan had been making the rounds in his congregation for weeks. Fitch's wife seemed to wear the resulting suspicion as a badge of honor. Because of it, people seemed to regard her situation with more sympathy and understanding.

Jessica and Julie decided they couldn't allow the injustice to stand without challenge. True, they probably had a stake in wanting to clear up misinformation about their role in Jack's life, but their primary concern was the unfairness of denying their friend full access to his religious devotions.

It took some chutzpah to telephone a stranger who presided over another ecclesiastical unit to meet with them about a private matter. Jessica made the call and told Bishop George Farley that she and Julie Bell had some information they believed he would want to know in relation to one of his ward members.

Crowded into the cramped bishop's office on the evening of the appointment were Julie, Jessica, and Jessica's husband, Dave, who had agreed to come along to testify about his implicit trust in the appropriateness of his wife's friendship with Jack Fitch.

Once the bishop had shaken hands with each of them and verified their identities, Julie explained that her husband also would have accompanied them had he not been in Idaho tending to his farm.

"Thank you for meeting with us," Jessica said as the blue-suited bishop folded his arms on his desktop and faced his visitors. "We wanted to speak with you about a very reputable person in your ward, Brother Jack Fitch. Our purpose is to clear up any mean and nasty rumors that may have been relayed to you about Brother Fitch."

The bishop nodded but remained silent.

"We just want you to know that Jack has become our friend and associate in working to save open space along the river bottoms," Julie said. "He has met with us in the company of other good people. And the three of us have spent time working on issues together. We want you to know that he is a very kind, respectable man. At no time has Jack ever said or done anything inappropriate. If Jack's temple recommend is in question, we felt you should know that anything that may have been passed on stating that Jack has been inappropriate in any way is incorrect."

SLAPPED!

Still attentive, Farley shifted in his seat. "I can't, of course, discuss the status of a member's worthiness to hold a temple recommend," he said.

"Understood, Bishop Farley," Dave interjected. "I want you to know that I totally trust Brother Fitch, Julie, and my wife. Jess works with many men because of her political activities, and she occasionally mentions individuals who attempt to cross the line. Never at any time has Jack done anything to lose trust with Jess or me. Jack is an honorable man. I consider Jack my friend. He's welcome at our home anytime."

Here, declining to comment on what had just been said, the bishop changed the focus. "I've had close association with June Fitch and her family for many years, and I know there has been a concern with Brother Fitch's mental illness."

Julie glanced at Jessica and Dave before speaking.

"In that regard," Julie said. "As you may know, Bishop Farley, Jack has been diagnosed as bipolar; psychiatrists no longer consider bipolar a mental illness because it's treatable. I know that Jack takes his medication. He's very conscientious about that."

The bishop paused momentarily. "I think what Jane and her children are concerned about is that Jack is spending the family's money on unnecessary expenses related to his concern for preserving nature."

Not wanting to emphasize disagreement, Julie and Jessica briefly described their perception of their friend as a frugal individual and noted that his contributions to their cause had been modest.

The bishop didn't argue. Neither did he indicate whether anything they had said had been persuasive. He had listened, and perhaps that was all the little delegation could expect.

As Jessica and Julie would later learn, a temple recommend would continue to be withheld from Jack Fitch until his eventual move to another ward and another stake. Ironically, there he would be welcomed, given several church assignments, and restored his temple privileges by a new bishop.

June Fitch's mindset had taken a decided turn toward resentment and animosity. She found it more and more difficult to keep her misgivings and distrust to herself, and when her children asked, "What's going on, Mom?" her bitterness sometimes boiled over in heated recrimination.

Upset and confused, the kids took their mother's side. Searching the house one day for some lost notes he had made on the river bottoms fight, Jack Fitch came upon a piece of scratch paper filled with an angry scrawl that he recognized as the handwriting of one of his daughters. The word *bitch* caught his eye. Then *slut*. The words were juxtaposed with two names—Julie Bell and Jessica Tobler.

Fitch crumpled the paper and threw it in a wastebasket. In all the years of his difficult marriage, never had he felt in a deeper hole. Was any of what he was doing worth this grief? Well, did he have a real choice? He wasn't going to quit fighting what he regarded as an unconscionable use of power by ruinous developers. And he wasn't going to give up on his kids; maybe someday they would understand.

Chapter 16
Fright Night

"Geoffrey's not stupid," Dick Munson told the *Salt Lake Tribune* in the fall of 1998, referring to his new boss, developer Geoffrey Henderson. Freed from the restraints of seeming to speak in a nonpartisan way for local government, Munson's tongue seemed to have been loosed as well. But just because you're being paid big bucks in the private sector doesn't mean you can ignore the rudiments of public relations.

Having failed to learn from another Dick's infamous explanation to the press (Nixon's "I am not a crook"), Dick Munson's use of the word "stupid" in reference to the owner of Henderson Development—even to deny that the word applied to him—wasn't exactly savvy PR.

In a series of articles, the *Tribune* had reported that Henderson Development was facing increasing public opposition on a new development front—up the road from South Jordan in bucolic Bluffdale, another small Salt Lake County community. The project—a seventy-five-acre "gateway" development at Redwood Road and Bangerter Highway—would ostensibly double the population of the town.

In order to quash resistance, the *Tribune* indicated, Henderson Development had hired a whole raft of former public servants to wield their influence to help push the project through.

In a piece headlined "How Do Wasatch Front Developers Navigate the Regulatory Maze? They Hire the Regulators," Henderson boasted, "I hired Keith Leeson (former city administrator of nearby Riverton), thinking that the city administrator of an adjoining city would carry some weight with the Bluffdale City Council."

In addition, according to the *Tribune*, Henderson had padded his development team with Larry Cane, the former city attorney of Bluffdale; Robert Unger, the ex-mayor of Mapleton; and of course, Dick Munson, who as city administrator of South Jordan had carried water for Henderson's RiverFront project.

"Geoffrey's not stupid," Munson burbled. "He's not afraid to get people who are qualified."

The result? "Influence peddling has hit the suburbs," the *Tribune* concluded.

Carrie Deco, vice chairwoman of the government watchdog group Utah Common Cause, was quoted as saying that in Utah, none of these things were against the law, "but in many states you'd end up in jail."

Clara Gaddis, state director of United We Stand, also spoke bluntly. "It's cronyism, and it happens all the time. Conflict of interest is the number one problem in this state. I mean, politicians think it's part of the job."

Loopholes in state and local laws invited such abuses. On the federal level, "revolving door" statutes required employees who left government service to wait a year or more before joining private companies that did business with the agencies where they were previously employed, the *Tribune* pointed out. Outside Utah, some state governments had enacted similar laws.

Meanwhile, the newspaper reported, Peter Stone, candidate for the Summit County Commission, was suggesting a "revolving door" clause be added to the contracts of county employees, citing the example of a county planner who had jumped to the staff of The Canyons ski resort to push for construction of a big hotel at the venue.

"Money corrupts," Stone said, "and there are millionaires being made every day out here."

As if to confess that Stone's thesis was indeed correct, Dick Munson was unusually forthcoming when the newspaper sought his response to its reporting.

He found no reason not to brag that he had been the subject of a bidding war among developers for his services and that Henderson was the ultimate victor.

"I had a couple of developers trying to hire me," he admitted to the *Tribune.*

And how did Henderson Development win the competition? The firm made the pitch during a hunting trip that Munson was invited on with company bigwigs, he acknowledged—a proposition he had accepted at the time. He told the *Tribune* the trip was an elk hunt conducted somewhere in northern Utah.

It wasn't clear whether *Tribune* reporter Carl Roy knew that Munson had previously admitted to Julie Bell and others that he had accompanied Geoffrey Henderson on an elaborate big game safari to Africa. Were there two separate trips, or was he changing the venue to minimize its importance? Whatever the case, Roy failed to question Munson's contention that he paid his own expenses.

Most significantly, however, was the time line Roy and the *Tribune* pried out of Munson, who said he had taken the hunt in the fall of 1995.

That meant that for three years while Munson was handling the most delicate of deliberations over the Jordan River business park project, he had already agreed to work for Henderson Development in the future and could therefore function as a stealth advocate for the firm's interests in city government.

In addition, as city administrator at the time of the 1995 hunting trip, Munson was in "complex negotiations" with Henderson on funding for Sterling Drive, which led to development of the upscale Sterling Village Apartments, Utah's largest complex at the time, with 880 units.

Munson's power base, from which he largely managed the major affairs of the city, was enhanced in the middle 1990s by the inaction of a weak mayor—Thurl Hollings (no relation to Marcus Hollings), who had suffered from hearing loss, poor eyesight, and debilitating old age and usually deferred to Munson's lead.

As a capper to Munson's interview with the *Tribune*, he was quoted as saying that while working for South Jordan City, he took ethics "very seriously" and had never done Henderson Development any favors.

Max McClellan, Thurl Hollings's replacement as mayor in 1996, was more involved in city affairs but didn't challenge Munson's support of the RiverFront project. McClellan told the *Tribune* he regarded Munson's exit from city government to accept the embrace of Henderson Development as a no-brainer.

"It's a free market," he said. "Munson left the city because of the amount of money he could make."

Unintentionally, the remark appeared to reflect McClellan's own checkered past, in which he had hopscotched in and out of public life— from state representative to state senator to lobbyist for a waste company and several other firms to mayor.

In the same article, after years of neglect, the *Tribune* half-heartedly attempted to dig beneath the surface of Marcus Hollings's double life as a district court judge and a real estate developer.

When questioned about a possible conflict, it was clear that Hollings was also grateful to take advantage of loopholes—the lack of explicit rules in the judicial code prohibiting his business activities. There was no reason, he told the *Tribune*, why he couldn't be a judge and a developer at the same time.

Nonetheless, he said, he was resigning from the bench for "practical reasons."

Surprisingly, at least one Utah developer cast a critical eye on the practice of influence shopping to procure former government employees to push private projects, telling the *Tribune* he didn't need help from political ranks.

Larry Teal, owner of Wasatch Pacific and a former partner in Draper's South Mountain project, called the practice unwise.

"If I hire Dick Munson and I work in South Jordan, it would be perceived as a conflict. I don't know if it passes the smell test or not."

SLAPPED!

With Halloween and November elections around the corner and SPACE still stinging from multiple rejections in city government and the courts, any indication that the media were finally picking up the stink of corruption among the group's opponents was at least a whiff of good news.

Always working new angles for positive publicity, Jessica decided it was time to have some fun for a change. Why not turn her backyard into a spook alley and invite the public to show up in costume?

If Geoffrey Henderson would come as a black-hatted villain, he wouldn't even have to change clothes, she mused.

Since Marcus Hollings was retiring from the bench, what better time than Halloween for the disrobing—as long as he wore something underneath. Dick Munson could sport the khaki shorts and pith helmet of an intrepid adventurer, and Griff Walters could show up as a weasel.

Aside from the fact that none of them would actually accept the invitation, what could be salvaged from such a scheme?

How about "Meet the Candidates at the Haunted Wetlands." Because real weasels, foxes, great blue herons, deer, and other wildlife species were endangered by development of the riverbanks, why not boost wetlands preservation by satirizing its opponents?

In addition, constituents could meet their potential representatives and question their environmental awareness. Weren't politicians the proper spooks for the season? Fear, fun, food, and politics—what could be better?

"Neighbors had talked about doing it for the trick-or-treaters," Jessica told the *Deseret News*. "One of them suggested inviting politicians to participate." (Something new to scare the kids.)

Another bonus—the great pumpkin (in fact several of them), five-hundred-pound monsters grown and contributed by Jack Fitch.

Both Salt Lake dailies ran short advance stories on the event. Channel 2 News gained permission to shoot a feature in Fitch's garden, celebrating his horticultural feats. How offbeat was it that an environmental crusader spent his off hours growing freak vegetables?

Two days before Halloween, Jack called Jessica, reporting the TV news cameras were on their way to his home. As SPACE's news magnet (her instinct for controversy attracting most of the group's sound bites on local television), Jessica wondered what it might be like to play bystander for once at a noncontroversial news event.

With Jack's invitation to "come on over and join the fun," she agreed it would be enjoyable for her kids as well as for a neighbor and her children. They all piled in for the ride.

Cameras were already rolling in the Fitch garden when the invitees piled out. The pumpkins were so outsized, they might have been grown by a mad botanist experimenting with mutant strains. Jack was smiling broadly in the pumpkin patch. Everyone seemed to be having a ball.

After touring the garden and marveling at the size of the vegetables, Jessica, her neighbor, and the children stood watching the TV reporter interview Jack.

Suddenly, a sudden commotion erupted at their backs. Turning to look, Jessica observed Jane Fitch descending the back steps, screaming at the top of her lungs.

"You keep away from my husband," she yelled. June was red-faced and shaking with rage.

Embarrassed and confused, Jessica retreated cautiously. Jack's wife continued her approach, pushing into Jessica's private space.

"June, please," she said. "What are you talking about?" She was attempting to keep her voice low, aware that the scene was under scrutiny by flushed and curious faces. One camera swiveled in the direction of the confrontation but hesitated as the cameraman had second thoughts.

"You just can't stay away from my husband, can you?" June said.

Then, her attention captured by her husband's TV interview—now in temporary abeyance twenty feet away—her face changed.

"There," she said. "Look at that!"

Obediently, Jessica turned to observe.

"He would have never gone on TV before he met you and Julie. He has so much confidence, and it's all your fault!"

Stunned, Jessica remained silent. There was no adequate reply.

Jack Fitch, meanwhile, was striding across the lawn, having abandoned his interviewer. "Look, June," he said calmly. "I invited these people to come."

Jessica, still flustered and defensive, seemed to fumble her practiced instincts for public relations, volunteering what sounded like a non sequitur. "June," she said, "your husband is a nice guy, but my husband is like Tom Selleck. Why would I want yours?"

June Fitch was not amused.

Mumbling an expression of gratitude to Jack for his invitation, Jessica moved toward her car, signaling her friend and the children. Over her shoulder, she saw June Fitch re-entering the house. The interview had resumed.

On the trip home, she kept silent, feeling explanations for her neighbor could only make it worse. She kept her eyes on the road, reptilian images swimming in her head.

June Fitch is a viper when she's mad—the snake in Jack's garden. As much as I sympathize with her predicament, that was one scary Halloween party.

Fortunately for everyone concerned, what the public saw that evening on Channel 2 News were only a few close-ups of giant orange orbs and Jack Fitch smiling in the pumpkin patch. Surreal but considerably less shocking than what a more exploitive scene might have revealed.

Still shaky after her experience in the Fitches' garden, Jessica wasn't certain she was up for Fright Night II in her own backyard. But the Halloween event turned out to be a palliative for her fears. A number of US Senate and Congressional candidates showed up, including Representative Farrell Brooks, plus aspirants for county commission, district attorney, and county sheriff.

One of the first things they encountered was a stuffed dummy in the Tobler front yard, wearing an enormous black cowboy hat. Although unlabeled, the effigy's resemblance to Geoffrey Henderson couldn't be obscured for most of the insiders. Julie Bell was the only one bold enough to break the code of polite silence about the other figure in the front yard. Only its lower limbs were visible, poking out from beneath a bush.

"I see that Geoffrey and Marc both made it after all." Julie winked.

On the banks of the little creek that ran through the Tobler backyard, Jessica, her husband, Dave, and their kids conducted tours through the "Bipartisan Haunted Wetlands," haunted (as the press had been notified) by developers and builders.

Drawing on her husband's taxidermy hobby and her friendship with an undertaker, Jessica had gone over the top, packing a coffin with fully realistic animal hides and stuffed torsos including a little red fox and raccoon labeled "Victims of Wetlands Destruction." Several of Fitch's giant pumpkins, gutted and carved, bore the SPACE logo with lit candles providing an eerie glow.

Neighbor Kids at Jessica's Haunted Wetlands

Jack's Monster Pumpkins at Jessica's Halloween Bash

The media were kind in treating the story playfully. The depleted SPACE kitty was replenished by contributions from attendees. The "trick" that had so very nearly backfired in Jack Fitch's garden had been balanced by a successful "treat." Jessica still knew how to have fun.

Chapter 17
Father's Day Massacre

In retrospect, Jessica realized she could have gone to her own Halloween event as Hester Prynn, the Puritan heroine of Nathaniel Hawthorne's novel *The Scarlet Letter*. It was the kind of dare she might have been attracted to had she thought of it in time.

While no one had yet suggested she be burned at the stake for her crimes, she had surely been branded a public menace.

"I feel like I have a big red letter—*L* for Lawsuit—embroidered across my chest," she told the *Deseret News* in December when a motion by Jessica and Julie Bell's *pro bono* attorney Lefty Gunderson to dismiss Henderson Development's $1.7 million lawsuit against them had been denied in third district court.

"But it makes me mad and more determined to continue fighting," Jessica said. "There should not be a risk to stand up for what you believe in."

Senior Judge Dudley Cornish, called out of retirement to preside over the case, often seemed befuddled in the courtroom. But he announced he had found the causes of action contained in written proceedings sufficient to move the claim up another rung on the legal ladder.

At one of the hearings preceding the judge's ruling, Jessica and Julie had found themselves in the same elevator with the judge. Breaking a strained silence, Jessica hoped to say something complimentary to the man who held their collective fate in his hands. "Pardon me, Judge Cornish," she said, "are we allowed to speak to you?"

"You're allowed to say, 'Hello, Your Honor' and 'Good-bye, Your Honor,'" he harrumphed. Lefty later warned his clients to "keep it zipped" during any other accidental encounters.

Jessica had received a phone call from an anonymous source suggesting that Cornish had maintained social contacts over the years with fellow Third District Court Judge Marcus Hollings. In fact, the source said, Cornish still had interaction with Hollings at the local chapter of Inns of Court, a national organization that sponsored monthly gatherings of attorneys and judges.

The discovery process, which would likely take several months, would involve attorneys from both sides requesting key documents, taking depositions, and seeking responses to specific questions.

Such processes could potentially be tainted if one of the plaintiffs in the lawsuit was an attorney with a pre-existing relationship with the judge, nurtured by social gatherings where food, drink, and conviviality were expected elements of the proceedings.

In a study by Tulane University, the American Inns of Court had been cited in several prominent cases as an organization that might provide unfair advantage to one side or another by allowing unfettered access to a sitting judge in a lawsuit.

"It is no secret that … well-heeled organizations are … able to create access to judges by holding social … events where they can become better acquainted and share information in an atmosphere of cozy informality," the study concluded.

"The process entails … meetings that are designed to bring lawyers and judges together under 'social' conditions and conducted under the guise of collegial exchanges. Such gatherings include but are not limited to private receptions for judges and the Inns of Court, from which many independent attorneys ('the Outs') and their public are ordinarily excluded."

In considering the Inns of Court issue, Lefty told Jessica and Julie he would forego introducing it before Judge Cornish since the judge would likely regard it as provocative and immaterial.

Meanwhile, at the disclosure that the lawsuit would proceed, Henderson Development attorney Griff Walters did his best impression of a carnivore licking its chops, a show of enthusiasm for the benefit of the press.

"We'll get right on it at the first of the year," he promised reporters.

Lefty Gunderson countered that as soon as discovery was finished, he would file a motion for summary judgment on behalf of his clients.

"We'll put them to their proof," he said. "We obviously want this resolved. It's a tremendous burden for my clients to have a claim for $1.7 million hanging over their heads because they wanted to preserve a little open space for their community."

Since the SLAPP suit had already been successful in scaring off dozens of SPACE supporters, the ruling made the blue highway Jessica, Julie, Jack Fitch, and their remaining loyalists were traveling in pursuit of justice rougher, longer, darker, and lonelier.

It stretched out inexorably to some unknown destination.

The next few miles of bad road would see Third District Court Judge Horace Wilkins deny a request for a temporary restraining order against a land trade between South Jordan and Henderson Development filed by Jack Fitch and Lew Chambers. The swap was crucial to the developers' plans, since it would make the Henderson properties contiguous, easing the way for building and extending the RiverFront project.

An appraisal paid for by South Jordan City had determined the property trade would be an even swap in terms of land values. SPACE, meanwhile, had cited as evidence an independent appraisal (paid for with $3,000 from the group's meager assets), which contended the deal would cost South Jordan residents between $237,000 and $2 million in lost land value, depending on whether the property would be zoned in future for residential or commercial use.

Examining the report by South Jordan appraiser Palmer D. Moranis, Jessica, Julie, and Jack Fitch discovered he had used Liquid Paper to white out several pertinent acreages from the map and had omitted a number of relevant facts, skewing his findings. They were briefly buoyed by the fact that the Department of Professional Licensing agreed to investigate the appraiser's competence at SPACE's request. The probe was quickly dropped but "red flagged" should Moranis ever decide to reapply for a license. As it turned out, he never did.

With SPACE facing gridlock or worse from public agencies and the courts, one ally in the Utah legislature, Senator Deron Blevins, R-Riverton, agreed to pursue another route to eventual justice. He sneaked a bill (SB27) through the back door of a senate committee, cleverly designed to hack away at the roots of strategic lawsuits against public participation (SLAPPs).

The first draft of the Blevins bill had been aimed at granting immunity to speech in public settings. Warned, however, by the Utah State Bar that the judiciary had been historically cautious in dealing with immunity issues, the Riverton Republican finessed that language and rewrote the bill to ensure that suspected SLAPPs would be granted a fast track to rulings in court.

Blevins testified that fifteen states had enacted similar legislation after the US Supreme Court determined in 1991 that SLAPP suits violated the US Constitution. The court ruled that as long as a defendant's activities were aimed at influencing some government action, the First Amendment protected them.

Under Blevins's bill, cash-poor defendants facing suit by plaintiffs with deep pockets could avoid piling up huge legal bills if they were ensured quick access to a judge's decision determining whether the lawsuit was a SLAPP.

During testimony before the Utah Senate Judiciary Committee, the bill received a surprising show of support from diverse and unlikely sources, including advance placement political science students from Copper Hills High School in West Jordan.

Blaine Prisbee, student body president at Copper Hills, testified that if the bill failed to pass, he, his classmates, and likely other young people would hesitate to speak out in certain public situations.

SLAPPED! 165

Without protection by the legislature, public-spirited citizens inclined to participate in the democratic process "will live in fear of these corporations," Tanya Tolliver, another Copper Hills student averred.

Prisbee and Tolliver's political science instructor, Darwin Rendell (former mayor of West Jordan), informed the senators that SLAPP suits were proliferating like a scourge.

"I saw them frequently as mayor," he said. "The corporation has a staff attorney, and the ordinary citizen doesn't have that resource. So the threat is intended to make the citizen shut up and go home."

Now that such suits were becoming an expected cost of doing business for many corporations, large firms were even budgeting for them, said Cleve Esperson, a board member of the Utah Citizens Education Project.

Responding to the expressed concern of State Senator Harry Spendlor, chairman of the judiciary committee and a real estate attorney by profession, that the measure could target legitimate legal actions, Esperson noted that corporate lawyers often hid SLAPP elements among other allegations.

A Provo resident, Billie Collins reported that a $12 million suit filed by Twin Peaks Development Corp. against her neighbors had tainted the community atmosphere and "chilled our neighborhood." She said that city council meetings—once packed with citizens—were now playing to empty galleries. People had given up on public participation.

Asked to supply further details, Collins said she herself had to be careful about her testimony since she could be tagged as a "Jane Doe" in the lawsuit, which had already ensnared as many as one hundred other citizens.

Although Jessica supplied a brief summary of the Henderson Development lawsuit, she also found herself tiptoeing around certain details so as not to further aggravate her own case.

"I expected harassment, ridicule, and vandalism, and all of that has happened," Tobler said. "But I never expected to be sued." She noted that "SLAPP suits were happening throughout Utah. People's lives are being destroyed."

It was typically honest Toblerian rhetoric, but it wasn't the quote that would later be cited as inflammatory and malicious.

Two days after the state senate testimony, the Utah Senate Judiciary Committee voted to ship Senate Bill 27 into "legislative limbo," as the *Salt Lake Tribune* reported—interim committees, where it was likely to perish.

"Basically, it's dead," said Cleve Esperson of Utah Citizens Education Project. "It was remarkable that the bill was defeated in committee … because there was no spoken opposition to it."

Tobler pointed out to the press that nearly all Utahns named in SLAPP suits were women, usually mothers. Then came the pithy accusation that would ire the opposition and later provoke the developers to threaten to increase the size of the suit.

"These people are mother-suers," she said. "What kind of men would want to bully, harass, and intimidate mothers?"

As spring blossomed into the summer of 1999, Jessica and Julie had ambivalently agreed to travel a legal back road to a dubious destination. Lefty Gunderson was at the wheel, steering them toward what he said might be a long-shot settlement of the Henderson lawsuit before the deposition process reached full bloom.

Meanwhile, with the aid of loyalist Lew Chambers, Jack Fitch was pursuing a different course—an attempt to convince the Utah Supreme Court to approve placement of two petitions on the ballot.

One petition sought a nine-member city council elected by geographical district to replace the five-member council and mayor elected at large. The other petition was to provide voters a chance to repeal a city council decision that flew in the face of the master plan, clearing the way for Henderson Development's RiverFront project.

Although certified by the Salt Lake County clerk as containing the requisite number of registered voters, the petitions had been rejected by the South Jordan City Council as "invalid." It had taken blood, sweat, and tears to get those petitions signed. While constantly rebuffed by local government and in the courts, Fitch had pushed SPACE forces to scour the countryside for signatures, and they had succeeded despite fears of litigation. Now the whole ball game was up for grabs with the supreme court.

These parallel routes to different goals would soon merge and collide at a strange and hastily assembled showdown on a Sunday in late June. Sitting around a conference table in Lefty Gunderson's law offices wasn't exactly how any of the participants had planned to spend an already overbooked Father's Day.

Henderson Development's attorneys had been piling on hundreds of interrogatories and documents during the discovery process, wearing the SPACE forces down and forcing them to list such minutia as every location where they had ever distributed a flier. Citizens who had contributed to SPACE in any way were badgered with the threat of further lawsuits.

The long-shot peace parley had evolved out of a series of phone calls placed by Marcus Hollings to Lefty and Senator Deron Blevins the day before. Apparently concerned about Jack Fitch's scheduled appearance before the Utah Supreme Court the day after Father's Day, Hollings dangled the hope that both sides might find enough wiggle room to compromise and reach a settlement. Just one condition—the huddle had to take place before the weekend was out.

Lefty agreed to attempt to recruit his clients, although it would wipe out a planned special day with his son. Starkly explaining to Jessica and Julie, he divulged that his run for mayor would place his services as *pro bono* attorney in jeopardy.

And should the lawsuit drag on indefinitely, their legal bills could end up bleeding them dry. He said they should contemplate the possibility of losing everything—friendships, marriages, and families.

"These people would like nothing better than to take your homes, cars, and wedding rings," Lefty said. "It may be in your best interest to settle, but if you settle, you won't be able to talk about the lawsuit."

Jessica was not persuaded. "It would be better to cut my tongue out so I wouldn't talk than voluntarily give up my rights," she told Lefty.

When Julie Bell got the word Saturday afternoon, she was baking a big pot of beans for her family's planned gathering. After hearing what Lefty had to say, she realized she couldn't exactly place a get-together of this significance on the back burner. She would just have to hope the showdown at Lefty's office would free her in time for the 2:00 p.m. family dinner.

Jessica was reached by Dave's cell phone at Nickelcade, where she was throwing a birthday party for her daughter Lexi. She also agreed to juggle her family obligations.

In a highly unusual circumstance, both Julie and Jessica and their spouses decided to skip Sunday services and send their children to church with neighbors.

Realizing his kids had never made a big deal of Father's Day, Jack Fitch said he could arrange to get away for a couple of hours.

While still at Nickelcade, Jessica took a second cell phone call, this time from attorney Doyle O'Reilly with more bad news.

He had just pored over the fine print in Henderson Development's proposed settlement document and was not pleased by what he saw. Jessica and Julie would be prohibited from contact with the media, talking to friends and neighbors about the case, speaking at city council or planning and zoning and would be subject to a $25,000 fine for each violation for four years. They would be barred from protesting Henderson's other developments and also barred from filing suit (while Henderson would retain the right to bring further action).

Recognizing the uncertainty in Jessica's voice about what it might mean to even consider a settlement, O'Reilly exploded with an expletive.

"Slimy bastards," he said. "I'm sorry," he apologized. "I make my living by delivering eloquent speeches and writing masterfully worded legal documents, and I do it without swearing. But these guys make me so mad. That's all I can think to say about them."

For a Sabbath morning, it was a little surreal. Jessica and Julie and their spouses wore their Sunday best. Although their opponents, who sat across the table from them, ostensibly shared the same religious affiliation, their facial expressions did not suggest communal warmth.

Sensing the tension, Lefty attempted to open the meeting on a frolicsome note, telling the congregants, "You can call me 'Mr. Mayor' if you wish." (It had been reported in the press the day before that he was about to enter Salt Lake's mayoral race.) Under frostily polite smiles, the gambit was not exactly an icebreaker.

Julie, Jessica, and Jack sat on one side of the table in Lefty's boardroom, accompanied by their spouses—Dave Tobler, Ted Bell, and June Fitch—and Marcus Hollings, Griff Walters, and Mills Homer (the lead partner in the Homer Walters & Hollings law firm) camped on the other side. Geoffrey Henderson was inexplicably AWOL. Lefty Gunderson and Deron Blevins were at the head and foot of the table.

As events progressed, it was difficult to tell which side of the divide June Fitch should actually have been sitting on. In trying to protect what she saw as her family's interests, she was playing a switch hitter's role, or perhaps a double agent. She had been invited to the meeting at the behest of Blevins, hoping that if she was able to observe Julie and Jessica in action it might dissuade her from her belief that they had been egging her husband on.

Homer's presence was also slightly unnerving, especially for Jessica. In another predictable link of the interlocking chain of relationships in the local Mormon maze, Homer served as president of the LDS stake (equivalent of a Catholic diocese) in which Jessica's brother Forrest resided. She had often mused on how difficult it must be for her brother to submit to temple worthiness interviews conducted by a man involved with a lawsuit against his sister.

By talking tough, Lefty signaled in his opening statement that a meeting aimed at a peace agreement would not serve as an excuse for mealy mouthed euphemisms or sugar-coated half-truths.

"Since we're all sacrificing to be here today," he began, "I'm mad as hell that Geoffrey Henderson didn't show up. I took time away from my son to get this abusive, vicious lawsuit settled so that we can all get on with our lives. Let's get down to brass tacks."

Turning to Hollings and his lawyers, he said, "Your lawsuit against my clients is ludicrous and baseless. Your settlement proposal is egregious and further illustrates that your action against two women trying to preserve some green space is a SLAPP suit. If this lawsuit isn't settled today, hundreds of thousands of dollars in legal fees will be accumulated on both sides. It will be an unnecessary drain on all parties involved."

Griff Walters shifted uncomfortably during Lefty's outburst but kept his eyes on his opponent. Responding, he managed a reasonably civil tone, but it failed to mask the malice.

"Your clients intentionally interfered with my client's contracts," he said. "They've continually harassed and made false and misleading statements to the media. Furthermore, they have taken advantage of a man who has a mental illness and have used and manipulated him to take time and money away from his family's precious resources to spend on their cause."

Walters's unsubtle reference to Jack Fitch hung in the air like a little cloud over the proceedings. Everyone seemed to be waiting to see what would happen next.

For his own part, Fitch looked almost amused. It was as if he wasn't in the room or existed only in the abstract. He was being trotted out as a generic example of instability without naming him or admitting to his presence.

Walters failed to meet Fitch's gaze and kept his eyes on Lefty.

"This mischaracterization of one of my clients does not raise my expectations of your intentions," Lefty said carefully. "What I'm going to do is suggest some shuttle negotiations. I will take my clients to another room to talk. We'll see if there's anything to talk *about*. Then I'll come in and talk to your clients. We'll see if there's any way we can walk out of here today with a settlement agreement."

En route to another conference room, Jack Fitch passed a corridor where he heard his wife's conspicuous whisper. Pausing to listen, he recognized the other voice as Marcus Hollings.

"It would be helpful if you could take some notes on what goes on in there," Hollings was saying. "Particularly anything Jack has to say. I'd appreciate a copy of your notes." June mumbled something that sounded like an ascent.

In the assigned conference room, Julie and Ted Bell, Jessica and Dave Tobler, and Jack and June Fitch were joined by Lefty Gunderson and Deron Blevins. Lefty glanced around the table and asked, "I need to ask if you're willing to have potential personal exposure."

What exactly did that mean? No one replied.

"If we're able to gain some concessions from their side," Lefty said, turning to Jack Fitch, "would you be willing to walk away from everything?"

"It's hard for me to answer at this point," Fitch said. "I've been left out of much of the negotiations. Under orders of my own attorney, I've been told to say very little."

"In that case," Lefty responded impatiently, "I don't know what the heck you're doing here. In my view, the way you've gone about some things is all wrong, but your efforts are admirable." Pausing for another run at the same hill, Lefty asked, "Are you willing to back off from your supreme court case tomorrow?"

"Not likely would I be willing to give that up," Fitch said.

"So be advised, you will not prevail at this point," Lefty said.

"I consider Henderson, Hollings, and Walters ruthless white-collar criminals," Fitch said. "If I were to settle, I wouldn't be able to live with myself. There is no chance I will not go to the supreme court tomorrow."

Lefty sighed, smiled, and said, "I admire the hell out of you."

Fitch wasn't sure how to take the compliment.

"I don't believe they will negotiate in good faith," Jack said. "It's all or nothing. I'm not settling. And I'll be there tomorrow morning—at the supreme court."

As the others watched, Jack Fitch left the table and walked to the door. Turning back, he said, "Jessica and Julie, I wish you'd come, but I understand if you can't. Sorry, but I've done what I can do here," he added and left the room.

With Fitch's exit, Lefty turned to Jack's wife.

"June, we can't help but notice that you've been writing something during these negotiations. Do you mind if I ask you what it's about?"

"I've been taking notes of this meeting," she said without flinching, "and writing down things Jack has been saying."

"Settlement negotiations are confidential," Lefty responded. "Who were you planning on showing these notes to?"

After a pause, "Mr. Hollings," June nervously admitted.

"June, you know that Marcus Hollings is on the other side of the table in these negotiations. Why would you show them to him?"

"He asked me to take notes and show him what Jack had said."

Lefty was incredulous. "You will *not* show Marcus Hollings what you have written. You will give me your notes right now."

Sheepishly, June Fitch produced the notebook.

Flipping open the cover, Lefty stared at the handwriting. "I can't read these notes," he said. "These notes are in shorthand. I commend you; shorthand is a lost art." He returned the notebook to her. "After you translate your notes into longhand, you will give me the only copy. Is that clear, June?"

"Yes, sir."

Now Lefty's focus shifted to Jessica and Julie. Individually, he asked each in turn if they would be willing to settle.

Surprisingly, Jessica deferred to her husband. "It's your money, Dave. If you want me to settle and to skip going to the supreme court with Jack, I will." Dave looked uncomfortable but said, "Let's at least try and get this settled."

"Okay," Jessica said, "if not going to court tomorrow with Jack would help promote a fair settlement, I'm willing to make that concession."

Julie didn't glance at her husband. She had already made up her own mind.

"If this is what it takes to help us settle, I guess I'm for it," she said.

Both women shared a moment of painful eye contact. They were breaking with a friend and staunch ally. Would he forgive them?

Lefty left the room to confer briefly with the opposition team. When he returned, he didn't look cheerful. "Let's join the others," he said.

Having compromised by promising not to appear at the supreme court, Julie and Jessica expected movement toward the middle from the other side.

Instead, Griff Walters took an aggressive tack. "One requirement for a settlement agreement is that Mrs. Bell and Mrs. Tobler agree to no longer continue association with Jack Fitch."

SLAPPED! 173

"Now, wait a minute," Jessica said, a half laugh frozen in her throat. "You're saying we can't talk to Jack?"

"Well, I suppose you could get together and tell him about homemaking meeting at the ward, but you can't talk about the lawsuit or anything that has to do with petitions or anything to do with any activities on the Jordan River bottoms."

The sarcasm and the audacity left both women angry and disgusted. They sat glaring at their opposites on the other side of the table. Was there a more transparent way to imply that Mormon women should stick to domestic chores and keep out of the public arena?

Meaning to be conciliatory, Deron Blevins interjected, "See, you ladies don't realize it. If you are nice to a person with a mental illness, he will try to please you and will go to the extreme. He will do anything you want even if it hurts his family."

It was a clueless and offensive remark from an ostensible ally—a man with a background in social work no less.

"What are you talking about?" Jessica shot back. "Jack has told Julie that our friendship with him has improved his self-concept, allowed him to feel better about himself, and helped give him enough confidence to get a job and have pride in himself. So are you saying that if a dog comes up to you and licks your hand, the proper reaction is to kick him?" Jessica's eyes were wet, and her voice shook with emotion.

"Well, Jessica you don't understand," Walters said. "You're not a psychologist. I'm just telling you, if you want to settle, you're not allowed to call Jack—not allowed to associate with him."

Julie Bell couldn't hold her tongue any longer.

"Mr. Walters," she said, "it doesn't take a pea brain to understand treating someone with respect makes the person feel good and builds confidence. Meanness tears the person down. Personally, I could never shun Jack. He is kind and a gentleman. Jack has done nothing wrong, and I consider him my friend."

"Lefty," Walters said, "I can see this is going to be difficult. Your clients are bullheaded and stubborn."

Smiling ruefully but resisting a strong retort, Lefty asked what would be the next step.

Walters plucked a half-bright idea out of the air. "Well, have your clients draft their own settlement proposal and submit it for our approval."

But before anyone could respond, Walters was already undercutting his own suggestion, piling on a whole new list of demands.

"Before we could look at such a proposal, your clients would be forbidden to talk to the media, attend city council meetings, or talk to Jack or their neighbors about *any* of Henderson's projects. Oh," he added, "and my client didn't appreciate your clients showing up at a public hearing in Bluffdale and speaking against Henderson's proposed development there. Nor were we pleased that they warned people in Bluffdale to be wary of Henderson Development and their former city manager, Dick Munson, who has joined my client's team."

"And finally, Jessica," Walters said, addressing her directly, "my clients didn't appreciate you telling a reporter that they were 'mother-suers,' which the *Salt Lake Observer* made quote of the week. Right now, they're considering adding a million dollars in damages to the lawsuit over that statement alone."

The dollar figure didn't appear to impress Jessica. It was a threat all right, but its blatancy cleared her head.

"Well, Mr. Walters," she said, "that *is* what they are; they are suing mothers. That makes them mother-suers."

It made for a good exit line.

Jessica and Julie told Lefty they would draft their own settlement proposal minus any response to Walters's demands.

As if the effort would make a difference. Settlement was nothing but a poisoned dream. Hopes had been massacred and loyalties betrayed. Peace could not easily be made with people who sought to limit rights of association and punish free exercise of democratic principles.

Chapter 18
SLAPPing Back

When you sit across the table from your adversaries, look into their eyes, and see their duplicity up close, shouldn't you be devastated?

Father's Day and its continuing fallout did produce a jolt for Julie Bell, Jessica Tobler, and Jack Fitch. Its effect was like a good, bracing slap in the face.

It forced them to wake up to the depth of their convictions and the ruthlessness of their opponents. Whatever ended up happening in the river bottoms, their personal lives had been harrowed up, and a date with some kind of destiny was coming, likely in court, where the developers' SLAPP suit would ultimately play itself out.

Jack was feeling the sting from several sides but wouldn't sit still for the punishment. Having been smacked around long enough, he was determined to find ways to fight back.

Facing a divorce action from his wife, he had filed an "alienation of affection" suit against Marcus Hollings, claiming the ex-judge had precipitated the breakup by meeting with June Fitch on his premises and convincing her that his "mental disorder" was grounds for drastic action. Jack's suit contended Hollings had pushed her to try to institutionalize her husband and to pursue a court order for conservatorship of his resources.

Divorce—the word had been rattling around in Jessica's head of late. Not only because Jack Fitch was faced with his wife's demand. But with Henderson Development threatening to take everything she and Dave had worked for, maybe she herself should think the unthinkable if it would protect their assets.

Late one night after the kids had gone to bed, she got into it with her husband.

"I'm the one who got us into this mess, Dave," she said. "You've worked seventy to eighty hours a week since we were married to allow me to stay at home with our girls. We finally have a nice home, a nice yard. And because Julie and I spoke up on this river bottoms thing, they want to take it all away from us."

Dave was staring at her, waiting for the punch line.

"I'm asking you for a divorce. It's not fair to you—for you—to lose all that we've worked for if they win in court. If we get divorced, at least nothing will be in my name. I could live in the basement if you'd let me. We'd have to be careful not to fall in bed with each other."

"Don't even go there." Dave snorted, touching his wife's arm. "Jessica, there's no way in the world I would divorce you. Let those scumbags tear this family apart over material possessions? Never."

A few days later, Jessica and Dave learned their kids hadn't been asleep as they had assumed. How much of the conversation they had overheard was unclear, but the word *divorce* had apparently sounded loud and clear. One of the girls had leaked the news to Jessica's parents. It took some doing to reassure her folks that nothing of the sort was going to happen.

Meanwhile, Griff Walters, Henderson Development's attorney, was spreading the rumor that Fitch was carrying around a "glamor shot" of Jessica Tobler in his wallet—supposedly a photographic keepsake from an improper relationship.

A "gag" photo Jessica had given Jack and other friends (too large for a thin wallet) did happen to exist. It pictured her in a business suit embracing a tree, meant to satirize her detractors' allegation that she was a "tree-hugging environmentalist." Glamor? Well, maybe if someone crawled onto a limb, insisting the bark of a cottonwood holds an irresistible allure.

While all of this was going on, Jack—with only a layman's knowledge of the law—was representing himself at the Utah Supreme Court. Here he sought a ruling that two petitions certified by the Salt Lake County clerk (yet rejected by the South Jordan City Council) should be allowed on the ballot.

"If citizens are coerced into silence, then there are no true public hearings," Jack told the justices, noting in passing that Henderson Development was suing him for his trouble. "In South Jordan, there are only public muzzlings."

While taking testimony, Justice I. David Stephens expressed "deep concern" about the lawsuit against Fitch, Tobler, and Bell. "He has every right in the world to be here," Stephens told attorneys representing the developers.

Mills Homer, speaking for Henderson Development, reluctantly agreed with the justice but characterized the lawsuit—pending in third district court—as an attempt to prevent Fitch and the other defendants from "interfering with my client's business dealings."

Watching the proceedings from the supreme court chambers at the Matheson Courthouse, Marcus Hollings was unruffled, deciding he had little to worry about from Fitch's countersuit. He was confident he could easily find a way to flick the "alienation of affection" charge off the court docket.

It was June Fitch who had called him (rather than the other way around). She had sought to enlist his assistance in discouraging her husband's involvement with SPACE and prevent him from further funneling funds from their bank account to Tobler and Bell's misguided guerrilla war. He would be honored to do so, he told her.

Of course, it was fortunate for Hollings and Geoffrey Henderson that Mrs. Fitch was a willing and generous source of information about what her husband was up to and what he was likely to attempt in the future. June Fitch had divulged she didn't trust Jack's relationship with Tobler and Bell (particularly Tobler).

In return, Hollings had suggested that in view of Mrs. Fitch's report that her husband suffered from a mental illness, his firm as a personal kindness and consideration could provide legal help toward a conservatorship. If his illness worsened and he had to be committed against his will, she ought to be prepared.

"And by the way," he had added, "it might be helpful if you run on to any documents, photographs, or information in your husband's personal effects that suggest some kind of inappropriate collusion with those women. Put them aside for safekeeping."

After the supreme court justices ruled without explanation the next day that South Jordan city officials were right to reject the initiative petitions that SPACE had mounted with such extraordinary effort, Fitch refused to falter in his public persistence.

"I'm not the least bit discouraged," he told the press. "This may all work to our advantage. We will probably do the petition drive again in August, September, and October—right before the election. We can combine signature gathering with campaigning for our candidates. We will get serious, get organized, and match the other guys dollar for dollar."

After a careful inventory by SPACE forces, what Jack called "our candidates" for city council almost all turned out to be from the leadership ranks of the organization.

Jessica Tobler, Julie Bell, Jack Fitch, and Lew Chambers, along with two lesser-known supporters of open space and managed growth—Spencer Gourley and Roger Hope—all committed to mount campaigns for council seats.

Unfortunately, six open space candidates for four at-large council seats meant that in some cases the allies would find themselves pitted against each other.

Bell and Chambers, for instance, were matched up in a race with West Valley City Finance Director Ronny Samuelson for a seat vacated by Larry Chapman, who resigned to replace Dick Munson as South Jordan city administrator.

The SPACE candidates were alert for signs of dirty tricks. Jessica remembered how Mayor Max McClellan's round wife Rhonda had eavesdropped on private conversations during Jessica's 1998 bid for a seat in the Utah House of Representatives and once was caught removing her lawn signs.

The election boiled down to a basic split between the age-old priorities of rapid growth, economic development, and new business (including the aggressive use of Redevelopment Agency funds)—pushed by incumbents and establishment figures—vs. an advocacy of open space and controlled growth policies by the insurgents.

Chambers and Tobler in particular campaigned vigorously against the use of RDAs, calling their fruits "corporate welfare." Tax breaks for big business at the expense of small businesses was wrong, Jessica said. "We absolutely should not do RDAs."

Their cries fell largely on deaf ears amid a wilderness of pro-growth rhetoric. Only Tobler, Chambers, and Hope survived the primary shakedown of an unusually large field of candidates. And in the general election all lost substantially. Ronny Samuelson crushed Lew Chambers with almost 75 percent of the vote, and Jessica got just 8.69 percent of the vote against five other candidates. Jack Fitch's optimism about matching the pro-development forces "dollar for dollar" had proven a pipe dream. Henderson Development and other developers had pumped big money into the campaigns of the opposition, while SPACE candidates had to largely fund their own candidacies after scratching long and hard for sparse individual contributions.

A major front-page story in a *Deseret News* Sunday edition might have had some impact on voters had it only appeared early enough. But it came on November 7, five days after the election. It reported the chilling threat of strategic lawsuits against public participation on American democracy, extensively quoting SLAPP experts, as well as Tobler, Bell, and Fitch.

What the article recounted was that citizens throughout Utah (in addition to open space advocates in South Jordan) were being SLAPPed by developers and that some of them were now SLAPPing back.

Double-bylined by Denna Crump and Mary Tristan, the story reported that James Draknik, a resident of the Clover Canyon Neighborhood Association in Draper—just east of South Jordan—was socked with a $45,000 lawsuit (plus punitive damages for defamation and interference with business contracts) after protesting a proposed housing development.

Draknik's attorney, Arnold Moore, told the newspaper his client was only doing his duty as a member of a local neighborhood association.

180   *Paul Swenson*

"He was a volunteer member of an advisory body, acting in that role. He was critiquing a land-use application. The developer didn't like the critique, so he filed suit," Moore said. "Anyone would feel threatened by this. They want him to be naked, to be exposed, and that's the big hammer they're using. It's a way to make a person feel vulnerable."

Even though Draknik was being sued individually as a citizen (not as an employee of the city), Draper had come to his defense, agreeing to pay his legal fees.

And now Draknik was SLAPPing back with a $2 million lawsuit of his own, the story reported.

Also cited in the *Deseret News* report was the case of Provo's Billie Collins, one of the citizens who had cautiously testified in favor of an anti-SLAPP bill before the Utah legislature, mentioning that she had to watch what she said to avoid potential litigation.

Although her worst fears had not yet been realized—she hadn't yet been named as one of one hundred John and Jane Does facing a $12 million lawsuit by a developer pushing a proposed housing project on the benches above Twin Peaks water resort—she *had* been subpoenaed, along with seven others, she said. Collins, as chairwoman of Committed Families of Provo, had helped circulate a petition against the development.

Tobler, Bell, and Fitch's fight with Henderson Development was the third case cited by the report.

"The litigation sends a message to people who oppose developers: shut up or get sued," the story summarized.

Noting that Fitch's name had eventually been added to the Henderson Development suit, the *Deseret News* reported that the developers had subpoenaed his mental health records and that the suit had cost him $15,000 to defend himself—"a huge chunk of his savings and income from a disability pension."

"It tore my marriage apart," the *News* quoted Fitch as saying.

Skimming the surface of a related issue, the story observed that Fitch's wife and father had petitioned the court to become conservators over Fitch in an attempt to quash his opposition to the development. They claimed in court papers that he had spent up to $3,000 to copy legal documents (an ironically insignificant sum, considering he was being sued for $1.7 million).

Meanwhile, Marcus Hollings, whose backstage maneuverings had happily stirred the pot of Fitch's troubles—all without close press scrutiny—stepped forward as a spokesman for Henderson Development to inform the *News* that free speech has its "limitations."

He claimed that Bell and Tobler had tried to persuade landowner Brad Wilkerson not to sell his property to the developer, which was "illegal."

Although eighteen states had passed anti-SLAPP laws intended to get quick rulings from judges on what constitutes a SLAPP, Utah had not yet passed such legislation, the story went on to point out.

Despite strong opposition in the Utah legislature that had killed the proposal, "I'm looking at trying again next session," Senator Deron Blevins, R-Riverton, told the newspaper. "There are already laws on the books dealing with frivolous lawsuits, and we want the law to meaningfully reflect that."

Opposition to the bill had been mounted by a number of lawmakers employed in real estate and by attorneys representing developers, the *News* reported.

Unsurprisingly, the paper noted, not a single developer mentioned in the story was willing to admit having ever filed litigation that could be legitimately considered a SLAPP.

Griff Walters, interviewed by the *News*, let it slip that his client, Henderson Development, had expressed an interest in filing a lawsuit that could be construed as a SLAPP. But Walters claimed the legal team at his firm had high-mindedly insisted that a narrower contract issue should be the basis for going forward.

Within the week the story was published (which would later win a Utah journalism award), Walters (under pressure from his clients) petitioned *News* editors claiming he had been misquoted. The *News* agreed to print a "clarification" in which Walters insisted Geoffrey Henderson "never contemplated filing a lawsuit" to prevent Tobler, Bell, and Fitch from exercising "their rights of free speech."

"We tried to keep the suit within boundaries," Walters had asserted in the original story. "We could have done a SLAPP. It's legal in Utah. But it wouldn't have been appropriate."

For those able to read between the lines, his air of wounded nobility likely wasn't all that convincing.

In *News* interviews with Penelope Canan, associate professor of sociology at the University of Denver, who coined the acronym SLAPP, and George Pring, professor of law at the University of Denver and Canan's coauthor of the definitive text on the phenomenon, their description of the earmarks of SLAPPs seemed directly applicable to the Utah cases.

SLAPP victims were sued, the authors said, for circulating petitions, testifying at public hearings, writing letters to the editor, and signing attendance sheets at public meetings.

The only solution, Canan told the *News*, was to slap back, as Draknik had done. Developers and other corporate abusers must be convinced they could be hit hard with stiff judgments in return for filing frivolous suits, she said.

"Citizen groups around the country are suing back and winning large damage awards. Juries understand the value and right to participate in government, and they are outraged that someone would take it away from them."

Examining the *Deseret News* story, which the paper had headlined "SLAPP Happy" and splashed across its front page along with a half-page photo of the defendants, Julie Bell and Jessica Tobler had mixed emotions. There *was* validation in the fact that local journalists were finally exposing the egregious tactic of crushing citizens' exercise of their constitutional rights, forcing them to spend money to defend themselves.

Although they empathized with James Draknik's fight in Draper, the fact that his city had paid his legal fees provoked pangs of resentment. Their own community, South Jordan, had not only failed to offer financial assistance but had effectively chewed them up and spat them out by joining forces with their abusers.

As a time-honored American tradition, the fruitlessness of fighting city hall was one thing. But fighting a *corrupt* city hall linked to powerful corporate interests was another.

When, if ever, would the Utah legislature take the excesses of SLAPP-happy developers seriously? And when would Julie and Jessica find their own opportunity to slap back at their corporate assailants in court?

Chapter 19
Bizarre Bedfellows

Some Utah conservatives had scratched their heads over the alliance of two Republican housewives from rural South Jordan and liberal attorney Lowell "Lefty" Gunderson from the decadent capital city. It was, however, even tougher to fathom the coming year's odd coalition shaping up to lobby the Utah legislature.

First, there would be a bittersweet breakup—the forced conclusion of Lefty's generous contribution of *pro bono* services to the environmental cause for which his grateful clients would continue to carry the banner.

Lefty was preoccupied with gearing up to run for mayor of Salt Lake City, and while he would keep his hand in with an occasional favor for Jessica, Julie, and the diminished forces of SPACE, his mayoral campaign would consume every waking hour.

Julie and Jessica had used a patchwork of paid and contributed legal help to keep their attackers at bay, but now they were losing their staunchest defender at a critical juncture. No substitute knight was available to saddle up a white horse in order to ride to their rescue.

Asked to counter the tainted settlement agreement presented during the Father's Day massacre with a proposal of their own, they no longer had the benefit of counsel—paid or unpaid. But when had Julie and

Jessica ever given up just because someone else wasn't stepping forward to help?

Upon learning that Lefty was out of the picture, the Homer Walters & Hollings law firm had craftily filed an amended complaint, demanding an answer within twenty days.

Julie and Jessica would have to answer the complaint themselves, conquering a steep learning curve to write and submit their own legal papers *pro se*. Jack Fitch, who had done his own *pro se* work in other proceedings, would help.

Huddling with Jessica in the small office off the kitchen of her home, Jack and Julie noted the scratched-out dates on the calendar reminding Jess she had bowed out of a planned weekend family getaway to address the emergency. Par for the course, she shrugged. They quickly roughed out an approximation of what they thought was important and then gave themselves the weekend to rewrite and polish it.

Handed a lemon of a settlement agreement, they would try to squeeze out lemonade. Attorneys would recognize what would emerge as a layman's effort, since it would be largely stripped of "legalese," the obfuscating language of lawyers.

Point by point, they denied each accusation contained in the amended complaint (providing evidence to the contrary and noting in the settlement agreement that they had not participated in the initiative petition drive). They stipulated that no fines or penalties could be attached to any agreement and precluded Henderson Development Company from filing suit again.

Noting that the SPACE leaders agreed to disagree with the developers, they consented to refrain from opposing Henderson Development agreements for two years. Specified in the proposed agreement was the fact that any settlement would *not* be confidential.

After numerous rereads and rewrites, the suggested settlement agreement was retyped, proofread, and signed. Julie and Jessica delivered it to the offices of Homer Walters & Hollings and the amended complaint to third district court.

And then they waited.

And waited.

After six months of the first year of the new century passed without response, Jessica called the third district court clerk, who said that Henderson Development had taken no action. There was no way to tell when or if the case would be kicked off dead center. Their efforts to lubricate the wheels of justice and comply with their part of the bargain had accomplished nothing; hundreds of well-chosen words thrown down a well without so much as a faint echo.

As a citizen lobbyist for environmental causes, gun rights, lower taxes, and countless other causes, Jessica Tobler knew every gilded chamber, corridor, and marbled hallway of the decaying Utah State Capitol, where the Utah legislature met in annual session.

Julie Bell had often joined Jessica at the legislature, but since she was now teaching kindergarten to bring in needed money and accompanying her special-needs daughter, Trish, to weekly therapy, her partner—with few exceptions—would have to carry the burden.

Representative Vickie Lawford had taken up responsibility for pushing a revised anti-SLAPP bill this time, adding a fresh face in support of Senator Deron Blevins's constant efforts, and Jessica was seeking new and colorful ways to focus the attention of the press and the public on the importance of its passage.

Haunting the halls outside the senate and house chambers on one of the few days Julie had been able to break away to partner with Jessica, they were buttonholing individual lawmakers and presenting any surprised member who would listen with a rubber surgical glove.

Legislators hesitant to accept such a strange gift were told it represented a slapping hand, since it was the legislature's duty to prevent outspoken citizens from being SLAPPed.

Marcus Hollings and other lobbyists for development firms had sent intimidating letters to lawmakers, calling supporters of the bill "liars" and implying that the bill would discourage progressive growth in the state.

While holding a fistful of surgical gloves in one corridor of a second floor hallway, who should Jessica run into but South Jordan Mayor Max McClellan. Sure enough, he was imploring representatives to oppose the bill. Quickly, Jessica found herself toe-to-toe with McClellan in a heated exchange.

"I'm ashamed of you, Max," she said, feeling his hot breath on her face in the crowded corridor. "You didn't stand up to the developers when you were mayor, and now you oppose statewide free speech guarantees for citizen participation in community affairs. You ought to know better than that."

McClellan, a former state representative, state senator, and then mayor/lobbyist, knew his way around the legislature. His influential voice was raised to protect his friends in business, and he seemed to have largely shut out citizen demands for protection of environmental resources.

"What I know, Jessica, is that you're determined to make waves and cause trouble wherever you go," he said. "You can't stand in the way of progress."

"Progress is accomplishing the greatest amount of good for the largest number of people," Jessica shot back. "That means being thoughtful stewards of the earth and its resources. As Americans, we have a right to express these opinions without getting sued for it. Shame on you, Max."

McClellan looked indignant and abashed but walked away.

The dirty work of the legislative session, however, fell to Marcus Hollings, who had apparently concluded he could take care of it in a phone call rather than having to show up to lobby in person.

"Tell you what, Deron," he said after reaching Representative Blevins, the Riverton Republican. "You ought to withdraw your support for a bill that denies our rights to protect our business."

"You know I won't do that," Blevins said.

"You wouldn't want it said that you were proposing legislation supported by an unstable individual, would you?" Hollings asked—again the old canard that implied Jack Fitch was mentally ill.

Blevins hung up on him.

As it turned out, Hollings needn't have bothered.

On the floor of the house of representatives on the last night of the session, Representative Craig Kirkus, an influential legislator managing the floor proceedings, kept moving the bill down the list of priorities. GOP honchos let the bill die shortly before midnight.

It was another case of "wait until next year." What would it take to finally pass anti-SLAPP legislation? It would take a colossal coalition to buck the shadowy alliances developers were able to make at all levels of private and public power.

Like a number of other power brokers from several levels of government, Craig Kirkus would end up professionally linked with Marcus Hollings, eventually working for his law firm—an important hire since Kirkus's political clout would dramatically upsurge with his elevation to speaker of the house.

An innocuous story in the daily press surveying occupations of the part-time Utah legislature noted the high percentage of real estate developers and attorneys among its members but didn't manage to name the names and map the connections that would have given the report greater relevance and context.

"You get the government you're willing to pay for," some newspaper editorial writers were fond of advising. The counsel was intended for taxpayers, but Jessica and Julie saw it more cynically. Geoffrey Henderson and Marcus Hollings had made the aphorism part of their business model: *it's easier to make government work for you if you can buy your own representatives.*

While the wheels of justice appeared to have ground to a halt in third district court—clogged with the sands of diminished capacity in a judge dragged out of retirement against his will—Jessica couldn't afford to spin her own wheels. Rather than sit around waiting for action on the environmental front, she would dig into other issues.

In her own eccentric version of spring break, Jessica had launched a preemptive strike in April, upstaging the Million Mom March for gun control planned for Mother's Day in Washington DC.

Organizing a rally on the steps of the Utah Capitol building, she dubbed it "Pistol Packin' Mamas," drawing thousands of female concealed weapon permit holders and other firearms supporters. Local and national press pronounced it one of the largest protest gatherings ever mounted at the capitol.

The coverage earned her an invitation to speak at a pro-gun rally in Washington DC on Mother's Day, sponsored by the Second Amendment

Sisters—a counter offensive to the much larger Million Mom event on the National Mall.

This was Jessica in her element, fighting for another cause she was passionate about. It kept her name and face before the public, a strategy that some open space supporters found helpful while others feared it might distract from or even blemish the image of environmental activism.

Then, through no particular fault of their own, Tobler and her pro-gun allies woke up one morning to find themselves crosswise with one of the most respected civil rights organizations in the world, ending up portrayed by the media as martyrs to mistaken and false accusations.

A clumsy functionary for the Simon Wiesenthal Center, internationally praised for its decades-long heroic work in identifying and hunting down Nazis and their sympathizers, posted a list of so-called "hate" groups on the center's website that included Tobler's Women Against Gun Control, among a number of other "kitchen table" gun rights organizations.

As local and national media attention swirled around her, Jessica called her florist and ordered a large bouquet of flowers to be delivered to the center's headquarters in New York City in the name of WAGC and then called the director and offered to travel to Manhattan to cook dinner for the board of directors, over which, she said, she would sit down with them and work out their differences.

Both the *Salt Lake Tribune* and the newly renamed *Deseret Morning News* published editorials demanding an investigation and apology from the center. Within days, the Wiesenthal spokesman admitted the organization's mistake, scrubbed its website of any mention of Women Against Gun Control, and removed other "kitchen table" gun rights groups from its "2001 Hate Groups" list.

Fresh-faced and nervy, Jessica bore some fleeting resemblance to the hippie innocence of young 1960s female peace activists who had brashly planted long-stemmed flowers in the gun barrels of National Guardsmen patrolling US campuses at the time. Ironically, of course, their stunt was brusquely anti-gun, while Jessica was an advocate for firearms ownership.

But she had again shown how a weed patch of public dispute could be converted to a garden of generosity. Even members of the Salt Lake Jewish community, as well as some of her detractors, had spoken up publicly in her defense.

Recognition of injustice sometimes brings people together. Perhaps it was a good omen, since the next and possibly final attempt to pass an anti-SLAPP bill was looming in the Utah legislature.

Titled the Citizen Participation in Government Act, again sponsored by Representative Vickie Lawford, the bill had been given the passionate endorsement of both Salt Lake City daily newspapers. In addition, e-mails from around the state were pouring into legislators' computers, demanding support. Maybe a better-informed and irritated public was finally ready to step to the plate.

The stripped-down bill essentially stipulated that citizens who believed they were the victims of malicious lawsuits—filed primarily to harass or intimidate—could petition for relief and dismissal and sue for damages.

Nonetheless, powerful forces were arrayed against the legislation. Outside the legislative chambers of the capitol, Jessica was informed by several lawmakers that Hal Ansel, president of the state senate and also president of the state's largest real estate firm, had vowed to kill the bill before it could attract momentum.

Catching sight of the great man himself in a nearby hallway, she followed in hot pursuit, only to see him glance over his shoulder at her and quickly duck into one of the capitol's old-fashioned marble-walled men's rooms.

Seized by an unwillingness to be ditched so easily, Jessica bolted through the entrance herself. Male sanctuary be damned! But as the frosted glass door swung open, another legislator—on his way out—stepped back in alarm, his brow furrowed. Then he raised a hand to bar access.

"You can't go in here," he said unsteadily.

Jessica retreated but camped a few feet down the hall.

Ansel peeked out the door minutes later. Failing to spot his stalker, he strode directly into her trap.

"I'm a citizen activist, Mr. Ansel, and I want to know why you're determined to kill the Citizen Participation Act," Jessica said.

"I know who you are, Mrs. Tobler, but that's not me. I think the person you should ask is Senator Mick Wallace. Now, if you'll forgive me ..."

"It better *not* be you," Jessica said.

Ansel turned on his heel and scurried toward the legislative inner sanctum, where lawmakers sought refuge from the public.

Trolling for Wallace, it took Jessica some time before she spotted him below, climbing the stairs from the ground level, one hand on a marble balustrade. After waiting for him to reach her level, she informed him that she had been told he was out to quash the anti-SLAPP bill.

"Oh, that's not *me*," Wallace said. "That's Hal Ansel."

Bait and switch.

It was becoming clear, even to old hands like Ansel and Wallace, that this time around pro-development forces were up against formidable opposition.

With the aid of Julie, Jack, and other SPACE citizen lobbyists, Tobler had mounted an almost shockingly diverse political coalition. It boggled the minds of even its most enthusiastic participants.

Had there ever been a cause in which students and professors from Brigham Young University found themselves yoked with the Utah Chapter of the American Civil Liberties Union, the extreme-right Eagle Forum, the Utah Progressive Network (UPNET), Women Against Gun Control, and Utahns Against Gun Violence?

Those eclectic groups only scratched the surface. Also on board were Cleve Esperson and the Citizens Education Project, the Sierra Club, Families Against Incinerator Risk (FAIR, later renamed HEAL), Republicans for Environmental Protection, Common Cause, Coalition for Accountable Government, the League of Women Voters, Citizens for Rural Bluffdale, Citizens for Smart Transportation, the Utah Gun Owners Association, the Libertarian Party, elected officials from neighboring towns near South Jordan, and of course SPACE (Space Preserves a Clean Environment).

The old cliché "strange bedfellows" didn't do the alliance justice. Sharing a bed with your ostensible enemies was supposed to be a bad thing.

But for once, organizations with multiple interests were cooperating to guarantee that citizens could not be intimidated for simply speaking their piece in public, no matter how widely opinions differed. Wasn't that the way democracy was supposed to work?

Meanwhile, Jessica was passing out Slap Stix brand caramel suckers to legislators near the legislative chambers, bearing the request, "Please protect citizens from being SLAPPed. Vote yes on HB 112."

In addition, she had managed to insert a copy of a *Salt Lake City Weekly* cover story on the need for anti-SLAPP legislation in every lawmaker's capitol mailbox. The next day from the gallery, she looked down to see several legislators reading the piece on the house and senate floors.

As it turned out, the jig was up for development forces. This time around, they couldn't find anyone willing to risk voter wrath in subsequent elections.

Under enormous public pressure, on the last day of the legislative session (February 28, 2001—a date to be remembered), both the house and the senate unanimously approved the Citizen Participation in Government Act. It was a foregone conclusion that the governor would sign the bill.

Stretching beyond the call of duty, Jessica Tobler stopped Hal Ansel in the corridor after the vote.

"Thank you and congratulations," she said. "I'm impressed you voted for the bill. You've done your fellow developers a public relations favor."

"I had no choice," he conceded. "You must have one hell of a phone bank."

While the passage of the bill and the governor's subsequent signature were unquestionable triumphs for free speech forces marshaled in the wake of the open space fight, Jessica and Julie might have guessed the opposition wouldn't accept defeat gracefully.

The mantra, "If you can't beat them, cost them money," appeared to motivate the developers.

Marcus Hollings's law firm would later question the legality of the Citizen Participation in Government Act before Judge Dudley Cornish, arguing (futilely) that it was aimed at a single entity (Henderson Development) and therefore constituted a Bill of Attainder (BOA).

Dating in English common law back to 1321, BOAs were used by English kings to nullify civil rights of prisoners and impose guilt and punishment without due process. Realizing that not even Cornish would likely fall for such a ploy, it would nonetheless be one more way for Henderson Development to briefly jam the wheels of justice while running up Tobler's and Bell's legal bills.

While the strategy would succeed under this narrow definition, it would fall flat with the public. With acceptance of the new law as popular policy, the ancient word "attainder" ("taint" in Old English) would end up sticking to the Henderson Development attorneys who had dredged it out of dusty law books.

Exploiting the public attention Jessica's star turn at the legislature had generated, the notoriously vociferous KUTV journalist, Rolf Devlin, invited her to participate in a tax debate on Channel 2's "Take Two," matching her against an attorney who supported a tax hike to better fund public transit.

Needing show-and-tell for a visual medium, Jessica produced a freshly baked lemon meringue pie, which she proceeded to cut the heart out of, saying it represented federal, state, and local taxes. The thin slice that remained she dished up for Devlin and the lawyer on a paper plate, producing plastic forks and suggesting they share it.

"Once you remove another ten percent for charitable giving," Jessica said, staring into the video camera, "all that's left for the public are crumbs. That's what happens when every level of government gets its fingers in the tax pie."

Devlin, scrambling for a foothold in the debate and licking meringue from an index finger, said Jessica's gambit reminded him of another maneuver on the house floor when she showered the legislators with caramel suckers. "Weren't you tempting them to break rules against accepting gifts from the public?" he asked. It was an affectionate tease, but Jessica was ready.

"I looked it up," she said. "Any gift under fifty bucks isn't reportable."

Devlin laughed; the lawyer rolled his eyes.

Chapter 20
Down by the Riverside

Among the folk songs Jack Fitch had learned to sing in elementary school were "Down by the Riverside" and "We Shall Not Be Moved." They represented two related but contrasting strains in American traditional music—one a paean to making peace and the other a demand to resist injustice.

The words to both had stuck with him and now grappled in his mind for dominance.

> *Gonna lay down my sword and shield*
> *Down by the riverside*
> *Down by the riverside*
> *Down by the riverside*
> *Gonna lay down my sword and shield*
> *Down by the riverside*
> *Ain't gonna study war no more*

After years of doing battle on the banks of the Jordan, Jack could have used a break from strategizing for combat. He'd had enough of that while serving sixteen years as a sergeant in the US Army. War was antithetical to one of his idealized goals—peaceful coexistence with nature. But then the words of the other song he had liked as a kid took hold.

> *We shall not—we shall not be moved*
> *We shall not—we shall not be moved*
> *Just like a tree that's standing by the water*
> *We shall not be moved*

Midway through the first year of the new century—despite the fact that construction machinery now towered over many of the hardiest of trees in the river bottoms—Jack, Julie, and Jessica were still standing, no matter how desperately the developers they opposed had hoped to fell them.

Midweek in the last week of July, South Jordan City Council members still wrangled over details as construction began on a five-lane highway to serve the $200 million RiverFront Development, a project now considered *fait accompli.*

Nonetheless, City Manager Chick Norris told the *Deseret Morning News* the office complex remained a "concept," since an official site plan had not yet been submitted for planning and zoning commission approval.

The paper reported that far from acquiescing to the inevitability of eventual defeat, Jack Fitch was launching several rearguard legal actions, attacking the flanks of what he regarded as an invading army intent on stripping citizens of their protections.

"I've lost my home, my savings, everything," Jack said. "But I would rather lose everything than surrender my rights under the Constitution."

One of Fitch's cases involved a $2 million suit against Henderson Development, Oquirrh Investment Properties, Brigham Investments, and Marcus Hollings. The suit charged Hollings with ruining Fitch's twenty-year marriage by embarking on a "savage campaign of judicial and personal abuse" against him.

Alleging "alienation of affection" on the basis of Hollings's secret meetings with June Fitch, the suit said Hollings's activities led to the breakup of Fitch's marriage.

The complaint also charged that Fitch's opponents sought to "blackmail him into silence" by seeking his private mental health files and prescription drug records in order to exploit the diagnosis of his manic depression. Hollings, the suit claimed, "… is long known for his habit of mocking and ridiculing Fitch" on the basis of the diagnosis.

Fitch told the *Deseret Morning News* that Henderson Development had stepped up its personal assault on him after his failed attempt to place a river bottoms protection initiative before South Jordan voters.

If the initiative had passed, Fitch noted, it would have substantially limited development near the Jordan River and hamstrung the developers' plans to transform the area into prime commercial property.

When the *News* sought comment from Marcus Hollings on the prospect of Fitch's lawsuit, the ex-judge shrugged it off with sarcasm. "He's so serious about it he has not even served me with a summons."

Hollings categorically denied the suit's accusations, responding with a string of generalities, intoned like a mantra. "Mr. Fitch has his facts wrong. This is not the first time he has had his facts wrong. In fact, most of the time he's had his facts wrong."

Although Henderson Development had since sold its interest in the property involved in the land trade for $19 million to Oquirrh Investment Properties, Hollings said the suit remained valid litigation before the court.

Why? "Because it cost us," he told the *News*.

Pressed to comment on the "alienation of affection" aspect of the suit, Hollings contended, "Mr. Fitch is trying to blame his personal problems on someone else."

The suit was the second legal action Jack Fitch had filed in 2000. In January, he had brought litigation against South Jordan City, alleging the land deal the community had negotiated was illegal partly because of a flawed property trade.

When the Utah State Parks and Recreation Board met in picturesque Moab, 240 miles and four hours south of Salt Lake City, Fitch and Julie Bell decided to make the trip in Fitch's ancient truck to oppose the proposed swap of a South Jordan City park in the river bottoms for a twenty-acre parcel of farmland.

The swap would allow Henderson Development acquisition of a Jordan River Parkway corridor south of 10600 South and west of the river.

Making a credible case in their presentation for the board, Jack and Julie succeeded in making the USPRB think twice about the deal.

The city was to wind up with 28.7 acres of property, about 6.5 acres of which would be within the river's one-hundred-year flood plain and therefore not feasible to build on, Jack and Julie told the board.

They also pointed out that the land trade would exchange pristine and undeveloped wildlife habitat for ground in use for years as farmland.

Nevertheless, when the USPRB board next met—despite additional heavy citizen lobbying against the proposal—it voted four to three to approve the swap. The win for Henderson Development guaranteed it a more consolidated layout of its land holdings.

Jessica and Julie had insisted it should have been kept to combine with the Wilkerson's land for a sixty-acre nature park. "It's one of the last places in Salt Lake County that is untouched," Jessica observed.

After the board's meeting that seemed to seal the park's fate, a board member on the losing side of the vote chose to complain about a less pressing but irritating aesthetic issue—the symbolic significance of Geoffrey Henderson's ten-gallon hat (kept clamped to his head throughout the session).

"My mom always taught me," the board member said, "that a gentleman takes off his hat inside a building."

Meanwhile, Jack Fitch claimed South Jordan had ignored the findings of a private appraisal that showed the city could lose up to $2 million if it continued with the proposal.

He also wanted a ruling to force review of the minutes of several closed-door meetings dealing with the land trade and public disclosure of any of the discussions. Nonetheless, that lawsuit had been thrown out of court in May.

"RiverFront Gets Ready to Rise"—that was the *Salt Lake Tribune*'s early August 2000 headline on the front page of the local section. It appeared to hammer home the linchpin of the SPACE forces' bad-news summer. By September, the *Tribune* reported, crews would start work on the first three-story structure just south of 10600 South and west of the Jordan River.

The Jordan River looking West to the Oquirrh Mountains before RiverFront development

Construction begins on RiverFront

In time, the 120-acre RiverFront Corporate Center (which was its newest name) would feature more than twenty buildings "ranging from single-story retail shops and restaurants to six-story office complexes," the *Tribune* reported. The complex would require ten thousand parking spaces.

While the story seemed to trumpet the clearing of all obstacles on the long road to construction of the glass and concrete city that SPACE had first opposed so long ago, a few loose ends were still flapping in the wind.

In July, *Tribune* staff writer Shawn Keeley had written a story reporting the curious fact that although the RiverFront Corporate Center had been hailed as the economic future of South Jordan, not a single tenant had signed to occupy the first building to be constructed.

"What was going to be a 1.7 million square foot, class A office complex under one developer (Henderson Development) has probably gone by the wayside" under another (Oquirrh Investment Properties), complained City Manager Chick Norris. He now feared the project would be built in a "hodgepodge" fashion.

Keeley's piece suggested that the glitch in the project's financial vision was a softening economy and a hardening of the stance by Jordan School District and Salt Lake County against taxpayer subsidies for the development.

The district and other taxing entities had been asked to forego any increase in their share of taxes generated by the new development for fifteen years for a total of $23 million. That increase would be used to pay off bonds sold upfront by the city to finance streets, sidewalks, and utility lines. It would funnel $13 million meant for school kids into developers' pockets.

"We are asking to be taken out of the middle of this thing (Economic Development Areas—EDAs—and Redevelopment Areas—RDAs) and not be required financially to bear the impact of development," Jordan District Superintendent Larry Newman told the press.

In addition, Julie and Jack made a twenty-minute presentation to the Jordan School District board, opposing the use of EDA/RDA funds for private development.

"As an educator in the public schools for twelve years, I have seen teachers spend their own money for school supplies we lack, all the while dealing with overcrowded classrooms," Julie said. "How can you even consider giving money meant for schools to developers?"

Ultimately, the Jordan District School board voted against releasing the EDA/RDA money for the river bottoms development. The move provoked a letter from City Manager Chick Norris to Newman, threatening to deny police and fire protection for school children if the funds were not made available.

At a meeting aimed at reversing the vote, Jessica's children and some of her nieces and nephews picketed with homemade signs in support of the school district. The board chastised the extortion threat and refused to change its vote.

The decision resulted in the only RDA ever refused by the district, citing the dearth of needed teachers in special education and the foolishness of siphoning RDA money out of the school system.

Weeks into August, tenants for the first RiverFront building were still lacking. In a moment of uncertainty—bulldozers on the riverbanks seemed to hesitate in their tracks—SPACE seized on an old issue that had lain dormant but had now again come to the fore.

Jack Fitch, the Friends of Cottonwood Creek, and the Jordan River Nature Center, Inc. asked for a "stop work order" on the riverbanks, contending that construction of a 350-vehicle parking lot crossed into a river meander corridor and thereby violated city ordinances.

Jerrilyn Caine, attorney for the complainants, quoted from a city ordinance that stipulated that land "located within the one-hundred-year flood plain and meander corridor ... shall continue to be designated as recreation, open space, or preservation areas."

"Wait a minute," contended a South Jordan City attorney in rebuttal, "parking lots *are* actually open space." The argument was just loony enough that Jessica Tobler briefly wondered if SPACE would next have to lobby for a new law defining open space as unobstructed by asphalt and automobiles.

RiverFront attorney Porter Langdon rushed to plunge a legal finger in what looked to be a bursting dike of media coverage, but he hit the wrong hole. He averred that the developer "is building this project exactly as permitted and is being careful to comply with all terms of the permit."

Not the point, Jerrilyn Caine quickly responded. "At this time, our dispute is with the city. We're alleging the site plan was unlawfully permitted by South Jordan."

To have their appeal heard, Caine's clients were told they had to fill out a request to appear before the South Jordan Board of Adjustment.

Ironic name for a city agency, Jack Fitch mused, since only a major attitude adjustment among city fathers in regard to the community's natural resources would change the path officials had chosen to follow. The appeal was based on real evidence of broken promises and breach of city ordinances. But like so many previous challenges, it was a long shot—a shot that had to be taken.

On the home front, things were no better. With Marcus Hollings as June Fitch's unofficial but willing marriage counselor, the Fitches' domestic situation had been quickly unraveling. June was intent on divorce and intent on shoring up the empathy and identification of her children she hoped they felt for her. She was correct to be concerned, the sympathetic ex-judge had assured her, that her husband's "mental collapse" would spell disaster for the family

It isn't easy to tell your kids that their father is crazy, June pondered. Of course, she didn't phrase it that way, but gradually she hoped they would get the picture. She hoped to make them see that it wasn't totally his fault; two women of low character from South Jordan had heavily influenced him. He had been weak and had played into their hands.

They had made their own interpretations of what that meant, she discovered, when a sign appeared on a bulletin board in one of their bedrooms: *Jessica and Julie are sluts.* What June Fitch didn't know was that her husband had also seen the sign.

Aside from a few sticks of furniture and two computers, Jack Fitch could assemble his meager personal effects in a couple of Hefty bags. Upon moving out of the home he had shared with his family for decades, he had already scouted a place to stay, but its urban location was far removed from the riverside environment he was still fighting to protect.

Friendship Manor was a decaying gray tower at 500 South and 1300 East in downtown Salt Lake City. The establishment housed mostly low-income seniors and the disabled, many of whom existed on Social Security or inadequate pensions.

Rather than seeing the move as a comedown, however, Jack found he liked his fellow residents at the Manor. In many ways, these were his kind of people. Since his legal fees had drained his bank account, he identified with their struggles.

In the final weeks of his shattered marriage, it would have been easy to fall into isolation and a long depression. Looking around and seeing his new friends at the Manor in even worse trouble, Jack remembered something he had heard attributed to the radical labor leader Joe Hill, who had ended his days in Salt Lake City in the early twentieth century: *don't mourn, organize.*

Within weeks, sans a law degree, Fitch was doing his own *pro se* and *pro bono* work as unofficial representative of the retired and disabled in his building. While he'd never had the academic training, Fitch was in every sense a paralegal, and it wasn't long before the Manor's owners found themselves served with a lawsuit for overcharging their residents for meals.

Jack Fitch, that seemingly inoffensive new resident, they discovered, had filed it on his own hook.

When the *Deseret Morning News* had quoted Fitch in July as saying he had "lost everything," it was a figure of speech that served as a suitable description of his situation. By late August, Marcus Hollings and his phalanx of associate attorneys at the Homer Walters & Hollings law firm had taken steps to make the phrase literal.

Hollings had obtained a motion for summary judgment in third district court, dismissing Fitch's "alienation of affection" suit on the grounds it was frivolous, and he had obtained sanctions against him, ordering him to pay $20,000 in attorney fees the ex-judge claimed he had incurred from hiring his colleagues to defend against the action.

Since nothing could have been gained by raiding Fitch's alleged bank account, a constable from the Salt Lake County Sheriff's Office showed up one morning at Friendship Manor with a court order to seize his minimal physical property.

Two junior attorneys from HW&H were also en route to monitor the seizure, but before they arrived, the friendly constable informed Fitch that they were particularly interested in making certain his computers were taken since it might deprive him of files he had been using to fight Henderson Development.

The constable told Fitch that according to his knowledge of the law, the attorneys for the defendants had no right to the intellectual property contained on his computers, so Jack succeeded in using a screwdriver to pry the hard drive out of one machine and was just completing the operation on the other when the dark-suited lawyers arrived.

Interestingly, they had driven to Fitch's door in a vehicle he instantly recognized; it was Geoffrey Henderson's huge white four-door pickup truck with its full-sized bed, fog lights, and a bank of flasher lights on top.

The luxury auto was in ironic contrast to Fitch's own mode of transportation, which the constable would be required to seize—the rusted-out 1969 Ford pickup he had nursed through numerous repairs for decades.

Papers the constable presented to Fitch declared, "You are directed to levy upon and sell the plaintiff's nonexempt personal property, described as follows: computer equipment … electronic equipment … office desks, chairs, furnishings, supplies, and any and all forms … of motor vehicle transportation."

For anyone with a taste for irony or black humor, the confiscation list turned out to be hilariously detailed. Included were Fitch's recently acquired and widely feared copy machine, his three-hole punch, his easel on which he had done some amateur artwork, a paper cutter, a pencil sharpener, two staplers, and his oddly constrained collection of classic videos—*Ben Hur, The Sound of Music,* and *The Ten Commandments.*

One of the two attorneys who came along for the ride in Henderson's monster truck to observe the raid would later mail a terse note to Fitch, informing him (without explanation) that he had quit the law firm's employ.

As if the city, the developers, and the courts hadn't done enough to shred protection for the river bottoms, one of SPACE's staunchest federal allies in the attempt to preserve natural habitat decided by fall to lay down the government's sword and shield.

Since South Jordan had reneged on a contract and failed to live up to an agreement city fathers had signed in 1997, the US Fish and Wildlife Service terminated its environmental restoration accord with the city.

The divorce of the two governmental bodies meant that 111 acres of historic floodplain along the river between 10600 South and 11200 South would not be restored as a preserve for migratory birds and other wildlife.

About $1.2 million in federal funds had already been spent on the restoration project. Another $650,000 that was available to complete the work would now be choked off.

"We're going to have to cut the cord and move on," explained Lisa Patterson, a Fish and Wildlife Service ecologist and project manager.

The decision was made after it became clear that city officials favored development over conservation along the river bottoms, blocking partners in the project from completing meaningful restoration there.

Patterson said FWS's determination to end its relationship with South Jordan was based on a number of factors.

In 1999, largely to help expedite the RiverFront Development on the west side of the Jordan, the city rezoned parcels of land on both sides of the river from "agricultural" to "commercial," increasing the value of the land, Patterson told the *Salt Lake Tribune*. The rezone destroyed a full mile of the river bottoms.

The price hike put about seventeen acres of the targeted lands "out of the ballpark of affordability" for environmental groups and for a federal agency that wanted to buy the land for conservation purposes, she said.

The Utah Conservation Council, a cooperating federal agency in the restoration, eventually came up with $1 million to buy those seventeen acres. However, the investment was contingent on a written city promise of due diligence in helping to complete the wildlife preserve, Mick Roland, commission director, told the *Tribune*.

The city assured Roland it would purchase $1 million worth of land elsewhere in the area targeted for restoration. But the city ultimately refused to sign conservation easements that would ensure the land's long-term protection from development. Instead, it proposed placing part of a golf course on city-acquired lands in the restoration project.

"A golf course does not provide anywhere near the diversity of habitat that the wildlife preserve was intended to provide," Roland said in what sounded like carefully phrased understatement.

Jessica had a more colorful rejoinder: "Putting a golf course next to that river is like putting glasses and braces on supermodel Claudia Schiffer," she told the *Tribune*.

Both Salt Lake dailies went on to quote her as saying that other south valley communities "see the river bottoms as a fertile breeding ground for vegetation and wildlife. South Jordan views the river bottoms as a breeding ground for taxes … or as a nice place for corporate America to smoke. The trees where the eagles and hawks once roosted are being replaced by towers where pigeons poop."

The commission's $1 million land investment, as well as about $200,000 the FWS spent for design and preliminary vegetation plantings were all for naught, Roland and Patterson averred, since the city failed to keep its commitments.

"We're disappointed," Patterson said. "This was a very good project that would have provided significant benefits for the river's natural resources. We worked very hard and did a lot of compromising to maintain the project. We can't compromise anymore."

Mick Roland reported to the *South Valley Journal*, a family-owned newspaper that provided news coverage specifically for the south end of Salt Lake County, "When South Jordan City rezoned land west of the Jordan River to a Commercial Freeway classification for developer Geoffrey Henderson's RiverFront office complex, that zoning inflated surrounding properties' perceived value, making it extremely difficult to buy and preserve the riverbottom properties for migratory bird habitat restoration."

A bright spot in the same *South Valley Journal* article informed readers that money was not the issue for all of the landowners who owned property near the riverbottoms who had decided not to sell their ground for development or preservation of wildlife. DaVerl Monson, whose family, Monson Enterprises, owned two parcels of ground extending south from

10600 South, had made his position clear at a South Jordan City Council meeting. "The Monson family is not interested in selling or transferring our property to anyone but us. We use it, it's been in the family for four generations, and we'd like to keep it that way," Monson said.

While South Jordan was kissing off its river habitat, the *Tribune* pointed out, West Jordan had recently embarked on a major effort with federal government support to restore the river's historic meanders and forty acres of wetlands. Meanwhile, Murray City was making a move to incorporate wetland and habitat restoration in its river parkway.

Par for the course, unfortunately, for the beleaguered residents of South Jordan. The city was betting that the prospect of a new expanse of manicured grass for the country club set to golf on was convincing evidence that local leaders cared about preserving "open space."

Now that a SLAPP suit and additional threats had scared off a number of activists, only birds and other wildlife were left to raise a hue and cry. And they had no votes.

Sandhill Cranes replaced by construction cranes on the Jordan River
Photo c. Rich Hagio

Chapter 21
Strange Encounters

Behind the flamboyant Western image of Geoffrey Henderson with his brass belt buckles, boots, and huge cowboy hats (black or white depending on his mood), it had been relatively easy for Marcus Hollings to recede into the shadows.

In the press coverage that SPACE had stirred up over the Jordan River project, Henderson was the more colorful icon, a throwback to a wilder West, a target of both admiration and ridicule, and the figure most often quoted in the newspapers or seen in photographs or on TV.

Marcus Hollings, meanwhile, was more than happy to maintain a low profile—the conservatively dressed and understated professional, befitting the image of a judge before and after his quitting the bench. He had found it wise to remain out of the spotlight.

So when the editor of an obscure Salt Lake County newspaper called to propose a profile, Hollings's instinct was to laugh it off. The *VOICE* seemed to appear only at periodic intervals when the publisher had scraped together funds for a press run.

Something, however, made Hollings reconsider. Maybe this was an opportunity for positive publicity, something folksy to counter the constant drumbeat of negativity in the daily press. The paper did claim to reach up to 40,000 residents in South Jordan, Riverton, Draper, Bluffdale, Herriman, and parts of Sandy.

The editor—a short, older, overweight man—showed up with a photographer, who turned out to also be the publisher (doing double duty). The latter wore a white shirt and tie, but the editor, who was to conduct the interview, was clad in a short-sleeved shirt and slacks, the sort of inappropriate informal attire Hollings had come to associate with journalists.

Once Hollings had been photographed at his desk (absentmindedly fiddling with a red pair of scissors he had idly picked up from the desktop) and the publisher had left with his camera, the interview began. It started benignly, with the editor asking questions about education, background, and various awards. But then there was a shift. The interview lasered in on the Jordan River project and Hollings's attitude toward what the interviewer called his "adversaries."

He asked about statements Hollings was alleged to have made about Jack Fitch's "mental instability," about his description of Jessica Tobler's supposed proclivity to go off the "deep end" on a number of issues, and about rumors attributed to him that Fitch and Tobler had a relationship that went beyond professional to something "romantic" or "sexual."

Faced with the questioner's persistence, Hollings swallowed hard and hoped that what he chose to say would sound forthright and candid.

"There are some mental health issues with Jack, you know," he began. "And they are troubling." He characterized Jessica Tobler as "a real maverick" (something he thought no one could argue with) and referred to Bell, Tobler, and Fitch as people who "look for a cause. They go from one cause to another." He tried to soft-pedal any connection to the buzz about a romantic liaison between Tobler and Fitch but did concede that he had heard the rumor.

One piece of the Marcus Hollings puzzle that the *VOICE* had failed to ferret out was the fact he had been floating a blatant public relations image as a friend of the mentally challenged, the disabled, the poor, and other minority communities at the same time he was using Jack Fitch's manic depression to discredit him, and taking steps to have his meager belongings seized.

While cozying up to June Fitch to convince her to seek a conservatorship for her husband's assets, he had also once tried to play the other side of the street by convincing Jessica she was aiding and abetting an "irresponsible" man.

Startled to find herself on the other end of a phone line with Hollings, who had called her home in the middle of the day, Jessica controlled her temper while listening to the ex-judge's description of a "mentally ill" individual who, he said, was collecting a government paycheck.

"Are you aware that you and Julie Bell are taking advantage of a disabled person?" he asked. Jessica hung up.

Meanwhile, Hollings was contributing five hundred dollars to Utah's Disabled Rights Action Committee while attempting to convince DRAC to join him in suing the communities of Bluffdale and Park City for an alleged failure to provide low-cost housing, which he said discriminated against people with disabilities. The developer's interest? Henderson Development was seeking a contract to develop high density housing on land it owned in both cities.

When the next edition of *VOICE* rolled off the press, Marc Hollings did a quick once-over and was surprised to find that the article occupied several pages of the little tabloid. He had been quoted extensively on Tobler, Bell, and Fitch, and the writer had even dug into the fact of Fitch's filing of an "alienation of affections" suit against him. But since the writer was forced to accurately report that the suit had been dismissed, didn't it raise the sort of credibility questions about Fitch's mental state that most people were likely to ask?

But the story quoted Tobler and Fitch as enjoying "jolly fun" at what they called an absurd insinuation that they were engaging in an extramarital affair. Let them laugh, Hollings thought. But then the ugly underlying implication of the piece became clearer—that *he* had spread the rumors and that readers should find *him* the butt of the joke.

The article contained far too many nettlesome details (only some of which were accurate, Hollings decided) about the inside business dealings of Henderson Development and the intermittent public opposition the firm was meeting in some communities throughout the county.

All in all then, another negative media report. Not a smart decision on his part to open up to a reporter. But would anyone of consequence pay attention? Not likely, he concluded.

One individual who would end up thoroughly inspecting and absorbing the community paper's report (paying rapt notice as well) would not have occurred to Marcus Hollings. She would find its contents so troubling that her response would come to profoundly affect his personal life.

As out of character as it had been for Hollings to meet with a journalist, his undeveloped imagination wouldn't have been able to conceive of the strangeness of the encounter the newspaper article would push into motion.

The voice on Jessica's answering machine said, "I know I'm the last person in the world you thought you'd ever hear from. But can we meet somewhere and talk?" The voice sounded quavery and unsure at first but steadied to a grim determination. Jessica played the recording again to make sure she hadn't missed anything. Then she saved it and dialed Julie Bell.

After hearing Julie's "hello," Jessica said, "Holy crap, Julie; guess who just called me."

The voice message belonged to Tamara Hollings. She had something on her mind, she said, that she wanted to share with Jessica and Julie, and she had begged to do it in person. It seemed an odd request, but how could they refuse? The wife of their nemesis wanted to talk? What about?

Jessica and Julie, used to skipping Relief Society homemaking meetings that conflicted with city council hearings where the future of open space along the banks of the Jordan River hung in the balance, often joked with each other about how their fellow LDS ward members might regard their religious and political priorities.

No need to check with each other to sort this one out. Individually, both decided to seek spiritual guidance through private prayers, and both got the same impression. They should listen to whatever Tamara Hollings had to say.

As a meeting venue, a public place was out. After a brief conference call among the three, it was decided to liaison in a church parking lot.

SLAPPED!

Midweek, empty lot in back of an isolated LDS stake center, hidden from view—no one was likely to be around to observe two cars parked side by side.

Julie hid a tape recorder beneath the driver's seat of her white Buick LeSabre. Jessica tucked a handgun into her purse. Having her pistol made her feel secure in an unpredictable situation. And the housewife-provocateurs of SPACE weren't at all sure what was going on. Would they be dealing with an informant or an infiltrator?

Having misjudged how long it would take to find the stake center in distant Sandy, Julie and Jessica were running late. A worried call from Tamara Hollings on Jessica's cell phone indicated she was concerned they had seen the maroon SUV in the lot and driven away, concluding it might belong to Marc Hollings. (The couple drove twin maroon SUVs.)

"No," said Jessica. "Pardon our delay. We're almost there."

When Julie and Jessica pulled up fifteen minutes late, the luxury SUV was still idling with Tamara behind the wheel. The scene suggested an added note of urgency.

While Julie was still struggling to fully park the LeSabre, Tamara had turned off the ignition and seemed to almost leap from the vehicle. Not waiting for specific invitation, she strode directly to the rear door of Julie's car, opened it, and collapsed into the backseat. Dropping her hand to the floor, Julie found the "record" button on the tape machine and pressed it.

The woman in the backseat had changed. Her dark beauty had been marred, damaged in some way; she appeared tired and anxious. This wasn't the serenely confident woman who had blocked Jessica's access to the drinking fountain in what seemed another lifetime. She had obviously been through a great deal, including a recent divorce, as Jessica and Julie had heard through the grapevine.

Her initial foray was more visual than verbal. Producing a packet of photographs from her purse and spilling them into Julie and Jessica's laps in the front seat, she said, "Look at these."

The images in the gallery were all of her. Some of them were gruesome. One was a close-up of her head, shaved and bloodied. Julie and Jessica didn't know what kind of reaction she expected from them, but they gasped involuntarily. Nausea might have been appropriate. Julie hoped they looked sympathetic.

Slowly, the narrative of the hike on which Tamara had been injured began to emerge—her confusion, the uncertainty, and finally the plunge. Julie and Jessica had shifted awkwardly to face her in the backseat. She took it for granted they had heard a report of the incident and her injuries. When she got to the point of her fall, she hesitated and saw the question in their eyes.

"I don't *know* for sure what happened," she said. "I can't remember if my foot slipped. Marcus was in back of me; his hand was touching my shoulder." She paused. "I can imagine what you're thinking. But we'll never know for sure."

She looked vulnerable and incensed at the same time. As if she wanted to say something she couldn't bring herself to utter.

"Was he concerned about how badly you were hurt?" Julie broke the silence to ask.

"I was groggy at the hospital when he spoke to me. Then he didn't show up for days. He didn't want to look at my wounds. Thank God my mother was there to take care of me. She brought me food when I tired of the hospital menu."

"It took a while for my hair to start to grow back." Tamara paused and wiped her eyes. "He told me I was no longer pretty," she said. "He called me stupid. He said some terrible things to me. He told me, 'You're not a whole person anymore. You've lost part of your brain.'"

Both women in the front seat looked shocked. Julie reached out to touch Tamara's shoulder.

Another brief silence followed. Tamara Hollings appeared to sense that another question—unasked—choked the car's interior.

"I've so needed to talk to someone about all of what has happened. I hope you don't mind that I came to you. For someone who wasn't one of those who thought Marcus could do no wrong, I was cowardly. I defended him for so long."

"It was that newspaper article in the *VOICE* that finally did it for me." She looked directly at Jessica. "That he could spread stories about you, that

SLAPPED! 215

he could make you appear to be a bad and disloyal person. That he tried to disrupt your marriage. That he called your friend crazy. I realized I had some complicity in what he's done to both of you—to *all* of you—because I knew about some of it before he did it. And I kept silent."

A pause.

"I could have done something all these years, and I didn't."

What followed was a loosely strung series of anecdotes laced with half-remembered pillow talk—husband-wife conversations in which Marcus had made her privy to company secrets. All because she had been married to a man with an ego, the power to implement his intentions, and no compunction against boasting, which often emerged in a rambling stream of consciousness.

In his arrogance, the ex-judge had never considered that his wife—now ex-wife—could cross him, despite his insensitivity to her needs.

He had frequently shared his disdain for Julie Bell and Jessica Tobler, Tamara said, referring to them almost as irritating gnats buzzing around his business interests. They could annoy him for a while, but they would ultimately be swatted flat.

"Once they've been sued and removed from the scene, anyone else who might consider trying to block our development goals will be scared off as well," Hollings had said.

When the women had shown no signs of backing down after the suit had been filed, Tamara's husband told her he had another card to play.

Staring at Jessica, Tamara held her gaze. "You particularly got under his skin," she said.

"What did he say?" Jessica asked.

"Ugly things. He told me he had decided on a solution to keep you quiet. He said, 'I'm going to go after Dave Tobler and his boss at his real estate firm, subpoena them or sue them, and then Dave will go home and tell his wife to leave Marc Hollings alone so he won't lose his job. Dave will make Jessica be quiet.'"

Tamara paused to let that story sink in.

"Well, guess what?" Jessica said. "Dave didn't, and I didn't."

216   *Paul Swenson*

Jessica recognized the resentment in her own voice. She still wasn't 100 percent certain that what Tamara Hollings was telling them wasn't part of some elaborate strategy from the enemy camp—a move to continue to put out the word and put on the pressure. It could be a pincer movement: the warning first passed through Jessica's sister from Griff Walters now reinforced by a seemingly innocent bystander.

But that didn't make sense, Jessica decided. The woman in the backseat looked as hurt and deceived as Jessica herself felt.

As she continued, describing the culmination of her recent divorce, Tamara Hollings appeared a defeated and broken woman.

After the threesome's highly implausible meeting ended, Jessica confessed on their way home that she felt foolish for having brought a gun. Fondling the tape recorder beneath her car seat, Julie felt a little shamefaced herself. "Well, I'm glad we taped it," she said. "The information could be important if we go to court."

Rather than head directly home, they opted for comfort food at an old haunt, the A&W drive-in. After ordering hamburgers, French fries, and frosty mugs of root beer, Julie retrieved the tape recorder and hit "rewind" and then "play." They glanced at each other in embarrassment. The muffled soundtrack of their conversation was garbled—an indistinct mishmash.

Oh well. Nothing to do but immediately sit down and commit to paper every word and detail they could remember.

The two hours it took to piece together what Tamara Hollings divulged in the church parking lot reminded Jessica of a half-forgotten bad dream, now becoming more vivid with the addition of new details. What Jessica and Julie had known from their own experience about their adversaries had been distressing enough. What they hadn't known—including things they were still unaware of—might actually be worse, she realized.

Since the ice had been broken between Tamara Hollings and the women she now regarded as confidantes, she continued to telephone Jessica on occasion to report issues from the past that still troubled her mind.

In one of these calls, she disclosed that she had been made aware that her ex-husband had offered money to the disabled and to members of black and Hispanic communities to show up at public meetings to claim they were being discriminated against because of a lack of affordable housing.

Tamara also reported that she had written anonymous letters to Summit County and to KSL Radio and TV, claiming that Hollings and his associates had lined their pockets by exploiting minorities to support their land and development deals.

How dark and disturbing would it be to know the whole truth? Jessica wondered. Were a conscience and a sense of human kindness foreign to Marcus Hollings and Geoffrey Henderson?

Struggling for focus in Jessica's recall was a blurred memory from the recent past—something large, white, and menacing. It was a truck, she realized. Henderson's outsized pickup. That enormous customized rig with all its bells and whistles.

Another strange encounter in a parking lot, she remembered—this one at city hall.

It had been a year or so ago when she was scheduled to testify at city council. As she was struggling to extract two easels, some bulky posters, and a handful of fliers from her car, the white shape loomed over her shoulder. After she had been able to get her arms around the materials and was setting out unsteadily on high heels toward the entrance of the building, Geoffrey Henderson's voice had startled her.

"Hey, Jessica, I see you have some big-time displays for tonight's meeting. You need some help carrying them in?"

Not possible, she thought, that Geoffrey Henderson was possessed of an instinct for benevolence. She half turned toward the man in the black Stetson. His attention didn't appear to be focused on her awkward burden. Instead, he was looking her over, from her freshly coiffed hair to her fashionable dress and heels.

"Very nice of you to ask, Geoffrey," Jessica said, "considering I'm about ten steps from the door. You mean you would actually be willing to carry your opponent's propaganda I intend to use against you at tonight's meeting? How chivalrous of you, especially since you've just filed suit against me for more than a million dollars."

"Oh, Jessica, I will give you one thing. At least you're a fun opponent, and you're not bad to look at. You're not an old lady with warts all over your face. It makes it more fun for us."

"Why, thank you, Geoffrey. Hey, is there room in the parking lot for you to park your truck? You know what they say about the size of a man's truck?"

Henderson paused at the door, his mouth agape, as if struggling for a reply.

Jessica had opened the door and was walking away with her displays. "See you in a few minutes," she said.

It was a memory she wanted to hold onto; it gave her a little lift.

Chapter 22
Desperate Housewives

Jordan River Lane, where Jessica Tobler lived in South Jordan, was not television's Wisteria Lane. Despite the vicious rumors that continued to circulate that Jessica's political alliances on behalf of open space along the river had led her to be unfaithful to her husband, her staid Mormon neighbors could never have been mistaken for prototypes of the characters soon to be seen on a racy hit TV show.

That show wouldn't premiere on television until 2004, and only later would the Wisteria Lane address become a code word for neighborhood scandal.

In September 2001, after the publication of the *VOICE* article had apparently stirred a hornet's nest inside Henderson Development Company, Judge Dudley Cornish emerged from hibernation long enough to file an order to show cause why Geoffrey Henderson and Marcus Hollings's SLAPP suit against Jessica and Julie shouldn't be dismissed for lack of prosecution.

Almost immediately, Henderson Development came out swinging with a surprise maneuver, filing before the court a Certificate of Readiness for Trial by October 15, 2001. In order to meet such a deadline—as Henderson Development undoubtedly realized—the SPACE founders would face a crushing blow.

220   Paul Swenson

For one thing, they were lacking an active attorney. Although the prospect was as welcome as eating dirt, Jessica and Julie dragged themselves into Julie's Buick LeSabre to pay a personal visit to Griff Walters's office, where they tearfully begged him to drop the case.

Sitting back in his leather chair, Walters smiled and then broke into a caustic cackle.

"Oh, I'm afraid not, ladies," he said.

"But what I *will* do for you is explain the hard realities of this case. You won't be able to handle it *pro se*. We're not only suing you personally; we're suing SPACE—Space Preserves a Clean Environment. Under current law, a corporation such as SPACE must be represented by an attorney." (Later, Julie and Jessica would realize that inclusion of SPACE in the suit had been intended as a poison pill to force the defendants to incur maximum legal expenses through hiring representation that would hopefully convince them to throw in the towel.)

On this occasion, however, it was the word *corporation* that sounded hollow and ironic to the housewives. If one were to cite a paragon of corporate influence, the grassroots group wasn't exactly a towering example; there was currently something in the neighborhood of ten dollars in the SPACE bank account.

"Oh, and one other thing," Walters said. "It would have served you well to have an attorney to advise you when you attempted to draft an answer to our proposed settlement agreement. Since you neglected to request a jury trial in case we found your settlement proposal unacceptable—and we did—the case will have to be decided by the judge."

The tactics were par for the course. They had been outmaneuvered again.

From the first, it had been the strategy of Walters and Hollings to bury Julie and Jessica in motions and legal documents, costing them money and time and forcing them and their attorneys to quit in discouragement. Meanwhile, the SLAPP suit, like a sword of Damocles, had hung over their heads for two years while they remained in psychological limbo.

Having abased themselves before Walters only to be treated as legal illiterates, Jessica and Julie concluded that descending one more humiliating rung into judicial hell couldn't make them feel any more foolish.

At a hearing for an order to show cause, they again pled their case for a dismissal, this time before a vacuous Judge Cornish. Neither Geoffrey Henderson nor Marcus Hollings had bothered to show up. Griff Walters stood in for his overseers.

"With all due respect, Your Honor," Jessica told the judge, "we are finding that justice is only for the wealthy."

"Oh no, it's not!" Cornish barked back. "That's why *I* am here. That is *my* job. Your job is to find a group that can supply free legal help. I know they exist."

Then he banged his gavel and announced he was setting a trial date for December 3, 2001.

Thrust onto the streets of downtown Salt Lake City after the hearing, Jessica and Julie thought about grabbing a sandwich and heading home to the south valley. Lefty Gunderson had won the election for Salt Lake City Mayor, nevertheless; the law firm where he had been a senior partner at Gunderson & Carpenter had continued business uninterrupted. They walked to the law firm's office, still located on west Broadway. There they asked for and received permission to copy hundreds of pages of pleadings he had prepared over the many months of representing them.

Using the Yellow Pages to make a list of nearby attorneys and their addresses and then lugging the legal papers in a couple of apple boxes Lefty's former secretary had dug out of a storage room, they hit the streets to make a series of "cold calls" (as salespeople might refer to them).

How likely was it that they would be able to find another knight on a white horse willing to provide *pro bono* assistance on a long-shot case? Not likely.

"Which means if we go forward with this, we're going to have to pay for an attorney," Jessica said. Glancing at Julie, she recognized the "evil glint" of stubbornness in her friend's eye that they had often joked about.

"Look," Julie said, "do we walk away and watch as they continue to abuse the system and abuse other people?"

"No," Jessica said. "Not even if it means losing everything we own."

At offices of the Utah Chapter of the ACLU at 355 North 300 West, Jessica and Julie were invited to sit down with attorney Stefan Kirk, who appeared to lend a sympathetic ear. They told their story and showed him documents. But once Kirk learned that that the trial date was looming in less than two months, he pointed out the obvious difficulty of carving out time to prepare a case.

At each subsequent visit where they were able to get past a secretary, the same scenario played itself out. "You appear to have a case," a few attorneys said. It was inevitably followed by, "We're not magicians in working against that kind of clock."

The worst thing was it made every kind of sense. It was a rare attorney who retained a streak of idealism strong enough to take on powerful forces on behalf of virtually indigent clients, even without the odds of ridiculous time constraints.

Rationally, it didn't appear that they had a chance. So, how did it work if you were a religious person and you believed in miracles? Did the grace of God apply only in the realm of church and family? In the secular world, what did faith have to do with courts, implacable judges, and reluctant lawyers?

It was not unusual for Jessica and Julie to ask for help in their nightly prayers. But this seemed overwhelming.

As children, they had watched members of their Mormon families fast for two meals one Sunday a month and contribute the money they had saved to a fund for the poor; "fast offering" it was called. The habit had continued into their own adulthoods. Occasionally, a longer fast was employed for someone who was very ill or if God's intervention was required to address a serious problem.

Going for long periods without food or water took something out of you physically but paradoxically also gave something back. A peace, a hope, a confidence—sometimes a sense of spiritual perspective—call it what you may.

Mornings after their husbands had left for work and their children were sent to school, Julie and Jessica began praying together, committing to fast two meals every day. They hadn't set a goal or a time limit on how long they would continue the practice. Somehow, an entire week of daily commitments went by. Was it surprising they hadn't felt weak or ill?

Neither of them had ever gone to this extreme (what they likely would have considered an extreme had it been attempted by anyone else). They agreed to extend one more day and then break the fast with prayer and food.

After breakfast, the name of an attorney—he had been on their original list but hadn't been reachable since he had been out of town—seemed to be on both of their minds. Del Gordon of Parker Anderton & Marsden.

A redheaded farm boy, he had grown up in Riverton, where he had served as mayor while practicing law. Reached by phone, he agreed to see them in his office.

Gordon didn't seem especially encouraging once he sat down to listen to their spiel and examine their documents. But he would take a closer look at the materials, he said, if they would leave them, and he would think it over.

Days later, when Gordon called and asked them to come in again, something in his voice seemed brighter. His examination of the plaintiffs' claims, he said, hinged on their assertion of "contractual interference," and he found no evidence of broken contracts by the defendants.

His firm would agree to take up their defense.

Julie and Jessica's relieved expressions of gratitude gave the attorney permission to grin broadly for the first time. Maybe Del Gordon was going to exceed expectations; well, they hadn't exactly formed expectations. Hope of finding competent and committed legal counsel for a risky, long-shot endeavor wasn't something they'd fully allowed themselves to embrace up to now.

"Are you desperate yet?" Gordon asked. Was he teasing, or did his tone also indicate he could imagine the depths of anxiety they had earned the right to feel?

His firm would require a $5,000 retainer, and charges thereafter would be billed at a reduced rate, payable in installments. Gordon assured them he was accepting a role as their protector, and his confidence that no breach of contract had occurred lent the impression that he considered the case a "slam dunk."

Jessica and Julie exchanged glances. *Miracle?* Something like that. But, as it would turn out, a much more expensive and protracted one than expected.

The first hurdle was the retainer fee, which they would have to split. Jessica was able to prevail (as usual) on her husband Dave to come up with $2,500 on her behalf.

Julie, however, didn't have the option of a supportive husband.

What could she do? Ironically, an offhand comment Ted made to his mother, suggesting his wife's involvement in a lawsuit had deepened her troubles (since she didn't have $2,500 to hire an attorney), became the inadvertent spark that ignited another small miracle.

"If she needs the money," Evalyn Bell told her son, "I want to give it to her."

Incredulously but gratefully getting the news, Julie told her mother-in-law she would work to return every cent. "No. This is not a loan," she replied. "I'm giving this to you."

Meanwhile, the immediate act of Julie and Jessica's new attorney was to file for a continuance of trial. Hard on the heels of that move, Gordon filed another motion requesting a jury trial. When Henderson Development vigorously opposed the move in a counter motion and Judge Cornish appeared to be swayed by SPACE's arguments, Griff Walters took a new tack—boldly suggesting that SPACE ought to be dropped as a defendant.

"If you rule that SPACE should be dropped from the suit, Your Honor," Walters told the judge, "so that Mrs. Tobler and Mrs. Bell are the only defendants, it would then be imperative that you deny them a jury trial."

When Gordon spoke up to demand Walters reveal the legal reasoning behind such an assertion, Cornish said he would like to hear the answer.

"These are housewives, Your Honor," Walters said. "Obviously, because of their status they would appeal to the emotions and positive biases of jury members. Only a judge would have the discernment to resist emotional influences."

"I beg to differ, Your Honor," Gordon said, struggling to restrain his indignation. "The Constitution of the United States guarantees the right to a jury trial for the defendants."

Cornish did not reply.

Following the hearing, written motions and counter motions flew thick and fast. Gordon had also demanded that his clients be granted the right to file a counterclaim against Henderson Development. As the weeks dragged on, suspense was killing Julie and Jessica. *Could the judge actually be considering denying them a right to a jury of their peers?*

When the rulings came down, Cornish had agreed to all three of Gordon's primary requests—a continuance to allow preparation for trial, the right to a jury, and the right of Bell and Tobler to file a counterclaim. However, SPACE had been dismissed from the action.

Del Gordon was living up to his résumé, which included recent recognition by his peers as one of the top one hundred attorneys in Utah in three different categories.

Gordon's competence was the good news. The bad news was the $15,000 it took to file several motions for a trial by jury and the hours it took to file a thousand-page counterclaim, jacking up the cost another $50,000 or so.

"Pay what you can when you can," he told his stressed clients. "Better keep this out of the media," he advised.

Basing the counterclaim on the new Utah anti-SLAPP statute, Gordon detailed the specific financial, constitutional, and mental damages ("emotional distress") his clients had incurred after the suit was filed.

Julie and Jessica were finally in a position to slap back at their accusers—not a "SLAPP" that would constrain their opponents' free speech guarantees (as their own rights had been quashed) but a court action that would hopefully allow a full airing of their grievances.

Even though the judge had granted at Del Gordon's request a restraining order prohibiting Henderson Development from piling on a continuous barrage of actions, forcing extraneous paperwork on the SPACE forces, Dudley Cornish was revealing himself at periodic hearings on the issues as dense and resistant to accepted judicial practice.

Willful and eccentric was one thing. His constant assumption of a peeved annoyance and condescension toward Jessica, Julie, and their attorney was quite another. For example, Cornish routinely allowed affidavits into evidence purely based on hearsay.

In the middle of a hearing on the counterclaim, peering from the bench over his glasses at the trio huddled at a table, Cornish announced, "You look far too glum down there." Failing to elicit a response, he added, "Now I want to see a big smile."

At another session, Cornish said, "I hope you're ready, cuz I'm not. Would you like to proceed?" (Translation: he had apparently not read the motions in preparation for the hearing.)

When Griff Walters launched a long rant condemning Tobler's and Bell's interference with Henderson Development's business affairs— capping his arguments by comparing their "crimes" to murder—Cornish sat stolidly and unblinking in his robes, waving away an objection by Gordon.

During a presentation by Gordon on how Henderson Development had worked openly and behind the scenes to limit Jessica's and Julie's testimony before the city council, Cornish cut him off.

"I know ... I know," he said mockingly. "I've read the pleadings. Your clients' actions just go on and on for pages. You needn't burden the court."

At one point, Gordon questioned the judge about his reaction to an argument the lawyer had submitted. "Are you reading the pleadings?" asked Gordon. "I don't read *every* document," Cornish replied scornfully.

How did the judge decide which documents to read and which to ignore? How insulting was it that a promised day in court had been shuttled down a blind alley of random jurisprudence?

Equally alarming, Julie and Jessica's attorney fees continued to accumulate at a desperate rate. Despite the firm's promised discount, the total was soon to reach $200,000.

But it was difficult for Gordon's clients to complain that he wasn't doing everything he could to obtain justice or in any way shirking his obligation to press an incompetent jurist.

It was obvious the old bird was resenting being hauled out of retirement. He had reluctantly returned with biases intact.

And it was clear from Cornish's ramblings which way the wind was blowing, influenced, perhaps, by Griff Walters, who had larded court records with damning statements of alleged fact unburdened by evidence.

He had charged, for example, that "Tobler/Bell's claim to be innocent victims is disingenuous at best. Tobler in particular is an extreme political and social activist. She demonstrates aggressive and often abusive conduct. She throws herself into the political vortex of every cause that comes her way. She lacks candor and ethics."

Walters added, "Tobler/Bell have acted as shills in the market for the Wilkerson property. They are lawless activists. They consider themselves above the law. They continued their wrongful conduct defiantly, intentionally, and arrogantly."

Once all the rhetoric and more than thirty pages of docket entries had poured over the dam, Judge Dudley Cornish dismissed the defendants' counterclaim and retained Henderson Development's SLAPP, ruling that since the suit was filed before the new anti-SLAPP legislation had been passed, the law did not apply.

To add insult to injury, Cornish shocked Jessica Tobler in open court by telling her he had read a lot of depositions during his career on the bench and considered hers "one of the most abusive I have ever read." Nonetheless, he said, he was constrained to rule against her

When it was over, Gordon struggled to find a silver lining. "At least with a jury trial," he said, "this judge won't be able to do as much damage. We got a good whiff of what he would be like if he ran the whole show himself. This is why we have jury trials under our system."

"If Judge Cornish had only read our pleadings," Gordon lamented to Julie and Jessica, "he might have understood the case—that the plaintiffs' strategy was a deliberate attempt to run up your legal bills and get you to quit."

Then Gordon filed an appeal of Cornish's decision with the Utah Supreme Court. There, it would languish until the summer of 2003. Had Jessica and Julie somehow foreseen the court would agree to review the case on interlocutory appeal—giving it approximately one in six chances of being heard—would they have taken heart? Or would they have regarded it as just one more long shot at justice? As likely to be dashed as all the others.

Chapter 23
Popcorn Popping

Jessica Tobler had never been deposed before, and she had only a vague and anxiety-laden clue of what to expect. Her attorneys had told her only to answer truthfully and not to be afraid to say, "I don't know" or "I don't remember" if she honestly didn't.

Griff Walters's protruding front teeth gave him a pronounced overbite. If Jessica could think of him as a funny little man (rather than as a predator) it might help calm her nerves. Peering through his tiny red Ben Franklin glasses, he reminded her of a weasel. Or sometimes of a mouse—more precisely, the cartoon character Stuart Little.

He could have been a villain in an animated Disney movie. But the scenario about to play out in Walters's cramped office—one of a nest of comfy tree-shaded cottages in the 9600 block of State Street in Sandy—would have a darker theme. Had she been an audience member rather than playing the lead, she might have wanted to smuggle in a large box of popcorn to munch during the stressful scenes.

One scenario began immediately after Jessica walked through the door. As producer of this extravaganza, Walters had already slipped a ringer into a "bit part" he was hoping she might not notice. Sitting to Walters's right at a conference table, armed with the accouterments of the court reporter, was none other than Vivian Hastert—Clare Jackson's sister, another married daughter of Brad and Delores Wilkerson.

Smooth move—hire someone to make an official record of the proceedings who happens to be a family member of the major landowners at the heart of the dispute. The Wilkersons had already falsely testified that Jessica and Julie had tried to pressure them to break their contract with Henderson Development. *Could there be a more transparent conflict of interest?*

Jessica ratcheted up her nerve. "Mr. Walters," she said, approaching the attorney and waiting until he made eye contact. "You either arrange for an unbiased court reporter or you can kiss my involvement good-bye. I won't be participating in these proceedings."

Caught off guard, Walters started to argue but thought better of it. It took him nearly an hour to round up a replacement and install her at the table. Looking confused and embarrassed, Vivian Hastert had already slunk out the door.

After this false start, the unfolding events would gradually reveal that the supposedly benign PG-13 script Walters had cooked up would produce a mundane musical number for the soundtrack. Strangely, that would turn the plot toward a sensationalized witch hunt, laced with hard-R innuendos.

But first, Mills Homer, senior partner, who had tagged along with Walters for the deposition, found himself overcome by sensory overload.

"Someone is wearing a perfume that is making my eyes water and my throat close up," he accused. "Who is it?"

After a two-beat pause, Jessica asked guiltily, "Is it me?" He beckoned her, and she reluctantly leaned her neck toward the attorney. "That's it," he said after taking a whiff and wrinkling his nose. "Please, go wash it off."

Taken aback with embarrassment, Jessica said, "It's my good luck charm. The scent is called Angel. I wore it because I need one today—an angel, that is."

Homer was still staring at her. "Okay," she said. "I'll go wash it off."

When a freshly deodorized Jessica returned to the room, Don Parker, a senior partner sent from Del Gordon's office to sit in on the deposition, leaned in to whisper, "If we go to trial, make sure you wear that fragrance."

A few minutes later, Parker decided he had more pressing business at another meeting and turned deposition questioning over to Lucie Gorman, one of the firm's junior attorneys.

Following this series of delays and looking sternly at Jessica across the conference table, Walters decided it was time to start.

Thank goodness for small favors, she reminded herself. Julie Bell was at her side, having given up her day and juggled her calendar in order to provide silent support. Walters had warned Julie she couldn't speak. Her own deposition would come the next day.

It occurred to Jessica that despite the ersatz hominess of the compound's architecture, the setting was a high-powered corporate neighborhood. In an adjoining cottage were Geoffrey Henderson and Henderson Development.

In a third look-alike chalet was legal eagle Marcus Hollings, every silver-blond hair in place, the very picture of the circumspect district court judge he had once been. While still on the bench, Hollings had managed to avoid conflict-of-interest allegations even as he cut legal red tape and real estate deals for the firm. The complicated charade required heavy-duty commuting between his downtown Salt Lake City courtroom and suburban Sandy.

Jessica was asked to state and spell her name for the record. Then Walters said, "I'm sure your attorneys have spoken to you about how a deposition is taken, but just to make sure you and I both understand it in the same way, I'm just going to go through some very basic things. First is it's critical that only one of us speaks at a time."

"Uh-huh," Jessica answered.

"You're going to need to use words like *yes* and *no* rather than *uh-huh* and *uh-uh* because these are sometimes difficult for us to actually read on the record what you meant."

"Okay."

"Also, you're going to need to not shake your head—well, you *can* shake your head if you want, but in addition to shaking your head, you're

232   *Paul Swenson*

going to need to verbalize your responses because the court reporter really doesn't try to take body language down, okay?"

"Okay."

"Good. Are you on any medication today that would prevent you in any way from …"

"No."

The supposedly substantive questions—when they finally started to come—seemed obvious, tedious, and inopportune to Jessica. Laboriously, Walters probed everything from her education record (Ricks College, Brigham Young University with a degree in communication), to postgraduate classes (producing the piercing revelation that she had been taught how to play the harmonica), her employment history, and her political activism and volunteer work.

To Walters's seeming consternation, she listed such activities as organizing Easter egg hunts, participating in a club called "Ladies at Home," helping to staff neighborhood watch groups, getting teenage kids out to church, constructing a float for Utah's 24th of July parade, planning a spook alley, and making cookies for maintenance workers, shut-ins, and the handicapped.

"Since I had given up my career to stay home with my children, I felt I should give service," Jessica said. "The world needs to be nurtured, and I get to pay something back."

Any other groups or activities, Walters wanted to know.

"An after-school group called"—here Jessica stifled an embarrassed laugh—"called …"

"Yes, go ahead. It had a name?"

"The Hot Pink Mamas … It really was."

Walters, puzzled, asked, "Was this a formally organized group?"

"Informal. It was a group of …" Having giggled a moment earlier, Jessica now caught a sob in her throat.

What did this show of emotion mean? What was she about to reveal? Walters looked like a cat eying a canary. What sort of naughty activity had she been involved in?

"Do you need a break?" Lucie Gorman asked Jessica. "I know there's a question pending."

"We're happy to take a break," Walters said. "Why don't we take about five minutes?"

"I don't want a break," Jessica said, regaining composure. "Look, the name was sort of an in-joke. We were a group of women who helped kids from broken homes. We met at my apartment. The kids sort of adopted me as their mom. Sorry. Can I get a Kleenex, please? I'm kind of broken up right now. One of their dads just died last month, and I sang at his funeral."

Walters's anticipation had evaporated. He asked a couple more pro-forma questions and let the subject drop.

"Tell me about your political work," Walters said once he resumed questioning. He was seeking gory details—how many fliers and yard signs did she make, how many meetings did she attend, how many "honk and waves"? Who designed her websites? Whose political campaigns did she work on? Who were her fellow activists? What was Women Against Gun Control, and why did she organize protests?

"You mean rallies?" Jessica said.

"How do you pay for your gun rights protests?" Walters asked.

"I'm going to object to the use of the word 'protest,'" Lucy Gorman said. "She has made it clear they were rallies."

After the interruption, Jessica said she had financed her activities by borrowing money from her grocery budget.

"Is it true," Walters asked, "that you once had a bumper sticker on your car that said, 'Too many causes, too little time'?"

"Words to that effect," Jessica said. "So many causes, so little time."

Walters paused as if her admission rested his case.

"My church teaches that we should be anxiously engaged in a good cause, and I take that literally," Jessica noted.

Abruptly shifting to questions about Jessica's husband's employment, Walters wanted to know what companies he had worked for and what positions he had held.

As Jessica hesitated, trying to adjust to the change in subject matter, Gorman jumped into the void. "While she's thinking of her answer—since you're going to depose Dave Tobler—why don't you ask *him* these questions?" she said.

Walters calmly replied, "I'll ask Dave these questions also. I just want to know what her memory is of his working." Anyone listening in might have assumed from the familiar use of first names that "Griff" and "Dave" were chummy, Jessica thought resentfully.

Baby glasses perched precariously on the end of his nose, Walters seemed to bore in particularly on Dave's previous position with Stenhouse Realty and its possible connection with Beck Development. What kind of conspiracy theory was he trying to cook up?

Jessica said she didn't know if there was a connection.

Did Dave work as both an agent and a broker for Stenhouse?

"I don't know," she said.

"Do you know what the difference is between a broker and an agent?"

"Yes."

"Okay. Why don't you tell me what you believe the difference is?"

"A broker oversees real estate agents."

"Is Dave a principal at Stenhouse Realty?"

"What do you mean by 'principal'?"

"Does he have an ownership interest in Stenhouse Realty?"

"I don't know."

Once again, Walters gave the deposition a 90-degree spin to produce a new line of questioning—a seemingly pointless meander through every apartment Dave and Jessica had rented as a young couple and every home they had ever owned from Murray to Midvale to South Jordan.

Eventually, he got around to lasering in on Beck Development as the developer of Jessica's neighborhood, including Jordan River Lane, the street where the Toblers resided.

"So Beck Development was the developer of your subdivision?"

"Yes."

"How many lots are on your subdivision? Do you know?"

"I don't know."

"Over fifty?"

"I don't know."

"Do you know if there were over one hundred lots?"

SLAPPED!

This kind of nit-picky inquiry about their home, their subdivision, Dave's work with Stenhouse Realty, the company's relationship to Beck Development, who worked for both companies—ad infinitum—went on interminably, and Jessica was getting irritated.

Finally, Lucie Gorman suggested a break in the deposition, and Jessica gratefully sought refuge in a corridor to talk to Julie.

Why was he asking all these questions that involved Dave and his business connections? So it was ironic that her husband made his living in the same profession as Jessica's accusers, but unlike them, he cared about protecting the natural landscape. He was an avid outdoorsman whose interests included taxidermy, painting landscapes, and writing songs about nature. It was as if Dave was on trial as well as her. Was it just a fishing expedition? If so, she mustn't take the bait.

They were apparently trying to use anything she might disclose, Jessica suggested to Julie, to place Dave crosswise with his employer. Griff Walters hadn't been kidding when he warned Cassandra he was going after Dave. He seemed to figure that if he could find something to put them both on the hook, perhaps they'd be too busy wriggling to make any more trouble for Henderson Development.

Jessica also remembered what Tamara Hollings had disclosed in the church parking lot. Hollings had said he was planning to subpoena Dave, hoping his boss would fire him or pressure him to keep his wife quiet. But Dave's boss had failed to cave, and Dave's support for Jessica had been unwavering.

After the break, Walters again shifted the line of questioning.

"When you met June Fitch, had you and Julie Bell already formed or put together the group that came to be known as SPACE?"

"I don't know," Jessica answered.

"Did you meet June Fitch at that time?'

"I don't think so."

"Do you know when you met her?"

"Let's see." Jessica twisted uncomfortably in her chair. "Man," she said, "you guys went from being too hot in here to being too cold."

Walters reminded her that her spontaneous comments were being recorded and would appear in the official transcript of the proceedings.

"Did you learn at some time that Jack Fitch was suffering from some kind of mental illness?" he asked.

Uh-oh, here it comes, Jessica realized.

"Yes I did."

"Do you know when you found that out?"

"When Julie Bell told me."

"How was that?"

"June Fitch called Julie."

"Do you know when that was?"

"I don't."

"So after this initial disclosure by June to Julie and then Julie to you and you guys discussed it, Jack continued to be involved with the SPACE group?"

"Jack had his own group."

"Wouldn't it be true that Jack perceived himself to be a member of SPACE?"

"You'd have to ask Jack."

Walters cited telephone records to document that Fitch and Jessica often spoke by phone several times a day. Then he paused briefly before making eye contact to launch a line of inquiry that Jessica regarded as insinuating and inflammatory.

"Did you ever perceive that Jack Fitch was infatuated with you?"

"No."

"Never crossed your mind that he was infatuated with you?"

"No."

"Did he ever write you poems?"

"He wrote me *a* poem."

"Did he ever write you a song?"

"To the tune of 'Popcorn Popping on the Apricot Tree,'" Jessica amusedly confirmed. "Called 'Jessica Riding.'"

Walters paused as if pleased. Maybe she shouldn't have been so quick on the uptake. Where in the name of reason was he going with this? How strange that he wanted a satire of a children's song—the original sung in Mormon primary—mentioned in the public record. The parody had been a private joke between Jessica and Jack Fitch. What could they possibly make of it?

This wasn't about popping popcorn. Walters wanted to pop Jessica's image as a serious activist and replace it with one as a scheming manipulator. *Pop a vein is more like it*, Jessica thought when she realized what he had in mind. *That's what he would like me to do.*

Walters produced a copy of Fitch's lyrics and handed it to her.

"Do you know when he gave you this poem?"

"He gave it to me when he saw me riding on TRAX."

Jessica suppressed a smile, remembering her avid public opposition to taxpayer-funded public transportation—a boondoggle in her opinion. Fitch had teased her about her hypocrisy; he had accidentally "caught" her playing passenger on the maiden voyage of light rail. At the SouthTowne station, riding TRAX north, he had glanced out the window and glimpsed Jessica on a TRAX train heading south. With that, the song parody was born.

"Have you had many songs written for you by men who aren't your husband?" Walters asked.

"Do I have to answer that?" Jessica asked.

It sounded as if she were evading the question, she realized, as if she had something to hide. Sometimes the truth was too complicated to explain.

Instructed to answer, she said, "There are men who are impressed with my courage and the fact that I stand up for what I believe in."

"And have these men written you songs?"

"Yes."

"Someone besides Jack Fitch who has written you a song? Who else?"

"I don't remember his name. I met him at a party. And he wrote me a song or a poem. The words are hanging on my wall because it means a lot; it's about a woman who stands up for what she believes in."

Walters looked annoyed. Serving up questions that she could hit out of the park was apparently not what he had in mind.

Carefully, he returned to prodding the implications of Fitch's banal lyrical tribute.

238   *Paul Swenson*

"Once again, when did Jack write this song for you? What time frame?"

"On the Free TRAX day. The day you could ride light rail for free."

"Was that in 1997?"

"I'm not sure—'97 or '98. It was in December, I think."

"Would this song indicate to you that Jack might be infatuated with you?"

"Absolutely not," Jessica said, exhaling audibly. "I find that offensive."

Walters's squint registered a brief blink before he doggedly pressed on. "I want to read a couple of verses and get your opinion.

> *"I looked out the window and what did I see?*
> *Jessica riding on the TRAX for free*
> *Winter brought me such a nice surprise.*
> *Light rail rider right before my eyes.*

> *"Mass transit riding is such a treat*
> *With a light rail rider who looks so sweet*
> *It was really so—what a thrill to see*
> *Jessica riding on the TRAX with me."*

Walters recited in a sing-songy voice lacking inflection or nuance.

"Okay," Jessica responded numbly.

"Were you riding with her—with him—on the TRAX?"

"No, I was not."

"So this is something he was seeing in his mind's eye versus something that actually happened, correct?"

"I was riding with Congressman Farrell Brooks."

Walters again looked fidgety and annoyed. "So you're saying this poem is about something that he's imagining, not something that actually occurred?"

"No, what he is describing, he saw. There is irony. Jack is pro-light rail, and he knows that I have fought light rail for years. Farrell Brooks—Congressman Brooks—knowing I was one of the most ardent opponents of light rail, asked me to accompany him on TRAX to see how it rode. We were departing from the SouthTowne station, headed north; Jack was coming the other way on another train. It's just like the song says. He looked out the window and saw me in the other train. Do you want me to sing it?"

There was a slight pause. Walters cleared his throat. Things weren't going the way he'd expected.

"No, that will not be necessary," he exclaimed. "I'm going to have you hold off on that. I'm going to hand you another, er, well, I believe this is a poem. The first poem is marked Exhibit 1. I'm going to have this one marked Exhibit 2. Do you remember getting this poem from Jack?"

Jessica quickly scanned the sheet as it was handed to her.

"Yes, I do."

"Do you think *this* poem evidenced that he was infatuated with you?"

"Absolutely not."

"Let me read it for you and get your opinion.

> *"Others cheated, but you were honest. Others lied, but you*
> *told the truth. Others were mean-spirited, but you were kind.*
> *Your friends love and respect you and always will."*

Griff Walters wouldn't likely be invited to recite from a university lectern; he didn't have the sensibility for it. The material was obviously prose, not poetry. The words weren't particularly inspiring, but his tone was flat and emotionless. The next lines—admittedly devoid of meter or poetic rhythm—sounded ludicrous in the way Walters read them.

> *"Neither the Salt Lake district attorney nor the Denver*
> *regional postal inspector is looking for your phone number."*

Walters coughed, again cleared his throat, and plodded on.

> *"In the end, truth will prevail. You will prevail too. You are*
> *a princess, a queen, an angel, a goddess. You were the real*
> *victor."*

Grasping that this was the closest to romantic pay dirt he was going to strike, Walters made a game attempt to invest the lines with feeling. His emphasis sounded silly, but he was almost gloating when he finished.

"When did he send this to you? Did he send it, or did he hand it to you?"

"I don't remember."

"Do you know when you got it?"

"To the best of my recollection, he wrote this to me after I lost my city council race."

"So that would have been …?"

"November or December 1999."

"In the line when he says, 'Neither the Salt Lake County district attorney nor the Denver regional postal inspector is looking for your phone number,' what is that about?"

"It's an inside joke."

Again, Walters's involuntary squint made it clear he wasn't pleased to be excluded from any scrap of information, meant seriously or not. "Okay, what *is* the joke?"

"Well, as I recall, a campaign piece had been sent out by my opponents in the city council race, and they had used an improper bulk rate postage stamp on their little sticker thing. And when we looked it up, it was registered to some sort of—I don't know—ministry."

Walters couldn't see the joke—inside or otherwise. He stared at her blankly.

"Who looked it up?"

"I don't remember."

"Did Jack Fitch look it up?"

"I don't remember."

"Was Jack working for you on the campaign?"

"Jack was running for office."

"Was he working with you on the campaign?"

"He helped me."

SLAPPED!

"So the Denver Regional postal inspector and the Salt Lake County district attorney were both investigating this bulk postage issue. That's what this is in reference to?"

"I think so."

Walters's exasperation was starting to show. His face was red, and the wheeze in his voice sounded like a teakettle—ready to blow. He couldn't pull anything of substance from the "I don't knows," "I don't remembers" and "I think sos."

He needed to steer things back from this bulk postage diversion to what he was looking for: something to show that Jessica Tobler and Jack Fitch had been playing post office for real.

"What was your response to this 'Angel/Goddess' poem?"

Before Jessica could answer, her attorney broke in. "Just a moment," Lucy Gorman said. "We ought to take a break.

Jessica shook her head and raised her hand. "No, I want to answer," she said. "Jack Fitch was being nice. He was being a gentleman. I'd lost two elections. It's no fun to lose, especially when the big boys target you because you're honest and you can't be bought and you tell the truth and you don't play games. That is what this poem—if that's what it is—means. I told the truth, even if it lost votes. Even if it meant that developers were going to donate to other people's campaigns.

"I have worked with hundreds of men in my political activities. There is not a finer gentleman than Jack Fitch. You can ask my husband. Jack was writing something to cheer me up. So this is a sin, is it? Trying to make me feel good? This is something wrong?"

The room was unusually quiet. Walters took a moment to respond, and when he did, the tension in his voice leaked through his attempted restraint.

"Mrs. Tobler, did you ever give Jack Fitch a picture of yourself."

From the corner of her eye, Jessica observed that Julie Bell looked as if she wanted to smack Griff Walters in the face.

"You know what?" Gorman interjected. "I'm going to object to this line of questioning. I don't know how it's relevant. I believe it is meant to harass my client. I can't imagine how it's relevant to the claims."

242   *Paul Swenson*

Walters turned on the attorney as if *she* had slapped him.

"Beg your pardon," he sputtered. "It's at the heart of it!" A droplet of spittle had escaped his open mouth. "If your client is claiming emotional distress damages against us, I believe this whole relationship with Jack—whatever it was—is caught up with emotional issues. We're going to get into what June Fitch was trying to deal with at the time and information that she—"

"This isn't about June Fitch," Gorman interrupted.

"It is. The emotional distress damages."

"This is *not* about June Fitch."

Jessica sat back in her chair, interested and grateful to be momentarily out of the line of fire. Watching Walters turn his wrath on someone else—another woman and her ally—and to see it rebuffed was heartening.

"Look," Walters said, trying to restrain his annoyance, "I believe Jack Fitch was obsessed with Mrs. Tobler and it got to the point that his actions were attributable to her—that he was doing whatever she wanted him to do."

As the witness, was Jessica invisible? It was as if she wasn't even in the room, or was an object.

"If Mrs. Tobler couldn't be in the forefront of everything, she could pull the strings and get Jack to do things," Walters said. He was facing Gorman, trying to stare her down. "I think the evidence is going to clearly show that whether Jessica perceived it or not, Jack perceived it."

"Anything Jack perceived is irrelevant to her claim for emotional damage," Gorman said evenly.

Walters had dispensed with dispassionate inquiry. His tone was argumentative and shrill.

"This is a litigation where she's saying that we were—or my clients were—wrongfully bringing a case against her for the sole purpose of harassing her," he said. "I think the evidence is going to show that there were multiple lawsuits going on that she was assisting and orchestrating, and Jack was helping her do that. Why would he do that? One of the critical reasons was that Jack came to have an unhealthy relationship with Jessica—a relationship she allowed to exist and didn't stop."

SLAPPED! 243

Having achieved a head of steam, Walters turned his attention back to Jessica. She met his gaze, silently fuming.

"And I don't care if she likes the questions or not," Walters said. "The defense of our case will bear on her emotional state and the emotional state she created around her with others."

Gorman was resolute. "Then I think we should discontinue this hearing and obtain a protective order."

(Since Homer Walters & Hollings had filed innumerable nuisance motions against Parker Anderton & Marsden, the latter had filed for a restraining order against the former, which the court granted. This led to orders to both sides to settle the case before January 3, 2002, and later with the help of a professional mediator, for which each side paid $2,000 in fees. Neither attempt succeeded.)

"Fine," Walters said. "Let's call the judge. "We've already put him on notice."

"All right," she replied. "Well, I think we're done."

Done? Deposed for a grueling seven hours and without a single question about the lawsuit. Tobler had survived, but she figured she'd had enough.

"We'll see you tomorrow," Walters told Jessica.

"Oh no," Lucie Gorman cautioned. "Under state law, a deposition is limited to seven hours. She's not coming back tomorrow."

"Well then," conceded Walters, "if we can't do her, we'll do Julie Bell."

As a verb, Gorman was thinking, Walters's word *do* (as applied to two female defendants) seemed not just grammatically questionable but casually insulting, perhaps purposely so. She had an impulse to call him on it. But no, it wasn't worth it at this point.

Jessica didn't envy Julie but on the other hand was happy to escape another round herself. She might not have felt quite so relieved had she known her accusers would eventually come after her a second time.

Minutes later on the sidewalk outside Walters's office, Julie, Jessica, and Lucie Gorman encountered Del Gordon, who had shown up for a brief postmortem on how the hearing had gone.

"Del," Gorman asked. "When I called you during the break to let you know what was happening, why didn't you tell me to object to their offensive line of questioning?"

"Don't you get it?" Del replied. "By asking such silly and abusive questions, they totally screwed up."

Oh ... understood, the knowing glances exchanged among the three women seemed to say. There was nothing else to add.

As the conversation among the sidewalk conferees wound down, Lucie Gorman disclosed she had advised Walters her client wouldn't answer additional questions or allegations regarding any alleged relationship between Jessica Tobler and Jack Fitch.

If Walters was inclined to use the deposition process as a naked exercise to dig dirt, they weren't about to supply the shovel.

Chapter 24
Costume Party

de pose
1. *vt* to remove someone from office or from a position of power
2. *vti* to give evidence or testify on oath in written or verbal form
3. *vt* to request and record evidence from a witness

Having had a ringside seat for Jessica Tobler's deposition, Julie Bell was quickly forced to associate the word *depose* with other dangerous "d" words—*divest*, *disrobe*, and *destroy*.

As a citizen who found her voice by fully participating in the democratic process, Jessica had attained a level of respectability in the community. Her activities had given her influence and a certain patina of power.

But in Griff Walters's relentless interrogatories, he had made it his mission to peel all of that away—to divest her of her positive reputation, to strip her bare, and to leave her naked to suspicion and innuendo. Jessica had been *deposed* in more ways than one.

Now it was Julie's turn. And before the first question could be asked, Henderson Development's legal team had done everything to make the process as painful and inconvenient as possible. Initially, Homer Walters

& Hollings had asked to depose both Tobler and Bell on the same day, September 11, 2002—the first anniversary of terrorist attacks on the World Trade Center and the Pentagon.

While Julie and Jessica were able to grasp the cunning nastiness of such a tactic, how many twisted games, they wondered, were their adversaries willing to play to try to psych them out?

When Del Gordon flatly refused to produce his clients on that date and demanded separate deposition dates, HW&H suggested October 30 for Tobler and October 31 for Bell. Only later, after they had agreed, did it occur to Bell that she had been tagged with Halloween.

She would have to divest herself of the costume she had planned to wear to her daughter Trish's school Halloween party; in fact, she would have to divest herself of the party altogether, a real blow to her special-needs child. Ironically, Julie had earlier signed up as the parent representative to help plan and carry out the festivities.

A parent of one of her daughter's friends would have to be willing to assume Julie's Halloween duties so that she could instead dress in a business suit and show up for a much more serious affair.

By staying cool, Jessica Tobler had partially succeeded in unmasking her interrogator as condescending and manipulative. But for Julie's deposition, HW&H was replacing Griff Walters with the firm's lead attorney, Mills Homer—reputedly a smoother operator. What kind of game face would Homer wear to the party?

Just as Julie had been Jessica's support at her deposition the day before, Jessica had pledged to be on hand for Julie's. She would be late, she had warned, since she was also performing classroom duties at a school party for one of her own daughters.

But when she arrived, she promised she would use a fashion statement to liven up the sober halls of justice.

When Homer, a tall man of medium build in a conservative gray suit, sat forward, he hunched his back, giving him the odd appearance of a rangy troll. While he affected an outward friendliness, it peeled away to a no-nonsense demeanor.

Del Gordon was on hand to represent Julie, and his bright blue necktie added a note of cheer. Julie had also added color to her appearance, wearing a red blouse and gold earrings. Before entering Homer's cottage in the little suite of HW&H offices, she had taken several deep breaths as a conscious relaxation technique.

When the participants were seated at a conference table, Homer requested the defendant state her name and address for the record. After she had done so, he turned to her, affecting a diffident smile, and asked, "May I call you Julie?" She nodded her approval.

The attorney's introduction was a series of seemingly standard questions about Julie's education and professional background. By his expression, Homer appeared either impressed or surprised by the MED (master of deaf education) degree she had noted in a verbal résumé of her experience.

Homer's alleged lawyerly polish wasn't necessarily in evidence during his early questioning, Julie observed. He was not as smooth as his reputation; neither was he especially subtle. His lines of inquiry were straightforward and predictable. Focused on Julie's political activities, he seemed thwarted by her report that she had not been an activist of any kind before getting involved in the fight to preserve open space.

It looked as if he itched to probe her candidacy for a seat on the South Jordan City Council but was abashed by her testimony that a single debate—plus a lone flyer and some lawn signs—had promoted her entire campaign.

After scavenging this largely barren terrain without notable success, he turned to Julie's eventual alliance with Jessica Tobler and their founding of SPACE. His interrogation lurched into motion with a less-than-scintillating exchange.

"Now, Julie," he said. "How did you become associated with SPACE?"

"I helped to form it," she replied.

"And what did you do in helping to form it?"

"Held a meeting."

"And when was that meeting held?"

"I believe the fifteenth of November 1996."

"And where was that meeting held?"

"At my house."

Staring at Bell blankly, Homer continued to reel off a succession of sterile questions. How could the answers she was giving produce anything of value for his purposes? Was his vacant expression meant to strategically conceal an ace or two he might be hiding up his sleeve? What Julie believed she was observing didn't so much seem to be a poker face as a void. Maybe Mills Homer was just a very boring guy.

As that thought crossed her mind, it was quickly followed by the guilty recollection that this tedious fellow was Jessica's brother Forrest's LDS stake president. Shouldn't she have more respect for a church leader?

"Who came up with the name SPACE?" Homer asked.

"I don't recall," Julie replied.

"And who was the person—I mean, did Jessica Tobler comment at any time during that meeting?"

"I don't recall."

"Did you comment during that meeting?"

"Yes."

"And what was your position during that meeting?"

"I had a great concern about the traffic aspect of the proposed development and how it would change our community."

Julie pondered. *This is what I skipped my daughter's Halloween party to enter into public record? Is he trying to lull me to sleep before he hits me with the heavy artillery?* It was hard to suppress a snicker.

At that moment, however, Jessica Tobler entered the chamber, and there was a brief lull before she settled herself by Julie's side. Her appearance had stirred a breeze in the room.

"She's quite flamboyant, isn't she?" Del Gordon whispered to Julie, having made a quick inventory of Jessica's outfit, his eyebrows arched.

She was wearing a knee-length white "country girl" wedding dress above a stylish pair of boots, topped with a white cowboy hat. Mills Homer's mouth was open. He looked flummoxed and peeved, as if an unwelcome guest in inappropriate attire (Reese Witherspoon in *Legally*

Blond?) had stumbled into his office to upstage his deposition with a surprise soirée.

Neither attorney seemed to immediately catch on. "Look," Jessica said, noticing they were staring. "It's Halloween. I just came from my daughter's school. Sorry for being late."

Homer cleared his throat, signaling a return to the business at hand. Ignoring the fact that the subject of his line of questioning was now in the room, he droned on in the vein he had been pursuing.

"Do you have any recollection of a sense of what Jessica's position was in those early meetings of SPACE?"

"Yeah," Julie said. "She wanted to preserve open space."

It was hard to suppress a smile at that one, and when Jessica turned to Julie, both of them grinned. Wasn't Homer aware he seemed to be casting himself as straight man and serving up laugh lines for his witness?

Maybe the interruption had finally clued Homer to something. Shortly after Jessica's arrival, he had climbed off his rhetorical treadmill and begun boring in on the events surrounding his clients' most serious allegation— that Julie Bell and Jessica Tobler had attempted to interfere with Henderson Development's contracts with Brad and Delores Wilkerson.

Homer's focus was the December 5, 1996 SPACE meeting, blighted by the snowstorm-forced absence of Mandy Fletcher of Utah Open Space. The attorney's purpose, however, was to probe the presence of both Wilkersons at the gathering.

"At that meeting," he asked Julie, "I take it that Brad announced to you that he was already under some kind of contractual arrangement with Henderson Development?"

"Yes."

"Did you inquire about what that contractual arrangement meant?"

"I don't recall inquiring about it further."

"Any discussions with Mr. and Mrs. Wilkerson about trying to void their contracts?"

"I think that the statement was made that if they did not get their rezoning and the options expired, they would be interested in having us help them find someone else. They were interested in having a park down there."

"Did you talk to the Wilkersons? Did you explore with the Wilkersons any alternatives to them complying with that contractual relationship?"

"I don't recall."

"You don't recall talking to them about that?"

"About that? Uh-uh."

"Did you understand at the time that the Wilkersons had committed themselves for a sale of that property if certain conditions were met?"

"Brad told us there were options."

"And what did you understand the conditions were?"

"The property would be sold if it was rezoned. They would sell if it was rezoned, and that's the only thing I knew. That's all they told us. That's all they said."

Homer's facial expression had changed from bored to exasperated. He obviously wasn't getting what he wanted from Bell. Here, he shifted his attention to a letter Henderson Development had sent Bell and Tobler on December 13.

"What, to the best of your recollection, did that letter tell you?" he asked.

"Accused us of interfering with contracts and several other things."

"What were the other things?"

"It was a warning to not interfere, I guess. I don't recall specifically the words."

"Are you opposed to avoiding interfering with other people's contracts?"

"Am I opposed to interfering?"

"Are you opposed to avoiding interfering with other people's contracts?"

Did attorneys go to law school so as to learn to speak in convoluted sentences that would baffle and confuse ordinary people? Julie Bell would not have been *opposed* to her attorney *interfering* with Homer's use of rhetoric as a weapon to mess with her mind. But she kept silent.

As Julie stared at Homer uncomprehendingly, he finally agreed to restate the question.

"At that time did you have an intention to interfere with the contract?'

"Absolutely not."

"Is it your testimony that you at no time ever encouraged Mr. Wilkerson to do something to void his contract?"

"Never."

Later, as Homer plunged into a new line of questioning, aimed, it appeared, to elicit information that could be used to discredit Jack Fitch, Julie sensed that because her interrogator realized he was behind on points, he was looking for a knockout punch. Even a sucker punch if Julie wasn't on her guard?

Under inquiry about Fitch's so-called "mental illness," she testified that June Fitch had told her that her husband had been diagnosed as "manic depressive" while in the army and had been discharged on that account.

"Did she tell you he was on some kind of disability from the military," Homer asked.

"I don't recall."

"Anything else she told you?"

"Yeah. She told me he was a very good man and that she loved him, that he had been a good father, and then she told me he often lived in the basement. She told me they were poor. I believe that's when she told me she wasn't happy that Jack had spent some household money on copies. She said there wasn't money to buy coats for her kids. Jessica and I collected coats to take to her family."

"At some point, Jack became an ally with you and Jessica—did he not—in opposition to the RiverFront project?"

"He acted as a member of SPACE."

"Did that give you any concern?"

"No."

"Anything else you did based on June Fitch's plea?"

"Well, sometime later she made another phone call to me."

"And what was said during that conversation?"

"She called up and started yelling at me about Jack spending money, and I felt she was out of line and way out of hand, and I asked her to please calm down so we could talk about it. I told her we had never asked Jack to spend any money whatsoever.

"I felt like he was an adult. Whatever I had learned of Jack after that first conversation, I saw no indication of mental illness at that time. I felt he handled himself very well. I didn't feel as an adult I had the right to tell another adult not to spend money. I did ask him to please not make copies for us, not spend any household money. I did do that."

Homer paused for a moment and then came back with an uppercut.

"You have heard that there was some concern that Jack may be a bit enamored with Jessica?

"Yes."

"Did that come up in any of those conversations with June on the telephone?"

"No."

"When was the first time you heard about it?"

Before Julie could speak, Del Gordon interrupted.

"I'm going to impose an objection. This is under rule 26, and I'm instructing her not to answer it." Turning to Julie, he said, "So this is one you don't answer."

"Okay," she replied.

"We are not going to go into the alleged amorous relationship between Jessica and Jack," Gordon said.

Homer looked hurt. "I understand what you are doing for the record, but I believe it is relevant in this matter," he said. "These parties have asked for emotional distress damages, and clearly a factor could very well be whatever that relationship was and whatever happened to Jack because of it. I'm not indicating there was anything wrongful on either Julie's or Jessica's part, but I think Jack stepped over the line on things."

Divide and conquer, Julie was thinking. *Jack was soon to be deposed, as well as his father (in an attempt to marshal his own family against him). Wouldn't Jack be the proper person to ask about this? But if they could coax something damaging out of Jessica or me, it could soften him up for further attack.*

Gordon was saying that while he understood Homer's position for the record, "I still think it's beyond rule 26."

"We may need to discuss that with the judge at some time," Homer said.

"Yeah," Gordon answered curtly.

Whereupon the parties agreed to break for lunch.

The afternoon session would turn out to be a patchwork of ill-fitting scraps from themes Homer had covered in the morning, as he revisited the sequence of early SPACE meetings; Julie Bell's contacts with various city council members, with Mayor Max McClellan, and with the press; Jack Fitch's mental state; and alleged SPACE interference with Henderson Development's contracts with the Wilkersons.

However, two new threads emerged. The last reminded Julie of the dirty tricks scenario familiar from Jessica's deposition, but the first presented a positive prospect.

To Julie's surprise, Homer's questions about her association with South Jordan City employees opened the door for her to bring up the cozy relationship between Dick Munson and Geoffrey Henderson.

"I want you to tell me when you had a contact of any kind with a city employee," Homer said.

"I talked with City Administrator Dick Munson."

"And what was said and by whom?"

"I asked Dick if it were true that he took an African safari with Geoffrey Henderson, because Geoffrey had told me that at the very first meeting at my house."

"And what did Dick Munson tell you?"

"He said, 'Yes, but I paid my own way!'"

This testimony presented a problem for Homer, although he wasn't about to concede it. Dick Munson had already told the press that the only hunting expedition he had ever taken with Henderson was a trip to the Uinta Mountains.

"Let's go back," Homer said. "So Geoffrey Henderson had already told you about that?"

"Yes, we ended up in a personal conversation, and we were talking about animals, and I asked him if he liked to hunt. He said he liked to hunt deer but that he also liked to hunt in Africa. He said he was rebuilding a large room that he was going to put his hunting trophies in. And he stated he had just gotten back from Africa and had taken City Administrator Dick Munson with him. I didn't know who Munson was at that time."

If Mills Homer was looking for any kind of rhetorical trophy to display as the result of this deposition (even small game could suffice), this was going to be his chance. He would have to get tough in order to score a kill. *Probe for a weakness, speak softly, dangle the hook.*

"Yesterday," Homer said, "we talked with Jessica Tobler about emotional distress. We feel badly we have to get into these things, but because of the nature of this lawsuit we do. I apologize if this causes distress, but I have to ask the questions."

There was a pause. "Okay."

"Julie, tell me, have you ever been under the care of a psychiatrist?"

"Uh-huh," she said. "Well, a psychologist."

Having established a clinical hook on which to hang his characterization of Julie Bell's past, Homer carefully marched her backward into it. He probed her years of teaching with Jordan School District, where she had consulted a school counselor and the continuing difficulties she had encountered with her sister from childhood through adolescence. Then forward again to her emotional meeting with a doctor at Riverton Mental Health; her struggles in carrying for her special-needs daughter; and her marital difficulties, which had led to therapy.

Playing a concerned tour guide to the most private and personal details of her life—all of which were now out on the table like little evidentiary exhibits—Mills Homer sat back and smiled paternalistically.

He was ready to ask the drug questions. "What has your doctor prescribed for you?"

She answered honestly: Wellbutrin as an anti-depressant, Premphase for hormone replacement, and Trazodone to allow her to sleep. No psychotropics, although Homer pressed her on this point.

"Did your doctor ever indicate to you that a side-effect of Wellbutrin might be …"

"Yes. She did tell me it was a possibility."

"Depressed libido?" Homer said.

"Yes."

Had Julie Bell exposed herself sufficiently? If a trial ensued, could her testimony be used to portray her as a psychologically addled individual under the influence of multiple drugs that had affected her decisions and damaged her marriage?

When the questions were over, Julie thought about it. The day hadn't been a total downer. Talking with Jessica as the attorneys conferred, she had to stifle an impulse to laugh. How could she not appreciate her friend's flair for fashion and spontaneity?

As Homer tucked his papers into his briefcase, Del Gordon beckoned Julie and Jessica to a corner of the room. "What's going on?" Julie asked. Conspiratorially, Gordon put a finger to his lips.

"Based on how well you stood up to him today," he whispered, "I believe Homer doesn't want to think about putting you on the stand in a trial. He was making a show of telling me how sorry he was that he had to ask you personal questions. What will it take for *you* to settle? And he means you, Julie, as opposed to Jessica. That's what he wanted to know."

Julie and Jessica exchanged a glance that let Gordon know. He didn't even have to ask what Julie wanted to do. "Okay," he said. "We'll keep fighting for justice."

Julie felt better now. If Jessica could show up for this pathetic legal exercise garbed as a country bride, Julie would never consider making a separate peace. Julie would wear a smile out of Mills Homer's office.

In his subservience to the instructions of unethical clients and his lack of qualms about hurtful questioning, it was Homer who had been unmasked. The emperor's new clothes were a good fit.

Chapter 25
Battle Scars

"I love a girl who has a good time," Dave Tobler had told Jessica Ann Jones on their first date at an Idaho rodeo in August 1984. A blind date—double-blind in fact since her family had blindsided Dave as a practical joke. When Dave knocked at her door, her sister Cassandra had answered and pretended to be Jessica.

Looking on as Dave fell for the gag had been dozens of family members on hand for a reunion. He had seemed pleased by the looks of the pretty brunette who was responding warmly to his conversation. Then as she and others had broken up laughing, a good-looking busty blond had walked into the room and announced *she* was Jessica. David Tobler's head had been spinning.

Once his dizziness subsided, Jessica had asked her blind date, "Do you mind if I wear my cowboy hat?"

"Uh, no," he had said. "Do you mind if I wear mine?"

In the stands at the rodeo, Dave Tobler had stolen a sidelong glance to be sure he had the right girl. His date's blond hair and her extremely clear and fair complexion had been very attractive under the hat.

During the calf-roping event, she had waved her hat, whooping it up and whistling as an aggressive cowboy leaped from his horse to hog-tie the bawling animal thrown to the ground with his rope.

257

"Oh, I'm sorry," she had teased when she noticed Dave appraising her out of the corner of his eye. "My mom told me it's not ladylike to whistle."

"I love a girl who has a good time," he had chortled. She had been able to tell he was pleased by the way he was laughing.

Nineteen years later, at 3:00 a.m., early in another August (2003), Dave Tobler rolled over in bed and found the opposite side vacant. He touched the pillow and found it stained with blood. What and how much had Jessica been hiding from him?

In his wife's anguish over the lawsuit and what her friends and strangers might be thinking about Marcus Hollings's insinuations of extramarital sex in the *VOICE* article, her face had broken out in an angry rash. Sores—some of them as large as an inch in diameter—would fill with blood and then ooze or bleed. They would last a month or more, draining pigmentation from the skin before leaving an ugly scar. Additional sores then started showing up on other parts of her body—her chest, her back, her neck.

Then the cycle would begin again. It would continue for months and years.

A variety of doctors and natural healers had surveyed the wounds and offered temporary and ultimately ineffective fixes, finally concluding their source was an overwhelming level of stress induced by accusations by their adversaries in legal documents and the press.

Jessica had covered what she could with makeup and turned aside Dave's inquiries. She was obviously embarrassed. His tender solicitations hadn't seemed to help; he had backed off his questions. Now it was clear the inflammation was severe, and he regretted his silence. That once beautiful complexion was absorbing the brunt of punishment.

Dave searched the house and found Jessica facedown on the living room carpet, sobbing. After kneeling at her side for a few minutes, he coaxed her to get up and sit facing him on the sofa.

Her face still partially covered by her hands, she explained that she and Jack Fitch had originally laughed about the absurd rumors of a sexual liaison, as the *VOICE* article had pointed out. But seeing the words in print—a widely respected ex-judge's blatant assertions that the rumors were true—was a totally different matter.

Now, with her face in ruins and having gained weight, she felt like a pariah—exiled, scarred, and disfigured.

Parting her hands slightly, she sobbed, "I can't stand the way I look. You must find me hideous."

Dave Tobler pried her fingers away from her face. Cupping her head in his hands and insisting on eye contact, he said, "Jessica, you are a warrior. All great warriors have battle scars. And you have been in battle. For the record, I find you beautiful."

She looked at him solemnly.

"You cannot listen to your political enemies. For every mean remark, every mean piece of hate mail you get, there are one hundred people who love you. You must ignore the negative feedback and pay attention to positive response. If you're going to stand up for what you believe, Jessica, you're going to have to grow some bark."

It wasn't as if she was thin-skinned, she realized. She had actually begun to appreciate hate mail, deciding it meant she was being effective. Some of the hate mail—packed with creative invective—was more interesting to read than fan mail.

But if being SLAPPed with a vindictive lawsuit and a court docket that now extended to more than thirty pages, if getting verbally assaulted by people she didn't know—if this was what was assaulting her body and playing head games with her confidence, it was time to take stock.

How many personal betrayals had Jessica suffered from neighbors and others after the suit was filed? What was life really about? It all came down to the loyalty of good friends—someone to stand by you when everyone else was bailing out.

If someone offered Julie Bell a million dollars, she wouldn't betray me, Jessica realized.

So in addition to her physical ills, there was her doctor's diagnosis of depression. Something had to give, but the last thing Jessica Ann Tobler was about to abandon were her struggles for free speech and open space.

She would have to find a way to get out from under this choking cloud of melancholy. Then maybe she could get back into physical shape.

As it happened, Jessica wasn't alone in her anguish. Her sister-in-combat was licking her own wounds, contemplating her need to heal.

Despite the fact Julie Bell's physical stamina appeared to be holding up, she couldn't ignore her mental free fall. As multiple motions of the lawsuit were filed and as she and Jessica studied and absorbed their implications, stress enveloped her like a shroud.

It was almost by accident, however, that Julie stumbled on the fact that her downturn was clinical, and it was going to be tough to find the resources to deal with it.

Unlike Jessica, her spouse didn't appear to empathize or offer emotional, physical, or financial support—a huge contributing factor. She fought envy over the fact that her friend could count on her husband's commitment.

Trying to explain to her husband her emotional state—that getting sued wasn't a picnic—Julie flinched at Ted's response.

"*You're* the one who got sued," he said. "It's *your* problem."

He makes me feel as if I asked to be sued because I stood up for my rights.

Thank God Jessica was an unwavering constant she could count on to stand by her side. Ironically, Dave Tobler provided more encouragement and support than her own husband.

When it rained, it poured. Amid all the chaos surrounding the lawsuit, her marriage, and the financial pressures at home, Julie's oldest daughter Cady had been regularly sleeping in, missing school. In Julie's LDS Relief Society, a powerful presentation on the symptoms of depression by Dr. Mary Tanner of the Riverton Health Clinic, brought her up short. Julie wondered if her daughter was depressed. She phoned Dr. Tanner's office and was able to secure an appointment to get Cady checked out.

In the meantime, studying her notes from Dr. Tanner's lecture, Julie had a flash of recognition. *I have every one of the ten symptoms of depression she talked about. What do I do about that?*

At the doctor's office, after extensive questioning, Cady was removed from the examination room to undergo a blood test.

"Now," the doctor said when she returned to speak with Julie, "tell me about *you*. How are you feeling?"

"Well," Julie stammered, "what do you mean?"

SLAPPED! 261

Tanner did not immediately answer but held eye contact, appraising her calmly. "It's obvious you have something going on."

The doctor's evaluation was like a dash of cold water. After shaking it off, she found herself describing the lawsuit she was facing and all the resulting stress.

The doctor listened knowingly. "We would like to conduct a test on you," she said.

It would be a marvel if I weren't depressed, Julie realized. *The way things are at home, the lawsuit, the accusations, attorney's fees, the fact that Ted is considering the need to file bankruptcy, the money issue—the whole mess.*

A mountain of legal bills had now topped $250,000. Adding to the stress, Julie felt guilty the Toblers were contributing the lion's share of funds toward paying off the debt. Despite essentially skipping Christmas for the kids, she could siphon off precious little from what Ted gave her for essential household items to apply to legal bills.

Cady Bell was eventually diagnosed with mononucleosis, which had apparently gripped her for several months. Tanner's test on Julie confirmed the prediagnosis. Her serotonin level was unusually low. Her depression could be medicated, the doctor believed. She prescribed *Wellbutrin*, an antidepressant.

The only problem was where was the money going to come from to pay for it?

Lack of funds was a surface manifestation of what Julie now realized was a much more serious business. Disturbing dreams and thoughts bedeviled her. She envisioned herself falling off a high balcony and on another occasion stabbed and bleeding on the floor, discovered by her traumatized kids.

What would her children do if she were to die?

These dreams, thoughts, and fears were signs of her depression, the doctor informed her.

Dying was not an option. She had to go on, if for no other reason than to care for Trish. Special needs required special care, and she was the only one who could give it.

On *Wellbutrin* for just over a month, Julie Bell ran out of money. Hoping to continue on even a limited basis, she cut the dosage in half. Would it help? Was it helping? Hard to tell.

When the passage of the North American Free Trade Agreement (NAFTA) flooded the Idaho market with cheap potatoes from out of the country, Ted was among many small farmers thrust off the land. Having moved to Utah and forced to consider bankruptcy—finally living under the same roof with Julie—he had quickly decreed there would be no funds for "extras."

Once Ted had taken over household finances, he provided no regular household budget. And since Julie was responsible for Trish's care, she could not seek work outside the home. Julie felt she had to ask for every dollar she spent. Ted would occasionally drive her to the supermarket to purchase groceries or take her car to gas it up. A stop at the pharmacy for her prescription was deemed out of the question.

Ted's presence on the premises had also exacerbated marital tensions. Once during a heated discussion, he demanded, "Just what have you contributed to this marriage?"

"Well," Julie replied, fighting tears, "I raised the children." She had given up her career teaching deaf children in order to stay home with the kids.

As depression set in, Julie had become increasingly emotional, she realized.

Since a half dose of *Wellbutrin* provided a minimal benefit (at best) and she was soon to run out, what were her options? *Am I coming to the end of my rope?* The old cliché seemed applicable.

Prayer was one of the last remaining options, and it had been a constant for Julie Bell. A week of entreaties produced what seemed like a random occurrence. *Call it the grace of God*, Julie later told herself.

Listening to the radio while doing laundry, her ears pricked at the mention of a local medical study of depression victims. They were seeking volunteer participants. Free meds would be provided over the course of an eighteen-month study. Participants would either be prescribed a promising new medication or placed in a control group and supplied placebos, offering no medical benefit.

Once accepted into the study, Julie observed after a couple of weeks that she was feeling and doing better. She had avoided the dashed expectations and stigma of the control group. The new medication was beginning to have a positive effect.

If she was anything, Julie decided—buoyed by a little surge of hope—she was a survivor. Her faith, her religion, God's grace—maybe a little luck—might see her through.

Unaware of Jessica Tobler's struggles with weight, infection, and depression, Marcus Hollings and Geoffrey Henderson were unsatisfied with a dearth of impact from what Hollings had implied in the *VOICE* was an improper relationship between Tobler and Jack Fitch.

Some people who had read the article in fact saw the allegations as a slur—a shameful characterization—and were instead asking embarrassing questions about the ethical boundaries of Henderson Development.

Something had to be done. Having had little luck with the small fry, why not rattle cages at a larger media outlet?

Jake Shelovey, the short, stout, but powerful editor of the *Salt Lake Tribune* was an energetic, eccentric curmudgeon given to a crusading spirit, mercurial moods, and bursts of journalistic enthusiasm. He was reputed to be death on reportorial misdeeds among any of his eclectic and sometimes undisciplined staff.

After spending a couple of weeks fencing with Shelovey's fiercely loyal and longtime secretary and public gatekeeper, Afton Forsgren, Marcus Hollings finally succeeded in obtaining an appointment with her boss.

One afternoon following the morning daily's editorial meeting, Hollings—with Geoffrey Henderson in tow—was ushered into Shelovey's cluttered office on the second floor of Main Street's *Tribune* building.

"To what do I owe the pleasure?" Shelovey asked brusquely, pointing to a couple of empty chairs.

"We've heard some things about a couple of your reporters that are of great concern to us, Mr. Shelovey," Hollings began ingratiatingly, "and we're sure will be of concern to you."

Shelovey rolled his wheeled office chair back a couple of inches and propped one foot on a desk extension where an ancient Smith Corona typewriter rested.

Does he actually use this thing? his visitors wondered to themselves.

He didn't look disinterested in what they had come to say, although one eyebrow was raised in what could have been skepticism.

"We've been told, confidentially of course," Hollings said, "that two of your county beat reporters have been supplied exclusives by a news source in exchange for ..." Here Hollings paused as if reluctant to mention a distasteful subject.

"For ... something improper and immoral ..." he trailed off.

"Oh come now, judge," Shelovey replied. "We're all men of the world here. Are you trying to say *sexual favors?*"

"Oh, well ..." Hollings sputtered, "you already know then?"

"I know nothing of what you're apparently alleging," Shelovey said. "But I've been in this business long enough to recognize someone trying to appear innocent while alluding to sex."

Hollings glanced at Henderson before plunging on. "Mr. Shelovey, as you probably know, Jessica Ann Tobler is a rather bold and blatant individual who uses her looks to get what she wants. We've been told she may have been sleeping with a couple of your reporters in order to obtain favorable news coverage—coverage that has damaged our business dealings in South Jordan."

"It's kind of you to come in," Shelovey said, abruptly getting to his feet. "I seriously doubt, however, that what you have told me has a basis in fact. I trust the reporters that work for me. But I will conduct my own in-house investigation and get back to you. Now, I suggest you leave. I trust I won't have to ask my secretary to show you to the elevator?"

Both visitors looked stunned. They stood up slowly but attempted to gather some shred of dignity before leaving the room. Huddled in their expensive overcoats, they appeared as debased animals, the editor idly contemplated, tails tucked between their legs.

Shelovey waited for his guests to turn and exit his office before he permitted himself to roll his eyes, take a seat, and insert a sheet of paper into his Smith Corona.

Chapter 26
Sweating It

Jessica Tobler's physician gave her a prescription for the rash on her skin. *Rash* was a euphemism of course; as the infection grew worse, the scabbing became more and more evident. Dr. Daniel Martin wasted little sympathy, although he did offer advice: please get some rest, take a vacation—anything to take the conflict she was involved in off her mind.

None of that was likely to happen, Jessica told him. She was thinking about well-intentioned people who often asked her ridiculously insensitive questions. "What is that on your face? Chocolate?" "Were you in a car wreck?" It was difficult to avoid those kinds of comments and the inevitable hurt that followed.

"One more thing then," he said. "You're an appropriate candidate for Prozac, and I would like to prescribe it for you."

Oh no you don't, she thought. Prozac was a *chemical*, and she wasn't about to introduce it into her body. "I'm not willing to do that," she informed him, "for health reasons." Although self-consciously realizing her own anxiety as she involuntarily touched one of the sores on her face, she didn't see the irony.

"I've heard too much about Prozac from friends," she said. "I'm not going to chance getting hooked."

Her physician said nothing but eyed her with what appeared to be analytical regard. Dan Martin was no ordinary doctor. Yes, he had a medical degree, but he also had a doctorate in psychiatry. Both Jessica and Julie Bell had been referred to him by the court, which in addition to a physical checkup had required a battery of psychological tests.

He had seemed to be satisfied with the results of the testing; in fact, Jessica detected he was sympathetic to their cause. He had even offered to defer payment until their lawsuit was settled. As the bills piled up, they were sweating every additional expense, which obviously increased the stress.

But Martin provided no panaceas. When Jessica asked about her weight gain, he offered no instant fix. It would be up to her to stick to the healthy diet she had pledged to follow and to carve out some time to take her exercise regimen seriously. Maybe it would help get the toxins out of her system. For her, physical activity was a more acceptable antidote for depression than chemicals.

Part of her anxiety, she realized, had to do with judgments people made about her. Even some of her admirers found her hard to figure. And her critics found fault. Those who didn't like her outspokenness in the public arena called her a loudmouth. Because she was brash and blond and sometimes said things that made people laugh, others dismissed her as a ditz. A portion of the public, however, actually seemed to think of her as a hero, which added its own pressure.

Incongruities multiplied. Her gun rights activism inspired and motivated one whole constituency and frightened and irritated another. One problem was that the same people who loved her for defending what they regarded as a Second Amendment guarantee to carry a concealed weapon were often aggravated and baffled by her fierce devotion to environmental causes—her ongoing commitment to save as much as possible of the Jordan River wetlands from development.

When she didn't hide her pride in the fact that the notoriously liberal Salt Lake lawyer Lowell "Lefty" Gunderson had volunteered a raft of his services *pro bono* in her fight against Henderson Development, some conservatives regarded the alliance as a deliberate provocation.

Others, who thought they had drawn a bead on her from her public persona, couldn't see the big picture. What sort of wife and mother—known to occasionally carry a handgun—would spend hours a day away from her home and children, quarreling with public officials in a land dispute?

The SLAPP filed against her should have shut her up, some thought. But it hadn't. If anything, she and her partner in protest—Julie Bell—seemed even more determined to stand their ground. *Their ground*—that was the point that many who scanned the daily press for hints of what Jessica was like away from the headlines didn't get. Jessica and Julie regarded the open space surrounding the river as a legacy for their children and their neighbors' children, as well as for future generations.

But the struggle had taken its toll.

Any public perception of Jessica Tobler as a bold and determined activist would not have included the possibility that she was a disheartened and almost broken woman.

Not only had Jessica been sweating the damage her reputation might suffer in the Mormon community and the larger culture from rumors Marcus Hollings was spreading about her personal morality, the SLAPP suit offered ambitious attorneys the legal invitation to pry into every aspect of her and her husband's lives.

Now she was often seized with the idea that people were laughing at her behind her back. Was any of this fair to her husband? How long would Dave be able to keep up a brave front that he didn't care about the fallout or that her activism might hurt his career?

Rather than blocking out current events, Jessica decided she would use her time at the gym to burn brain cells as well as calories, to analyze what was going on in the news and everything else she had to keep up with to remain in the thick of the fight. She could—and would—multitask with the best of them.

When Jessica walked into SouthTowne Fitness—a stone's throw from the river she had come to love like one of her own children—she was nervous and apprehensive. She didn't relish the commitment her husband had persuaded her to make to sign on with a personal trainer.

Immediately, her eyes were drawn to a tanned thirty-something muscled guy with a pearly white smile, wearing a blue "SouthTowne" T-shirt. *Oh no*, she prayed. *Don't let it be him.*

Jessica was painfully self-conscious of what she herself was wearing—M&M pajama pants emblazoned with "I Love Chocolate" on the butt. The only sweats in her closet that weren't too tight for comfort. *Please*, she pleaded. *I want someone normal looking. Not a Mr. Beautiful accustomed to training and dating bikini models.*

The man was walking toward her, making eye contact.

"You must be Jessica," he said, extending a big paw. "I'm Luke White."

"Hi," she said. "I'm the depressed out-of-shape forty-year-old." (*Dang, now it's definitely too late to leave.*)

Gratefully, White didn't immediately take her to one of the intimidating machines. He installed her at a desk in the back, where she filled out forms. As he asked her questions, Jessica began to relax. The details of her innumerable diets and then the particulars of her activism—the fight to save the river bottoms, the lawsuit—began to spill out in an insistent flow. Was she talking too much? But White didn't seem put off. He seemed, in fact, strangely interested.

She realized they had been talking for more than an hour, and people were starting to notice, particularly a gaggle of attractive young women in workout attire.

White finally took her to the weightlifting equipment and briefly demonstrated the basics. Jessica did some preliminary lifts.

"You're strong," he said.

"Is that good?" she asked.

"Yes, it's good to be strong."

After watching her for a while, White said, "Tell you what. I'm usually sixty dollars an hour, but for the first few weeks to get you started, I'll charge you twenty-five dollars an hour. Just don't tell anybody."

Jessica was surprised to suddenly feel the sting of hot tears and tried to hide them. "Thank you," she said. "You're kind. I'm sorry I'm crying. When people are nice to me, it makes me cry."

SLAPPED!

269

"Don't worry," White said. "I'll be mean to you soon enough when I get your butt into shape." He was smiling. "I'll see you here tomorrow morning, and I suggest you don't wear clothes that say 'I Love Chocolate.' It's the wrong motivation."

The next day, preparing to meet her trainer, Jessica caught sight of herself in the mirror. She had taken a shower, washed and curled her hair, applied makeup and perfume, and was donning earrings when the absurdity hit her. What was the point of gussying herself up in order to work up a sweat?

Was she the same person who yesterday had dressed herself inappropriately to make her first appearance? A good thing people who believed she was someone who couldn't care less what other people thought, couldn't see her now.

They might get the feeling she was insecure.

Walking into the gym, she popped a breath mint into her mouth before she realized she was already chewing gum. She spent some time on the treadmill, and then Luke White steered her toward the leg-lifting machine.

"Your legs need work," he said.

White watched with a patiently neutral expression as she ground out increasingly laborious lifts.

When her leg trembled and she hesitated, he insisted, "Give me two more, please."

"I can't," Jessica said, panting a little. "I'm sweating in front of you. This is so embarrassing."

"It's not embarrassing to sweat. It's normal. C'mon. Exhale."

Jessica puffed out a couple of tiny breaths.

"Let's hear you *exhale*."

"I don't like making weird noises in front of people."

"What I'm asking you to do is not weird," White said. "You're exhaling. You're building up muscle and losing fat. See that guy over there with the bulging muscles in the yellow striped spandex shorts and the wife-beater T-shirt? He's about to try to bench-press 450 pounds."

"You mean the one with what looks like—is that a sock stuffed in his shorts?" Jessica said, glad to have the attention shifted away from her. "Obviously wants to impress the ladies—or maybe the guys." She laughed.

Odd, she thought. This kind of talk was making her less self-conscious rather than more.

White looked at her quizzically but laughed as well. "Yeah, that guy. Now listen to him. He comes in here every day. He tries to impress people by lifting a lot of weights. And to call attention to himself so that everyone sees how much weight he can lift, he *really* exhales loudly. I call him the Screamer. And those guys that let their free weights drop to the floor without gently setting them down, they're the Pounders. Screaming while lifting weights, making *ugh* noises every time they exhale."

"Gross," Jessica said.

"The Screamer doesn't think so," White said. "He thinks he sounds sexy and strong. So your little exhaling noises aren't going to be noticed. They're normal. In fact, they're kind of fun. By the way, you don't have to smile and make cute faces while you're lifting weights. It's okay to strain your face muscles."

"Like this," Jessica said, tightening her face in fake exertion.

"Yeah, like that. Now give me two more."

It was strange. As time went on, during these kinds of interchanges with her trainer, she felt more comfortable, even if he constantly corrected her or emphasized her coyness or idiosyncrasies—like the time Jessica was cowed by an apparatus that she realized would require her to straddle a bench in order to grab weights from above to work the lateral muscles—and she backed away in dismay.

"I don't think I can straddle a bench in front of the opposite sex," she said. "Would you please look away?"

She attempted to delicately sit sidesaddle on the bench and then very slowly lift her left leg over.

White was looking at her in consternation, rolling his eyes. "Oh man," he said. "I feel sorry for your husband."

At another exercise machine that required Jessica to lie on her stomach and lift weights with the back of her calves, working her hamstrings and behind, she had another attack of embarrassment. "Look," she said, "I'm going to drape a towel over my backside."

Calmly, White said, "Your self-consciousness is succeeding only in drawing more attention to yourself. People will focus on the towel over your butt in order to try to see what in the hell you're up to."

As time progressed, she observed that Luke—she called him that now—was always amused by her reading material on the treadmill like the day she brought in a huge court deposition.

One serene morning, en route to the gym by bicycle (there was more than one way of sweating it, Jessica told herself), she came around a corner near the Jordan River to confront the freshest horror—a bulldozer ripping up centuries-old trees from the river bottoms and tossing them aside like matchsticks.

Bulldozer ripping up trees along the Jordan River bottoms
Photo c. Ray Wheeler

Without conscious thought of consequence, she found herself flinging down the bike and charging ahead of the machine in a rush of rage and adrenaline. Extending her arms and positioning herself within its path, she screamed, "What the hell are you doing?"

The mechanized destroyer coughed and hesitated in its progress. "Stop!" she yelled. "You're ripping up these trees!" Her impassioned statement of the obvious seemed now to have affected the bulldozer operator. "How can you do this?"

The hard-hatted driver—a handsome young man, she now realized—turned off the engine and climbed off the machine.

He looked stunned but impressed as she explained she had worked hard to preserve "these precious resources."

"I'm sorry, ma'am," he said. "I'm just doing my job. We're preparing the ground for parking spaces; thousands of them will be needed for the office complex."

Backing off a bit in the face of his implacable naiveté, Jessica found her cell phone and placed a call to *Salt Lake Tribune* columnist Saul Jolley.

"They're ripping out these trees down here, Saul," she told him. "Can't you guys stop this? I'm sick about it."

While he felt her pain, Jolley said he was a reporter, not an activist.

Jessica's next call was less impassioned—more a plea for understanding and concern.

"This is one more knife to the heart!" she cried to Julie Bell.

Julie agreed and commiserated.

"Now you know the pain I feel when I look out my picture window every day," Julie said, observing that it was a very different view from the same window that had earlier launched her career as an activist—the ducks, the deer, and other wildlife.

The vision of a potential nature center or children's museum was now obliterated by bulldozers, backhoes, and a coming concrete and asphalt jungle.

"You're late!" Luke griped when Jessica arrived from her rage against the machine. "Run stairs!"

After she ran to the top of the stairs, she descended with the exaggerated motions of a supermodel. Luke commanded her to stop.

"What the hell are you doing?"

"In a beauty pageant where I won Miss Congeniality, I learned to walk down stairs like a lady."

"Well this isn't a damn beauty pageant. It's a gym! Now stop acting like a contestant and *run* down those stairs. And since you're treating this experience like a walk in the park, try it an extra five times—up and down. Now *run*!"

Over a few weeks' time, pounds began to melt away, and Jessica's complexion began to clear. Her spirits were lifting.

Wanting to show her gratitude to Luke, she fell back on an old people-pleasing instinct—baking.

If some purists at SouthTowne had known what she started smuggling into the fitness center in her gym bag, they might have compared it to sneaking a bottle of wine into an Alcoholics Anonymous meeting. But Luke seemed happy to accept the cookies and cakes she brought him, hustling them to a back room, where he confessed to her that he scarfed them down in private. A couple of times, Luke had the audacity to eat the cupcakes she had brought him at his desk in full view of the diet-conscious patrons. He had been especially appreciative when she once showed up with a nine-by-thirteen-inch pan of coconut cream coffee cake.

As their arrangement went on, Jessica and Luke settled into a comfortable routine and something resembling friendship. She noticed that when they had long talks at his desk, the beautiful people who came to the gym—at least most of the females—often stared at them (at *her*?) with something that looked like exasperation.

Or was it envy?

As her depression lifted, her face cleared, and her body shed pounds and developed musculature. Could it be? That surge of something Jessica was feeling? Yes, self-confidence.

Chapter 27
Big

Geoffrey Henderson did not think small. Even before he got into land development, while he was still forced to grub out a living as a fire extinguisher salesman, ambition burned like a fire in his belly. He saw himself as a champion of capitalism, confident he would soon ride to his destiny astride the powerful white horse of money and imagination.

While attending seminars conducted by corporate real estate giants and gurus of the self-made-millionaire movement, he admired their luxury cars, their expensive suits, and their expansive egos.

Driving through wealthy neighborhoods in the suburbs, he esteemed colorful plastic flamingos peeking from garden greenery, concrete sculptures of Greek gods, and the occasional statue of a Negro gatekeeper—a fading relic of what he thought must be the lost legacy of the South.

But Henderson was a man of the West. His own estate, once he had built it, would reflect the masculine art and heritage that more nearly symbolized his aspirations. In dress, style, and decor, he would exude machismo—the kind that would dominate man, beast, and nature and bring them to heel.

His first Sandy residence, despite the nearby corrals and riding paths for his stable of horses, had not come close to fleshing out the image and grandeur of his original vision. The house was a little run-down. He had, of course, stocked the living area with stuffed animals, most of which had been killed by his own hand. At first, this had made his third wife, Lila, complain it made her feel a little creepy. But as she grew accustomed, she claimed she felt protected—and all the more vulnerably feminine in her variety of spandex outfits.

But the place couldn't be distinguished from its middle-class neighbors by anyone who hadn't ventured past the front door. It didn't fit the financial reach of its occupants.

Finer, grander homes were being built farther up the hill in Sandy. News quickly spread that Henderson's eye for prime real estate, combined with the resources he needed to procure it, had allowed him to stake out a magnificent piece of ground long coveted by others.

Suddenly, everyone was buzzing about the construction of a south valley mansion, the likes of which hadn't been seen before. People were more than willing to go out of their way to make sure Jessica and Julie knew all about it.

While conducting church assignments, during political events, on shopping trips, at weddings—whatever activity or venue—the monster house on people's minds always seemed to come up.

Late in 2001, as the home was being completed, while Jessica and Julie—LDS visiting teacher companions—were meeting with a woman on their teaching list, her young husband interrupted their conversation in the kitchen, eager to inquire about the SLAPP suit Henderson Development had filed.

"You might be interested," the man said after he had asked a few questions, "that as a contractor, my father is acquainted with the builders who are constructing Geoffrey Henderson's new house."

"Oh," Jessica said without pretension, "what is it like?"

"Well," he replied, "my father says it's worth about ten million dollars."

SLAPPED!

277

Within weeks, additional details seemed to come her way while she knocked on doors in Riverton, stumping for candidate Deron Blevins in his re-election campaign for state senate.

"Aren't you Jessica Tobler?" a man asked after she had made her spiel on his doorstep.

"Well, maybe," Jessica parried, "depending on whether you're mad at me for anything."

The man laughed. "I recognize you because you're the woman Geoffrey Henderson sued, and I know from the news you're a gun rights activist," he said. "We've had experience with Henderson because he's sued people in this town, and a lot of people are afraid of him. I know him a little bit since he subcontracted me to do the cabinet work on his $12 million house."

Oh, thought Jessica, *it's getting more expensive.*

Something must have shown on her face, because the man apologized for keeping her on the doorstep and invited her in.

Once they were seated in his living room, he proceeded to ask an odd question. "Have you ever seen two stallions fighting over a mare?" Although she was raised in the country, Jessica had obviously skipped that chapter of her education, and her puzzlement must have been obvious.

"Well, that's what Henderson has in front of his big house," the man said. "Huge bronze statues of two stallions on their hind legs and the mare in the middle, also rearing."

"You're kidding," she said. "Disgusting!"

"No, it's true," the man offered. "Not so different from the power grab he's using to get what he wants with Henderson Development." Jessica headed for the door and they shook hands. "Hey, good luck in your fight," he said. "A whole bunch of people you don't know are praying for you to win and to stop them from using lawsuits to abuse more citizens."

"Thank you," Jessica said.

Halfway down the sidewalk, she realized she hadn't made much of a pitch on Deron Blevins's behalf.

Next to add to the legend of the McMansion in Sandy within Jessica's earshot was a clerk in a fireplace store. Dave and Jessica were considering installing a wood-burning stove as a hedge against Y2K energy concerns, and the guy behind the counter recognized their last name.

"Aren't you the woman who Geoffrey Henderson sued for opposing his development?" he asked. "Haven't I been reading about you in the newspaper?"

Dave smiled deferentially, knowing what was coming next and stepping comfortably into his supporting role as the husband of the main attraction.

"That's me," Jessica replied. "We've both been in the line of fire. Our whole family, really. What do you know about Geoffrey?"

"He's been in here a lot looking for fireplaces. Huge guy in a black cowboy hat. He bragged he was building a new house. He looked at everything we had in the store and then informed us our fireplaces were too small for his home."

"That's Geoffrey all right," Jessica said.

"I thought it was pretty arrogant," the clerk said. "He filled out some paperwork describing the dimensions of what he wanted in the hopes we could order something bigger. *Big* was a word he used a lot. He wanted to make sure we knew how *big* his house was."

Words like *big* and *opulent* were on everybody's lips.

Julie Bell told Jessica that on Mother's Day, while visiting at her mom's house, her sister-in-law Brenda jumped into Julie's conversation with her sister Sammie when she heard them discussing the horse statue in front of Henderson's house.

"Oh, I've been there," she said. "My friend's mom and dad are in Geoffrey and Lila Henderson's ward. They asked the Hendersons if they could hold my friend's wedding reception in their backyard, and Geoffrey said, 'Sure, why not?' And so I got invited as a friend of the bride.

"You should see the house. It's so *big*," Brenda enthused. "Enormous chandeliers and a gigantic fireplace. The kitchen is bigger than my friend's apartment—over 1,300 square feet!"

Brenda continued, "And you should see all through Geoffrey's house, filled with stuffed animals he has killed all across the world, especially in Africa and the Rocky Mountains. His African animal collections include a full-sized giraffe, stuffed zebra heads, a warthog, a wildebeest, a white rhino head mounted over the kitchen bar, water buffaloes, cape kudus, a sable, an impala, and a collection of other African antelopes.

"His animals of North America include a big stuffed brown bear, caribou, Rocky Mountain bighorn sheep, and even a porcupine. But there's just too many to name," she said.

"The highlight," Brenda bragged, "was a collection of the great cats of the world, including a pair of African lions, a leopard, and a mountain lion."

A few of Geoffrey Henderson's trophies
Photo c. iStockphoto Alija

"And the outside," she continued, "in addition to the swimming pool, their own lake and waterfalls. Unbelievable."

Julie couldn't keep herself from asking. "So how much do you think they spent on the place?"

"Ten, fifteen million—I don't know, but it was plenty. And the furnishings for the interior—a lot of what they used was imported from Europe. They also had a collection of sculptures and other treasures they have collected from around the world."

"Yes, I heard that," Julie said.

Thinking about Geoffrey Henderson's reaction had he been listening in on this conversation, she imagined him licking his chops. *Just the kind of talk he would love, realizing we're spending our time out here getting green with envy. Okay then. Shut my mouth.*

How many more people she knew or ran into were going to approach Jessica with breathless reports of the Henderson estate as the most luxurious setting for young couples celebrating their nuptials? Now it was her musician friends, Ricki and Tim Hoskins, in demand to play at weddings all over the valley.

"Hey, Jessica," Ricki said when they bumped into each other in town. "What's the name of that developer who's suing you? Isn't it Geoffrey Henderson?"

"Yes, why?" she replied, expecting what would come next.

"We're playing at a wedding at his house next week. In fact, this is the second gig we've played there. Want to come along? You could come in with the band and check out his house and yard. It's quite the place."

"Crazy idea," Jessica said. "I could wear a disguise. It would be fun to sneak in. You could tell Geoffrey Henderson you're my friends." She laughed. "Actually, that's the worst thing you could do. If the word got around, you could be blackballed from future gigs. It's a tempting idea though to ambush him in his own home. Thanks, but no thanks." Ricki looked only slightly disappointed.

"And don't worry, I won't hold it against you—the fact you'll be eating cake with the enemy," Jessica said.

When Jessica looked up from her weeding in the backyard of her South Jordan home one July day in 2002, she found Julie twirling a ring of keys on her finger.

SLAPPED! 281

It was oppressively hot, her knees were sore, and she had a pain in her lower back. It was clear Julie had something in mind, and whatever it was Jessica didn't much care. She would be up for it.

Jessica not only needed a break from the heat and the weeds; she'd just spent several days getting her mother out of the hospital and on her feet after an eight-bypass heart surgery.

"Guess what I've got in my hot little hands besides my car keys," Julie said. "Geoffrey Henderson's address. Want to take a little ride to Sandy?"

Jessica had been fighting further curiosity about Henderson's house for months now, but she realized guiltily that it hadn't worked very well. "Let's go," she said. Since Julie had proposed the trip, it seemed like a lark; the least she could do was go along for the ride.

It had been six years since they had climbed into Jessica's red Integra to find Geoffrey's old house in Sandy (and yes, she still drove the same car). They had no housewarming gift for Henderson this time—no fox in the box. Would he regard it as a lapse in etiquette that they were paying a visit empty-handed? Likely not, since he would hopefully never discover they'd dropped by.

Jessica got into the spirit of a modest disguise by donning a hat and pulling her hair up into it. Julie was wearing dark glasses. Both were in a fine mood by the time they had wound their way into the Sandy hills and found the desired cul-de-sac, known as Happy Gardens Circle.

It wasn't difficult to recognize the house. It looked like a castle, with an iron weather vane turning on one of the medieval turrets, and gargoyles perched on the edge of the roof. Larger than life, the three bronze horses reared ominously above Julie's car as she slowly eased by.

One of Jessica's many informants had reported the sculpture alone was valued in the neighborhood of $350,000.

A sumptuous guest house had been constructed adjacent to the main structure's looming fortress. And as Julie followed the curve of the cul-de-sac around the house in an attempt to allow a peek into the backyard, the two women were astonished to come upon a forty-foot concrete wall topped by six feet of barbed metal fencing.

"Must be exciting for the neighbors who used to have a view of the valley," Julie noted.

On further exploration, the women found a little side road. Before it dead-ended, it revealed a cozy little acre stocked with live—rather than brass—horses. Julie parked the car and found a ditch area that allowed a somewhat unobstructed view of the Henderson backyard.

"Look," Jessica pointed at the swimming pool and the man-made lake, the latter contained by huge boulders with little waterfalls trickling over them. Peacocks, ducks, and other birds browsed nearby.

It could have looked idyllic had the elements of the scene not clashed so jarringly. The juxtaposition of the horses and adjoining corrals to the huge house made it appear as if the designer had located a ranch alongside a castle. The peacocks and the ducks were a nice touch for someone who was bent on destroying wildlife habitat on the Jordan River. And the swimming pool next to an artificial lake made both appear superfluous.

What a spread. It was *big* all right and meant to impress; the man who lived here was, no question, a big-time operator.

As the two women glanced at each other, Jessica allowed herself an expletive she hardly ever uttered. "Hollllyyyyy Shitttttttt!" she said. "I guess we got what we came for! Wealth and power is what we're up against, and he has enough of both to destroy us."

"All the more reason," Julie affirmed.

"Meaning?" Jessica asked.

"We have to do the right thing."

Chapter 28
Poseurs at the Deposition

The bigger they are, the more deliciously are they deposed.

Jessica and Julie had run the gauntlet of intense interrogation at their own depositions and had not only survived but had made strong arguments for their case. After the welcome private distraction of their clandestine adventure at Geoffrey Henderson's estate, the housewives would now be stepping back into the glare of the public arena to witness Henderson, Marcus Hollings, Dick Munson, Brad and Delores Wilkerson, Clare Jackson, and other "bigs" from the opposition face deposition.

In addition, Jack Fitch had yet to be deposed, and he would be challenged by June Fitch and likely by his father, Edward Harper Fitch, in separate depositions.

It could be advantageous or dangerous depending on how well the developers' case held up under scrutiny. It could be fun or infernally frustrating. But there was no question it would be expensive.

Thirty-five subpoenas had been issued, and even though only sixteen individuals ended up being deposed (Jessica Tobler twice), big money would flow to attorneys for the opposing sides. One deposition could cost between $5,000 and $10,000, based on how many billable hours were filed by how many attorneys. Lawyers got paid no matter if they were deposing their own witnesses or those from the other side. Eventually the lawsuit's legal bills for defending Jessica and Julie would reach over $400,000. It was likely legal bills for Henderson Development were even higher.

Even false starts had a price tag. When Lew Chambers arrived for his deposition, he was informed by the powers that be that they had decided he need not be deposed. But Julie and Jessica, who were on hand as well, were told they would still be charged for their attorneys' time and gas money.

Why even show up for that kind of financial abuse? Well, they couldn't sit home, wondering what was going on in their absence. They would put on their activist game faces, dress with care and a certain fashion sense, and be a strong and confident presence at the table as their allies and adversaries took the hot seat for questioning. Of course, some of their valiance was a pose; they were alternately hopeful and scared, but they kept their apprehensions hidden.

The real poseurs at these proceedings, Jessica and Julie assured themselves, were those witnesses for the plaintiffs who would take the stand willing to lie or fake evidence.

At the deposition of Clare Jackson, the married daughter of Brad and Delores Wilkerson, Julie and Jessica watched as she embraced the role of loyal defender of the purity of her parents' land dealings—transactions that had ultimately led to the development of the river bottoms. It was a part she had seemingly been born to play.

Evidently, she had been coached in deposition protocol by her court reporter sister, maybe coached a little too well. She paused to spell the name of every person she mentioned. Jackson had apparently not been warned, however, against transparent references to LDS ecclesiastical connections, repeatedly referring to herself throughout her testimony as "young women's president."

She testified she kept two journals—a personal record and a "farm journal." She produced a volume that she said was the latter and read aloud from it. "Julie keeps going over to my mom and dad's house to get them to breach their contract," she intoned. Asked on what date that entry occurred, Jackson explained the journal did not contain specific dates. Continuing to read, she said, "Why doesn't Julie just leave us alone? I asked her, 'How would you like it if some environmentalist tried to get your husband to break a contract to sell a farm to get it developed?'"

To distract themselves from their incredulity, Julie and Jessica found themselves rolling their eyes and passing notes to each other.

Watching Jessica's sour expression when Jackson appeared to contradict herself, Julie messaged her to keep a poker face. *Don't make faces. Don't let on. Give no clues.*

Here they come, Jessica messaged back. *More fabricated journal notes. It's like she prepared a talk. Interesting how Clare's journal seems to be only about land deals, unmixed with anything else. I'm trying so hard not to laugh.*

A journal with no dates, Julie scribbled in return. *Great history.*

Funny as hell, Jessica wrote back. *Keeps this up, she'll rot there.*

When "Lefty" Gunderson was Jessica and Julie's attorney, he had deposed Jackson's parents, Brad and Delores Wilkerson. Delores had been so nervous that she had been unable to put together more than a couple of coherent sentences in a row. Her questioning was mercifully cut short. Brad Wilkerson, meanwhile, had stumbled badly in essentially admitting that he had played all parties against the middle to get the best deal. "Haven't you ever heard of horse trading?" he had asked defensively.

The Wilkersons were not allowed to sit in on each other's depositions. Brad had lost his cool under questioning, angrily attributing his inarticulateness to the tactics of a "tricky attorney"—Lowell "Lefty" Gunderson.

This deposition, however, was not included in the mounting legal bills for Jessica and Julie. Amazingly, a court reporter named Angel who had read about Jessica and Julie's fight to save open space, volunteered her time during the Wilkerson's deposition. She also prepared the write-up of the expensive depositions at no cost.

Former South Jordan City Councilman Robert Warren, now city manager of a small California community, was flown into town for his deposition at Jessica and Julie's expense. His testimony proved memorable, confirming that Henderson Development had threatened to sue the city at one point, convincing some council members they were in danger of litigation if they didn't rezone the property as Henderson Development had requested.

In an amusing footnote, he also reported he had been falsely informed that he had been burned in effigy at Jessica's infamous Halloween bash.

Dick Munson's less-than-memorable deposition was notable chiefly on two fronts. He averred that community master plans were meant to be "living documents," forever changing as the city grew. He also admitted he had accompanied Geoffrey Henderson on a hunting trip but denied Africa as their destination and said he had paid his own expenses. Nodding in Jessica and Julie's direction, he said, "I can prove it by producing my receipts," something he subsequently failed to do.

Geoffrey Henderson's deposition proved to be enlightening. Under questioning, he spent most of his time on nuts-and-bolts issues, outlining the various players behind Henderson Development's investments and leaving the ethical and legal issues for his partner, Marcus Hollings, to later address. He boasted that the development company hadn't even needed to put money down on the property; it was simply passed on to the developers that succeeded them. He also revealed Henderson Development made $19 million on the sale of the ground.

In addition, Henderson managed to slough off on his partner the major motivation behind the lawsuit against Jessica and Julie. He said that personally he had lost his taste for the litigation and blamed Hollings for initiating the lawsuits.

Absentmindedly, perhaps, Henderson also ungraciously bit one of the hands that had been extended to support Henderson Development's version of the land wars, unguardedly referring in his testimony to Clare Jackson as "a fussbudget."

Posers, poseurs, and those who had been assigned to depose major and minor players in the legal tangle over open land and free speech had staged what amounted to often innocuous warm-up acts.

Now came the finale. What kind of strategies or surprises would Marcus Hollings employ under questioning? How calmly or rationally could June Fitch mask the bitterness of her marriage while attempting to undercut her husband's motives? Would Jack Fitch's father bolster his son's credibility or damage it? And Jack Fitch himself. As the x-factor, he could turn out to be the linchpin—either for one case or the other. How would he perform?

Chapter 29
A Brilliant Madness

It was almost Christmas, and the legal pleadings were piling up and so were the legal bills.

In Julie Bell and Jessica Tobler's protracted fight to preserve green space along the Jordan River and defend against the SLAPP suit, the sheer volume of documents produced by the case was killing trees and helping to denude the landscape. How crazy was that? Trees, of course, were among the resources they were trying to save.

To prepare and obtain a court-ready document through several rewritings, one had to waste reams and reams of paper. Then copies of the document had to be made for all the clients and the principals involved on the legal teams of both plaintiffs and defendants. Used a few hundred times in a document, the word *the* could be expensive.

Julie and Jessica spent hundreds of hours at Del Gordon's office, plowing through paperwork and then boxing documents and hauling them home, where they exhausted thousands of additional hours poring over them again. Before the case would be settled, it would take thirty boxes to contain the paper trail being generated.

Then came more paper, bearing invoices for expenditures on paper, production, and photocopying. Attorneys bill their clients for every scrap of paper they produce—not to mention postage—and every word of advice uttered from their mouths. If two attorneys from Del Gordon's firm attended the same hearing, the cost could amount to as much as $1,000 an hour.

A fraction of the paper used for the SLAPP. Destruction of beautiful trees became stacks of legal paper.

While Jessica and Julie were struggling to make a monthly dent in their burgeoning attorney bills, they were driving old cars they couldn't afford to fix; the air conditioning on Tobler's 1989 Acura Integra had failed, and a window on Bell's 1989 Buick LeSabre refused to roll up or down.

On the morning of Marcus Hollings's deposition, with both of their cars laid up, Jessica and Julie decided to take TRAX (light rail) to Salt Lake City. Struggling to be sure they arrived on time, they hopped on a downtown train without fumbling for change to feed the ticket machine at the TRAX station and were of course challenged by a jowly uniformed woman named Helga. She was not impressed with their explanation of a pending appointment at a judicial hearing.

"Look, you're lucky I'm not calling the police on you. Get off at the next stop, buy a ticket, and reboard the train honestly," she said. A twenty-minute wait for the next train made them conspicuously late entering the hearing room.

Inside the room, what met Jessica's eyes reminded her of a scene from *Erin Brockovich*. On one side of the table were Griff Walters, Mills Homer, Geoffrey Henderson, and Marcus Hollings; on the other side were Del Gordon, Don Parker, and Mark Marsden, a third partner in Gordon's firm. Glasses and jugs of ice water had been provided for the participants. Hollings was being grilled by Gordon.

Under his questioning, *fixation* was a word Hollings was using to describe Jack Fitch's devotion to saving open space around the river. He apparently knew the term wouldn't fly with an unbiased observer (were it applied to Jessica and Julie's efforts). But he thought he could make it stick to Fitch by connecting it to allegations of mental illness.

"June Fitch has told me on many occasions that she is unhappy with Jack's *fixation* about the RiverFront project," Hollings said for the record. "And obviously," he redundantly rambled on, "I'm involved with the RiverFront project, and June has indicated she's unhappy with his fixation. She'd like it to end."

On several occasions during the deposition—circling back to the subject when Hollings least expected it—Gordon asked what kind of influence he may have had in persuading June and Edward Fitch to seek a conservatorship of Jack's resources.

"Have you, Geoffrey Henderson, or Henderson Development—ever suggested to June Fitch or Edward Fitch that they ought to appoint a conservatorship or guardianship?"

"We have had discussions about the appointment of a conservator," Hollings replied. "I don't think we've ever made the suggestion. However, I'm being careful in how I answer it ..."

Later, Gordon asked, "If you, Geoffrey Henderson, and Henderson Development had obtained a conservatorship—had filed and gotten it appointed—the hope was, wasn't it, that the litigation between Mr. Fitch and you would end. Is that correct?"

"Yeah," Hollings said. "The hope would be that basically Jack Fitch would not be interfering with our business activities."

Nervously distracting herself from the testimony, Jessica was drawing pictures of the adversarial team across the table. She and Julie were also exchanging acerbic notes with each other.

Look at his eyes; he's lying.

I want to laugh out loud at some of this stuff.

That's two of us.

Then there were the difficulties of their own attorney. Del Gordon (sharply dressed in a dark suit, starched white shirt, and tie) had placed several different colored Sharpies in his breast pocket to mark exhibits. As he extracted and replaced the markers (sometimes forgetting to cap the pens), little dots of green, red, black, and blue began to stain his shirt. It was difficult not to bust a gut at this sight, but Jessica and Julie managed to hold it in.

After several more exchanges between Gordon and Hollings, the latter confessed he was hopeful the judge would appoint a conservator " ...for a number of reasons, and it's not all self-interest. I genuinely believe Jack suffers from a mental defect and disability. I honestly believe that from the evidence I have looked at. I've been a judge for sixteen years, and I adjudicated a lot of people that had mental illnesses. I see many of the same things in Mr. Fitch."

The hearing room was unusually quiet, and all eyes were on the ex-judge. The blatancy of what amounted to an accusation of dementia hung in the air.

In a rush of reassurance, Hollings then moved to emphasize how much he personally *liked* Jack Fitch. "I think he's a fine individual," he said. "Be that as it may," he noted, "a lot of fine people do have mental problems. Mr. Fitch does. It's clear."

Warming again to the attack, Hollings said, "I think he's made his mental problems *our* problems in a business sense, and furthermore, I know it's been a tremendous problem for South Jordan City and the taxpayers, since we had to front a lot of money to deal with Mr. Fitch and his fixations."

At the lunch break, Jessica and Julie were walking with Gordon down a corridor when another lawyer asked him, "Are you kicking his ass?" Without missing a beat, Gordon thrust out his chest and replied, "Yes I am!"

Julie and Jessica used the break to descend in the elevator to Crossroads Mall, the level below the hearing room and there, in a novelty store, found a mechanical peacock that made bird noises when a button was pushed, its feathers fanning out in a colorful circle of male finery. They later presented it to Gordon with a note: *Strut your stuff, Del. Proud as a peacock.*

When questioning resumed, Gordon asked how Hollings had responded to the worry June Fitch had expressed about her family and their possible liability in a telephone conversation between the two.

"I told her that what her husband was doing was idiotic and legally risky and that he was putting her family at great risk. I told her, in essence, we probably wouldn't be pursuing any litigation."

"I've been told that you said that you wouldn't take her house," Gordon asked. "Is that correct?"

Hollings modestly lowered his eyes as if to cast himself as the rare benevolent creditor out of a nineteenth-century Dickens novel. "Correct," he replied. "I said, 'June, our desire is not to make your life more difficult than it already is. We don't want to put you out on the street. We *could do it*. I believe we could. We're not going to do that.'"

As it continued, Hollings's testimony was carefully constructed to connect a series of damning dots—Fitch's "fixation" with a lost cause and his willingness to flout his family in favor of a flirtation or fascination with Jessica Tobler.

Gordon asked what June Fitch and her attorney, Kit Effington, had said to convince him of the need to appoint a conservator or guardian.

"June believes that Jack has been manipulated significantly by Jessica Tobler and Julie Bell," Hollings said. "I believe that to be correct, but I formed that opinion independently from what they stated.

"They indicated Jack really is a puppet of Jessica Tobler. They are very concerned about her manipulations. They've told me that Jessica's been asked by them to leave Jack alone, but she refused to do so."

Knowing that his own association with June Fitch had already been raised as a red flag, Hollings asserted, "I'd like to point out a very important fact in our relationship. I don't think I ever once called June on the phone. Every communication was initiated by June. She was calling *me*. I wasn't calling *her*. I don't think I ever once called her."

Gordon paused to regard him sternly.

Feeling perhaps slightly flustered under Gordon's gaze, Hollings faltered, "If I did, it was only *once*, so I mean … I can't even remember a time."

Near the end of the deposition, Gordon asked, "Do you have any firsthand knowledge of Mr. Fitch's mental health?"

Hollings was forced to admit he did not. "Just the *manifestations*," he said. "I mean we've been the *subject* of his fixation."

Another point Gordon pressed Hollings on was whether he had paid any of the legal fees incurred in the conservatorship proceedings

"No," he said. "Of that I am confident. We—meaning Geoffrey Henderson or myself or any related entities or friends, family, or associates—we haven't paid any money."

Not that Henderson Development hadn't *tried*, as it turned out. One thing that emerged from June Fitch's testimony during her deposition was her declaration that Hollings had indeed offered to pay some of her legal expenses to seek a conservator.

"He said, 'I would be willing to help you out,'" she testified. She said she had rejected his offer because she felt payment was her own responsibility.

Despite this revealing tidbit, June Fitch proved an overall credible witness against her husband under questioning of attorney Jeri Lane, a colleague of Del Gordon's at Parker Anderton & Marsden. (Del Gordon was on hand but turned the interrogation over to Lane.) Although somewhat naive and soft-spoken, June Fitch came across as sincere. She ended up raising several complex and problematic issues that Gordon realized could cause trouble at a guardianship hearing or a trial.

During questioning about her husband's mental health history, June said a red flag was raised for her in 1982 while Jack was in the army, stationed in Vogelweh, Germany. While living with him on base with three small children, June said she had received a call from his commanding officer, who claimed her husband had disobeyed a direct order.

Jack would be evaluated in an army hospital, the man told her, and if the diagnosis dealt with mental instability, he would not be charged for disobeying an order. If he were found to be well, he would be dropped in rank.

The diagnosis came back "manic depressive," and her husband wasn't charged, she said. When Jack was released from the army in 1988, he was given temporary disability army retirement pay, she noted.

By 1992, when Jack's father did the necessary paperwork to initiate Social Security disability income for Jack, the money went into Edward Fitch's account as representative payee, June Fitch testified. Two years later, she added, Jack's father petitioned Social Security to make June representative payee.

"The money went into our joint account up until January 1999 when without my prior knowledge, Jack took it out and put it into his own personal checking account," June asserted.

Pressed by Ms. Lane, the witness conceded she had obtained her husband's medical and psychological records from his father and had coughed them up on request to Henderson Development's attorneys.

"Did you have Jack's permission to proffer his medical or mental health records to the developers' counsel?" Lane asked.

"Did I *have* to have permission?" she queried.

"I'm just asking the question."

"Well, I didn't know that I had to have permission. I was told I should turn over whatever I had in my possession."

Pressing June about testimony she had given that Jack Fitch was unable to manage his property and affairs effectively, Lane asked, "Is it your belief he can't care for himself either financially or physically?"

June Fitch's answer was so direct and detailed it carried a subtle punch. "Up to this point, no. Well, physically he can do laundry, and he can clean, and he can feed himself, you know; he can get his own meals. I don't know about financially."

"Does he currently have a job?"

"I don't know."

"You don't *know*?" Lane sounded incredulous.

"He doesn't tell me. He had a hearing last summer; he was starting vocational rehabilitation. He hasn't worked for eleven years. He started vocational rehabilitation the day after the hearing, and I don't know the status of that. I've asked him several times, and he'll say, 'Oh, I don't know.'"

Del Gordon could imagine what this kind of testimony would sound like at trial. In her off-handed, unassuming way, June Fitch painted her husband as a barely functioning ne'er-do-well obsessed with far-out causes at the expense of his family's welfare. Jurors could wonder if he were witless about his own proclivities and/or knowingly deceptive and evasive with his wife.

June continued to other firsthand observations of Jack's mental state that Gordon realized it might be tough to challenge.

"When Jack is not sleeping, there are times when he does not think properly," she said. "He paces the basement; his eyes are glassy." Jack's LDS bishop, who had told her he had noticed his glazed-over stare in church, could corroborate this, she added.

Asked what she planned to tell the judge if there was a trial, June replied, "Well, I plan on telling him that I don't think Jack is competent in taking care of his finances. I'm going to tell him that I don't think Jack is competent period."

Pressed for specific evidence of this assertion, she referred to a document in her possession that indicated her husband had filed two petitions for a summons to include himself in Henderson Development's SLAPP suit. *I am the true John Doe No. 1*, he had written. In effect, this amounted to asking that he also be sued for $1.7 million.

"To me, this is in total disregard for the welfare of himself, his family, and his home," June said.

Stated this baldly in court, Gordon and his colleagues might find it difficult to convince a judge or a jury otherwise.

It wasn't that Jack Fitch didn't have a rationale for his actions. But its essence was more difficult to communicate. Was someone necessarily crazy if one's devotion to saving open space and fighting injustice were so great as to insist on standing shoulder to shoulder with one's friends when they were under legal attack by a corporate bully?

If June's testimony could be used as convincing evidence before a conservatorship hearing or in court, wouldn't corroborating testimony from Jack Fitch's own father be the *coup de grâce*?

That was undoubtedly the thinking of Kit Effington and his colleagues in deposing Edward Harper Fitch. Although he shared a certain ingenuousness with his daughter-in-law, Edward, as it turned out, was also given to overstatement.

Asked by Del Gordon why a conservator should be appointed for his son, the elder Fitch said straightforwardly, "Because Jack has wasted many, many dollars on his obsession with environmental projects." In addition, he said, "Jack is a manic depressive, and it's well-known that manic depressives are irresponsible with money—that's their trade."

While Edward backed June's testimony that Jack's spending on opposition to the RiverFront project hurt his family, he seemed to stumble in using the word *greed* to describe a motive for his notoriously penny-pinching son.

"It's Jack's greed for money for his own purposes," his father said, that caused him to siphon funds away from his family.

"It's the money he's spent on this environmental thing that's caused the problem," Edward asserted. "That's why he transferred the veterans' money to his control so he could spend it freely. He didn't have to clear it with June."

Jack didn't spend enough money to cause problems "until he got messed up with the environmental project," his father said.

Gordon did succeed in eliciting from Edward Fitch a confession that during a telephone conversation with Marcus Hollings, the ex-judge had boosted the idea of obtaining a conservatorship as a way of "getting Jack off his (Hollings's) back," or words to that effect.

On several occasions during the rambling deposition, the elder Fitch was asked about his son's mental state and alternately described it as either "manic depression" or "bipolar disorder." But then in contrast to his daughter-in-law's testimony of Jack Fitch's ineptitude, Edward said, "No, he's competent. As a matter of fact, he's brilliant."

Asked what he meant, he supplied the session's one good laugh line: "He regularly beats me in Scrabble." Edward didn't seem to notice that the others at the table were smiling or suppressing laughter.

Expanding on the word *brilliant*, he then extrapolated in another direction.

"Look," he said. "Patty Duke has written a book; it's called *A Brilliant Madness*, and it describes manic depressives. They're brilliant people, but they go off the deep end on some things."

Edward went on to say that he had read the book and given it as a gift to both Jack and June Fitch. Now he was recommending it to Del Gordon. "If you haven't read it, you'd be well advised to," he said, because it would help to understand his son.

There were actually *two* books with that title, as Gordon later learned. One was by Duke and Gloria Hochman, subtitled *Living with Manic Depressive Illness*. The other chronicled the life of famous mathematician John Nash and would be made into an Academy Award-winning movie, retitled *A Beautiful Mind*. Nash's illness was not bipolar but paranoid schizophrenia.

But as described by leading psychologists cited in Duke and Hochman's book, bipolar had no relation to insanity. Jack Fitch was eccentric—maybe sometimes extreme in his passionate dedication to what he believed—but he wasn't mad.

While it appeared that Edward Fitch had failed to grasp his son's ailment, the misunderstanding was a common one—the sort of misperception that might later confuse jury members at trial. If it came to that, it would have to be watched for.

But the phrase *a brilliant madness*—its ironic quality suggested it could possibly be adapted and used to persuade objective observers that Jack Fitch was instead an asset to his colleagues and community.

In fact, there would be no need to wait for answers to Fitch's suitability as his own best character witness. His assets would be on persuasive display for both his allies and his detractors during his deposition. This despite the fact that his testimony would be coerced under the cruelest and least conducive circumstances for establishing a basis for truth.

Jack Fitch was required to show up for the proceeding the day after major foot surgery, and he rolled into the hearing room in a wheelchair. Although Judge Cornish had allowed delays in depositions for both Marc Hollings and Geoffrey Henderson because of business obligations, he denied Del Gordon's petition for a postponement for Fitch. Before even arriving, Fitch had accomplished his own physical marathon on public transportation, transferring with his wheelchair from a bus to TRAX and having to negotiate the chair's wheels out of grooves near the TRAX station, where they had become stuck in the pavement.

Upon his arrival, his attorneys were concerned that he was without pain medications, but he informed them he didn't want his testimony called into question by opposition attorneys on the basis that he was drugged.

During much of the proceedings, Fitch refused to be cornered by aggressive interrogation and instead went on the offensive himself, alleging that Hollings and Henderson had reprehensibly attempted to turn his father against him with half-truths and that their statements were untrustworthy.

Griff Walters made the mistake of floating a question to Fitch he thought he couldn't answer: "What could you have meant by your quote the *VOICE* published, 'We've cost Henderson Development millions of dollars.'"

Fitch replied that it was his pleasure to explain the corporation's business to its attorney. "The grassroots activism of SPACE (Space Provides a Clean Environment) prevented Henderson Development from grabbing the $22 million of taxpayer RDA money you wanted to fund your project."

Fitch was also asked to explain another quote in the *VOICE* article, "I supply Jessica with the bullets, and she fires them."

"Were those real guns and real bullets?" Walters baited him. "Ridiculous question," Fitch replied. "A figure of speech."

If only all the depositions could have ended this decisively, Del Gordon was thinking. With the plaintiffs' attorneys out of ammunition and nothing left to shoot but blanks.

Blank. That reminded Gordon of something—the look on Marcus Hollings's face after his deposition and his oddly melodramatic exit from the courtroom. As if called upon to play the role of emissary of the Christmas season (not exactly typecasting), he had raised his hands in an expansive gesture, murmuring vaguely to the assembled, "Let there be peace on earth."

Another blank and empty threat.

Chapter 30
What Would Jesus Do?

If it were not for a weekly respite, how could Julie Bell survive? The week was sliced up into meetings with her attorney, poring over legal papers, taking Trish to therapy sessions, sparring with Ted over their precarious finances, and, of course, opening a fresh batch of bills. Her habit was to quickly slide them into a cubbyhole of her desk as if placing them out of sight might keep them out of mind.

Thank goodness for Sunday. A splash of March sunlight from the large window in the church foyer brought out gold threads in the carpet at Julie's feet. It was strange but pleasant to be sitting comfortably on a couch in the foyer with her husband in the unusual circumstance of having arrived early for sacrament meeting, waiting for members of the other ward they shared the building with to conclude their services and vacate the chapel.

Julie was wearing a blue dress, pantyhose, and heels. Ted—freshly shaved and showered—looked almost boyish in a dark suit and white shirt.

If she closed her eyes for a moment, she could remember what it felt like to recognize the pull of attraction shortly after they met. That seemed a long time ago.

299

While talk between them was often on the surface, they could still find a way to grapple with an issue that affected them both. This morning, they engaged in a short conversation about Trish's need for emotional support, prompted by a glimpse of Royden Ross, who had waved hello while passing through the foyer. Ross had been one of the few adults in the ward whose unusual kindness to Trish had created a bond that their daughter depended on.

Their daughter. Every now and again, Julie was buoyed by the fact that they still shared mutual concerns and interests. But frequently, a distance yawned between them. Even now they sat apart on the couch.

On occasion, Ted would listen to something Julie had to report about a development in the lawsuit, but it couldn't go much deeper than that. If it threatened to, Ted would inevitably make it clear that it was *her* problem, not his.

Late Saturday night, Del Gordon, Julie and Jessica's attorney, had telephoned Julie to read her the content of a newly produced affidavit filed against them by Tim Christopher, a Salt Lake County attorney and former South Jordan city councilman.

The news was like another little backstab of pain that went to something personal and vulnerable. Christopher lived in an adjoining neighborhood and was a priesthood leader in Julie's LDS stake. In fact, he had only recently been released as a member of the stake high council and had delivered several assigned speeches in the Bells' ward sacrament service. She hadn't really had much contact with him—either at city hall or at church—but had always regarded him as a decent and honorable man.

Now what would it be like to encounter "Brother Christopher" at church? A more likely happenstance than less, she realized, since he belonged to the ward that shared their church building.

As the thought percolated in Julie's brain, the hypothetical became reality. Tim Christopher, tall, slender, and balding, was exiting the chapel in a powder-gray suit, his amiable pregnant wife, Roxie, on his arm, her brown hair cut short. As the daughter of Mayor Max McClellan, Roxie had her own community-insider status. The Christophers stopped to converse near a small table in the foyer and had not yet noticed Julie and Ted. He looked dignified and untroubled by any exterior concern.

The appearance of the couple had attracted Ted's attention, Julie noticed. He glanced at her as if to evaluate her intentions. "I don't know if I can sit here and keep my mouth shut," she said, shuffling her feet.

It was the Sabbath day. She was in church—a sanctuary of peace and remove from the cares of the week, hardly the place for a confrontation—yet a cloud of injustice and anger hovered from last night's phone call. Maybe church was just the place to tell truth straight and without apology.

Ted was looking at her quizzically. "It's so hard to sit here and not say anything," she said. "And the longer I sit, the more my blood boils."

"Well," Ted said. "Go say something then."

It seemed an uncharacteristic show of support from her husband.

Should she take it as a sign? Julie noticed she was getting to her feet.

On the walk across the foyer, she observed Roxie Christopher fortuitously choosing that moment to leave her husband's side. She was walking away. Tim Christopher glanced up just as Julie reached him.

His mouth was halfway open to say something, but Julie beat him to it. "You know, Tim—and everyone does know—we did nothing wrong." His face was frozen between smile and grimace. "How could you have written that affidavit against us?" He didn't speak.

"Also, Tim, as you must realize, Jesus would never have sued anyone."

She wasn't going to wait around for a reply, but just as she turned to walk back across the foyer, she shot him a last imploring look, meant to punctuate what she had said.

Sitting back down on the couch, Julie felt a flood of validation and relief. Her eyes were wet with sudden emotion. After she explained what she had said, even Ted looked pleased. "Come on, Julie. I'm going to sacrament meeting," he said. "Are you coming?"

"Maybe later," she said. Out of the corner of her eye, she could see Christopher fidgeting, stealing a look their way yet avoiding eye contact.

As Ted walked away, Tim Christopher seemed to make up his mind about something and headed purposefully across the foyer toward Julie.

He didn't meet her eyes until he had stopped in front of her, looking down to say, "If we can talk about this as adults, I will talk with you."

Well duh! she thought. "I thought we *were* adults," she said. He looked uncomfortable. "Well, sure, let's talk," Julie said, gesturing to the sofa cushion next to her.

Christopher didn't sit; instead he remained standing. Was he signaling this was going to be a brief conversation? Or was the arrangement that made it necessary for Julie to look up to him a conscious or unconscious way of maintaining his authority?

As he began to talk, he did lean back against the hip-high table adjacent to the couch, slightly altering the stiffness of his posture. Oddly, it seemed to Julie, his opening remarks appeared to be an attempt to explain how a city council governs.

Christopher seemed at pains to point out from his experience as a city councilman how difficult it was to serve in that capacity—trying to represent different constituencies, listening to citizens' demands and complaints.

"Decisions cannot always be made on the basis of what the majority of citizens want," he said. "Citizens aren't always aware of all the information that we receive, so the government is set up to allow *us* to make the decisions."

Julie nodded half-heartedly, not wishing to challenge these less-than-salient points. But it was dawning that Christopher intended to ignore what she had said to him; he wouldn't defend or apologize for the enmity of his affidavit. Instead, he abruptly veered to offer a piece of personal advice.

"Julie," he said, "if you are smart—if you and Jessica Tobler are smart—you will get out of this lawsuit. You will lick your wounds and cut your losses."

Was there any possible way to respond to this condescending remark? It was obvious he intended his affidavit as one more weapon to pressure Julie and Jessica to resume their domestic duties, as men of his stature expected good Mormon housewives to do. Julie stared at him with what she hoped was cool but uncompromising disdain.

SLAPPED! 303

"I will tell you this much," Christopher said. "Marcus Hollings has informed me that the reason he sued you is simply to get you out of the way."

What was his purpose in divulging this information? Was he offering it as a juicy tidbit to convince her that he was capable of empathy? Or was it one more "shut up" message passed through Christopher on Hollings and Henderson's behalf?

"Marcus told me he was sure that if he threatened to sue you, you would go away," Christopher said.

Duh yes, Julie thought. *Tell me something I don't know.*

"So then he actually filed the lawsuit, and you still didn't go away. He got mad at that."

Julie tried to suppress a rueful smile, knowing that Christopher himself had development interests and undoubtedly had some of his own money involved. She didn't respond but gazed at him expectantly.

"Marc also told me that he was adamant to keep the lawsuit going until you *had* to give up, since you would either be out of money or emotionally broke. What he told me is that money wins; he's got it, and you don't."

"If this goes to a jury trial, everybody knows you would win," Christopher continued. "Instead, he wants to make sure he can financially and emotionally destroy you."

A few people were passing by in the foyer, glancing at the tall man—one buttock now resting on the table—and the seated woman. Those who recognized Tim Christopher and Julie Bell might have wondered if she were seeking informal counsel from priesthood authority. Or was it just a friendly chat?

"So," Julie said, "you must be close friends with Marcus Hollings and Geoffrey Henderson."

"I've been friends with Marc for years," Christopher said candidly.

"Well, does that mean you were friends back when you were a city councilman?"

"Yes," he said. "I was close to him while he was still a judge."

Julie let his reply hang in the air for a moment, alive with all its implications. But Tim Christopher didn't look sheepish or embarrassed.

From down the hall, where primary kids' voices were singing, she recognized the notes of a simple hymn, "I Am a Child of God," which had come to represent for some Mormons the innocent core of a childlike faith.

How preordained and carefully crafted Henderson Development's strategy must have seemed in the beginning. Cultivating relationships and contacts in government and community—Geoffrey Henderson taking Dick Munson on an African safari; Marcus Hollings finessing the loyalty of his friend, Tim Christopher, to accomplish his purposes. It must have looked so simple—a slam dunk.

That was, before Julie and Jessica came along.

"Marc Hollings sued you to get you out of the way," Christopher reiterated. "But he once told me he was sorry he had launched the suit. He said that if he had it to do all over again, he probably wouldn't have done it."

Again, Julie paused to ponder Christopher's motivations. Why was he spilling this curious information? Was it even true? It didn't sound like the Marcus Hollings she had come to know and loathe. Was it possible that these men—whose public posture of total surety and self-confidence was so much in evidence—could it be they sometimes struggled with the dichotomy between what they professed in their church callings and what they practiced in their private and professional lives?

Julie recalled that Jessica had mentioned her own confrontation with Christopher at an All a Dollar Store where she was shopping with her kids and other neighborhood children for birthday party favors.

At the All a Dollar Store, Jessica had rounded a corner in the party favors section and bumped into Christopher, who breezily offered, "Well, Jessica, how are you doing?"

Conscious of the fact that her increased weight and the sores on her face had registered with the man, she had said, "You know what, Tim? I'm not doing all that well. And when I remember that you didn't do a damn thing to speak up for Julie and me when you were on city council, I frankly don't know how you can sleep at night."

Christopher had looked surprised. "Way to go, Mrs. Tobler," her kids' friends had chimed in. "Yeah, Mom, that was cool," her own children had added after the man had left.

Now, towering over Julie on the couch, Tim Christopher looked imperious. How could she not ask the pertinent question?

"Do you believe it was okay for Hollings and Henderson to sue us when they knew—and you know—we didn't do anything wrong?"

Christopher didn't flinch. "Yeah. It's okay to sue anybody for anything. But of course you *were* wrong in opposing the project."

When Julie spoke again, she was surprised to recognize the steeliness of her own voice. "As I recall, you were a high councilman when you wrote your affidavit. You lied about us, and you knew we had not done what you said we did. In fact, I've never even talked to you before."

"I'm not a high councilman now," Christopher said. After a moment of silence, he shifted his weight on the table, looking to Julie as if he might have regretted the implications of his words.

Then, abruptly changing the subject, he recounted his All a Dollar Store encounter with Jessica, casting himself as an empathetic observer of her plight. "I understand she has depression and other problems," he said. "And it has cost her family a lot."

There was another pause before Christopher looked at Julie and said, "I just can't understand why you didn't quit. When this whole thing is over, do you really believe you will have accomplished anything worthwhile?"

"Well," Julie said, "our real intent all along was to do something good for our community. God knows that, and that's all that matters."

"Hmm," he murmured. "I can see that's what you believe, and I admire you for it."

Was that sincerity in his voice? Had he softened some? No, she decided. *You're going to hell for lying, buddy.*

"But, Julie," he said. "I just can't understand why you didn't settle when you had the chance."

On Julie's telephone table at home when she returned from church was a copy of the *Ensign*, the official monthly magazine of the LDS Church. On the cover was a seventeenth-century master's painting of Jesus kneeling in the Garden of Gethsemane.

Who was he praying for in that most agonizing and inclusive of all prayers? Could any plea to heaven for the redemption of humankind really cover the sort of casual perfidy observable on a daily basis? *Well,* Julie thought, *I hope he was praying for all of us. We need it.*

She dialed the home number of Del Gordon, hoping he wasn't already sitting down for Sunday dinner. When he came on the line, he was surprised to hear that she had just spent nearly two hours in conversation with Tim Christopher.

She repeated as much of the exchange as she could remember, believing Gordon might find it useful. Most of Christopher's affidavit had been sheer hearsay—as a rule, inadmissible in court. Gordon had made a motion to quash it, but Judge Cornish had denied it. Gordon pointed out to Julie that Christopher had obviously been coached what to write in several instances, most likely by Marc Hollings. He had testified that Julie and Jessica had intruded on Henderson Development's contracts with the Wilkersons through inappropriate contacts.

The latter—at the heart of the matter—was prevarication, first because such contact had not occurred and second because Christopher had no personal knowledge of whether any such contact could have occurred.

Gordon thanked Julie for the information and said he had a follow-up move in mind.

In midafternoon the next day, he called back to say he had spoken to Tim Christopher on the telephone, and after he pointed out to him some discrepancies in his affidavit, he had agreed to come to Gordon's office and file an amended statement.

How's that for a turnaround, Julie thought. But after she had slept on the news, the next morning Gordon called to report that Christopher had changed his mind. He wouldn't be coming in to the office after all. He felt comfortable with the original document.

It wasn't difficult to deduce that the attorney may have engaged in a little chat with an old friend.

On the following Sunday at church, Julie noticed Jessica's excited wave as she entered the building from the parking lot. She was obviously bursting with some kind of news.

"Guess who I just spoke with out there?" she said. "Tim Christopher. He wasn't happy to see me. I suppose we've got to stop meeting this way."

Julie noticed the look in her friend's eye and laughed. "Tell me about it," she said.

Spotting Christopher after she had exited her car, Jessica had realized he was cutting across the lot to his home, almost directly behind the church.

"Hey, Brother Christopher," she had said. He had turned away from her slightly, halfway frozen in his tracks, as if on recognizing her he had hoped to avoid contact.

"Hey," Jessica had said again. "You should know how much we appreciate you lying under oath in your affidavit. Not a nice thing for a high councilman to do."

Christopher hadn't said a word; he had just kept walking.

Would this mean that their ex-high councilman would likely lay low for a while and take extra precautions at church? Maybe, they both concluded.

Two months later, Julie picked up her telephone to find an agitated Jessica on the line. What did Tim Christopher have in mind now, she asked. She had almost gotten over the intensity of her feelings about the man, when—surprise, surprise—just that morning, upon opening a fat hand-addressed envelope, she had found a detailed letter from Christopher, defensively explaining his offending affidavit and raking up all the old emotion.

In it, he referred to his affidavit as "carefully constructed," asking how a person who believed in speaking out (presumably Jessica) could criticize him for his own free expression.

He explained that as a friend of Marc Hollings, he had taken offense at the reporting in the *VOICE* article, which he said had made his friend "sound like a Mafia member" and city council members sound "mindless and corrupt." He charged that the *VOICE* had lied about Geoffrey Henderson taking Dick Munson on an African safari and had "delved into private lives, including yours, reporting false hearsay."

As a witness for Marcus Hollings's integrity, Christopher noted the two had worked together on "international family policy." Hollings is, the attorney wrote, "a good, decent man who has given much to the church and community."

He wanted Jessica to know that he and Hollings had "even met with general authorities" (of the LDS Church). This was, of course (he expected they would realize), the ultimate trump card.

"I mean you no harm," Christopher wrote. "I do not harbor any animosity or ill will." As an additional sop, he advised that he didn't approve of or condone the Henderson lawsuit. "Although probably legal, it was a big mistake," he said. "A developer should not sue private citizens, even misguided citizens who attempt to interfere with private contracts."

Well, there it was, Julie told Jessica. The reason he could presumably sleep at night, having willingly bought every lie Marcus Hollings had told him.

How do you swallow something like that? Julie wasn't just thinking about Christopher. She and Jessica were choking on their own bile. *How do you make that go down? A spoonful of sugar wouldn't do the trick. Or would it?*

A few days later, Julie couldn't remember if it had been her idea or Jessica's, but they found themselves on a walk to Tim and Roxie Christopher's house, each carrying a huge box of a local brand of donuts made with potato flour—"spudnuts" they had been called in the old days.

Watching Tim Christopher's face as he opened the door to find Julie and Jessica on his doorstep was an experience in itself. And watching a few of the Christophers' fifteen children lick the sugar off their lips as their parents looked on awkwardly, allowing them to dig into the boxes, took some forbearance.

But Julie's mood had lifted. She and Jessica laughed a bit on the way home.

Chapter 31
Heels, Deals, and Repeals

Was it the pink high-heeled sandals? Was it Rod Hubbs calling the cops because Jack Fitch went over time on the two-minute limit he had been given to address the planning and zoning commission? Or was it simply that Hubbs rubbed people the wrong way and for once had ended up rubbing the wrong person?

Whatever the case, the Hubbs hubbub—first reported by the *Salt Lake Tribune*, even though no *Tribune* reporter had been assigned to cover the hearing—became a week-long media circus. Someone had tipped *Tribune* columnist Saul Jolley, who passed it on to a colleague on the news desk. The yarn was the kind of entertaining distraction that caught fire in the public imagination just long enough to actually illuminate one little-known hiccup in the long since *fait accompli* RiverFront project.

It was ironic that the first time Jessica Tobler had said a word in planning and zoning for five years (not since that last commission meeting when Henderson Development had asked audience members to join them in suing Jessica and Julie) that a few rhetorical sparks caught fire.

Argon Group, the new owner of RiverFront once Henderson Development had unloaded it, had insisted on building a parking lot within 125 feet of the Jordan River's one-hundred-year flood plain (a clear

310   *Paul Swenson*

violation of city ordinances). Jessica had decided to make an appearance at the hearing to speak against RDAs and to call attention to Argon's violation of the law.

Now that South Jordan had green-lighted the project, oblivious city officials had seemed happy to grant de facto acceptance to almost anything the developers suggested.

Thanks, however, to what happened at the hearing, the violation got a little accidental press.

Julie and Jessica had found a spot on the aisle where they could sit together. Observing that one or both of them was about to speak in a zoning meeting for the first time in years, Julie had passed a note to Jessica on a yellow sheet of paper that proclaimed, *We're back!*

Jessica laughed. It called to mind the horrific image she had seen in a movie preview of Jack Nicholson's insidious grin at the ax-shattered bathroom door in *The Shining*.

Then, in a shocking turn of events, Jack Fitch was pitched out of the hearing, ordered to leave the room for his failure to yield the microphone fast enough for Commission Chairman Rod Hubbs's liking. Told that a strict time limit had been established for each public comment, Jack was given a police escort to the parking lot.

Walking to the front of the room for her turn to speak, Jessica was steaming. As she passed Hubbs, intending to give him the evil eye, she noticed *his* eyes were fixated elsewhere. Was he staring at her legs? More precisely, her shoes? She had just reached the podium when he stage whispered, "Don't fall off your heels, honey."

Insensitive, cocky, or sexist? Well, all of the above—insult heaped on the injury of Jack's expulsion. Forget flood plains and RDAs for a moment. If there was a *heel* in the room, it was Hubbs, she thought. *Keep your voice steady*, she reminded herself as she turned to face him.

"I think, Mr. Hubbs, you are rather arrogant in your actions here tonight. It is no wonder so many citizens become discouraged from getting involved in their local government."

A stir of comment and nervous laughter could be heard in the audience.

"*I'm* arrogant?" Hubbs shot back. "I'll have you know that *I'm* here week after week, listening to citizen complaints. I have a wife and two little kids at home, and I've hardly even been home for two days. So I don't have to listen to your bull crap, you ignorant wretch!"

Reaction in the audience sounded like a collective gasp.

"What did you call me?" Jessica seemed stunned. "You're referring to me as 'ignorant' and as 'a wretch'? On the public record?"

Red-faced and sputtering, Hubbs said, "You heard me."

As long as we're about it, we might want to get "honey" onto the record as well, Jessica mused. The thought helped to steady her composure. She said not to "pave paradise and put up a parking lot," quoting the Joni Mitchell song, "Yellow Taxi," and citing the ordinance that prohibited intrusion on the flood plain. These remarks would actually survive to surface in some media reports, although what most of the coverage focused on was the Tobler-Hubbs face-off.

After a spate of *Tribune* reportage and commentary, the controversy became juicier. Both Salt Lake dailies and two local TV channels were covering it, digging for details.

Asked by the press whether he had actually used the offending characterization of Jessica, Hubbs stumbled, "I don't remember one way or the other."

In one report, however, he colorfully referred to Tobler as "a rock-the-boater, goat-getter, and a liar," digging himself a deeper rhetorical hole. Then he re-emphasized he would *not* apologize for anything he had said. Nor would he consider another zoning commissioner's call for his resignation.

As a final dollop of irony, one media outlet reported that Tobler and Bell had obviously intended to poke fun at the city commissioners by writing, *We're back!* on the yellow sign-up sheet used to signify the order of public comment for the meeting.

Oh goodness no. Julie laughed to herself. *It was a private joke meant for Jessica. Why did I have to use that piece of paper?*

Just when the embers of the story appeared to be dying, a TV reporter from Fox 13 learned that planning and zoning hearings were routinely

312 *Paul Swenson*

audiotaped in South Jordan, and obtained the official recording. On the tape, "ignorant wretch" rang clear as a bell.

Meanwhile, Jessica's *phone* was ringing—off the hook—with calls from South Jordanians and residents of other cities, claiming they were among dozens of citizens treated rudely by Hubbs over the years.

Within a day or so, Hubbs informed the planning and zoning commission he was resigning his eighty-dollar-a-month position for "personal reasons." No connection with the controversy, he said. And by the way, no apology would be forthcoming.

The *Salt Lake Tribune*'s editorial on the brouhaha took a lofty approach, appealing to the nobler instincts of government officials and citizens, asking that they treat each other "respectfully."

KALL Radio went the other direction with a sardonic one-act radio play helmed by long-time satirist Tim Burnessi, who cast himself as a hubristic Hubbs. His girl Friday, Peg Bradshaw, played Tobler, adopting a high squeaky voice reminiscent of Betty Boop. Missing, however, were appropriate sound effects—the clickety-clack of Jessica's high-heeled sandals.

Listening on her car radio, Jessica laughed so hard that she had to pull off the highway to collapse behind the wheel. The next day, she told the *Deseret News* she had forgiven Rod Hubbs and moved on.

Four days after the planning and zoning meeting, seeking release from stress, Jessica opened her gym bag at SouthTowne Fitness.

Three days before, the newspaper had contained a local section story headlined, "Official Says He Won't Apologize," reporting the titillating news that South Jordan Planning and Zoning Commission Chairman Rod Hubbs had called citizen activist Jessica Tobler "an ignorant wretch" during a public meeting. Criticized by several officials and the public, Hubbs had responded that he "wasn't sorry" for the remark and wasn't about to resign.

The day after, however, the follow-up story in the *Tribune* indicated he had done *just* that even though Jessica had been quoted as saying she saw no need for him to vacate his barely compensated eighty-dollar-a-month post.

Extracting the newspaper from her bag and turning to the opinion page, she found the editorial titled "A Civil Tongue," eager to catch up.

"Ignorant wretch," it began. "People engaged in heated arguments over emotional issues have been called far worse."

Jessica adjusted the treadmill's control setting to "easy grade" and picked up the editorial's continuing text.

"Neither obscene nor sexist, the label attached by Rod Hubbs, since resigned as chairman of the South Jordan Planning and Zoning Commission, to activist Jessica Tobler, even containing a note of pity in its anger, suggesting its target is a sad, unfortunate person rather than an evil one."

Well, thanks for nothing, Jessica considered.

She glanced up to notice that she wasn't the only one sublimating scenery on her run with words on a page, but the reading material couldn't have been more disparate.

On the treadmill on her left, a willowy brunette with long legs was glued to a copy of *Glamour* magazine. And on her right, a matron was using a thick hardbound novel as her distraction. When she had to briefly remove the book to turn and secure a new page, Jessica observed that it was the one piece of fiction that might almost qualify as LDS Church approved—*The Work and the Glory*.

"You're reading the newspaper *again*?"

It was her trainer Luke White's voice at her elbow, and she missed a step on the treadmill, wobbling slightly.

"You must be the only woman at SouthTowne who reads the paper while she's working out."

Jessica couldn't tell if she detected admiration or disdain in White's voice, but he *was* smiling. She considered pointing out that the piece she was reading was about her but swallowed the impulse, fearing he might think she was bragging, or worse, pleading for sympathy.

White adjusted the control to "moderate grade" and left her alone to leg it out another twenty minutes before he would be back to monitor the rest of her workout.

Jack Fitch had also followed the Hubbs hubbub as it played out in the media. He got a laugh from the radio play—a good thing, since it would turn out to be the last note of levity in his life for a while.

June Fitch, frustrated at the slow-moving crawl toward a hoped-for conservatorship for Jack's resources, had apparently decided to play another angle. Face-to-face with Jack in their modest living room, she suggested she might defer filing for divorce. But he would have to agree to sign over to her the house and all financial resources (including his bank accounts).

Divorce was a threat June had used regularly over a long period, and this too was a bluff, Jack reasoned. *There's not a chance she's serious.* She was staring at him, waiting for a reply. Holding her gaze, he didn't answer. June finally broke eye contact with a shrug.

Despite their differences and frequent disagreements, Jack was convinced his wife shared similar religious convictions about the sanctity of the marital bond. Divorce was a bad deal—a moral issue for a conscientious Mormon. Faithful friends they were both acquainted with didn't dissolve their marriages on a whim.

Having to deal with the possibility that someone else might be appointed to control his finances—the almost surreal aggravation that both his wife and his father would commit to public record the claim that he was incapable of managing his own money—the threats had been quite enough for Jack Fitch.

Denial was a psychological term Jack understood well, but it would not occur to him to apply the concept to his own state of mind. He was a trusting person; family members had their own agendas, but he couldn't imagine anyone close to him purposely trying to hurt him.

Jack also trusted American justice. While venal individuals and corporations could use nuisance lawsuits to punish citizens inclined to challenge their grandiose plans, in the long run fair dealing would triumph. *What goes around comes around.*

Still, his father's attitude had been hard to take. Why couldn't he just stay out of the suit to appoint a conservator? "Dad, this is wrong," Jack had pleaded. "It's crazy. It just isn't right."

Edward Fitch had vacillated about whether he should intervene or involve himself in his son's family affairs and environmental activism. Eventually, June's entreaty that something had to be done to preserve family financial stability had prevailed. And Marcus Hollings, in his guise as generous and benevolent family advisor, had importuned Edward to take a stand.

When Jack realized what had happened, he cut his father some slack about the steps he had taken under Hollings's influence. Edward confessed to his son that Hollings had telephoned him and suggested he would not only be willing to shell out for all expenses associated with obtaining a conservatorship but would also pay Edward's attorney fees.

That information, passed on by Jack to Del Gordon, had shocked and outraged the attorney, since it was a direct contradiction of Hollings's deposition.

Jack realized his father had swallowed Hollings's assurance that once a court had defined Jack as "incompetent"—allowing his finances to be governed by a conservator—the judgment would serve as a protection against other lawsuits that had been filed against him.

A disgraceful deception at best. Hollings was the obvious source of all these suits, so in effect he was running a protection racket, pitching an implied immunity from his own threats in exchange for getting Jack Fitch out of his hair.

But wonder of wonders, Edward Fitch had eventually come to his senses. The allowances Jack had made for his dad while acting under Hollings's influence had ultimately been justified by a surprising affidavit the elder Fitch stepped up to file. Inserted in the record at third district court, the document effectively repealed all the damaging statements he had previously made.

"On or about June 1, 1999, I spoke by telephone with Mr. Marcus L. Hollings of the law firm of Homer Walters & Hollings," the affidavit stipulated. "Mr. Hollings had me act as a petitioner in a lawsuit against my son, Jack Fitch … to have the court declare Jack incompetent to handle his personal affairs and to place Jack under the control of a conservator.

"Mr. Hollings represented to me that this lawsuit would be a means of protecting Jack and his family from financial harm in the lawsuits that had been filed against him. He assured me that I would incur no legal expenses.

"I was led to believe that Mr. Hollings had Jack's best interests at heart. I was not aware at the time that Mr. Hollings was the principal figure behind the lawsuits against Jack," Edward Fitch averred. His plea for seeking a conservator was based on his belief that doing so "was a legitimate way of protecting Jack and his family."

Edward had since learned, he said, "that the conservatorship lawsuit against Jack was an inappropriate use of the law," and he was therefore taking steps to have the suit dismissed.

Significantly, Edward Fitch asserted he had concluded he had been duped. "I was the victim of cynical manipulation on the part of Mr. Hollings. I find Mr. Hollings's actions to be deeply troubling," he wrote.

In addition, having read the affidavit of June Fitch, he now believed "this document presents a misleading picture of Jack and June's marriage. I also believe it is characterized by omissions, half-truths, and exaggerations. Some statements in the affidavit show a style of writing, vocabulary, and tenor uncharacteristic of June. I would question the circumstances under which the document was created."

With healing of the lingering hurt underway with his dad, Jack could begin to acknowledge that his relationship with June would have no silver lining. Right up until the day he received the divorce papers in the mail, he had been convinced she wouldn't go through with it.

Now that it was reality, what could he do? Nothing, he concluded. This was one battle he wouldn't prolong.

There was a growing tumor on June's brain, diagnosed long ago but thought to be so slow growing that it would not affect her materially for several years. But who knew how she might have suffered and how her thinking might have been impaired?

What became clearer to Jack as he pondered these things was how much Hollings had also manipulated June and how little he could hold her responsible. He would try to do well by his kids while remaining a friend to his ex-wife. Facing lawsuits, loss of financial control, and who knew what else, he couldn't afford to burn bridges.

Then came the next surprise. Someone had not done his homework, Del Gordon informed Jack by telephone. In all the advice and supposed expert legal help Marcus Hollings had supplied for June Fitch, he had not carefully thought through the ramifications of her pending divorce vis-à-vis the conservatorship.

With Edward Fitch repudiating statements in his deposition and withdrawing support for appointing a conservator for his son's finances, June's testimony was all that was left.

Once she had divorced, however, Gordon explained, June had no standing in the lawsuit. Once the divorce became final, the lawsuit had to be dropped. While busy spending time revving up his legal team for another swing at Jessica in a disputed second deposition, had Hollings taken his eye off the ball? Whatever the case, he had struck out.

Jack could feel the grasping hands being slapped away from his pockets. Divorce had its bright side after all.

Chapter 32
Hardball

The tall man Jessica would face across the table at the offices of Homer Walters & Hollings wasn't the Weasel; one startled glance would tell her that. He had silver-gray hair, a fashionable haircut, an expensive suit, and piercing blue eyes.

Braced for the toothy but familiar visage and grating monotone of Griff Walters as interrogator at her court-ordered second deposition, Jessica was thrown slightly off stride when the stranger introduced himself as John C. Bradley and indicated he would be representing Henderson Development.

Bradley was ruggedly good-looking, almost irritatingly so. He had a disconcerting air of self-assurance and a deep, mellifluous voice. Listening as he chatted briefly with Lucie Gorman, the attorney Del Gordon had sent from Parker Anderton & Gordon (Gordon was now a partner in the firm), Jessica could imagine what she would be up against.

It had taken her a moment to recall what she had heard about Bradley. He was a hotshot criminal defense lawyer whose background had also included real estate development. He had been plucked out of private practice by Marcus Hollings as just the kind of guy who could be depended on as an intimidator to ramrod through tough cases.

319

It occurred to Jessica that in a way, it was some kind of backhanded compliment that Bradley had been brought in as a high-powered relief pitcher for Walters to try to "brush her back" as she came to the plate for the second time.

Thank God that Julie Bell was already seated at the table. No matter what happened, Julie would be at her side, Jessica realized.

The fact, however, that Henderson Development and its legal team had been granted another shot at her was not reassuring. Del Gordon had won a ruling that Henderson's lawyers couldn't haul her back for more questioning the day after her original seven-hour deposition as they had asked.

Walters had contended that she had avoided questioning on substantive issues by feigning loss of memory. Odd argument, Gordon responded, since it was Walters who had dithered away his chances by avoiding the core of the lawsuit, wasting the allotted time with questions about so-called "love poems" and other irrelevant material.

Now, however, without explanation, Judge Dudley Cornish had sent the proceedings into extra innings, and it was clear that John Bradley was here to play hardball.

His high hard one—his money pitch—would soon be made clear. Bradley came back to it over and over again. As a founder of SPACE and a community activist, how much did Jessica know about "what it meant to interfere with someone else's economic relations" and business contracts?

His approach was to alternate variations of this question with "off-speed" pitches—a wicked curve or an unexpected knuckle ball.

A typical curve ("Let me ask you this. Are you an environmentalist?") looked like a fastball until it reached the plate, but then it took a plunge as Bradley worked to connect any confession of conservationist leanings to membership in or alliance with groups such as the Sierra Club, which was widely distrusted in conservative Utah.

When Bradley tossed a knuckler, it was often a beauty: "Did it cause you any personal conflict or trouble that you were organizing against the development of open space and yet your family's income came from development of open space?"—a reference to the irony of Dave Tobler's profession as a real estate salesman.

SLAPPED!

This particular pitch got away from Bradley, however. He had at first misstated the question ("Your family's income was derived from developing open space and at the same time you coordinated opposition to open space?") Having to restate it correctly, he ended up sounding foolish. Then, although Jessica didn't hit it out of the park, she managed to blunt the impact of his insinuation of hypocrisy.

"We—neither Dave nor his company—do business that way," she said.

She found herself suppressing a chuckle at the idea that just because Dave was in real estate, he'd have to compromise his principles for the good of his business. "I'm just laughing," she said, noticing Bradley was staring at her, "because ..." Pause. "*Whatever* Dave's company would say, or anyone else, I would say, 'Sorry, I'm on the side of the citizen.'"

Bradley looked incredulous but moved on.

Grasping for information that would put Tobler and Bell in inappropriate communication with Brad and Delores Wilkerson once the couple had contracted with Henderson Development to sell their land, Bradley pressed the point from several angles.

"Were you concerned that you might be interfering with a deal that Henderson and Mr. Wilkerson had?"

"No."

"Why?"

"Because there was no way I was going anywhere near Brad if he had an option on his contract."

And yet, Bradley insisted, hadn't Bell and Tobler on different occasions taken cookies and Easter baskets to the Wilkerson home?

On *one* occasion, Jessica recalled, as they had often done as a neighborly thing for other residents.

"Had you taken Brad Wilkerson cookies before?"

She said she had once invited Wilkerson to a neighborhood watch meeting she had chaired.

"No," said Bradley. "Had you taken him *cookies* before? That's a yes-or-no question."

"No."

"Had you taken him Easter baskets before?"

"No."

"Have you brought him cookies or Easter baskets since?"

This line of questioning was surreal, Jessica thought. Did Bradley think she had hatched some clever gustatory conspiracy, appealing to the Wilkersons' secret sweet tooth? Was he suggesting a few cookies might trump the big bucks Henderson Development had dangled for their land?

"No," she said.

Failing to catch Jessica's hand in the cookie jar (his insinuation of petty bribery), Bradley now tried another backdoor approach to potential contract meddling—a phone call she had made to Brad Wilkerson for permission to allow two prominent Salt Lake County commissioners to look at his land.

"Did you call and clarify as to whether there was any agreement or understanding between the Wilkersons and Henderson Development?"

"I think I called Brad and said, 'Hey, is it okay if I bring Andy Nakamura and Kent Overman down to look at the property?'" Jessica said.

"Hadn't you received a letter from Henderson Development in December of 1996 that said, 'Don't mess with our contracts'? Right? Do I fairly characterize the letter?"

"Probably."

"I'm interested in what steps you took to make sure there were no contracts, oral or written."

"I may have had a copy of it—his option contract thing," Jessica said.

This oblique sidestep provoked another question from the attorney as to whether she had not been concerned that her actions might intrude on an agreement between Henderson Development and the Wilkersons.

"No," she said.

So what had been the purpose in showing Nakamura and Overman the property?

"What happened was, I was at 7-Eleven one day, getting Slurpees with the kids, and Andy Nakamura was there. He said, 'Hey, Jessica, I see you're trying to preserve some open space. Why don't you call my office? We have funds for that, you know. Let's see what we can do.' So I called and made an appointment."

John Bradley made a mental note to ask more narrowly focused questions. Give Jessica some rope and ... rather than hang herself with it, she twisted it like a lariat to round up some improbable personal anecdote that made it appear as if public officials sought her out at convenience stores to do their bidding.

"So after you take Nakamura and Overman by, what's your next contact with the Wilkersons?"

"Oh, by the way," Jessica said, ignoring the direct question, "when we came by to look at the land, Brad Wilkerson had us up to the house. It was very cordial. And then, later, Delores—his wife—brought me some homemade salsa."

Did this woman rehearse these irrelevant diversions ahead of time to avoid dealing with substantive issues? After the dead end of the cookies fiasco, Bradley wasn't about to touch anything concerning food.

"So, what was your next contact with the Wilkersons after that?"

"I think it was when Delores brought me the salsa," Jessica deadpanned.

The witness was maddening. There was no way to predict what would come out of her mouth next. Accustomed to cracking tough nuts on the witness stand, never had Bradley—in all his trial experience—encountered anyone who could set his teeth on edge like this breezy blond.

Plodding on with an exaggerated patience, Bradley did succeed in badgering Jessica to admit that she possibly hadn't done enough due diligence to learn that the Wilkersons had signed a *second* contract with Henderson Development in November of 1997 after the first option on the land had expired.

But in attempting to walk her through a chronology of various contacts with the Wilkersons, he consistently found himself stymied, since the witness trotted out arcane incidents that made her appear an innocent bystander rather than schemer or manipulator.

Tobler and Bell's confrontation with Clare Jackson, the Wilkersons' married daughter—what had precipitated that?

324   *Paul Swenson*

It was Jackson who had confronted *them*, Jessica testified, although it was her parents who had invited them to the scene of the episode, the fence line between the property of the Wilkersons and a neighbor. Jessica and Julie had been recruited to help resolve an irrigation dispute involving a head gate.

As Bell, Tobler, the Wilkersons, and the neighbor were chatting at the fence line, Clare Jackson had stormed out of her parents' house. "Yelling at me," Jessica said.

"What did she say?" Bradley asked.

"She said, 'You leave my parents alone! I'm so tired of you harassing my mom and dad. My mother can't even sleep at night.'"

"What happened then?"

"Brad Wilkerson said, 'Clare, I *asked* them to come here. They're trying to help me. If I didn't want them to be here, I wouldn't have asked them.'"

"When was the next time you had contact?" Bradley asked.

"With Clare or her parents?"

"With the Wilkersons."

"Delores Wilkerson called and apologized that her daughter was rude to me."

Bradley nodded indulgently, hoping his faint smile covered his frustration.

At this point, both lawyers agreed to a ten-minute break.

"You're doing great," Julie whispered to Jessica in the hallway. "Keep after him."

Returning from the break, Jessica felt refreshed, having brushed her teeth with a new toothbrush she had purchased en route to the deposition. Because it had been a two-for-one deal, a second new one remained in her purse.

Purely on impulse, she pulled it out and extended it to John Bradley, who was sitting alone at the table.

"Would you like a toothbrush?" she asked, proffering the item. His hand moved and then drew back as he looked at her a little oddly. "Take it as a memento," she said, explaining the reason for her dental largess. Finally, he smiled and allowed her to place it in his hand.

"Just don't tell Henderson I took a gift from you," the lawyer said.

Maybe Bradley wasn't exactly the Big Bad Wolf he pretends to be.

"Mr. Bradley," she blurted, "why exactly are you working for Henderson? Are you his in-house attorney?"

"No," he said.

"Oh, are you his outhouse attorney?" Realizing what she had just said, she uttered a nervous laugh. Jessica hadn't meant it to come out that way. Now it was too late. He looked away, and it was clear that if he thought it was meant as a joke, he didn't think it was funny.

When the questioning resumed, Jessica noticed her interrogator wasn't smiling. From a file folder, he withdrew two thick sheaves of paper, noting for the record that they were transcript copies of a deposition taken from Brad Wilkerson.

Turning one of the copies over to Jessica, he said, "I'm handing you what I've marked as Exhibit 2. I want you to take a look."

He referred her to a paragraph dealing with a meeting that he said Julie Bell and herself had attended, along with the Wilkersons and another property owner, Ken Edwards.

"I'm going to read what Brad Wilkerson has to say, quoting from paragraph ten." Bradley waited while Jessica found the passage in her copy. *"Throughout the meeting Jessica and Julie repeatedly encouraged me not to perform on the first real estate purchase contract that I entered into with Henderson Development."*

"Was that a question?" Lucie Gorman interrupted to ask.

Bradley looked perturbed but kept his attention on Jessica.

"Was that true?" he asked.

"No," Jessica said.

"So Brad is either mistaken or lying?"

"Yes."

Quoting again, Bradley read, *"Jessica and Julie also encouraged Ken Edwards and me not to sell to Henderson Development and to get out of our contracts.* Is that true?"

"No."

"Never said anything like that?"

"Never."

"Brad's either mistaken or lying?"

"Yes"

"Paragraph eleven, *Jessica and Julie stated that if I would get out of the contract with Henderson Development, they would find other buyers for the project.* Did you tell Brad Wilkerson that?"

"No."

"So he's lying or mistaken when he claims that?"

"Yes."

Like a dog with a bone, Bradley continued to toss around the phrase *lying or mistaken*, inviting Jessica to repeat it like a mantra as she attempted to distance herself from Brad Wilkerson's deposition testimony. At trial, could Bradley cite the steady accretion of the phrase and her denials of sworn testimony to imply that she herself was *lying or mistaken*?

But when the attorney tried to tighten the screw a quarter turn, attempting to force Jessica to decide whether Wilkerson was "simply mistaken" or "deliberately lying" about a whole series of disputed events, she broke the trap.

"What do you think?" he pressed. "Tell me your opinion of what's going on."

"I think he's being coached," Jessica said.

"You think he's being ..." Bradley paused. "*Manipulated*?"

"Yes."

"By lawyers, that sort of thing?"

"Mhm," she murmured. The answer seemed so obvious. Jessica didn't think it required a formal reply.

Bradley had taken the word *lawyers* out of her mouth, and since he was one of the attorneys who might have been in a position to apply pressure, the miscue was doubly embarrassing. He flushed slightly, recovering to ask, "So, he's not truthful. He's lying when he says those things?"

"Do you know what?" Jessica mused, mulling a new insight, "in Brad Wilkerson's mind, he probably *is* telling the truth."

It was another brain twister fresh from the tongue of Jessica Tobler. Now who was adroit at pitching a curve? Half of what she said seemed to come out of left field.

"So he's just mistaken then?"

"*Very* mistaken."

Clearly, Bradley himself was mistaken while continuing to underestimate the witness's ability to play catch-up. She could squeeze bunt out of tight situations and steal an occasional base he thought he had covered.

He had another deposition card to play but hesitated briefly. Perhaps another mention of the Wilkersons' nettlesome daughter. She had obviously gotten under Jessica Tobler's skin. Might it unsettle her and provoke an intemperate admission she wouldn't mean to let slip?

"Please refer to paragraph twelve," Bradley said. "*During the period that the real estate contract was in existence, I was informed many times that Jessica and/or Julie had been contacting my daughter Clare Jackson to get her to encourage us to break the contract with Henderson Development Company.*"

"Is that true?" Bradley asked. "Did you contact Clare Jackson?"

"Never."

"Never? Not a single time? *Ever?*"

"I never contacted Clare."

"Did you ever *have* contact with Clare?"

"Yes, when she came out and yelled at me."

"Other than that …?"

"Never."

Now Bradley shifted to a new tack—questioning why the defendant balked at accepting several reasonable settlement offers even though she claimed to be under tremendous stress.

"Threatened with a lawsuit just weeks after getting involved with trying to save something beautiful and having that hang over my head— that I could lose everything I own—of course we were stressed out," Jessica said. "But you have to do what's right. So we continued to oppose the project because you can't give in to someone who uses lawsuits to silence people."

"You've deliberately cultivated a reputation for taking controversial stands," Bradley said. "Do you agree with that?"

"Deliberately? No. I was speaking up for something I believe in, something I didn't feel was right, and something that abuses taxpayer dollars. I'm here nine years later because I did nothing wrong. *That's* my reputation," Jessica said.

"Why," Bradley asked, "was the settlement offer to keep your mouth shut for three to four years and not go to city council meetings, not talk to the media, unacceptable?"

Finally, a softball pitch from an experienced attorney who should have known better.

"It's my town," Jessica said. "I have an obligation to get involved in my community. You can't restrict my freedom of speech in the media, my right to public dissent. I won't quit talking to my friends, my family, my neighbors about issues. You can't reserve the right to sue me again and prohibit me from suing you and then fine me $25,000 if I do."

"What of the total billings?" Bradley asked.

"Around $400,000, I think," Jessica said.

"How much of that have you paid?"

"Close to $100,000."

"And did that come from the second mortgage on your home, or where?"

"Second mortgage and half my husband's paycheck."

"Why do you owe them $300,000? Why haven't they made you pay?"

"Because—they just took us on. It hurts me how much money we owe them. I don't know why. They just haven't dropped us yet ... It's embarrassing. Every time I get a bill, I almost go into cardiac arrest over how much I owe my law firm."

"Why not dismiss this case and stop the bleeding?"

"Because I *did not do* what they said I did."

Sensing Jessica Tobler was emotionally vulnerable, worn down physically and mentally, Bradley took the risk of asking if she had anything to say about "ailments" she had suffered.

"I suffered anxiety every time I went to the mailbox and found legal bills," she said, "making me afraid of a piece of paper. I'm tired of the people suing me prying into my life, trying to convince a judge I'm some kind of troublemaker mom in the community, driving around in a minivan with the license plate slogan, 'So Many Causes, So Little Time.' Yes, my husband gave me that license plate holder as a good-humored gift, but I don't even own a minivan."

The hearing room was quiet. Jessica had spoken with emotion but had kept her voice under control.

As a hardball attorney with years of experience in the criminal courts, John C. Bradley's deposition of what he considered an uppity housewife—who had chosen to put on airs as a social activist—should have been routine. He had habitually eaten her kind for breakfast.

But somehow—was it innocence, naiveté, or sheer luck?—she had held her own. He hadn't even been able to induce her to admit that her constant advocacy in public and the media was activism of any kind.

"I'm just a concerned citizen." Jessica had shrugged.

Since 2001, she said, she hadn't been as active in pressing her concerns in public.

"It is not fun having $400,000 in legal bills hanging over my head," she explained.

So why, Bradley had queried, wouldn't she agree to a settlement in which both sides would walk away without further damages?

"Pay my legal bills, and I'll think about it," she had suggested. "I don't have a million dollars, but I have a voice. And if you use that against me, you're wrong for doing that. At the very least, every American has the right to go to a public hearing and make a statement. You think I'm going to walk away from something that serious after nine years in which every word out of my mouth has been used against me in court?"

So be it, thought Bradley. *See you in court.*

Chapter 33
The High Court Hustle

Can't win for losing. The old saying used so casually by others in everyday conversation had become all too literal for Jessica Ann Tobler. In the summer of 2004, everything had seemed to be coming apart at the same time—her health, her emotional stability, her finances. And maybe even her marriage.

Asked by nosy individuals if their parents ever fought, the Tobler children habitually replied, "Only about the lawsuit," but offered no details.

Gossips who wished they could be a fly on the wall of the Tobler household might have been slightly disappointed at what they would find. Some of the tension in a typical exchange between the couple was about how best to support each other.

"I'm sick of them treating you like crap," Dave often said, "and it makes me want to beat the shit out of them."

But the more serious division was about whether to settle. "You *have* to settle," Dave would say. "It's killing our family. I'm tired of seeing you suffer. I want my old wife back—the one who didn't cry all the time, who wasn't always worried about losing everything. They're destroying our family emotionally, financially, and physically."

"Dave, I'm so sorry," Jessica finally replied. "I hate myself for what I've done to the family and that any extra money goes to pay attorney fees. But what more do you want, Dave? You have a nice big truck. You get to hunt and fish. We have a nice house, a dream backyard. What more do you want? I'm sorry you married a crusader. You should have married the domestic goddess your mother wanted you to marry."

"Here's what I want, Jess," Dave said. "I'm going to pay the latest settlement offer of one hundred dollars tomorrow, and you're going to have to keep your mouth shut like they demand."

But after a night's sleep, Dave was repentant. "I'm sorry, Jess. I realize you can't settle. You're not giving up your free speech rights. Forget what I said."

Jessica Tobler was caught in the middle of competing sociological and economic pressures. Her self-image—as a respectable member of her Mormon community—had been shaped by the traditional definition of a woman's role as "stay-at-home" mother and housewife. She had been a devoted church worker, community volunteer, and activist but had resisted taking employment outside the home.

Nevertheless, she often felt inferior to career women who could point to a string of accomplishments and whose income could provide financial benefits for their families. And compared to successful men who built homes and highways and invented labor-saving devices, she sometimes felt she had contributed little of lasting importance.

Depressed by mounting legal bills, public criticism, and vicious rumors of infidelity spread by her opponents, she was tempted to a double-edged paranoia.

Is it wrong for me to be involved in my community? she pondered. *I thought I was being a good person, and now people are convincing a judge I'm out causing trouble, calling me a whore. Am I supposed to be like every other Mormon woman? Okay, I'll take up scrapbooking! I'll learn to make quilts! Then will they leave me alone?*

Wasn't it frustrating enough that she had been essentially denied free speech rights for nine years? *If a reporter asks me a question, I have to call*

SLAPPED!

my attorney to ask if I can comment about an issue. And every time I call my attorney, it costs me more money.

At first there had been a sliver of what seemed like genuine good news, raising the hopes of both Jessica and Julie Bell. Nearing the end of a very long judicial road, they might actually be accorded something resembling justice in the Utah court system.

Calling the move "a long shot," Del Gordon had filed an interlocutory appeal before the Utah Supreme Court, saying there was maybe a one-in-six chance the court would agree to hear the case. As unusual as it was for an appellate court to agree to hear an appeal *before* a suit goes to trial, Gordon wanted a high court fix before the lower court (i.e., Judge Dudley Cornish) could muck it up any further.

Three months later, when the news came down that supreme court justices would actually hear the case, Jessica and Julie didn't know whether to exhale or hold their breaths. They were both suffering from depression and physical and financial exhaustion, staring every day at the growing mountain of debt from legal help, now topping $400,000.

Del Gordon was doing his job, furiously submitting motions and filing papers for the interlocutory appeal, but that meant the meter continued to run, piling on even more debt with every tick of the clock.

But Julie and Jessica were finally getting an invitation to the big dance. Wasn't that something to get mildly excited about? The Utah Supreme Court wasn't exactly the junior prom.

For the masses, the classic image of blindfolded justice, a noble female form balancing a scale on a fingertip, represented the ideal of American jurisprudence. But here it would be three men and two women in black robes, taking, perhaps, their own sweet time. And all the while, holding lives and futures in the balance.

Fortunately, maybe, Jessica and Julie were too close to their own difficulties to focus on just how long the process would take. Hurry up and wait. The high court hustle was a dance that put a premium on patience. Holding their breaths would never have been an option.

Questions and motions from the dueling law firms of Parker Anderton & Gordon (representing Jessica Tobler and Julie Bell) and Homer Walters

& Hollings had been descending on the justices for months. How would the court ultimately rule? Del Gordon said he was unable to predict. Some of the signs from the queries the justices were posing pointed in the direction of a reversal of the district court's rulings. Yet others suggested they were skeptical of the arguments Gordon was advancing.

There was disagreement at the court over whether the anti-SLAPP Act passed by the legislature should be retroactive. By the time the case was finally heard in November 2004, there was still little indication which way the wind was blowing.

November 1 dawned crisp and sunny. Jessica and Julie checked their kids out of school to accompany their parents to what would likely be a once-in-a-lifetime appearance before the Utah Supreme Court. At 8:45 a.m., as the two families climbed out of their respective vehicles at the Scott M. Matheson courthouse in downtown Salt Lake City, their children were dressed spiffily, the Tobler girls and Cady Bell in attractive dresses and Brandon Bell in dress slacks and a white shirt.

Fifteen months after being informed that the supreme court would hear their case, Jessica and Julie were finally getting their day in court.

"You look nice," Dave Tobler told Jessica as they entered the building. She wore a pastel pink suit, matching pearl earrings and necklace, and pink high heels.

"Don't look *too* pretty," Jessica's mother had warned her. "The justices will think you're too much and rule against you." Pretty enough was not *too* pretty, Jessica mused.

Today, court was a family affair. Jessica's sisters Cassandra and Lelauni were there (along with Lelauni's husband), as well as Jessica's brother Forrest, just off an all-night work shift. Julie's husband, Ted, and her firebrand father, Marvin, who had spent years mouthing off about common sense politics at city meetings, also showed up. As did Jessica's and Julie's LDS bishop, Ronald Hadley, an attorney who had taken time off work to lend support.

"Well, here we go," Julie said as they traversed the marbled hall to the fourth floor hearing room. "This is a big day."

Julie and Jessica followed their attorneys into the courtroom and sat behind them in the front row. The three male and two female justices, including Chief Justice Charlene Duran, were elevated above the appellants, seated against benches of elegant dark wood. Onlookers, Jessica noticed, were straining their necks a bit to glimpse the occupants of the raised platform.

It was announced that each side would be granted ten minutes, followed by ten-minute rebuttals. Then the justices would ask questions. *This is what it all comes down to*? Jessica considered. *After nine years of legal work, ten minutes to make our case?*

Surprise number one was Don Parker standing up to present the case for Jessica and Julie. Both had assumed Del Gordon would handle the honors. Surprise number two was that he seemed to be garbling some of the facts.

"Holy crap, we're dead," Julie whispered to Jessica.

But within minutes, Parker seemed to have eased into better form, sketching the case's broad outlines. His clients, he said, were concerned citizens trying to save open space. The suit brought against them by deep-pocketed developers was intended to silence them, thereby wreaking long-term emotional and financial damage.

Opposing attorneys responded that the women were meddlers who lied, misrepresented facts, and harassed landowners to violate their contracts.

In response to a question from justices, Parker conceded that Judge Dudley Cornish had ruled that the SLAPP Act was not retroactive, focusing on the words *continued* or *commenced* in his statement to the justices.

Any damages "should be before the enactment of the SLAPP Act or only after?" a justice asked.

"Damage should be for the commencement of the act (in part)," Parker replied, "for either or both commencement and/or continuation. Let's stop this thing before you destroy people, before they lose their homes. The appellants were participating in the elements of the government, speaking in planning and zoning meetings. The city and the appellants were trying to get the money to purchase the ground."

Parker argued that Henderson Development knew there was no wrongful interference by Tobler and Bell but continued the lawsuit.

Mills Homer, representing the developers, contended that since the SLAPP Act was enacted in 2001, it did not apply since the actions in question took place in 1996 through 1998. He also claimed Tobler and Bell made "repeated contacts" with the Wilkersons, advising them not to honor their contract.

"He's lying," Jessica's sister Lelauni leaned forward to whisper in her ear, causing her to almost miss what a justice asked next.

"These facts are disputed, aren't they?"

"They *are* disputed, Your Honor," Homer admitted. "They claim they never made these actions."

"So what would be the appropriate result," female justice Jane Paris asked, "if we let the claim go to the jury and the SLAPP counterclaim goes to the jury, letting the jury sort out if that claim is in fact with a substantial basis in law and fact? Then I suppose you prevail on the claim. And if the jury disagrees, then maybe they find for the appellants on the SLAPP claim?"

In making the developers' case, Homer had a number of exchanges with the court that focused on the minutia of the SLAPP Act and often found himself fighting a rearguard action against justices' probing questions.

Homer argued that the SLAPP act had established "a certain threshold that had to be met" in defining whether a lawsuit fell under the definition of a SLAPP.

A male justice inquired, "Well, but don't you claim that the standard applicable to recovering attorney fees is also applicable to whether or not the suit itself should be dismissed under SLAPP?"

"No, no," Homer answered. "I don't claim that if the suit does not meet other standards of law then it could be dismissed, that's correct."

"There's really only *one* standard," the justice replied. "It's fair and convincing proof that its primary motivation was to harass these people. Is there some other basis on which it would be dismissed under SLAPP? I mean that's what the SLAPP act is all about."

Homer conceded the point, noting that if one were to convince the trial court by clear and convincing evidence that Henderson Development's "only purpose in suing these folks was to chill their activities as they related to the governmental process," the suit could be dismissed on that basis, although the defendants may or may not recover attorneys' fees.

Later, Homer asserted that if a judge awarded attorney fees, the jury could decide compensatory damages. "I suspect attorney fees would be an appropriate issue for the jury," he said, "but determining whether or not a matter has a substantial basis in fact and law is clearly a legal issue to be decided by the judge."

"Why wouldn't you just instruct the jury?" a justice asked.

"Because then in doing so, you're instructing the jury in how to be experts on the law," Homer explained.

"Isn't that what we always do to a jury?" the justice responded, eliciting laughter from the courtroom audience.

"Let me ask you another question," interjected Justice Jane Paris. "The appellants claim summary judgment was inadequate because you didn't comply with Rule 4-501 by indicating facts you disputed, giving appropriate references, paragraph by paragraph as they were required to do. You were completely silent in respect to each argument. I'm wondering if that means you're conceding it, just forgot about it, or what?"

"No, Your Honor," Homer said, looking shaken. "Not forgotten, not conceding it in any way. The lower court judge didn't perceive any difficulty in determining facts or allegations."

"Is this not the precise reason," Paris responded sternly, "that demonstrates the reason behind the rule? You've got one view of the facts; they've got another. Ships passing in the night."

During these exchanges, which occupied a large chunk of hearing time, Don Parker was content to sit back and watch his opposite number sweat it out.

After Homer's verbal bludgeoning by the justices, Parker took the floor for his own turn on the hot seat.

Chief Justice Duran advised him that "there is some claim that the price the developer was required to pay in the second REPC contract was artificially inflated because of some misrepresentation your clients made to the Wilkersons."

"No," Parker responded, "if that were true ... I mean, I dispute it. If it was artificially increased, it was the city that put more restrictions on the property before they would zone it and before they would change the master plan. The injury, if there is one in this case, was caused by the city council."

Each side made some seemingly salient points during the hearing, and both attorneys took their lumps; Homer, it seemed, more than Parker. Jessica and Julie pondered the absurdity of having to fork over upward of $400,000 to defend themselves. How the justices would ultimately evaluate the testimony could be anyone's guess.

When Jessica and Julie turned to look at each other as the hearing concluded, the same questions were in each other's eyes: *Did we win? Did we lose?* Who knew?

Leaving the courtroom with her brother, Jessica almost collided with Mills Homer. "Brother Homer," she said, purposely using church vernacular, "you know my brother Forrest? You're his stake president."

"Oh, hi," the lawyer said, looking like a fish out of water but offering a clammy hand. As his ecclesiastical leader walked away, Forrest himself looked dazed and disoriented, Jessica noticed. But her concern for him was immediately consumed by the mounting agitation of another sibling; her sister Cassandra was rushing toward her with a look of hurt and dismay.

"He didn't even *look* at me," Cass wailed, her face red.

"Who?"

"Griff Walters. I held the door open for him, and he walked right past me! All those years sharing the same church building, and he didn't even acknowledge me."

Poor Cassandra, Jessica mused, getting another disturbing glimpse of a man she had once esteemed. Despite the same conservative dark suit he wore on Sundays, Walters must now appear to her like one more lawyerly fish caught outside the comfort of mutual respect, wriggling on the hook of his own hypocrisy.

Chapter 34
Pyrrhic Victory

Fall dragged into winter and a hesitant spring of 2005. On June 14, Don Parker, head of Del Gordon's firm, telephoned Julie Bell with the news the supreme court was passing down a decision. In the court's initial summary, the news looked promising. It had reversed Dudley Cornish on three major issues of the case.

Brimming with relief, Julie couldn't wait to call Jessica, but there was a problem. All of the Toblers were on the Green River near Moab, Utah, on a family trip. When Julie reached Jessica's cell phone voice mail, she kept her voice steady and noncommittal, saying only, "Call me now," not wishing to spill the beans to a machine. Jessica, meanwhile, picked up the voice mail (along with a message from Del Gordon) but couldn't return the calls since she would have no service until they got off the river two days later.

Dirty and exhausted once the family reached their campsite, Jessica was ready for some good news when she placed the call. "We won!" were the first words she heard Julie say, her exuberance bursting after having managed to restrain it for forty-eight hours.

On returning home from the trip, Jessica told Chuck Short of the *Salt Lake Tribune* she didn't care what else in the supreme court opinion was

340   *Paul Swenson*

upheld as long as the SLAPP suit claim held up. "This part of the ruling tastes so good," she said.

Meanwhile, however, slogging through dense legalese in the forty-five-page decision once court clerks had provided copies, Del Gordon discovered how thoroughly bad news was intermingled with the good.

"We hold," the justices wrote, "that the district court erred in denying Tobler and Bell's motion for summary judgment on Henderson Development Company's first and second claims for intentional interference with economic relations because HDC was unable to establish facts sufficient to satisfy an essential element of each claim, and Tobler and Bell's actions in petitioning the city council fall under the Noerr-Pennington Doctrine. We affirm the district court's denial of summary judgment on HDC's third intentional interference with economic relations claim because HDC established a genuine issue of disputed material fact.

"With respect to Tobler and Bell's counterclaims, we hold that the district court erred in granting HDC's motion for summary judgment on Tobler and Bell's SLAPP Act counterclaim because Tobler and Bell pled a cognizable claim under section 78-58-105 when they alleged that HDC continued after the SLAPP Act to pursue its lawsuit against them in order to punish them for their opposition to its zoning application.

"However, we hold that the district court did not err in granting HDC's motion to dismiss Tobler and Bell's counterclaims for intentional and negligent infliction of emotional distress because they failed to allege an element essential to both claims.

"Finally we remand to the district court for resolution, in light of this opinion, HDC's motion for summary judgment on Tobler and Bell's abuse of process counterclaim and their claim for punitive damages."

In other words, the court had slapped Judge Dudley Cornish's hands, ruling he had erred in three major provisions of the case wherein he had favored Henderson Development, but was dumping the whole thing back in his lap for another look and a new judgment.

What the court had granted with one hand, it seemed to have taken away with the other. This kind of justice was as old as human history, Del Gordon pointed out. Flashing back to the Pyrrhic War in 280 BC, he cited the complaint of King Pyrrhus of Epirus, whose forces suffered so many casualties in defeating the Romans at Heraclea and Asculum that one more triumph of this kind would utterly undo him. Hence the origin of the bitterly ironic phrase, *Pyrrhic victory.*

So, Jessica and Julie wondered, at what wounding and expense had their success been achieved? *Can't win for losing.* While the court had seemed to recognize defects in the judge's reasoning process, the justices obviously hadn't fully confronted the possibility that a judge hauled out of retirement to hear the case was himself defective (having lost some measure of mental capacity), rendering him unable to make fair and equitable decisions.

After the June ruling, Jessica, Julie, Del Gordon, Don Parker, Lucie Gorman, Griff Walters, Geoffrey Henderson, and Marcus Hollings were all called in for a conference in Cornish's temporary and claustrophobic office in the Scott Matheson Courthouse.

"I know I was overturned on some issues," Cornish explained, furtively eying the housewives, "but I don't care what the supreme court said. I still believe Geoffrey Henderson has a case against you." If there had been any question which way the judge would be leaning next time around, his words seemed designed to erase all doubt.

For Julie and Jessica, all the air seemed to have gone out of the room. Henderson, Hollings, and Walters remained smugly silent.

"I'm going to set a trial date for January 2006," Cornish announced.

When the women and their attorney raised the issue of egregious court costs, Cornish floated one of his airy judicial aphorisms meant to end all debate. "Be neither sick nor bad," he said, "but if so, be rich." As clueless as Cornish often was, even he could not have been unaware of the irony. One side of this dispute had plenty of money, and the other side didn't.

Which neatly explained why the developers and their attorneys left the room smiling.

Now facing what appeared to be the inevitability of the case extending for months through a costly trial, Parker Anderton & Gordon sent Jessica and Julie a letter in October 2005, informing them that unless they received a check for at least $100,000 toward resolving their debt, they would be forced to withdraw from the case since it threatened to bankrupt the firm.

What now? *Desperate times*, the housewives remembered from another moldy aphorism, *demand desperate measures*. For two months, Jessica and Julie applied themselves to long hours in front of Jessica's computer, establishing a website and researching organizations committed to free speech and open space, hoping to solicit donations and to locate attorneys willing to work *pro bono*.

As the new year dawned, a few nibbles but no bites. Even the few lawyers sympathetic to their cause and willing to talk pointed out that time constraints would make it impossible for them to get up to speed quickly enough to prepare for trial. There was also genuine doubt, as the lawyers noted, that a jury would return a verdict that allowed the defendants to recover their legal costs.

Another letter from Del Gordon and associates informed the women that with deep regret they would be forced to withdraw.

Then two things—happening in close proximity—tightened the noose. A constant drumbeat of newspaper publicity over the case, combined with backdoor pressure from Marcus Hollings, finally weakened the resolve of Dave Tobler's employer. Dave was notified he was being let go—*fired*.

Although Dave was putting in sixty hours a week for his employer, his boss had used Dave's moonlighting at a second job in order to help pay legal bills as an excuse to cut him loose. Now he had no full-time work and no benefits.

Likely aware of Dave's predicament through informants, Hollings and Henderson chose this juncture to extend a settlement offer of $50,000. *Get the nettlesome women off their backs for cheap at a time when they must be at the end of their ropes.* The supreme court decision had made it less than certain the developers would necessarily prevail with a jury. It was an opportunity to end the whole grotesque affair with a single stroke.

In a burst of overconfidence, Hollings opted to write a $50,000 cashier's check to Parker Anderton & Gordon and hand-deliver it to their offices. The check was drawn on the account of one of Henderson Development Company's shell companies in order to avoid court inquiries about previous testimony that HDC lacked adequate funds.

While the strategy had the desired effect (on hearing the news, Dave Tobler told his wife he thought it was time to throw in the towel), he probably should have known such a proposal wouldn't be the end of it. While the so-called settlement money was a drop in the bucket of their legal bills, it would move toward paying off the nearly $120,000 Dave had already invested in fighting the lawsuit. "Wouldn't it?" he asked Jessica. After all, having lost his job, Dave had no source of income.

"No," Jessica pleaded. "Don't take the money." She was suddenly emotional. "We have to stick with this to trial. We *have to* recover our legal costs. After everything we've been through, this is the hardest and most humiliating—owing our attorneys so much money."

Dave was standing very close to her now, looking determined but confused by the tears on his wife's cheeks.

"You would be stupid if you didn't take the money," Dave insisted. "It would help us in getting back on our feet. Don't be stubborn; we're completely broke. Don Parker called me to ask that I talk sense to you. He said we should take the money and pay it back to them later."

"I cannot—and will not—take it," she said. "Owing them more money that we have to pay back would just add to the humiliation."

Pushing past him in the narrow space by the breakfast bar, Jessica was crying harder, losing control. She grabbed her purse from the counter. "I'm leaving," she said. "I don't care if we're dirt-poor. We have to get ourselves in a position to pay our debts. But if you accept this money, I'm leaving and you won't know where I am."

She was almost to the garage door before Dave caught up and took her by the arm. "Look," he said, "if that's the way you feel, I'm willing to listen. Please, don't leave. We'll work it out."

Accompanying her husband back into the kitchen, Jessica watched with gratitude and admiration as he placed a call to Don Parker. "Listen," Dave said, "I'm going to honor my wife's wishes and not take the money."

When Jessica told Julie what had gone down, her friend added her own awe and respect for Dave's support and said, "You know I would back you up in whatever the two of you think is right."

As the days of December 2005 peeled off the calendar toward another lean Christmas (virtually no money to put presents under the tree for either family), they used the time to think about what it would mean to abandon the fight and accept a mere $50,000.

Although the check had not been cashed, Marcus Hollings was claiming a settlement had been reached and that Parker Anderton & Gordon was holding the money while refusing to concede.

"Oh my gosh!" Jessica informed Julie. "Now Hollings and Henderson are threatening to initiate disbarment proceedings against Gordon and the others. After everything they've done for us for four years—held off on insisting we pay them—how bad would that be if we didn't settle and their incredible kindness and generosity got them disbarred?"

At this juncture, Griff Walters and Don Parker got together to place a conference call to Judge Cornish. Hearing them argue their respective sides over the phone, Cornish listened for a while but finally demanded all parties meet in his chambers at the Scott Matheson Courthouse the first week of January 2006 to work things out.

Jessica and Julie speculated they were about to be "taken to the woodshed" and pledged to each other not to be bullied into settling.

Crowded together before Cornish's imposing desk, they quickly realized they weren't here for a negotiation—instead, another lecture from the blindside.

"Here's the way we will proceed," Cornish said and then laid down a rant that made it clear he believed Henderson Development had the stronger case and would likely prevail.

Cornish then asked Henderson and his team of attorneys if they would mind leaving the room for a few minutes "so I can talk in private to these ladies and their attorneys."

Stiffly facing the lawsuit's defendants once the door was closed, he asked, "So just how much would it take for you to settle?"

"Judge, no amount of money could or would compensate us for the stress and emotional damage we have absorbed," Julie Bell said bitterly.

"Well," replied Cornish, "in court, we talk dollars. Let me ask again. In dollar amounts, how much will it take to settle?"

"Oh, about a million," Julie said. She didn't smile.

"Well, obviously, you're not going to get that," he said, refusing to recognize the sarcasm.

After a whispered conversation with Jessica, Julie said, "We'd like at least $100,000, since $50,000 would barely make a dent in our legal obligations."

Cornish glanced at Del Gordon and his attorney team, seeking their reaction. "Let's not worry about our fees at this point," Gordon said, "while we try to get this settled."

The judge then suggested that Henderson and his attorneys should replace them in his office and that Julie and Jessica should huddle in a corner of the courtroom to consider their options.

By the sheer strength of his own bias, there was the possibility that Cornish could prejudice a jury if the case went to trial, they concluded. And even if the jury ruled in Jessica and Julie's favor, Henderson Development Company may have hidden money in shell corporations, and the judgment might not even be enough to cover attorneys' fees. Of course, Henderson Development would have the option of appealing a verdict they didn't like.

Additionally, if the jury ruled *against* the housewives, they faced the possibility of losing everything, including their homes. They wouldn't be able to appeal because there would be no money *left* to fund an appeal.

Furthermore, Henderson Development was threatening to challenge the new SLAPP law and to fight to the finish to have it ruled unconstitutional. The last thing Julie and Jessica wanted to see happen was anything that would endanger that legislation; it had taken three years of extremely hard work to get it passed. The process could go on for years.

When Hollings, Henderson, Walters, Homer, and Bradley emerged from meeting with Cornish, Julie saw Walters speak to Del Gordon in the hallway outside the courtroom, and in a moment Gordon entered to inform Julie and Jessica that the developers had flatly rejected paying more than $50,000 to settle the lawsuit.

"What now?" Julie asked.

Desperately, Jessica asked to use Parker's cell phone. "I want to try to follow up a few leads for new attorneys," she told Julie. After a series of calls, she reported that the few she had been able to reach said pretty much the same thing: "There's no time to prepare for trial."

Grasping for one last straw, Jessica phoned her youngest daughter, Sydney, asking her to comb the Yellow Pages for additional names of attorneys she could call.

As she waited for Sydney to find the listings and call back, the ultimate futility of this ploy began to settle in.

"Mom," Sydney said, finally returning the call, "there are all these different categories—accident, bankruptcy, divorce, criminal, defense attorneys," Sydney said. "What are we looking for?"

"Never mind," Jessica said. Pressed by her daughter for an explanation of what was going on, Jessica admitted their plight. "Mom," Sydney implored, "*don't* settle."

Numbly, Jessica thanked her daughter and handed the phone back to Parker. She was teary-eyed. "My daughter is begging me not to settle," she said. "Don't worry," Parker consoled, "I'll reassure her later."

Overhearing a sliver of the conversation, Lucy Gorman held up the $50,000 check for Jessica's inspection.

"Look at this," she said. "This is real money. And it's a *lot* of money. Please understand: *you win. They paid.* They've never paid before. They've never backed down before."

Julie and Jessica excused themselves and left the room to find a quiet corner of the corridor. What to do? On this cold January day in 2006, they had endured nine years of hoping for justice. For almost a decade they had sought a trial by a jury of their peers to examine massive accumulations of evidence of harassment and emotional distress. Who could they appeal to now?

By mutual suggestion, each took a turn at voicing a whispered prayer to God for guidance. Then, for the better part of an hour, they continued to mull their options.

The media were poised to cover such a trial, Jessica pointed out; several reporters had assured her of the fact. Hollings and Henderson would be exposed by numerous witnesses; there was even a possibility Hollings's ex-wife would agree to testify against him, despite the fact Hollings and Henderson had threatened to "destroy" her—go after the settlement money she had obtained in her divorce from Hollings—were she to interfere in their business dealings.

Jessica and Julie had overwhelming evidence; Hollings had none, except for Clare Jackson's concocted journal notes and affidavits, all of which would easily be discredited. In a deposition taken by Lefty Gunderson, Brad Wilkerson had admitted that Jessica and Julie had never asked them to breach a contract, that he had been playing them against the developers to get the highest price for his ground.

"Haven't you ever heard of horse trading?" he had asked Gunderson.

Nevertheless, Jessica and Julie were worn out. They had no financial resources to draw on. The tug-of-war over the lawsuit, they tearfully admitted to each other, would have to be over.

It was a short walk to Cornish's chambers, but it seemed more like the last mile. They informed Del Gordon, Don Parker, and Lucy Gorman they were out of options.

Jessica was wiping her eyes. "Wait a sec," she said. "Before the others come back, I need time to compose myself. I don't want them to see me crying. Is my mascara smeared?"

A few minutes later, Hollings, Henderson, Walters, Homer, and Bradley were summoned into the room. Cornish followed.

Before revealing their decision to Cornish, Jessica and Julie pointedly asked their opposing attorneys, "There's no confidentiality in this settlement agreement, right?"

Short pause.

"None whatsoever," Hollings blurted before his attorney could respond. "Tell the world, in fact. Tell the media. Post it on a website. Write a book if you want. We don't care."

Glancing over to gain some hint of visual assurance that Marcus Hollings meant what he was saying, Julie Bell waited for him to look her in the eye. Instead, he kept his gaze focused on the judge. Not once, she realized, had either Hollings or Henderson made eye contact during the entire meeting.

Turning to the women, Cornish asked, "You're accepting this settlement?"

"We *are*," Jessica said but then nudged Gordon to ask the judge for an extension until noon tomorrow to sign the papers.

In what seemed an ironic and unseemly gesture for an ex-judge, Hollings could be seen tugging at the coattails of Griff Walters, urging his attorney insist the judge deny the request. But glad to reach closure, Cornish hadn't noticed.

"So be it," he said. "Noon tomorrow."

Beaten down as they were, Jessica and Julie had not wanted to perform the official act so publicly. Despite the fact they had been deemed victors, taking up the pen in full view of their antagonists would feel too much like capitulation.

There was a tiny thrill in observing the peevish regret of the developers and their attorneys, forced to wait overnight. Were they afraid the South Jordan women might pull one last rabbit out of the hat? Three of the five stalked from the room, shoulders hunched, the door slamming behind them (by neglect or design).

A rather shamefaced Mills Homer had lingered. He approached, offering to shake hands but avoiding eye contact.

Jessica wasn't about to let him off easily.

"You know we did nothing wrong," she told him. "And you should have known better than to put us through this. After all, you're a stake president for heaven's sake."

The admonishing reference to his ecclesiastical calling seemed to strike a nerve. He shrank toward the door.

Last came John C. Bradley, the snakily handsome criminal defense attorney brought on board by Henderson Development as a hired gun to defend the developers against the SLAPP claim. Having played only a silent cameo role in the day's proceedings, he felt no compunctions against trotting over for a handshake.

"You did the right thing," he said, "settling, that is."

SLAPPED! 349

"If we didn't settle," Jessica said evenly, "they were going to hurt us, weren't they?" Bradley nodded almost imperceptibly before turning to the door.

A few minutes later, Jessica was glad to observe that Don Parker hadn't forgotten his promise to call her daughter.

"Sydney," he told her when he got her on the phone, "you can be really proud of your mom today. She's a winner, and she won. And here's the proof: Henderson, Hollings, and Walters skulked out of the courtroom and slammed the door! She's a winner, Sydney. No more will you have to see your mom stressing under the weight of an abusive lawsuit."

"Really?" asked Sydney. "That's awesome."

Chapter 35
Behind the Green Door

Early on the morning after the long day's melodramatic scenario had played itself out in Judge Cornish's chambers and adjoining rooms, corridors, and alcoves, Jessica was gripped by an unsettling dream.

She was in a hall of mirrors. Like in a carnival fun house, the shiny glass surfaces offered distorted reflections of herself and her surroundings—fat, thin, happy, sad, confused. And in the shadows of the silvery mirror images lurked malformed ghosts of developers, attorneys, and family members, plus a variety of doorways.

Where did they lead? She wanted out—out of the fun house, out of the dream, out of her confusion. But she didn't know which door to open, and there was a feeling of *deja vu*. Hadn't she repeatedly been forced to make these same choices before?

As Jessica opened the door she thought would lead her out, she discovered Geoffrey Henderson's secret den where he displayed his most prized trophy animals from around the world. As she glanced past the mounted rhinos, elephants, and tigers, she screamed in horror. Hanging on the wall above a giant marble fireplace, she saw her own head stuffed with green glass eyes and a Cheshire Cat smile and locks of curly blond hair framing her face. As she turned to run, she saw Julie's and Jack's heads similarly displayed.

Jessica's screaming awakened her. Once she had shaken off the nightmare's immediate emotional effects in the dimly lit bedroom of morning's first light, Jessica sat up and carefully climbed out of bed to avoid waking Dave.

In the bathroom, splashing cold water on her face, she thought about the dream. *Unsettling.* Ironic, since the noon deadline loomed just ahead for her and Julie to sign the settlement documents.

The persisting *deja vu?* Well yes, of course. They had been pushed to the brink of settlement so many times. That had to be it. How many exactly?

In the kitchen, as Jessica poured granola into a bowl, dressed in a flannel robe, recollections came trickling back. In 1998—that was the first try. Lefty Gunderson had informed Henderson and Hollings that his clients wouldn't pay them a dime but suggested an agreement could be reached if the developers merely apologized. Jessica and Julie had arrived for a meeting at Lefty's office, but no one from Henderson Development had shown up.

The women, however, brought Lefty the proposal that if the developers would agree to donate a few acres of land for open space and drop the lawsuit, they would agree to stop protesting their project. Lefty had advanced both bids to the plaintiffs and was soundly rebuffed.

The Father's Day meeting at Lefty's office (ending in the infamous massacre) was the third unsuccessful attempt, followed by Julie's and Jessica's visit to Henderson Development's corporate offices with an offer to "make lemonade out of lemons."

"Yeah, right," the developers had basically scoffed, sourly rejecting the prospect.

After replacing the granola box in the cupboard, Jessica returned to the bathroom. In the shower, she abruptly remembered the aftermath of the *VOICE* article's publication. At that point, she and Julie had lacked a lawyer. Responding to a letter from Henderson attorney Griff Walters threatening to take them to trial, Jessica and Julie had confronted Walters in his office and suddenly found themselves openly sobbing, begging him to drop the lawsuit since their families were being destroyed mentally and financially.

He had basically laughed in their faces. "Either find an attorney, or make us an offer on your own and agree to keep your mouths shut," Walters had responded.

He then had claimed that SPACE had never filed a response to the lawsuit.

"What do you mean?" Jessica had inquired. "Yes we did."

"You may have filed a response, *pro se*, as individuals, but to represent an organization (SPACE), the law required you to hire an attorney."

The frustration from the memory was enough to dredge up old emotions, and in the shower, Jessica couldn't tell which drops were coming from the showerhead and which from her eyes.

A grand sum of ten dollars was in the SPACE bank account at the time, yet Jessica and Julie were forced to hire an attorney (Del Gordon) to advocate for SPACE. He pressed for a jury trial; Henderson Development then asked Judge Cornish to drop SPACE from the case, and maddeningly, he proceeded to do so, leaving the women to defend the suit as individuals.

Under the US Constitution, Gordon argued, the defendants had a right to a jury trial, while Henderson Development contended that would be "unfair," since as housewives, the defendants would appeal to the "prevailing sympathies" of a jury. Cornish then ordered another settlement conference before the scheduled preliminary court hearing of January 3, 2002.

My gosh, thought Jessica as she toweled dry, that would make seven times between 1998 and 2002 that they had been pressured to settle.

But wait, Jessica considered. *What about the time in 1999 when Lefty Gunderson was about to end his pro bono legal services and run for mayor and suggested that without his help we would really get hurt financially and emotionally? He said we would have to keep our mouths shut (in the press and city council) for four years. We said no, of course. That would bring it to *eight*.*

354   *Paul Swenson*

And then, in March 2002, another settlement offer from Henderson Development, served up with a little obvious and gratuitous gift horse bestowed on Jessica's sister's family.

Jessica had been caring for her mother while she was sick, and one day, Griff and Ann Walters began ferrying meals to Jessica's sister Cassandra after her husband, Roland, lost his job. Wonder of wonders, Griff then offered Roland a cushy advertising position at a new business he was launching, knowing it would get back to Jess.

Realizing Jessica was stressing over her mother, Walters then asked Del Gordon to settle, requesting a few thousand dollars plus a promise to keep quiet in the future.

Del had left a phone message for Jessica to pass on the settlement terms and to ask her to think about the offer. When she had called him back, he said, "Don't bother. I already know your answer. Not only no, but *hell no!*"

Measured out in torturous individual doses like pseudosettlement secretions from a bottomless tube, she identified this one as love potion number nine.

The "biggie" was number ten. Judge Cornish had ordered both sides to pay for a professional mediator to try to settle. Parker Anderton & Marsden had shelled out equally with the Henderson Development attorneys for a retired judge, Orson Roush, to mediate. Attorneys from both sides, as well as Jessica and Julie and their spouses, gathered with the plaintiffs around Del Gordon's conference table. Both sides had proclaimed confidence in winning should the case proceed to a jury trial. But the mediator's presence, along with a murderers' row of heavy hitters, had exerted tremendous pressure to reach agreement.

When the negotiations began, the plaintiffs' attorneys said it would take $50,000 from the defendants to bring settlement.

"Okay, Del," Jessica had pleaded. "At this point, you're supposed to give us that motivational speech saying that money and material things don't really matter. That what counts in the end is that we fought the good fight and did the right thing."

Gordon had looked at her as if to question whether she was serious or simply indulging in whimsical irony. "Sorry, Jessica," he had said. "I'm not much of a speech maker."

Nearing 3:00 p.m. and the end of the day, compromise had flipped the numbers so that Henderson Development would owe the defendants $10,000 on settlement and could not gag their free speech. It appeared that Marc Hollings was now willing to accept a settlement on these terms.

Then, Jessica recalled (right when it appeared a deal would be made), Judge Roush had re-entered the room to relay the news that Geoffrey Henderson wouldn't agree.

Through the open door, his angry voice could be heard from another room. "I won't pay them *any* money," he had been shouting. A door had slammed, and it appeared the bellicose developer had left the building.

Each side had paid $1,000 for the mediator—$2,000 in total. Attorney's fees on the defendants' side totaled around $3,000 for the six-hour settlement conference. With the addition of attorney fees for the plaintiffs—well, it had probably been a $10,000 day.

One day's costs in a multiyear fight that had already likely totaled more than a million dollars for both sides, Jessica thought. A lot of open space could have been saved for that amount.

Later in the morning, after she dressed and was contemplating joining Julie for the drive into town to sign the settlement papers, Jessica found herself operating a vacuum to calm her nerves. The machine's motion seemed to loosen her memory.

The eleventh settlement side step had come while both sides were waiting to hear whether the Utah Supreme Court would hear the case. It was Don Parker's contention that if the justices turned down a hearing, Henderson Development would hold all the cards going into a prospective trial. Jessica and Julie had held firm, however, and turned down the settlement.

After the supreme court ruled, Henderson Development made another settlement offer (number twelve) insisting the defendants pay one hundred dollars and maintain confidentiality. That was at the point that Dave had told Jessica, "You're *not* giving up free speech rights. We're *not* settling."

Sometime between July 30 and November 1, 2004, in a meeting at Don Parker's office, he managed to levy extreme pressure to settle, this time dragging scripture into the conversation and suggesting the proper spiritual course was one of "forgiveness."

Again his reasoning was that if there was a trial, Jessica and Julie would go to court without bargaining chips and would likely fail. "If this continues," he said, emphasizing the onerous cost to his firm, "it could bankrupt us."

He likely sensed both women had a burden of guilt, knowing it was Del Gordon who had agreed to take the case and was therefore under pressure from Don.

Nonetheless, Julie told him, "We're not going to fail. If this goes to jury, we will win this case," and Jessica added, "Don, why would we quit now? We have to trust the system."

Another Henderson Development offer boiled down to "you go your way, and we'll go ours," dismissing payments by either side but still demanding confidentiality. Jessica had taken a fat black Magic Marker and had written in cursive on a sheet of paper, "You'll have to pry my free speech from my cold, dead voice box!" and faxed it to Del Gordon.

Counting in her head, Jessica realized that would make a total of fifteen failed settlements.

Oh yes, and how about the squeeze play after Mills Homer had beaten Julie up at her deposition, attempting to bait her with an offer for a separate settlement? She hadn't wavered in refusing to leave me to fight the lawsuit by myself.

Oops and double oops. After Jessica finished vacuuming, she stole a few minutes to play some soothing piano music to relax her nerves. As her mind became lost in song, another previous settlement shuffle that had eluded Jessica surfaced through the melody. This one predated her mother's illness, pushing all the others up one notch to seventeen total.

Huddling with Del Gordon, as well as Martin Hernandez, another attorney who had briefly represented them *pro bono*, along with Marcus Hollings, Geoffrey Henderson, Griff Walters, and some of their junior partners in a hearing all parties hoped would lead to settlement, something dramatic had happened while they waited for a judge to arrive.

Suddenly in the back of the room, two or three uniformed police officers had laid their hands on Jack Fitch, handcuffed him, and escorted him out of the building. They had produced a bench warrant for his arrest based on the charge that he had failed to show for a hearing in his alienation of affection suit against Marcus Hollings.

Outside, Fitch denied he had ever been notified of the hearing. Told the offense demanded a fine of two hundred dollars, Jack had pulled out his wallet and paid them directly from cash he happened to have on hand. In a few minutes, Julie and Jessica looked up to see him re-enter the courtroom—uncuffed and unescorted.

After the disruption, Jessica's and Julie's attorneys walked them into a back room for a settlement conference. As Jessica was vocally resisting settlement, Julie broke down into tears. "I feel so guilty," she said to Gordon and Hernandez. "I just want to be able to pay you guys back for your time, and I believe that if we go to trial …" The words caught in her throat.

Gordon placed a hand on her shoulder. "It's all right, Julie. We're not settling. Just pay what you can when you can."

Jessica and Julie later heard that some of Henderson Development's junior partners had quit over what they considered an abusive lawsuit.

So, with yesterday's proceedings in Cornish's court, Jessica reflected, the final settlement, eighteen strikes at the piñata before it bit the dust!

Who could have known there would be all those false exits before the women could choose the right door? And now that they had gone through it, was it really the right one?

Of course, hadn't they always made the correct choice, right from the beginning? Free speech, clear water, clean air, a green future for their children, and a commitment to open space for continuing generations had always been their goal. So, yes, the green door was the right one.

Whatever might lie beyond it, there would be no going back.

Chapter 36
Settlement

What did it mean to settle? With all of its connotations, the word carried a lot of baggage, and for Julie Bell and Jessica Ann Tobler, some of it wouldn't be unpacked for years.

The day before signing the documents (on their way home from the Matheson courthouse in downtown Salt Lake City to the south valley in Julie's vehicle), they had decided to celebrate with their favorite comfort food—hamburgers and French fries at an A&W drive-in. So why hadn't they felt all that celebratory or comforted?

The fact was, although the food had been satisfying, there was an aftertaste—unresolved emotion. Neither of them seemed able to put it into words. Was it relief, disappointment, or just a jumbled mix of feelings held in for too long?

"If we were drinkers," Julie had said, "I suppose we would sit here crying in our beer." She had glanced at her friend, hoping to tease away the uneasiness neither seemed ready to talk about. "Our *root* beer?" Jessica said, trying to force a smile. "We better get home."

Talking later in the week, both would confess they had suffered from lack of sleep and at least one night when the dam had broken and left them crying into the wee hours. And both had found it difficult to think of a good reason for getting out of bed.

So this is what a hangover feels like, Julie Bell pondered the morning after settlement. She was dealing with a stupor of thought and the dull throb of an all-over body ache as she struggled to get Trish ready to put her on the bus for school. Julie was somewhat buoyed by the thought that her special-needs daughter had developed a friendship with a boy named Isaiah in her ninth grade class. They had created a partnership for some class projects.

Julie's day would be dictated by a few routine occurrences—picking up Trish from school, transporting her to speech therapy, deciding what to fix for dinner, and getting it on the table for the family. Maybe the very ordinariness of such a schedule was a good thing. She was going to get back to the basics of her life—a life that had imploded. What would it be like not having to fight through the daily far-flung confusion and exhaustion of wondering what the developers were going to throw at them next?

Maybe now she could begin to focus.

So why wasn't she hopeful or relieved? A sort of bedevilment. Recriminations and second thoughts. *Why did we settle? After promising ourselves and each other we would never do it. We did it anyway.*

If there was a silver lining in the dark clouds, it would be they had faced down an old boys club to win a huge victory at the Utah legislature. The new law guaranteed that private citizens who challenged large corporations by exercising their constitutional rights and got sued for their trouble would get a fair shake in court.

How much was the pang of real regret, and how much could be attributed to long-range depression? After all, Julie was continuing on the antidepressants her doctor had prescribed for her. And while they were helping, they weren't a cure.

Okay, give yourself some credit. We didn't want to settle, but we had to; the dollars weren't there to keep going. Pathetic that Ted didn't even ask what transpired in court; I had to tell him.

But why shouldn't she think of it *this* way: Marcus Hollings and Geoffrey Henderson were forced to settle as well! This was the first time they ever had to shell out as losers in a lawsuit. *Isn't that something we ought to feel good about?*

Still in her pajamas as midday approached—depressed and devastated—Jessica found herself wishing she could think of someone—anyone with a listening ear—who hadn't been directly involved in her near decade-long struggle. How about her friend Jake Paulos? A war historian and public relations specialist, he had always been a calming influence throughout her years of activism. Could he offer an objective assessment of how things had ended?

"Jake, thank heavens you're there," Jessica said when Paulos answered on the second ring. Did he have time to talk? Yes, he said, picking up the anxiety in her voice. He listened attentively while Jessica told her story of the events leading up to the agreement, interjecting "okay" from time to time or asking an occasional question.

"So, be honest, Jake. Did we do the right thing?" Jessica asked, pausing in her rambling narrative.

"Let me tell you something, Jessica," Paulos said. "Life is not like the movies. People don't get fairy tale endings. Even Erin Brockovich's story was 'Hollywoodized' on screen."

"Yes," she said, "but for nine years I wanted those guys to pay for what they did. I wanted to make them face a jury of their peers. I wanted to at least get back the money we spent on attorneys in trying to save the river bottoms and preserving free speech rights.

"We mortgaged our house trying to fight them off, and for years we devoted half of Dave's paycheck to attorneys' fees. We went without Christmas gifts. We sacrificed material things to protect what we believe in."

"Yes, you did," Paulos said.

"I wish I could talk to them without my attorneys."

"Who?" Paulos asked.

"Henderson and Hollings," Jessica said.

"What good would that do?"

"I would ask them, 'What do you want from us? You've gotten everything you asked for. The river bottoms are all torn up. There is a five-lane highway running through what was once open space. You've got your high-rise glass office buildings. There are ten thousand parking spaces. You got your way! You made $19 million on the sale of the property. And even that's not enough.

362   *Paul Swenson*

"Every town you go into you make tens of millions of dollars more. You drive the nicest cars. You live in castles. You take extravagant vacations. You have high church and community positions.

"Do you need another house? Do you want mine? Do you want my broken-down car? What is it? What more do you want?'"

Paulos was silent on the line.

"I think I know what you want, and you will never get it," Jessica continued. "You will never get me to give up any of my rights. What you want from me you cannot buy. And what I want is not for sale. You can't buy rights at the mall. The only way you can get rights is to fight for them. Now, all I ask is that you leave me alone."

Paulos still didn't speak, apparently trying to process her rant. "I see what you mean," he finally said. "What you may want to remember," he offered, "is that the courtroom is the biggest crapshoot in the world. There's no guarantee what a jury would have done. Especially in conservative Utah. Even if you had won, you might not have received a substantial judgment.

"Maybe in another state it could have been different. Where a majority of folks don't consider it taboo for women to 'meddle' in men's business dealings. Public perceptions would have lent more support.

"In 'green states,' where environmental activism is accepted and admired, you two ladies would have been hailed as heroes."

Erin Brockovich's case was only one among many environmental fights that had captured the nation's imagination. There was also *Anne Anderson, et al., v. Cryovac, Inc.*, a court fight over industrial toxins in the water supply of Woburn, Massachusetts, in the 1980s. It had led to a long and highly publicized struggle, Paulos said, dramatized in the 1998 film, *A Civil Action*, starring John Travolta.

Heroism hadn't been on their minds, Jessica insisted. "At the end of the day, we just wanted to stop Henderson Development from inflicting more abuse on other citizens and other cities," she said.

For Jessica and Julie, the war might be over. But even in war, "there are no real victors," Paulos said.

Casualties were a reality of the battlefield. While the housewives had been badly wounded, didn't the old cliché still hold? What had not killed them—hadn't it made them stronger? And what they had done for free speech rights might make it possible for others to stand up more confidently next time.

"Think about what your courage and persistence inflicted over time on your opponents," Paulos said. "You made them choke on their cornflakes and coffee every morning while they read their morning newspapers. Coffee or Postum—whatever those guys drink. Their reputations have been reviled," he observed.

"They had to pay dearly for their own attorneys, even though they were in-house. They were forced to spend time on legal issues rather than hustling new business. They got no *pro bono* work and no reduced rates, despite the fact they could write off attorney fees as a business expense on their taxes."

"What this very public battle has done to their egos can't be measured," Paulos argued. "Some of the most powerful men in the state, beaten. Beaten by two stay-at-home moms. They sought huge damages from you, and instead they had to pay *you* to settle."

Settle. Maybe the word sounded a little more gratifying coming from the mouth of Jake Paulos.

"Thanks so much, Jake," Jessica said. "Got to go. Have to take Tuxie to school."

"Tuxedo, your cat?" Paulos said. "Obedience school?"

"No," Jessica laughed, explaining the pet would be used as "product placement" for her daughter Lexi's marketing class. "Her teacher hates cats, but as her class assignment, he's agreed to having Lexi try to persuade him that a cat who's a classy dresser—black-and-white fur formal wear—makes a fashion statement for its owner."

"Wow." Paulos laughed. "That's marketing."

"For me and my smart daughter, all in a day's work," Jessica said.

Jack Fitch had not been in Judge Dudley Cornish's court for the last round of the grueling fight, and on the day after the papers were signed and he had heard the result from Jessica by phone, he wasn't easy to mollify.

"No," he groaned into the receiver. "If we had been able to put it to a jury, we would have been able to take them down," he said.

Jessica found herself arguing the other side of the equation. "Listen, Jack," she said, "we won. We should shout it to the world."

Reluctantly, Jack came around, and when he did, he was on it like a kid in a candy store. By noon the same day, he was camped at Del Gordon's office, begging for a copy of the ruling. Characteristically, he then hightailed it to Kinko's to run off several copies of his own and delivered them by hand to the newspapers.

By late afternoon, Jessica and Julie had been flooded with calls from reporters. It was clear from the questions they were being asked that the press was stunned that they had not only won a $50,000 in payment but had managed to wangle a nonconfidential agreement and hadn't had to sign away free speech rights.

On the morning the papers published, there were also editorials that didn't flinch from describing the women as heroes.

Under the byline of Dirk Jansen, the *Salt Lake Tribune* reported that neither Jessica Tobler nor Julie Bell "will see a penny of the settlement. Instead the $50,000 cash will help pay off a legal tab that reached upward of $400,000."

Jansen quoted "an emotional Tobler" as saying that "to go to trial, it would have taken another hundred thousand. We ran out of money. That's basically it."

Ironically, Marcus Hollings, asked by Jansen why Henderson Development had settled, also offered a poor-mouth explanation. "We knew it was going to cost us more than $50,000 to try the case. We made a business decision in everybody's interest to end it once and for all."

Hollings conceded the company was "worn out" by the legal odyssey and claimed it was depleted by Henderson Development's recent purchase of Geneva Steel. He refused to characterize the case as a SLAPP action despite the fact that the suit was considered a precursor to the law enacted by the Utah legislature in 2001 to protect citizens from strategic lawsuits against public participation.

"In 1991," the *Tribune* recalled, "the US Supreme Court set their standard for managing SLAPPS," ruling that "as long as a defendant's activities are aimed at influencing some governmental action, they are protected by the petition clause of the First Amendment."

Jessica Tobler told the *Tribune* the developers had portrayed her "as a stupid stay-at-home housewife" who likes to protest things. "I don't have a million dollars, but I have a voice," she said.

In the *Deseret Morning News*, Julie Bell characterized the lawsuit as "long and grueling," adding that she was "relieved I can go on with life now." She called it "sad" that the developers continued to abuse the public trust. "The only way they could ever be stopped is if someone has lots and lots of money."

On the *Tribune* editorial page, the newspaper declared that "the debt the people of Utah owe to activists Jessica Tobler and Julie Bell is even greater than the debt those two owe their lawyers. The two refused to knuckle under to Henderson Development and its abusive SLAPP ... In the meantime, legislative and judicial action cracked down on such horrible abuses of the courts, making it much harder for the next deep-pocketed developer to so abuse the system."

In upscale, environmentally conscious Park City, where citizens were under siege from as many as eleven Henderson Development lawsuits against residents of both the city and Summit County because they had denied zoning changes for high-density development, interested parties invited Jessica and Julie and their spouses as guests of honor for dinner at a ritzy restaurant and requested a copy of the $50,000 settlement check to display as evidence that the development monolith could be beaten.

The framed copy of the check, the event sponsors said, would offer inspiration that ordinary citizens could resist the efforts of corporate power to transform the pastoral quality of communities with cookie-cutter developments.

Additional phone calls from Salt Lake County residents followed the media reports, with messages of congratulation and gratitude for Jessica and Julie's hard work. It felt good for a while, until the women thought to wonder where some of these people had been earlier when they really could have used their support.

In the immediate wake of the settlement agreement, Jessica wondered if she'd ever dip her toes into activism again. And then, less than a month after the final papers were signed, she found herself swept back into the public arena by a new flood of controversy.

A downstate Republican legislator from Panguitch, Senator Tim Hutchins, was about to unveil a bill making it next to impossible for citizens to launch land use referendums.

Why was it that operatives in Jessica's own political party seemed to constantly be involved in efforts to limit public participation in grassroots citizenship? As much as she wished for a period of detachment from hot button issues, this was something she couldn't leave alone, she decided.

Jessica brought together several diverse organizations, including Space Preserves a Clean Environment, Save Our Communities, Save Our Canyons, Concerned Citizens of Draper, Bluffdale United, Riverton United, and Citizen Coalition for RDA Reform to fight the proposed measure, calling the group Utah Alliance for Citizens' Rights.

Predictably, Marcus Hollings and other large developers were prepared to support Hutchins's proposal, as well as a land use bill in the state senate pushed by Senator Hal Ansel, a Sandy Republican.

Hollings was quoted in the press as backing Ansel's measure in order to "rein in bad-boy cities" that abuse their zoning powers, referring specifically to towns in Summit County that Hollings was suing.

Ansel, a real estate broker and former Utah State Senate president, tried to tamp down public comment about his bill by refusing to be interviewed by the press. But environmental groups were rallying to oppose it.

The measure would "basically create no end to development" on the slopes of surrounding mountains, charged Tish Smart, president of Save Our Canyons.

"There's a real-life story behind each and every provision in the bill," Hollings vaguely told the *Salt Lake Tribune*.

The article noted the developer's previous position as a third district court judge and pointed out that Speaker of the Utah House Craig Kirkus was employed as the lead partner in his law firm. In fact, Henderson Development, the company's lobbyists, and the law firm all shared cozy business cottages in the same complex on the 9600 block of State Street in Sandy.

Ansel had intended to hide provisions of his measure and Hutchins's proposal in a "Boxcar Bill" without a name or number to keep details from the public. But once the press let the cat out of the bag, the wind was knocked out of the developers' sails.

Earlier in the process, Jessica had telephoned Ansel at home (his wife had gotten him out of the shower to take her call) and told him, "I just wanted you to know I've put a coalition of groups together to fight your bill."

Later, she had submitted a hard-hitting op-ed commentary to the *Tribune*; it was held from print once the "Boxcar" was derailed.

By April, another potential threat to one of the land use accomplishments Jessica and Julie had fought for reared its head in the public arena. Rumors were flying that South Jordan City was toying with selling four acres of the twenty-acre city park at 11050 RiverFront Parkway that SPACE had managed to preserve as open space.

Sale of park acreage would mean one more encroachment into the "spectacularly beautiful" Jordan River bottoms, Jessica told the *Deseret Morning News*. "The park is a haven for people, and every night something is going on down there." A sale would be an "outrage," she said, making citizens further "mistrust their city leaders."

When a spontaneous protest was planned to challenge the sale, City Manager Chick Norris recognized the strength of the opposition and backed off. No, he said, there were no plans to convert the site to office space, warehouses, or other commercial use.

He disclosed that The Church of Jesus Christ of Latter-day Saints had been briefly interested in the land as a site for a stake center, but the proposal was no longer in the works. Norris said the city was not disappointed to have dropped the idea.

"Let's chalk it up to the process working," said area resident Tim Atkinson.

Protest signs—already painted and ready for erection—were junked, and instead the public celebrated a victory at the park.

The open space of the park was popular for kids' sports, dog walking, picnics, and recreation, the *News* pointed out, quoting Jessica to bolster its opinion: "It's a playground for people to find some peace and solitude," she enthused.

Those very qualities had been in short supply in their own lives, Jessica and Julie realized. But as quickly as additional controversy had briefly flared came breathing space. Everything seemed to settle down, and a couple of months later, to celebrate Jessica's birthday, the two found time to have fun together, deciding to rendezvous at their predictable old haunt.

"Let's go to the A&W," Julie suggested, "sit in a booth, and order those thin and crispy French fries with fry sauce—the best anywhere."

"Best anywhere except for real potato fries from Idaho," Jessica corrected. "But A&W is the place; this mama's got to have a Papa Burger."

The signature item on the A&W menu, the Papa Burger, included two beef patties, two slices of cheese, lettuce, tomato, onion, pickle, and Papa sauce.

On the premises, relaxed and happy, Julie and Jessica alternated between laughter and tears. Between bites, wiping their mouths with paper napkins, they found things to talk about that hadn't floated to mind for a long time.

Like the unexpected lift they had received at one of the lowest points in their journey, disappointed and distraught after seven years of struggle. Out of the blue, their LDS stake president had encouraged them to dig in for the long haul. "Take these developers to the mat if you have to," he had urged.

In addition, their supportive bishop had treated the women and their husbands to dinner and made it clear that he appreciated what they were going through.

These were things they should never forget.

"Remember once when we were in Lefty Gunderson's office and I found that note from a woman in one of his books?" Julie asked.

SLAPPED! 369

"Remind me, why were you poking around in his things?" Jessica said.

"He had left the room, and I was always curious about the books he had on his shelves. This one had a red cover, and when I picked it up, a note fell out. Without thinking, I read it, and then I felt embarrassed I had looked. It was a note signed with a woman's name, and she was thanking Lefty for the 'love-hate relationship' they had always had."

"That could have been me," Jessica deadpanned.

"Yes." Julie laughed. "You did have a little crush on him once."

"Wait a minute," Jessica replied. "It was *you* who said you wanted to grab his face and pinch his honest little *cheekies*."

"I was grateful for what he had done," Julie demurred.

"Well, we both were. I once pasted his photo on a Wheaties box that said 'Breakfast of Champions' and gave it to him."

"That must have been before you took him those weird Halloween cookies and his parrot—what was his name …?"

"Cordoza," Jessica said.

"Yes, Cordoza—his parrot—bit you," Julie said.

"Oh my gosh! I remember. Cookies shaped like blood-stained eyeballs, cherry-flavored frosting for the blood. That was at his house. He said he was grateful, but then I told him I would like to see his parrot since I had one of my own. He took me upstairs to show me the cage in the bedroom. Foolishly, I reached through the bars to pet it."

Julie was laughing now.

Look," Jessica said, holding out her finger, "I still have the scar."

Julie examined the mark and tried to stop smiling.

"As if we hadn't already had enough trouble with *your* parrot, Mr. Green," Julie said. "Remember all those squawks and parrot noises on that tape Lefty asked us to make when we interviewed the landowners on the telephone?"

Both women convulsed with paroxysms of laughter.

When the hilarity had passed, Jessica asked, "Am I weird? Isn't my life pathetic that the pleasure I got from watching Lefty in his starched white shirt depose Brad Wilkerson was almost orgasmic?"

That brought on another wave of hysterics.

Curiously, Lefty Gunderson was now mayor of Salt Lake City, a highly controversial figure—today more so than ever. And among the scars *he* bore among a very few unforgiving liberal friends who were fending off GOP criticism of the mayor, was the stigma of having devoted months of *pro bono* legal help to two Republican housewives from South Jordan.

Yet, on a prominent shelf behind his desk, he still proudly displayed a miniature Jeep containing two mostly naked Barbie dolls, clad only in bullet-bedecked bandoliers.

"That's the only thing I've ever done that was 'crafty' in any way," Jessica said. "You are the crafty one, Julie. You sew, you quilt, you can stuff. You bottle fruit."

"Well I used to." Julie sighed. "Maybe I can get back to it now."

After the frivolity, the friends were momentarily quiet. Julie was feeling a little tremor of guilt that she and Ted had been unable to contribute even close to equally with Jessica and Dave to pay down their legal bills.

Then, glancing at Jessica, she felt a wave of gratitude; through it all they had been totally supportive of each other. This was a friendship that had been tempered and steeled in the fires of endurance and opposition. Nothing in the world could take that away from her, and there was nothing she would trade it for.

"Well, Julie, one thing I finally know for sure," Jessica said. "I've pretty much got activism out of my system. No more causes for me."

"Okay, princess," Julie said, patting her friend on the shoulder. "Tell me another fairy tale."

Epilogue

Under a leaden November sky, a lone American bald eagle plummets low over the Jordan River, looking for prey. Its shallow descent near Jordan River Lane in South Jordan, Utah, once prime wildlife habitat along the riverbanks, presents to view a heavy concentration of man-made artifacts—automobiles, asphalt, glass, concrete. Climbing swiftly to a higher altitude, the rare bird shifts its course north by northwest toward the Great Salt Lake.

The sprawling development on the ground is called RiverFront. Contemporary medium- to high-rise office buildings of virtually identical design feature glass facades bisected by rectangles and ovals. "Executive suites" in the project are marketed to well-heeled corporate tenants.

Higher learning is also marketed here. The University of Southern Arizona (USA), a nonprofit school headquartered outside Phoenix, operates a satellite "campus" behind the windowed walls of several floors of a high-rise RiverFront structure. In April 2010, USA took steps to substantially expand its presence there by breaking nearby ground to build a $23 million, 125,000-square-foot structure that will house a nursing school.

In another RiverFront high-rise, an obscure institution called Newman University advertises its scorn for liberal arts education with the slogan,

"Learning the Important Stuff," which turns out to mean courses in aeronautical engineering.

Paradise Paved with Parking Lots
Source: Google Maps

Also interspersed on the property are a variety of smaller buildings where upscale restaurants, wellness centers, fitness facilities, and other shops beckon consumers.

Several signs along the highway advertise "space available" in the complex, seeking to recruit new tenants. After the development had leased more than one million square feet, including a Jungle Safari Grill and a Dan's Deli, there was a decline. With national and Utah economies struggling to forestall further financial downturns beyond recession, small business occupancy rates at RiverFront were down. Leases for the development's executive suites were also depressed after their November 2008 launch. In early 2009, however, management reported that corporate leases were picking up and that about 80 percent of the executive space was filled.

Having lost the fight to preserve much of the Jordan River bottomlands (now occupied by RiverFront) as open space, grassroots activists, environmentalists, and a few far-sighted public officials turned their attention to enhancing existing improvements of the river channel and to saving it from further encroachment.

On the other end of the river, Salt Lake City's huge planned youth soccer complex near the Jordan at 2200 North remains one of the most contentious ongoing disputes, pitting environmental groups against sports and recreation boosters. Activists have pressed the city to find land farther from the river for the project, but the city council remains committed to the location and is considered likely to approve the rezone that will green-light its approval.

In June, 2010, a quarter-size hole in a Chevron pipeline in Red Butte Canyon spilled at least thirty-three thousand gallons of oil into Red Butte Creek that reached other creeks and streams in Salt Lake City and the pond in Liberty Park and eventually spread a sheen of oil on the northern reaches of the Jordan River—a new and unique befouling of the waterway. Hundreds of birds, fish, and other wildlife were affected. Fortunately, the trails escaped pollution. The river was closed to the public briefly between 500 North and 1300 South while crews monitored and collected oil from the surface.

Meanwhile, Utah state planners have proposed extending the river's existing trail system, covering forty-four miles along the Jordan Parkway (through and between twelve communities), aided by support from the mayors of Salt Lake City and Salt Lake County. Since the federal and Utah governments appear to be slashing expenditures for trail systems, the largest barrier to progress on the ground remains money—locating sources of new cash to pay for the project.

Significant funds are needed to purchase land, circumvent infrastructure roadblocks and construct new trails. Under state plans, the Jordan River itself would become a "water trail" for boating, kayaking, and canoeing.

Some of the very improvements that citizen activists most vigorously advocated during the bottomlands dispute—nature centers, protection of flood plains, and preservation of open space—are now seen by state planners as crucial to the Jordan's future, along with equestrian trails, maps, brochures, and standardized signs identifying the river's features.

Salt Lake County is in the process of completing the first Jordan River master plan in more than thirty-five years, aimed at finishing the last 20 percent of the trail system, thus creating a route running from Utah County through Salt Lake County to Davis County and connecting with east–west corridors as well as the Bonneville Shoreline Trail.

Master plan goals would also target cleaning up river pollution, upgrading riparian zones along its course, and improving water quality. How quickly such far-flung ambitions can be fulfilled will obviously depend on the political and financial will of government bodies, private and public leadership, and a committed citizenry.

As the Jordan River rolls toward a more hopeful but uncertain future, aftershocks of the battle of the bottomlands still reverberate. The controversy effectively challenged and changed many personal, political, and business lives. While some wounds may have begun to heal, others have been exacerbated. Free speech issues persist.

Henderson Development, which continues to accumulate valuable properties for development and eventual sale at substantial profit, has not abated its use of public lawsuits as a coercive business tactic in order to pressure communities and individuals reluctant to silently acquiesce to the company's advance.

On Henderson's behalf, Marcus Hollings has brought suit against the cities of Riverton, Bluffdale, South Jordan, Tooele, West Valley City, Fruit Heights, and Provo. Of twenty-three active lawsuits against Utah's Summit County, launched by various interests and individuals, fourteen can be traced to developers—nine of which originated with Henderson Development.

Many of these actions seek to wipe out zoning ordinances in western Summit County that developers oppose. One of these suits has attracted considerable media attention since Hollings and Henderson Development are seeking $40 million in damages against the county, contending the planning code violates the Utah Fair Housing Act.

The county attorney's office argues that the development firm did not apply for a land use variance on any of the properties in question, as outlined in the code, and instead proceeded directly to litigation, citing a county official who claims that Hollings told him his firm didn't "believe in filing applications … just lawsuits."

Hollings, meanwhile, has attempted to seize moral high ground in the dispute by soliciting support of civil rights organizations on the grounds that certain county zoning laws discriminate against minorities by blocking construction of low-income housing. These efforts were taken at face value by officials of the Utah Chapter of the National Association for the Advancement of Colored People (NAACP), who gratefully presented Hollings with a "Man of the Year" award.

In 2007, Mountain States Super Lawyers, an organization of attorneys recognized as preeminent by their peers, also added to Hollings's résumé by granting him membership.

Lowell "Lefty" Gunderson, having served two tempestuous terms as mayor of Salt Lake City, left public office to found a national educational and advocacy organization, High Road for Human Rights, which addresses solutions to climate change and global warming and works to oppose torture, human trafficking, sexual slavery, and genocide. He also ran for president of the United States in 2012 on the Justice Party ticket.

On a personal level, some other participants in the river bottoms fight have left the battlefield or changed status.

Two journalists who covered the on-going river bottoms story, Dan Booker and Joe Orr, are dead. Former South Jordan Mayor Max McClellan, seventy-four, also died of complications related to cancer in November 2008. His wife, Rhonda McClellan, preceded him in death by a few months.

Representative Vickie Lawford was elected first female speaker of the house in 2010.

Griff Walters, the Henderson Development attorney who had once ridiculed Jessica Tobler's activism against light rail, used the Utah Supreme

Court's decision on the Tobler/Bell/Fitch extraordinary writ petition to help him launch a petition against the Utah Transit Authority's TRAX system when it threatened to affect his own neighborhood.

John C. Bradley, the attorney that Henderson Development brought on as a hired gun during the last days of the settlement process, went on to become lead counsel for several polygamists facing bigamy and statutory rape charges.

Rita Baylor was elected on her second try to South Jordan City Council in 2009 after speaking up on open space issues during the campaign and citing her previous work with SPACE.

Both Marcus and Tamara Hollings found new marriage partners after their strained and problematic divorce. Tamara's beautiful hair was shaved again as she battled and won a fight against breast cancer.

After settlement of the SLAPP suit her ex-husband brought against Jessica Tobler and Julie Bell, Tamara treated her new friends to a celebratory meal at the same Denny's Restaurant where they had once supped less satisfyingly with Marcus Hollings and Geoffrey Henderson. Denny's then became the traditional meeting place for the three women, often for late-night snacks while catching up on the latest gossip.

The website of the Mormon Places reports Hollings remains a high-profile member of the LDS Church, having served until recently as a "gospel doctrine" instructor in a Draper, Utah, ward. His business partner, Geoffrey Henderson, also continues in church leadership positions.

Henderson Development's website calls Geoffrey Henderson a transformational figure who takes "difficult dirt" and turns it into profit. Raw parcels of land that other developers have shunned because of wetlands status or because of uncooperative municipalities and problematic easements are patiently processed by Henderson and his legal team until they have obtained "proper" zoning and platting, and then they are sold to builders who are "happy to pay a little more for a property ready to build," the company statement explains.

The company cites the hiring of Marcus Hollings as a turning point for Henderson Development's reach. Soon after Henderson and Hollings became acquainted, while the latter was still a third district court judge,

"Marc was working with Geoffrey to resolve various entitlement issues," the statement notes. "With Geoffrey's business acumen and Marc's legal background, Henderson Development was ready for larger scale projects. Today, Geoffrey is actively involved in the company's management, strategies, project direction, acquisitions, sales, and funding."

Some corporate plans have failed to pan out. The Real Salt Lake professional soccer team rejected Hollings and Henderson's offer to deed thirty acres of "cleaned-up" Geneva Steel land in Vineyard, Utah County, for the team's new stadium (where Henderson Development hoped to profit from collateral business opportunities), choosing instead a Sandy location.

As events have progressed, an anonymous public relations writer's use of the phrase *difficult dirt* in describing material the firm processes in its subjugation of the landscape may have proven an unfortunate choice of metaphor.

After failing to carefully track or investigate conflicts of interest inherent in Marcus Hollings's employment by Henderson Development while he was still a third district court judge, the press is finally becoming more alert to patterns of overlapping influence between the powerful developer and the Utah legislature. As that occurs, some reporters are also digging dirt of the recent past.

In 2007, Utah House Majority Leader Craig Kirkus, a partner in Marcus Hollings's law firm (Hollings Beard Kirkus & Ashton) got into a series of scrapes that focused media scrutiny on Kirkus as well as the law firm and ultimately on Henderson Development.

"Henderson Development had a very good year at the Utah legislature," wrote *Salt Lake Tribune* staff writer Jeri Fraley. "With its close ties to Kirkus (identified by the *Tribune* as 'perhaps the most powerful member of the ... legislature'), it was able to push through key parts of a pro-development agenda while remaining under the radar."

Key legislators elected partially through Henderson Development's contribution of $43,750 to their campaigns were able to shepherd to passage three pro-development bills Speaker Kirkus had tagged as priorities, the *Tribune* reported.

Kirkus and Henderson also had their way with a fourth bill that forced US Steel to pay a much higher proportion of the clean-up cost of the Geneva Steel site ($29 million) than its new owners, Henderson Development (required to chip in only $10 million).

Conflicts of interest were a fact of life in a part-time legislature like Utah's, Kirkus said but claimed he didn't "insert himself" into legislation backed by Henderson.

In November 2008, voters decided to clear up any lingering questions about the house speaker's legislative conflicts by defeating his re-election bid at the ballot box. But by the time the next legislative session rolled around in January 2009, Kirkus had returned to his old state capitol stomping grounds, this time as a lobbyist. After exiting his senate office, he retained $400,000 in his campaign account.

Before eventually leaving Hollings's law firm, Kirkus's lobbyist registration listed his clients as Altria, the parent company of Phillip Morris USA, the largest tobacco company in the country, as well as the Utah Transit Authority, Intermountain Healthcare, the Utah Sports Commission, Gold Cross Ambulance, and, of course, Henderson Development.

As a Brigham Young University graduate and former missionary for the LDS Church (which opposes tobacco use), Kirkus's ties to Phillip Morris drew attention in the press.

Those reports came hard on the heels of another public relations hit for Henderson Development. When Salt Lake County Councilman Donald Wade implored the county to use part of the $48 million taxpayers raised in an open space bond to buy and preserve 3,500 acres of remaining pristine land around the Jordan River, *Tribune* columnist Roberta Wolfe wrote: "Too bad he wasn't around ten years ago in 1999."

In jogging Utahns' notoriously short memories, Wolfe raked up a whole decade of muck that the RiverFront fight had generated.

"That's the year Henderson Development sued a group of neighbors for trying to stop the parking lots, high-rise office buildings, and chain restaurants from covering willows and wetlands in South Jordan," she recalled. "You can mark it on your calendar. The day the Jordan River Parkway almost ended."

"One side wanted to preserve something beautiful," Wolfe quoted Jessica Tobler as saying. "And one side wanted to develop the heck out of it."

Recalling Henderson Development's SLAPP suit against Tobler and Julie Bell, Wolfe detailed the subsequent attack on citizens' free speech rights.

"In the end, speech held out," she wrote. "But the river corridor was blanketed in asphalt. Cowed by the litigation, South Jordan City caved, rezoning the property for commercial development. And the rest is office complex and strip mall history. It's just dumb luck and good timing that the rest of the river corridor hasn't been tarred and graveled."

And the personal fallout? "For Henderson Development, money was always the bottom line," Wolfe concluded. "The company sued the neighbors for $1.7 million, going after their assets, using quotes in the newspaper against them. Corporate and nonprofit sponsors interested in preserving the river corridor melted away. The suit turned Tobler into a recluse. She drove a clunker, racked up $400,000 in legal bills, and stopped talking."

Renewed hope of the Jordan's reclamation obviously comes as a ray of sunshine.

"Rivers are sacred ground," Tobler told Wolfe, "the lifeblood of communities. Man can go to the moon. But man cannot recreate nature."

Despite the fact that Jessica Tobler's interview with Wolfe in December 2008 was her first public mention of the struggle in two years (since the $50,000 settlement agreement), neither she, Julie Bell, nor Jack Fitch required a trip to the moon for daily reminders of the damages.

News of one of the most egregious dirty tricks that opponents had played on Jessica emerged late in the game when a friend informed her that that someone had been inserting her name onto a variety of pornography sites on the Internet.

Counter-balancing this indignity to some extent were calls from pastors of several protestant churches, informing Jessica and Julie that their congregations had followed their ordeal in the press and had prayed for their success and safety.

Fitch was reduced by his divorce and the financial drain of court proceedings to his Social Security income. But the significant decision he had gained at the Utah Supreme Court, where he had gone without a lawyer (*pro se*) ruled in essence that municipalities cannot deny citizens the right to circulate petitions and referenda in their respective cities. Later, citizens of several communities used the ruling to petition their overreaching governments.

Fitch currently lives alone in a modest downtown Salt Lake City apartment and is serving a local mission for the LDS Church.

Julie Bell worked long hours selling advertising for a Salt Lake Valley phone directory company (where she was among the top three in sales) and later launched another sales business out of her home. Julie's husband, Ted Bell, continues to sell residential real estate.

Special-needs daughter Trish Bell graduated from Bingham High School and continues to look to her mother for extended care, as well as spiritual and financial support. In February 2009, the eighteen-year-old was voted by her classmates at Bingham as queen of the school's Sweethearts Ball.

Julie's son Brandon graduated from the University of Utah and was married in 2011. He is pursuing a dual master's degree.

Daughter Cady was married in 2008, and she and her husband, Trevor, are parents of two daughters. She graduated from Utah Valley Univeristy with a business degree.

Jessica Tobler, after emerging from years of painful isolation from public commentary on community issues, again finds herself wading energetically into such causes as political campaigning, legal immigration, gun rights advocacy, activism against cell phone pornography involving minors, opposition to RDAs, EDAs, and team sports hazing while continuing to support efforts to slash government taxation. She remains a staunch champion of preserving open space. She also led efforts to repeal a law the legislature made in 2011 that basically made government records off-limits to the public and received the 2011 Roy B. Gibson Freedom of Information Award for her work. Jessica also supports legislation in states without anti-SLAPP laws to protect citizens who are still in danger of being SLAPPED!

Dave Tobler, who worked years of overtime to pay off legal bills from the Henderson SLAPP suit, is currently managing director of a commercial real estate firm.

Lexi Tobler graduated from Utah State University and works at vacation resorts, plans recreational events, and composes her own piano music. Her sister, Sydney, an exceptionally close friend of Julie's daughter Trish, took time off from attending Brigham Young University where she is majoring in recreational therapy and dance to serve a mission for The Church of Jesus Christ of Latter-day Saints in the Iowa Des Moines Mission.

In the close-knit suburb of South Jordan, seldom a week goes by without Tobler, Bell, or other family members encountering individuals at church, in school, or at community gatherings who may serve as painful reminders of past grievances.

Since Jessica's daughters were the same ages as the offspring of Glen and Sue Edwards, as well as sons and daughters of several city council and planning and zoning commission members, they ended up establishing friendships and performing together in school productions and other events.

The Toblers and the Bells shared a church building with Mayor Max McClellan and Tim Christopher and then were moved to another building, which they still share with Brad and Delores Wilkerson, Clare Jackson (the Wilkersons' married daughter), and Glen and Sue Edwards.

Over time, it has been necessary for the two women—whose longtime partnership in the river bottoms battle made them lifelong friends (they currently serve in LDS Church callings as visiting teacher companions and both teach children in primary)—to learn a thing or two from their kids about the difficult process of forgiveness and letting go.

Jackson had been particularly resented for her unsubstantiated testimony that Jessica Tobler had opposed the rezone of Jackson's parents' land so that her husband, Dave Tobler, could acquire it for development—an allegation Tobler and Bell had to legally defend against. (Dave Tobler's real estate boss had stated he had no interest in the property because it was in a flood plain.)

Disinformation as revenge? The Toblers and the Bells learned that a female friend of Jackson's who worked in Dave Tobler's firm had attempted to sue the company's boss for discrimination, protesting a promotion she had coveted that was instead given to Dave Tobler.

These enmities from the past made Jackson's continuing interaction with Toblers' and Bells' children a bitter pill to swallow. Ironically, however, observing the generational change in attitude by their offspring, they came to wonder if their kids hadn't somehow absorbed and applied the most admirable aspects of their parents' training.

After a school dance, when Julie's daughter Cady accompanied some friends to a party hosted by Clare Jackson, she vanquished potential awkwardness by treating her mother's erstwhile antagonist with simple politeness.

Jackson was the school librarian for both Jessica Tobler's and Julie Bell's children throughout their grade school years and was librarian at the high school both Julie's and Jessica's kids attended. As a member of the Centennial Celebration Committee, she had constant contact with Sydney Tobler, a student body officer.

Sydney told her mother she liked the way Clare Jackson dressed and often complimented her on her outfits. "What does she say?" Jessica asked her daughter. "She tells me, 'Thank you. You're sweet.'" Sydney found Jackson's lost ID card on school grounds and returned it to her.

As for Jackson's parents, Brad and Delores Wilkerson, whose land was at the heart of a Henderson Development accusation that Tobler and Bell had tried to persuade them to break a contract to sell, Jessica and Dave stumbled into an opportunity to make a fragile peace.

Standing in line to buy cookies at a neighborhood fund-raiser for special-needs kids, the Toblers observed the Wilkersons approaching the party. Jessica's first instinct was to leave, and when the couple noticed the Toblers, they walked away.

Changing her mind, Jessica Tobler bought a couple of extra bags of cookies, and she and Dave found the Wilkersons.

"Hi, Brad. These are for you," she said. His face registered shock. They hadn't spoken in ten years.

"Now, who are you people?" his wife, Delores, asked. She hadn't recognized them.

After sorting out the confusion, the couples talked briefly about inconsequential things.

"I met your daughter Sydney," Brad Wilkerson said. "She sure is a happy kid."

After the Toblers returned home, Jessica broke down in tears. A decade had disappeared. How monstrous that neighbor had been turned against neighbor, she mused. "I feel lighter," she said recently. "A milestone in my life—a healing experience."

That quality of healing moment has not quite occurred for Julie Bell. She is saving it for a private excursion, perhaps to Jordan River Park, the one parcel of open ground that she and Jessica Tobler had been able to save in the river bottoms fight.

"Our forefathers and foremothers paid a price to save open space and free speech rights for us," Julie said. "Jessica and I tried to walk in their shoes. Someday, perhaps our grandchildren will run and play on this beautiful piece of land."

The healing moment on the Jordan River
Photo c. Ray Wheeler

Endorsements

Calling all Mormon housewives: your story is told in the new novel, *SLAPPED!*, and to my knowledge it has never been told better.

The channeller of this true story was accomplished journalist, editor and novelist Paul Swenson, but its tap root was interviews with Mormon husbands and housewives, thick binders of newspaper articles about real-life events, legal documents and court records. Except for name changes to protect the innocent from further persecution by the guilty, it is an acutely granular portrayal of life within three prototypical Mormon households in the prototypical Mormon suburban community of South Jordan, a bedroom community of Salt Lake City, the world headquarters of the LDS (Mormon) faith.

It is a fascinating story on many different levels. It portrays with empathy and affection the heroic daily lives of Mormon housewives as they raise children, participate in church activities of every kind, run errands, keep a household--AND battle a powerful corporation and the entire entrenched power structure of a tightly-knit theocratic community, risking everything including their own welfare and that of their families, to stand tall for the values of free speech, democratic government, and preservation of some small remnant of the natural world in their small community.

In the real life version of this story, one family was totally destroyed and a second nearly bankrupted. One devout Mormon lost his temple recommend after his personal reputation was slandered with false allegations of adultery as punishment for objecting to corruption in government and for obstructing the agenda of a powerful developer. This is in part a classic horror story of government corruption viewed at very close range. Along its labyrinthine path we encounter persecution by malicious gossip, character assassination, vandalism of homes, lawns and cars, torture and killing of pets. We see bullying of citizens exercising their constitutional rights to free speech, by means of "SLAPP" litigation ("Strategic Lawsuits Against Public Participation") by powerful and wealthy corporations. We see at very close range the endlessly revolving door between government and the private corporations it pretends, unconvincingly, to regulate. We see bribery offered and accepted by public officials, profound conflicts of interest, cowardice and venality across the gamut of public life. And we see the underlying values of that made the Mormon pioneer culture and civilization unique in its respect for wild nature and good stewardship of the natural environment. To anyone curious about the origins of corruption in government, or the complex realities of a highly inbred faith and culture, this book is a fascinating read.

For non-Mormons it is a rivetingly real, microscopically detailed and nuanced anthropological report on life within a typical Mormon suburban community in modern times.

It stands with the very best writing about historic and contemporary Mormon culture, including that of Wallace Stegner, in *Mormon Country, The Gathering of Zion* and many other books and articles, or of John Krakauer in *Under the Banner of Heaven*.

—Ray Wheeler, *Cosmos West Literary Review*

When I read *SLAPPED!*, I was amazed and perplexed that this scenario could happen in our country. I naively thought that as citizens we could sleep peacefully under a blanket of political protection.

I couldn't believe that these folks who just wanted to save a piece of ground…just a small tidbit of land provided by Mother Nature for others to benefit and take pleasure from…could be harassed by greedy and powerful developers.

While reading this informative and very interesting book, I ran the gambit of emotions. I laughed at their mischievous capers and cried at what these women went through.

I loved this book and couldn't wait to read the next chapter. *SLAPPED!* is the best novel based on a true story I've ever read.

—Jodi Lyn Peterson Webster, Colorado

"They say you can't fight city hall." I guess these Utah housewives had never heard that idiom. Because they did fight city hall. And their story is truly compelling.

SLAPPED! has every element of a great fiction novel—intrigue, violence, love, humor, theft, blackmail, power, greed, and even forgiveness. What makes this story even better is that it is based on a true story. The events of *SLAPPED!* take place in a suburb of Salt Lake City, Utah, where two women were naive enough to believe they lived in a community that protected the First Amendment of the U.S. Constitution—freedom of speech, the right of the people to peaceably assemble, and to petition the Government for a redress of grievances.

Religion and politics are strange but familiar bedfellows especially in Utah where the predominant religion is The Church of Jesus Christ of Latter-day Saints (Mormons). The housewives struggle to keep these two issues separated so as to not destroy their faith or their love of country.

This story reminded me of events of "Watergate" as told in *All the President's Men*. I was instantly transfixed and read this suspenseful book in one sitting. Shortly after reading *SLAPPED!*, I visited the sites from the events depicted in the book. It was some sort of incredulous pilgrimage; sitting in the booth at Denny's, visiting the homes of the main characters, and then finally standing in the enormous asphalted parking lot that had once been acres and acres of a beautiful riparian corridor.

SLAPPED! is an incredible story that everyone needs to read and think deeply about. It is a lesson in courage and resilience that will make you question how far you would go and how much you would sacrifice to defend something you value—and to stand up for your rights as well as your fellow American's rights.

—Val B. Darrington, Professional Educator, Hershey, PA

Buy this book only if any one or all of the following matter to you: A) You love a good underdog story, B) You haven't quite completely given up to "The Man" and/or C) You're convinced that good, old-fashioned gumption and grit, exercised by citizens who give a rip, still are important elements of the ongoing American experiment. Written with a "get real" perspective, humor and a distinctly fresh voice, *SLAPPED!* will inspire you to roll up your sleeves and make a difference.

—Adam Hansen, Principal and VP Innovation, Ideas To Go, Inc.

About the Author

Paul Swenson was born the youngest of ten children in 1936 in Logan, Utah. He began his writing career at age 22 as a crime reporter for the *Deseret News* in Salt Lake City. Later, he took up the editorship of *Utah Holiday* magazine where he became known for producing important investigative journalism about Utah politics. Many successful writers, including Nevada Writers Hall of Fame inductee Phyllis Barber, and Pulitzer Prize nominee Linda Sillitoe got their start under Paul's editorship. He also edited *The Event* magazine, and wrote for the *Salt Lake Observer*. Many of his other articles were published in the *Salt Lake Tribune, Sunstone, Dialogue: A Journal of Mormon Thought*, and other publications. During his later years, Paul followed in the footsteps of his poet sister, May Swenson, producing many poems. Paul wrote many news stories about the real-life events that inspired this book and became so intrigued that he spent four years researching and interviewing the people involved in order to produce this novel. He died shortly after completing it in 2012.